Blue Dusk

Blue Dusk

Susan Goodman

MICHAEL JOSEPH
London

MICHAEL JOSEPH LTD

Published by the Penguin Group
27 Wrights Lane, London W8 5TZ, England
Viking Penguin Inc., 40 West 23rd Street, New York, New York 10010, USA
Penguin Books Australia Ltd, Ringwood, Victoria, Australia
Penguin Books Canada Ltd, 2801 John Street, Markham, Ontario, Canada L3R 1B4
Penguin Books (NZ) Ltd, 182–190 Wairau Road, Auckland 10, New Zealand

Penguin Books Ltd, Registered Offices: Harmondsworth, Middlesex, England

First published in Great Britain in 1990

Typeset in Monophoto Lasercomp 11 on 12½ pt Photina
Printed and bound in Great Britain
by Richard Clay Ltd, Bungay, Suffolk

A CIP catalogue record for this book is available
from the British Library

ISBN 0 7181 3266 1

To Regina

PART 1

Paris

Chapter 1

Long after they were married, Robin Faraday would sometimes tell people – smiling, teasing, looking at Kate with love – that he had picked her up one fine spring morning on the Boulevard St Germain in Paris. He had seen her across two marble-topped tables at the Deux Magots while he was sitting in the sunshine, drinking coffee, watching the world go by. And fallen for her.

'But it wasn't like that at all,' Kate, who entirely lacked Robin's breezy self-confidence, would say – colouring, mildly embarrassed. Put on the spot, she was inclined to duck her head. 'It gives *completely* the wrong impression . . .'

'All right, then,' Robin would acquiesce, his hand protectively on her left arm, the bad one, which drooped when she was tired. 'Let's just say we met there.' His blue eyes searching out her dark ones. 'Is that better?'

'That's better . . .'

He was in Paris for a week's holiday, long overdue, owed him by the merchant bank for which he worked in London. The previous January, skiing in Switzerland, he had met an attractive, zany French girl who skied almost as well – and certainly took as many risks – as he did himself. The girl, Manou, proved exotic company in the evenings too. A bachelor, thirty-two and fancy-free, Robin had always grumbled to his friends that he never seemed to have any luck meeting nymphomaniacs. Until *this* girl . . .

Robin reeled back to London and during the following months, they kept in touch with a couple of hasty postcards. Late one Saturday night the phone rang. It was Manou. She *'meessed'* him *'ter-r-r-ibly'*, she purred. And why – he could visualize the pout – did he not come to Paris to see her? Hadn't they had a good time together last winter? No? Manou's megawatt sexuality beamed undiminished across the Channel . . .

Pleased, rather flattered – why not indeed? thought Robin, and they made a date for dinner in Paris two weeks hence.

'That's settled then,' Robin said, a bit heated after yet more of Manou's fractured English blandishments. 'I'll drop you a line when – er – I've fixed a hotel . . .'

It did occur to Robin, briefly, to wonder what on earth a girl like Manou was doing alone on a Saturday night – telephoning *him*, for God's sake. But used to attracting the opposite sex – and possessed of a healthy ego – he quickly dismissed the thought.

When he walked into the small, discreet hotel near the Madeleine two weeks later, he was in the best of spirits. For a few days, he would forget the office and the job that was beginning to frustrate him seriously. *'April in Paris . . .'* he hummed under his breath as he paid the taxi, felt about for documents, dealt with the luggage. *'Holiday feeling under the sun . . .'*

He had come upon a Paris sparkling in bright sunlight, swept with green, brilliantly alive. Pink and white candles iced chestnut trees which lined the great avenues; the noisy, chaotic traffic swirled, choking even the narrow side streets. People were sitting at tables outside cafés. There was a delicious feeling of spring about – a true whiff of balmy Southern warmth. The grey chill of London that morning already seemed a world away.

The man behind the desk looked up as Robin strode in. *Anglais*, he deduced on sight. It wasn't so much Robin's looks – although these were what continentals would think of as characteristically English. Tall, with good shoulders; a well-set-up young man with a confident manner rather than handsome. His light brown hair, very straight, was slicked down with an exact parting. He had a square jaw which he was inclined to thrust forward – as he did then. But it wasn't entirely his looks – nor was it his clothes. Grey flannels and

4

a well cut navy blazer; the sort of subdued striped tie associated with schools and clubs ... It was something else that gave away his Englishness – the air he exuded of being totally at ease in his surroundings, delighted to be there – and matter-of-factly expecting everyone else to think the same.

'Mr Faraday ... of course. We were expecting you ...'

Formalities over, he handed Robin his key – and with it, a letter. Robin glanced down. Manou's flamboyant writing ... H'mm. He smiled broadly at the boy who was carrying his case and followed him to the small, creaking lift.

In his room the smile froze. In disbelief, he re-read the brief lines of stilted English – then he crumpled it, aimed it towards the wastepaper-basket and sat down on the bed, arms crossed, legs stretched. Glowering.

'That bitch. That absolute bloody bitch ...'

Because she was 'si, si désolée, mon cher Robin', but after a terrible quarrel with Jean-Claude – who was, he must under-stand, the love of her life, hadn't she told him in Verbier? – he had that day returned, begged forgiveness and insisted on whisking her off to the country for a weekend of loving reconciliation ... 'Enfin ...'

In other words, he'd been duped. Good and proper. That was definitely the first mention of any Jean-Claude ...

He roundly wished the pair of them everything bad, caught sight of his furious face in the mirror – and started to laugh. So much for his romantic week in Paris, fool that he was. At least he had the grace to see the funny side. He looked round the room. It was made, he thought wryly, for just the kind of assignation he had had in mind – quiet, dark embossed wall-paper, dull gilt furniture. A large bed, square pillows, immacu-late white linen. Old-fashioned; just a bit seedy. He liked it. Pity.

He squared his shoulders. To hell with Manou anyway ... He had never spent more than a couple of days at a time in Paris, en route to the faraway, exotic destinations he had hungered after since he was a boy. He would eat well, explore, walk, visit museums ...

And he also had contacts. Of course ... Last year, he had struck up a good working relationship with his opposite number in a deal they were structuring, a young Frenchman who worked for an American bank. Pierre ... Pierre ... *Duval*. That was it. Amusing; perfect English. He looked at his watch and picked up the phone. Ten minutes later, he had an invitation to dinner on Monday evening at one of the most amusing restaurants in Paris – which would include, Pierre hoped, his clever young law student cousin, Monique. It was a beginning ...

That night, Robin dined well – alone – and was in bed by eleven, struggling to get the gist of the news on television; the book which he had brought, but not expected to read, to hand. Once or twice he glanced at the unoccupied side of the bed with amused regret. He slept marvellously.

He spent most of Sunday in the Louvre. Bright and early on Monday morning, he was out on the street ready to start making the rounds of Paris sights. He scarcely knew the Left Bank at all and it seemed as good a place to start as any ...

So, after wrestling with the Metro, he emerged half an hour later into the misty morning sunlight of the Place St Michel. He consulted his map and his green Michelin guidebook as the world jostled round – and got his bearings. The morning was everything a spring day in Paris was supposed to be. Blue sky, soft pale clouds, a hint of morning mist burning off. He looked over at the curtains of ivy hanging down the walls of Notre Dame; watched a pleasure boat nosing under the bridge. One by one the bookstalls along the quaysides were opening up.

He stopped and unhurriedly bought a *Herald Tribune*, thinking of the chaps in the office well into the problems of a Monday morning by now. He grinned. Perhaps Monique would turn out to be attractive as well as clever. Good old Pierre ... He could do with a coffee and turned into the Boulevard St Germain. He passed a church, crossed a cobbled square, and looked up at a large café-restaurant on the corner. Le Café des Deux Magots ...

He sat down at a table along the side beneath a striped awning. Robin ordered a coffee, opened his paper and sat back, easy in the pleasant morning warmth, watching the colourful parade stream by.

And that was when he first saw Kate.

Chapter 2

She was sitting alone, two tables away – reading from a green Michelin Paris guide. Exactly the same as his. It was her stillness, so peculiarly Kate's, which attracted him instantly. And her delicacy. Her dark hair fell just to the collar of her white blouse. She turned a page, absorbed, and without looking up reached for her coffee cup. Wrists like a bird's, he thought as she raised it. She wore a very fine gold chain round her neck.

Robin lowered his paper a little.

Kate, who had been bending forward, sat back in the wicker chair and crossed her legs. The thin blouse skimmed her narrow arms and shoulders, dropped to a 'V' between her breasts and tucked neatly into a wide, red leather belt. She glanced up briefly at the people walking by on the sunny pavement, the cacophony of traffic – and returned to her book. She twisted a strand of hair neatly behind one ear. She seemed to be smiling.

Staring over the top of the *Herald Tribune*, something quite discernible happened to Robin's emotions at that moment. His heartbeat quickened and his throat felt tight. He could make out – just – that her guidebook was in English. She seemed so young . . . He looked round quickly – was there a boyfriend? A father? A companion of any sort? . . . Seeing no one – the café was still quite empty – impulsively, without premeditation of any kind, he got up. He slipped his guidebook in the pocket of his jacket, put his map and paper under his arm and went over to her.

Kate, who had been concentrating on her reading, rather enjoying being on her own at the side of the noisy, lively street, hadn't noticed him at all. So when she glanced up, startled, and saw this good-looking young man standing over her, obviously about to speak, her first reaction was one of slight social panic. Who was he and what on earth did he want? He looked so familiar. Did she know him from some-where? Could he be one of her twin sister Laura's flock of young men who streamed through their London flat and their parents' house at weekends? She was hopeless at names, always had been. 'You're so vague, Katie-Kate,' Laura often chided. 'You simply don't pay enough attention to people . . .'

She didn't. So *did* she know him? No name, or place, sprang to mind. So in those first seconds which seemed to go on and on, she lowered the guidebook and smiled up at him uncertainly.

'Look – I'm not in the habit of accosting young women in public places,' he began in a pleasant, ingenuous manner. 'Do please excuse the interruption. But I've left my guidebook in the hotel, the same one you're reading actually . . . there are one or two places round here that I wanted to visit . . . I wondered whether you would be kind enough to let me check . . .'

The oldest ploy in the world. Pathetic. Even Robin, never backward at coming forward, was abashed. It came out without his even thinking about it. But it would have to do.

'Oh do, please,' Kate said, relieved. Thank heavens. *That* was all he wanted. She wasn't supposed to know him after all, apparently. And he looked perfectly respectable. English. Well dressed in an informal way. Nice voice. Really rather hand-some. 'How maddening for you – and they're so good, these guides, aren't they? Here . . .' She held it up to him with more warmth than she might otherwise have done.

'How very kind . . .' Robin took the book but his other hand was by then firmly grasping the chair next to her. 'I'm at a bit of a loose end here as a matter of fact, and I'd planned to do some of the sights . . . stupid of me to have left behind the most valuable prop . . .' He saw she had noticed his proprietory hand. She looked a shade disconcerted. But he stood his ground. And at that moment, as luck would have it, the waiter appeared with his coffee and took in the situation at a glance. Two young people, both clearly *Anglais* and *bien élevée* . . . Having seen everything there was to see around these tables many times over, he allowed only the hint of a raised eyebrow, a tiny shrug – and slid the tray onto Kate's table. *Eh bien* . . .

'Oh I say . . .' Robin began with apparent diffidence. But he was already pulling out the chair and Kate was automatically removing from it her bag and sweater; watching him, her dark, slightly almond-shaped eyes enormous. Robin sat down. Again, some strange and powerful feeling overcame him. A kind of inner recognition. Dropping all pretence he looked straight at her and said quietly,

'I'm afraid the line about the guidebook was a complete fabrication. I expect you knew that anyhow. I do have one. It's in my pocket . . . here . . .' And he pulled it out.

'Then why . . . I mean, I don't quite understand . . .' Puzzled, Kate stared at the second, and identical, Michelin now lying on the table between them.

'I saw you sitting here. Alone. And I was alone myself . . . and I suddenly very much wanted to come over and join you.' She was staring at him by then, the corners of her mouth twitching. 'I'm sorry to sound such an idiot. Just say the word and I'll push off.' He placed both elbows firmly on the table.

She broke into a merry and delightfully amused smile which lit her eyes and brought a bit of pink to her cheeks. What an incredible thing to have happened. So suddenly. Laura would laugh and laugh.

Robin started smiling too. They looked at each other – both, in their different ways, astonished at the surprising situation in which they found themselves.

Kate always said she thought that everything between them came about because they were both feeling how good it was to be alive, to be in Paris, to be young, on that warm and golden spring day.

'That's the strangest thing I've ever heard,' Kate almost gasped. 'It's the sort of thing you'd never believe if someone told you . . .' She couldn't help being amused – and a little flattered. 'Because, you see, when I saw you were obviously going to speak to me I thought, Oh God, I know I've met him

9

before somewhere – I thought you were probably a friend of my sister's, and I couldn't remember and I'm hopeless at names anyhow and I wondered how on earth I was going to bluff my way out of it . . .'

Then it was Robin's turn to laugh and say that that made him feel a bit better because she didn't feel she'd been accosted by someone frightening – at least he looked familiar – and wasn't it a perfectly glorious day and a divine spot and shouldn't they have a go at this excellent coffee . . .?

'Are you here for long?' Kate asked politely. It occurred to her that she was drinking coffee with a man she had never set eyes on before – and perhaps, suddenly uneasy, it wasn't something she should be doing. And although his appearance was so conventional, she sensed something different about him; the way he had removed himself to her table for a start.

'Only for a week – a bit of a holiday from the office I slave for in London.' Noticing her slim fingers, Robin decided that she had something of a ballerina look about her – the oval face, the slender neck and thin, sinuous arms. It came to him that she would have beautiful shoulders and a long and lovely back. 'And I got here the day before yesterday. As a matter of fact, I was intending to meet a French girl I bumped into skiing last winter. It was all arranged. Only once I got here, I discovered that she'd gone off with her boyfriend and stood me up.'

'What an awful way to behave,' Kate said indignantly. 'And when you'd come all the way over. Did you mind very much?'

'Not a bit,' he said cheerfully. 'At least, not after the initial shock to my pride. It's the sort of thing a bachelor has to put up with.' He smiled so broadly that deep creases fanned out from the corner of his eyes. Kate noticed and thought how nice he looked. Laura, she felt, would think the same. 'And if it hadn't happened that way, I wouldn't be here now, would I?' Sitting in a sidewalk café on this great Parisian morning – with you – his look implied. Kate blushed. 'That's me . . . now won't you tell me what you're doing in Paris . . . please?'

'Well, really, it's part of a twenty-first birthday present – from my parents. A very belated one as the next is only a few weeks away.'

So she was, as he had thought, very young. If anything, she looked younger than nearly twenty-two.

Sunlight dazzled the traffic honking and grinding up and down the wide boulevard, and fell across the grey stone façade of the apartment houses opposite.

'You see, we were having a big twenty-first party – Laura, my twin sister, and I. Unfortunately, something nasty happened to my back a couple of weeks before and it was too late to cancel the marquee and the band and everything . . . so as I had to miss the whole thing, my father promised they'd make it up to me later on. What with one thing and another, the months went by . . . until this spring, I had some spare time, and I decided I'd like to come to France for a while. . .'

But what Kate didn't say was that her severe back trouble had been a direct result of minor damage at birth which had left a marked weakness all down the left side of her body. What she also didn't say was that during the time of the party, and for weeks afterwards, she was lying in traction, flat on her back in the local hospital. On the day of the party Laura, who was passionately devoted and protective, had decorated her hospital room with flowers and streamers and balloons. And that night, far too late for Matron's liking, she had come charging in with a dinner-jacketed boyfriend on either arm – wearing an extremely low-cut black dress of which their mother disapproved – all three carrying bottles of champagne for Kate and the nurses . . . and stayed on until their father, who was a doctor, had come in wearing his stern professional look and firmly chased them off Kate's bed and back to the revelry.

'What bad luck. Poor you. But you're not here on your own surely, are you?' Robin asked. Although she had seemed so still sitting there reading, almost like a statue – when she spoke, her features were surprisingly animated.

'Oh no . . . I'm staying for three months with family friends . . . a professor at the Sorbonne and his wife. They're absolutely charming. They have a delightful flat not far from here . . . The wife, Madame Berger, gives English conversation lessons and I've been helping her. It's fun, and I rather like it. They're having a dinner-party tonight and as there's a lot of cooking

11

and preparation going on, the lessons were cancelled. So I decided to do some wandering about on my own.'

'I see. Just like me. Funny we both wandered into the same sidewalk café, isn't it?' They smiled brightly at each other. 'How long have you been in Paris now?'

'Since February. This is my last week but one. Then I'm going with the Bergers to their farm in Normandy for a bit. I'm also supposed to be improving my French – which I think I am.'

Robin smiled sympathetically. 'My own French is pretty rough,' he murmured. Would Pierre try and fix him up for a date with Monique? Watching Kate, he somehow rather hoped not ... She looked so charming, sitting back in the wicker chair, striped with sunlight, chatting away like a schoolgirl, fingering the gold chain. A bit old-fashioned in that strict white blouse; she reminded him of a sepia photograph from the turn of the century. He had an instinct that she was more forthcoming with just one person; that she would be shy and quite withdrawn in a crowd.

'I've done a secretarial course,' she went on, making a face. 'I got through it somehow. I've had one or two temporary jobs. And when I get back I'm going to start looking for something permanent.' In fact, her back had been extremely troublesome for the whole of the year and only now was her father – and her various specialists – satisfied that she was fit enough to consider full-time work.

'It's far too marvellous a day to think about work ...' He caught sight of the two Michelins lying by their now empty cups and said abruptly, 'Look – since were both intending to soak up a bit of Left Bank atmosphere, why don't we take our respective guidebooks and do a bit of exploring together? Would you mind? And by the way, my name is Robin Faraday ...'

'I'm Kate Holford.'

They shook hands, Robin saying, 'It's about time – although as you thought you knew me, perhaps we really have met before. But I think – in fact I'm sure – that I would have remembered ...'

'I honestly did think you were a friend of Laura's. She's got

12

so many friends. But seriously, if you'd like me to show you round for an hour or so – I do know this part quite well – I would . . .' – and her chin rose slightly – 'be happy to.'

I'm being very bold, she thought. It amazed her how much more open, more confident, she had become in these months away on her own with the Bergers. *Robin Faraday*. She liked the name; even that sounded familiar. But I don't know him, Kate told herself, trying to feel shocked – and failing. Laura, who always watched her like a hawk, wouldn't be pleased.

'Marvellous . . .' He could hardly believe his luck. Without giving her time for second thoughts, he picked up both bills, pulled out some notes and signalled a waiter.

'Oh no, please . . .', Kate began, leaning forward, appalled. 'There's no need. That's quite wrong . . .' But it was too late, all done, the waiter smiling at them both, pleased with the ridiculously large tip, Robin gathering paper, map, both guide-books, getting up, pushing back his chair . . . He stood courteously behind her as she picked up her bag and sweater. Then she held onto the table firmly, as though to steady herself, and stood up slowly. She was wearing a full, grey-and-white striped skirt which draped pleasingly from the slim waist clasped by the red belt and fell almost to her ankles. He saw that she was wearing low-heeled red shoes. She was above average height.

She stood perfectly still for a moment or two before she turned to him over her shoulder and said, 'All right. Shall we go? . . .' The shiny dark hair swung round her face.

'Absolutely. Lead on.'

Only a foot or so behind her, he noticed the limp immediately. When she was younger, several delicate operations on her tendon had been reasonably successful. She had had constant therapy; her shoes were specially built up by the most skilful man in London. But the limp remained – and always would. Yet it varied in degree, as her family was aware – affected by many things: her state of mind, whether or not she was tired, if she was in unknown territory. Public places – particularly walking in and out of restaurants – were always slightly stressful. She needed to concentrate.

But today, as she threaded her way carefully past the tables – mostly full now – and onto the busy pavement, she felt confident and calm. And steady. Years of remedial dance lessons had given her a superb carriage. She held her head high and her narrow shoulders back; the skirt fluted gracefully round her calves. She was a pretty young woman with an indefinable air of distinction about her – even then. She attracted glances.

Following closely, Robin was astounded – and not for the first time that morning – by sudden forceful emotions over which he seemed to have no control at all. He knew then that his heart, or whatever it was, had been fatally pierced. Nothing Kate had said as they were talking, not even her reference to a bad back, had led him to think that she had any physical disability. And yet, following in her slightly uneven step, he found himself catapulted into a state of passionate protectiveness – which he had never remotely experienced towards another human being before. His body was tensed towards her. If she had so much as stumbled by an inch or brushed into a table he would, he knew without doubt, simply have grabbed her and swung her up in his arms.

Nothing of the sort happened. Poised, Kate reached the pavement just ahead of him and turned, squinting in the sun. She slung her scarlet sweater in a loose knot round her neck.

'Now where do you suggest?' she asked. 'Or will you leave it to me?' She glanced at her watch. 'It's still early . . . I thought perhaps Notre-Dame, a walk round the Ile de la Cité and a wander through the flower market . . .'

Then she saw Robin's face. And she knew – at least something of what had been going through his mind. She had years of experience in reading different people's reactions to the way she walked. She was expert in choosing the best approach. She invariably met it directly. It has to be dealt with, she thought, often wearily. And then perhaps we can forget all about it. Right?

Now she said lightly, 'Oh – so you noticed my poor old leg. Some people do, some don't. At least, not to start with. I've lived with it most of my life, by the way. It doesn't usually worry me, so I always think it shouldn't worry other people.'

'I'll remember.' He tried to match her naturalness and gaiety; but everything about Kate including – no, *particularly* –

14

her slight physical imperfection had sensuously aroused him. He was sweating; his heart was pounding; his breathing wasn't quite steady. But he kept cool and said jauntily, 'What you suggest sounds fine to me . . .'

'Aren't you tired?' Robin asked as they emerged into the brightness out of the vast, dark chasm of Notre-Dame. It was after midday and the sun was beating down. Surprising for early May. They had been walking for an hour – through narrow streets, along the Seine, across the Petit Pont to the Cité; dawdling in the brilliantly colourful flower market . . . and finally, into the cathedral. Even there, in the hallowed gloom, light filtered through the great rose window and irradiated the flickering votive candles.

'Not really.' Kate faced him – that smile with the gamin quality again; unexpected in so demure a young woman. 'I don't think you worry about being tired if you're doing what you want to, do you?'

'Perhaps not. But all the same, we've done a fair amount of pounding pavements . . . it's a bit early, but you wouldn't think about having lunch with me, would you? Unless you've got other plans, of course . . .'

Amazing how nervous he was of being turned down flat. A week ago – hours ago – he would never have believed it possible.

'Oh no, I haven't, not at all,' Kate assured him quickly. She shaded her eyes as they watched a pleasure boat glide past them up the river, loudspeakers droning. 'The Bergers said they'd expect me when they saw me . . . I'm sure I'll be able to help them a bit later on . . . they've got quite a lot of guests for dinner . . . but do you know what I'd really like . . .?' – spinning round towards him, her skirt billowing. She sounded breathless. In fact, she was slightly intoxicated at being on her own, doing exactly as she pleased, for once, without the loving, anxious looks of her parents and Laura.

'What's that?'

Her cheeks, which were inclined to be sallow, were flushed. 'A picnic. It's just the right day for one, isn't it?'

'And picnics should be spontaneous . . .'

15

'Absolutely . . .'

'So a picnic it is. But where?'

'Oh – in the Luxembourg Gardens. Have you been there yet? They're heavenly – and they're not very far from here. But on one condition . . .'

'Which is?'

'Half and half. You buy the wine and I'll buy the food.'

'Done.'

Their shopping finished, they were both relieved to step out of the heat, the traffic and the crowded pavements into the coolness of the gardens. It had been a long and quite steep walk up the noisy boulevard. On the way, they had chatted about their lives in London. And when Robin mentioned his old Cambridge college, Kate asked him if he knew a particular friend who would have been there about the same time, she thought. Robin remembered the name and knew him by sight.

'So you see, you could have met me somewhere after all,' he teased. 'Perhaps in somebody's rooms or at a May ball . . .'

Kate laughed. 'Quite right . . .'

Glancing at her anxiously from time to time, Robin noticed that she had shifted her bag and the shopping she insisted on carrying to her right arm. But other than taking the incline at a slightly slower pace than he would do normally, he was in no way particularly conscious of Kate's limp – which in any case was at its least discernible that day.

The stiff lines of the towering chestnuts in the Luxembourg Gardens gave welcome shade. They chose a sun-dappled bench overlooking the wide breadth of the pond which was encircled by statues. Children played nearby; opposite sat an old lady dressed entirely in black, still as one of the statues, her wrinkled face lifted to the sun.

Robin, who had also bought a cheap corkscrew and two tumblers, opened the bottle of red wine. He took off his jacket and rolled up his sleeves. Kate had laid paper napkins on the bench between them; she reached into her assortment of plastic bags, and put out a long baguette, coarse pâté, a wedge of pale yellow brie and two large apples.

'There's only one knife so we'll have to share,' she told him.

'Here.'

Robin handed her a glass and she took it saying gaily, 'I'm sure we ought to toast something . . . I mean, just look . . .' Her arm traced an arc taking in the trees, the elegant view, the sunshine. Paris. 'Aren't we *lucky* to be here, in exactly this spot, today, having a picnic?' She tossed back the fine dark hair. She had delicate features – nice cheekbones, a straight nose and rather a wide mouth. Her skin was smooth olive – already warmed by the sun. There was a trace of perspiration on her upper lip. '*Look* . . .'

She collapsed against the back of the bench and turned to him. Robin had an absurd desire to lean over and kiss her throat, or perhaps lower down, where the neat white blouse made a division between her breasts. He swallowed hard and raised his glass.

'Let's drink to that – being here on a spring day in Paris . . .' He would have liked to have added 'together' – but refrained.

If Laura could only see me now, Kate thought guiltily, she simply wouldn't believe it. Picnicking on a park bench with a man who – let's be honest – had picked her up in an outdoor café on the Boulevard St Germain just a couple of hours before; and, what was more, enjoying every minute . . . 'You must stop being so shy,' Laura was always telling her. Mother too. 'Show more of an interest in people – and then they will in you . . .' For years, since she was about fourteen, she had been stuck in a cloying, youthful relationship with, literally, the boy next door. David. It had eventually petered out on both their sides. No one who knew her at home would recognise this new, reckless self. It must be something to do with being abroad.

'Can I have some more wine, please?' She held out her glass.

Between mouthfuls, they revealed much of their selves to the other. Robin thought that the absence of formal introduction encouraged such openness; there were no inhibiting social factors to be cut through first. He found himself telling her how fed up he was with the merchant bank. 'It's unbelievably dreary, hanging about, never really getting your hands on the good deals, waiting for dead men's shoes, everything blanketed in gentility and tradition . . .'

17

So why, Kate enquired, if he felt like that, didn't he move on to something else?

'Good question.' He took a piece of brie, perfectly ripe, and broke off a crust of bread. 'My old man is completely self made – much to his credit. Came up the hard way, left school at thirteen, supported his widowed mother, almost a cliché ... and when the steel holding company he worked for went bankrupt, he somehow managed to persuade the local bank manager to lend him the money to keep it going. That was in the thirties when things were very rough in the Midlands. Well, he kept it ticking over through the war and after, by some fluke, he got into supplying television aerials. It took off in a big way. He sold out a few years ago and he and my mother moved to Jersey. I'm an only child ... Dad's always been very generous financially and in every other way ... and of course I've had all the education, the chances he never had ...'

'I still don't see why you have to stick with that stuffy bank.' She could tell that he hated the sight of the place.

'I don't, really.' Robin sighed heavily. 'The trouble is that being the first generation with some education I feel I want to make my own mark in the world somehow ... Guilt perhaps. And Dad, who's still got his good broad accent, gets a terrific kick out of flaunting the name of the bloody bank ... he was very proud when I got my rowing Blue as well ...'

'That doesn't seem to be a very good reason for hanging on, just so your father can say you work for so-and-so's even if it is so prestigious. You sound ambitious ...'

'I am that.' His chin squared. 'And in all fairness, the bank did put me through Harvard Business School. I'm considered to be one of the younger employees who they're grooming, so to speak, for a plum job. Not that you'd think it from the work I'm given,' he added gloomily.

'In that case, wouldn't you be much better off working for a company you enjoyed? Cambridge and Harvard must have given you the best training there is. Here ...' She passed him a piece of apple.

'Thanks. You're absolutely right of course. And as a matter of fact, I've been approached by an outfit just starting up, doing the same kind of thing – mergers and acquisitions – but in a much smaller way. A couple of go-ahead friends that I was at university with. I won't bore you with it all, but they reckon there's a market to be tapped – dicier, leaner firms who need a leg up or a loan or perhaps a merger situation or even a management buy-out but who don't want the full power – and the fees – of the big boys . . .'

'There you are then,' Kate said lightly. 'That's the sort of thing you should be looking out for. What else do you like doing – apart from work?'

'That's easy.' He grinned at her, his blue eyes crinkling, and splashed the rest of the wine into their glasses. 'Skiing, tennis, squash . . . tramping over moors and mountains. Travelling to odd corners of the world, the wilder the better, with a tent and rucksack on my back . . .' He had a restless, sporty look about him, Kate thought. He obviously kept in good shape physically. She could imagine him hiking through some rough faraway country, a desert perhaps. 'And what about you – do you like travelling?'

He remembered her leg and cursed himself for being tactless. But Kate just smiled serenely and said that no, she didn't think she was a traveller but that she, too, had lots of pleasures away from bashing at a typewriter. She began to peel another apple.

Robin watched. 'Tell me the things *you* like doing . . .'

'Oh – arty things, I suppose you'd call them. I love paintings. I'd like to study art history really. My father is a doctor, but he's interested in art as well . . . we have rather the same tastes . . .' They were very close, those two, and for years he had been taking her with him to galleries and museums. 'Oh – and clothes, I do enjoy the idea of clothes – but I expect that sounds dreadfully frivolous.'

'Not at all.' He allowed himself a lingering look over the strict blouse which had a pleasing fullness at the shoulders; the wide red belt and the flowing skirt. Neat red shoes. 'I think women should look good. It makes life pleasanter for everyone – women and men. And I don't think that sounds too sexist.'

'No it doesn't. I agree. I've always known exactly what I wanted – and what colours – ever since I was little. I used to drive my poor mother mad.' She had – and made shopping expeditions into a wearysome chore. Chubby and easy-going, Laura as a child had accepted whatever dress or sweater was suggested. But not Kate. *She* would insist on a bottle-green velvet dress, please Mummy, not navy again ... and a red cardigan, please oh please, not beige like Laura's. And Felicity Holford, knowing that another operation wasn't far away, would give in. On this, at least. And over clothes, Kate never changed. Later in her life, when she could afford it, she was just as definite. She didn't buy a lot – but whatever she did buy was carefully thought out.

'Pictures and clothes. That's a good start. What else then?' Robin leant back comfortably, his arm stretched along the top of the bench towards her. He was already wondering how he could persuade this beguiling girl to keep him company through the afternoon. His fingers rested a couple of inches from her shoulder. He wanted, badly, to touch her. The thought of her walking away from him – to the flat and the family she was staying with – was beginning to disturb him seriously. So he held on to the last of his wine and played for time and tried to think ahead; a plan she wouldn't be likely to refuse ... 'What else?'

Kate, relaxed by the sun and the wine, was looking dreamily towards an enormous round bed of pink and blue forget-me-nots around a statue of Pan. 'Flowers and gardening, perhaps. Isn't that bed enchanting? Everything over here is so much further ahead ...'

'We're a good deal further south, after all,' Robin said seriously, looking up at the great blossoming chestnuts.

'You sound very professional,' Kate teased, eyes alight. 'I think you must be an explorer manqué, not a banker, a sort of present day Dr Livingstone ...'

Robin laughed. 'Definitely ... you've hit on my favourite fantasy. An explorer in the 1800s when there was still some decent unknown territory in the world. I'd have loved that, despite the dangers and the discomfort. Hacking through the tropical undergrowth, bearers to carry the stores. And who knows, I might even have discovered something ...'

'An island? Or some straits?' So she had been right in her

vision of him striding determinedly through the bush. Kate leant forward slightly – lips parted, laughing too. Her shoulder brushed his fingertips sending an electric current right up his arm.

'Why not a mountain?' he demanded. 'Mount Faraday has a nice ring about it . . .'

'Or a river. The Robin . . . H'm – doesn't sound quite right . . .'

It was the first time either of them had used the other's first name. Robin immediately came up with an idea – and pounced. He wasn't going to lose her yet, not if he could help it. He seized her hand in a very friendly way.

'Speaking of rivers, you wouldn't be kind enough to introduce me to the Seine, would you? It's a marvellous way to see a bit of Paris . . .' Kate drew back, hesitating, very conscious of his large hand covering hers. Also – pleased by it. 'Oh do, Kate . . .' Her name; he'd said it. 'On an afternoon like this . . . and if you haven't got anything pressing . . .' He already knew she hadn't, not until later. 'You can phone your French friends and tell them when to expect you . . . please . . . Kate . . .'

Laura would faint dead away with shock, no doubt about that. Mother too. But he was so nice, this stranger who didn't seem like a stranger at all; such fun to be with. And he looked so solid, so trustworthy; all her instincts told her this. Also his smile – and he was smiling then – was quite hard to resist. Laura would certainly agree with that.

'Well – all right . . .'

'Marvellous.' Robin turned his wrist slightly without letting go of her hand. 'It's only a quarter to two. Shall we dump all this stuff, find you a phone and start making our way?'

Chapter 3

When they reached the embarkation point, they just had time to buy tickets and rush aboard before a sailing. 'That was a close shave,' Robin remarked as the boat started to move off almost immediately. 'Here we go . . . I've wanted to do this for years . . .'

'The last time I did it was very dreary – it poured the whole time,' Kate said, looking up at the wide blue sky and getting out in her sunglasses. 'We're off . . .'

Moving out into mid-stream, caught up in the fun of it, they were like a couple of kids on a holiday outing. They sat in the open, in the bright sunlight, licking ices, pointing out the sights to each other as they came into view. A stiff breeze whipped their hair. They passed under bridges, along wide quays, past ancient stone walls hung with curtains of ivy. Rounding the nether side of Notre-Dame, Kate drew his attention to the intricate buttressed stonework; Robin squinted up at the terrifying gargoyles. 'Now that's the stuff of night-mares . . .'

Coming back down river, they went and stood by the rail – Kate leaning over; Robin, arms folded, balanced with his back against it, trying to pinpoint landmarks.

'What's it like, being a twin?' he asked suddenly, looking down at her.

'I can't answer that question, can I?' – pushing her sun-glasses on top of her head, grinning up at him. 'I've never known anything else. For example, what's it like being an only child?'

'Good point.' He laughed. 'Are you two identical?'

'Yes we are. Only nobody thinks so because we've got such

different personalities.' And because Laura, she thought – sighing inwardly as she sometimes did – didn't have to contend with her unreliable, and frequently troublesome, left side. 'She's considered much more outgoing than I am, more of a party girl. Also, she's fatter.'

Most people are, thought Robin. She was leaning on her elbows in such a way as to push her thin shoulder blades out against her blouse. Like a skinny child standing on a beach in a bathing suit. Her hair had fallen forward exposing the nape of her neck. Childlike and terribly vulnerable. Robin experienced a surge of tenderness. He crossed his arms even tighter.

Over the years, there had been so many girls. Only one serious relationship, with the wife of a visiting professor from England when he had been at Harvard – a passionate and secretive affair which had ended painfully for them both. And now, two years after, he had found Kate – so young, elegant, a bit waif-like – sitting reading in the sidewalk café, just two tables away from him. He turned and leant on the rail beside her. The boat slid on down the wide river, slicing Paris through the heart. The sun had already begun to lose warmth and the water turned inky.

'As you're so well up on art,' he began cunningly, after a long and friendly silence between them, 'perhaps you could begin to educate me in the artistic treasures of Paris. I slogged round the Louvre by myself on Sunday but I've still got four and a half empty days ahead . . .'

Excitedly she said, 'The Jeu de Paume. Oh – definitely. You must go there . . . it's a divine place, all the most wonderful impressionists . . .'

It was also one of the places which Robin had marked down as a 'must' before he set out that morning.

'Any chance of us going together tomorrow?' he asked hopefully. 'It's not much fun on one's own.'

Kate straightened and shook her head. 'I'm so sorry,' she said apologetically, looking up. 'But we're chockablock with conversation lessons tomorrow to make up for today.' She sounded, and felt, regretful. He had behaved perfectly after – well – after they had eventually met properly. They even laughed at the same things; he could so easily have been someone she knew at home. The day had gone by in a flash . . .

Damn and blast, thought Robin, irritated. A whole wasted day . . .

'Perhaps . . .' Kate began. She saw that when he wasn't smiling his mouth looked severe. His eyes were a clear blue. Kate thought his face seemed suddenly flushed.

'Perhaps what?' He could see that they were ending up, and preparing to berth, at the bridge where they had started. There was no time to be lost. 'What, Kate?'

'I suppose I could,' she said slowly and gravely, 'if Ina doesn't mind, get off a bit early . . .'

She was thinking: I must have gone mad. Laura would be furious. Her heart was thundering now. One thing to have a bit of an adventure by day – but to actually make a date. His arms, beneath the rolled up sleeves, were almost touching hers.

'How early?'

'Sixish . . .'

'Not until *then*?'

No mistaking his disappointment. Kate drew her breath. They faced each other, very close. Passengers were starting to disembark. Neither moved. More than anything else in the world Kate wanted to fling herself at his chest, her arms tight round his neck.

'You could come and meet the Bergers,' she said faintly.

They could continue the white lie she had already told on the phone about knowing him before. And he would like them – and they him. That would make it seemly. Wouldn't it?

'All right. I'll pick you up – we'll have dinner.' He sounded resigned. 'Look – we've got to get off this thing . . .' An official was advancing towards them. He took her hand and they descended onto the quay. Without speaking, still holding hands, they started walking across the bridge to the Left Bank. Half way over, Kate stopped and put on her thick sweater, buttoning it right up to her chin. She was shivery. Warning lights flickered. She suddenly started to feel achingly exhausted. Her left leg was dragging.

Robin, doing some quick thinking – noticing none of these things – was wondering if he could press her further and try for an earlier meeting tomorrow. On the other hand, she was obviously very sheltered and he didn't want to put her off completely. Her address and phone number were essential.

'I enjoyed that. It was great fun. Thank you so much for coming,' Robin said politely. 'We are going in the right direction, aren't we?'

'For me – yes . . .' She could feel her energy draining rapidly. She thought of the evening ahead. She had looked forward to the party for days. She must rest. If only she could reach the flat before she felt worse.

Then – sickeningly – came that dreaded pain. Hot and sharp. All down her left side, pulling at her fingers, her arm, her hip, her leg. She had done too much. *It* knew. It was never, never fooled. And it was no time to fight. Not against this all too familiar adversary. Father knew that. And *he* knew that *she* knew. Yet today, she had broken all the rules.

'Could you get me a taxi please, Robin? Now. I think there's a rank across the road.' Her voice was always one of the first things to go. It was ragged and whispery.

'Kate?' One glance was enough. She was ill. 'Wait here. Don't move. I see a taxi. I'll come back and get you.' He was off, dodging traffic, arm raised, wrenching the door of a waiting cab. He raced back and grabbed her, half carried, half handed her in – and got in after her. She gave the address – 33 Rue Napoléon – to the driver quite steadily. Then, huddled in a corner, she tipped back her head and closed her eyes. Her face was pinched and drawn.

Robin stared. He was acutely alarmed – and yet he felt helpless. He could hardly believe that this was the same girl who, some ten minutes before, had been standing laughing with him at the rail. Christ, how could he have been such an insensitive bastard? She was exhausted, probably in pain. He had seen she was slightly lame, almost from the beginning. But she had made so light of the fact, spoken of it almost gaily, wanted him – so he thought – to ignore it. And for most of the day, he had. She had seemed so well, so full of life.

The taxi lurched and bounced, occasionally stopping in a screech of brakes. As they came to a stop, Kate turned her head towards him, opened her eyes and managed a bit of a smile.

'I'm dreadfully sorry ... this happens to me sometimes if I'm not careful ...' Almost a croak. She slid her hand, her good right hand, over the worn leather towards him. 'I didn't terrify you, did I?'

'It's *my* fault,' he said quite violently. 'Dragging you half across Paris ...' On the edge of the seat, his back to the driver, eyes never leaving her face. He took her hand, which was icy cold, and chafed it between both of his – his breath was coming so hard that he had the sensation of choking. Tremendous feelings of protectiveness, all mixed up with sexual excitement, had taken possession of him.

There were bluish shadows under her eyes; her left leg, painfully thin, stuck out awkwardly. And he who had never known a day's illness in his life ...

Kate closed her eyes again and moved her head.

The taxi finally stopped with a jolt.

'Hold on. I'll come round and get you.' Kate was groping for her bag. 'Don't move yet. Please.'

The taxi roared off and left them standing in a narrow street somewhere, Robin judged, between the Boulevard St Michel and the river. They were outside a fortress-like façade and an ancient, nail-studded door. To the side, he saw a row of bells.

Her left shoulder was drooping badly as she rummaged awkwardly through her bag and pulled out a key.

'You're sure there's someone there?' he insisted. The thought of her disappearing behind that formidable door made him desperate. 'Look – can't I come up with you – at least to the flat?'

'No, no ... Tomorrow. About six. It's Flat 2 – ring the bell here and I'll come and get you.' Her voice sounded wan; no sign of the charm and animation she had shown all day. A plain, pale little face above the bright sweater.

'But what about the phone?'

He scribbled it down in his diary, writing the name of his hotel, tearing out the page and giving it to her. She took a couple of steps with difficulty and put the key in the lock. The door swung open with surprising ease. Inside, Robin was amazed to see a pretty courtyard with blossoming trees and a fountain playing in the centre.

'Thank you for bringing me back,' Kate said. Her eyes betrayed the mixture of pain and tiredness she felt. 'And for the whole day. It was like nothing I've ever . . .'

'For me too,' Robin broke in.

They stared at each other for almost a minute.

'Well then – until tomorrow . . .'

He knew that he had to walk. And for a long way. He felt stifled, bursting with undischarged energy. He made his way down to the river and started striding along, past the bookstalls. He recognised the different bridges now. He decided where he would cross over to the other bank; memorised streets and squares and landmarks. Soothed, as always, by strenuous exercise.

Oddly, he did not think of Kate at all; or of anything else very much. He couldn't – yet. He was revelling in the cool early evening air, and the sounds and smells and sights of Paris. He had a talent for absorbing new places. He couldn't get enough of them.

Further on, he stopped at a bar where he threw down a Pernod. He jumped on a bus that seemed to be going in his general direction – and when he found it hopelessly stuck in traffic, jumped off again. He walked the rest of the way to the hotel.

'One minute Sir . . .' The girl at the desk stopped him as she handed him his key. 'There is a message . . .'

'Oh – thanks.' He put it in his pocket and headed for the creaky old birdcage lift. He felt in a state of mild elation and thought that another Pernod would go down nicely.

The message was from Pierre. He had tried to get him several times during the day. Would he please ring him at his home? He did. His cousin Monique had arrived and was free this evening; they were having dinner with some other friends at an amusing restaurant in the Rue Maboeuf, not far from the Étoile – and would he please join them?

Going through the pockets of his jacket when he changed, Robin pulled out two slim green Michelin guides. Holding one in each hand, he stared down at them. And only then did his mind clear and the day finally come into focus.

Chapter 4

It was very quiet as Kate had let herself into the sprawling family flat late that afternoon. There was no one about. The preparations for the evening finished, Ina must have taken herself off to rest. Intensely relieved, Kate made her way painfully down the long corridor to her room. She kicked off her shoes, undressed and put on a dressing-gown. Then, in the small adjoining bathroom, she shook out two of her strongest pills, poured a glass of water and swallowed them. She got onto the bed – still shivering, still feeling faintly sick – put a pillow under her left leg, and pulled up a blanket. She lay on her back, eyes closed, arms crossed over her chest – and waited. If she was lucky, the pills would start working, she would drift off for a bit – and apart from feeling weak and shaken she would start to mend. Her whole body permanently out of kilter, muscles and ligaments strained easily. Usually, her acute early warning system alerted her in time. But not today . . .

She was beginning to doze already . . . no harm done. No more than there was already . . .

Her mother had had a late first birth; a long labour and a difficult delivery. Twins. Laura was born – lusty, a goodish size. Then – Kate. Forceps used on her shoulder with too heavy a hand; it was only a matter of a little too much pressure for a few vital seconds. She was tiny and floppy, hard to get going. There were anxious moments with her breathing. But the trauma had already occurred. Her father picked it up first; seeing her kicking in the bath, one leg very slightly shorter and less well developed than the other. And when she started to reach, always favouring her right side; noticeably less strength in her left arm. They took her to the teaching hospital in London where he had trained. Her father's observations were confirmed. But there was absolutely no sign of any mental impairment whatsoever. It was a question of watching and waiting and taking appropriate steps. Her good right side would compensate naturally. Later, there were operations – a series, carried out at different ages, to build up and strengthen the left leg – and therapy. All of which she had had, with at least partial success.

But her constitution was never robust. Childhood illnesses knocked her out; colds lingered and frequently became bronchitis. Worry about Kate's health was never absent within the family for long. She was a patient, quiet child. Keeping up with Laura from the first, as she did, taught her determination. Beneath her gentle exterior, she always had courage – whether it was learning to ride a bike or play tennis at school or facing another spell in hospital. As she grew up, she learnt to deal with her condition with common sense and optimism. Most of the time she got the balance of what she could and could not expect to do, right. And coping with minor disability, she had so many small victories in her everyday life. It could, after all, have been very much worse. In their different ways, her parents and Laura were all intensely proud of her. Kate knew this; it was the source of her considerable inner strength.

She very nearly slept . . .

An hour or so later she saw – or so she believed – Robin sitting on the side of the bed. She was just going to tell him that he had gone off with her Michelin by mistake when his figure faded and she realised that she was still dreaming. She opened her eyes again and moved her left leg experimentally. Everything ached. But the nausea had gone – and with it, the deathly tiredness.

She was lying perfectly still when Ina Berger knocked lightly and stuck her head round the door. She spoke in French.

'Kate? All right, my dear? I heard you come in, but I was in bed resting myself.'

Kate smiled at her sleepily. She, too, spoke French.

'What time is it? I was just thinking that it was about time I got up and began to dress.'

'There is no hurry . . .' She stood by the bed, looking down at Kate, her eyes showing concern. 'You are quite well? You are sure?'

'But absolutely. I'm going to get up,' Kate said, pulling herself up, leaning on her elbow, making an effort. 'He's very nice, the man I told you I met. Robin Faraday. We've got mutual friends . . . wasn't it a strange coincidence meeting like that on the Boul Mich?' Sounding natural, she thought.

'But so lucky.' Ina shrugged eloquently. 'And such a lovely day and you had company . . .'

'Yes . . . and Ina, he's taking me out to dinner tomorrow. I told him to pick me up here about six. I do want you and Louis to meet him. Will that be all right? And with the lessons too?'

'Of course, darling. We'll be finished by then . . . but now I must go and get ready . . .'

When she got to the door Kate, who was reviving quickly, was suddenly conscience-stricken. 'I've been no help at all today, Ina. Do tell me, please, what I can do . . .'

Ina smiled at her affectionately. 'Be charming. That's all.'

A long soak in a warm bath gave Kate another boost. She was going to be all right; she wouldn't give in. Her will-power rarely let her down. She had been intending to wear a new red dress she had bought in a small dressmaking shop in a nearby street. But she didn't feel up to it. Not tonight. She moved cautiously about the room. Her limp would be bad this evening. She frowned. She would have to be especially careful passing drinks or handing anything. She took out a long, floaty pair of black trousers that looked like a skirt – which she had borrowed from Laura. A creamy silk shirt. The trousers were much too big but she could pull the waist in with a black and silver belt.

When she was dressed, she looked in the mirror – and seeing how pale she was, added colour to her cheeks. That looked better and healthier. She brushed her hair until it fell on either side of her face in dark wings. She would do. A miracle when just a couple of hours ago . . .

All the time she was dressing, she had been conscious of

sounds from the other end of the flat – footsteps, voices, glasses clinking. Preparations in full swing; expectation building ... At last, the bell shrilled – and she heard Ina calling anxiously to Louis. The first guests were arriving. Then something she remembered made her smile. It had, after all, been the most extraordinary day ... She tucked a mild pill, just in case, into her black velvet evening bag. But she was feeling human again. 'Thank you God,' she murmured fervently – head up, shoulders back, steeling herself. And as she opened her door she was thinking: where is Robin now?

The flat was ablaze with light. It had the comfortable feel of a much lived-in family home – as it had been throughout the forty-odd years of the Bergers' marriage. It was crammed with books and pictures; well worn chairs and sofas; everywhere, photographs taken down the years of the four children and now *their* children. Generations of students had passed through.

Hearing Kate behind him, Louis Berger – tall and silver-haired and patrician – immediately took her by the arm and drew her into the small group, introducing her as the English girl he had known since she was a child – when he and Ina had first met her parents in Normandy. And now here she was, a cherished guest who was also proving a valuable addition to Ina's classes.

Kate shook hands acknowledging friendly greetings – and silently hoped that her French would be up to the occasion. Wine was offered from silver trays. The bell again, and again; more guests, laughter. Ina, chic in black, welcoming, introducing. People gradually moving from the wide hall into the sitting-room, softly lit and decorated with enormous bouquets of spring flowers and blossoms. And everyone wanting to talk to Kate who had such charming manners, who spoke French so prettily – and who looked delightful.

The telephone rang in the hall just before dinner was to be announced. One of the maids came up to Kate and whispered, '*Le téléphone . . . c'est pour vous Mademoiselle . . .*'

Kate excused herself. It was unlikely to be Laura or her parents to whom she had spoken last Sunday. Then who . . .?

31

She passed the dining-room where candles were being lit at two large round tables covered to the ground in white damask. The phone was on a low stand near the door. She picked it up, ''Allo . . .'

As though from very far away there came a crackling sound – the buzz of background conversation and clattering plates. Some shouts, then, 'Kate?'

She hadn't, not for one moment, thought that it would be him. And yet as soon as she heard his voice she remembered all the things she had to tell him, thoughts tumbling into her head one after the other. She said nothing.

'Kate? Kate, is that you?'

He must be in some public place. There was clearly lots going on all round him. He seemed to be speaking very close into the mouthpiece.

'Yes. Wherever are you?'

'Somewhere. Some restaurant with friends.' Dismissively. 'But I've been worried . . . are you better?'

'Yes. I'm all right now. In fact . . .' her voice warming, 'I'm feeling absolutely fine.'

'Good. You sound it.' He was both immensely relieved and at the same time dismayed, however preposterously, to hear that she was enjoying herself – without him. 'Has the party started?'

'Yes – yes, we're just going in to dinner.' She set down her wine glass. 'I'm sorry about today – at the end. I'll explain to-morrow.'

There was a pause as coins clinked and whirred at his end and then he said, 'Don't go . . . I'm missing you . . .' He was. The group he was with, although friendly enough, meant nothing to him. He could picture, precisely, the narrow wrist and the long fingers holding the receiver; in some dingy flat behind that improbable medieval door.

'Are you?' she whispered. Her cheeks flamed. The noise behind him, whatever restaurant it was, rose to a crescendo.

'*Yes,*' he boomed.

Then she remembered one thing, at least, that she wanted to tell him. 'You know, you did go off with my Michelin after all . . .' She practically shouted; it seemed so very funny.

'I know. I know. I found it in my pocket when I changed.'

He was laughing too. 'I'll bring it tomorrow. It's mad, isn't it?'

Much later Robin thanked Pierre for his hospitality and arranged to lunch with him at the end of the week. Then he strode away, alone, into the fine night, past busy cafés and banks of brilliant neon lights. Down the wide avenue, crossing streets, weaving in and out of the crowds strolling, as he was, late in the mild spring air.

And all the way back, hardly noticing his surroundings for once, his head was filled with the possibilities of Kate.

Chapter 5

'So now you know,' Kate said to Robin across the table at dinner the following evening. They were in a well-recommended neighbourhood restaurant which Robin had chosen as being both off the tourist track and close to the Bergers' flat. 'That's the medical history of my left side in a nutshell ... Very brief. I've left out the boring bits. But although Father thinks I know how to manage *it* – and myself – best at this point, I do make mistakes. And it happens on the good days, when I forget, like yesterday. And then, suddenly, I go to pieces. In every way. As you saw.'

'Poor Kate.'

Her hand, so slender, lay on the pink cloth. Robin experienced a wave of excitement and, at the same time, feelings of intense protectiveness. Because he realised, with astonishment, that Kate was that rare breed, practically unknown nowadays – a physically delicate young woman. He had thought there was something attractively old-fashioned about her from the first. In comparison with her, the girls he knew were tough creatures – back-packing through Greece, thinking nothing of working ten-hour days in the City and then partying half the night. His own rugged good health, which he had always taken totally for granted, briefly discomforted him.

'It's not so bad. Honestly. I've learnt to be a great survivor ...'

The way she looked, now, proved it. Her attractively gamin smile was full of verve. She was wearing her new red dress with a wide neckline, soft sleeves and a long row of small, covered buttons all down the front. The colour lit her face and only the still dark shadows beneath her eyes gave any sign of yesterday's exhaustion. She had worked steadily with Ina's students all day, leaving herself only just time to change before Robin arrived.

'So I see.' His hand took hers and stayed there until the waiter arrived with his *filet de boeuf* and veal for Kate. He had been up by seven and had systematically explored several quarters of the city, using the Metro extensively and walking for miles. He was starving. 'Aren't the Bergers charming?'

'Nice people,' Robin agreed. He had enjoyed talking to the Professor who had once dined in his Cambridge college; he found Ina Berger warm and attractive. Both he and Kate had referred discreetly, just once, to their imaginary mutual friends. 'They obviously love having you there . . . and Madame was extremely complimentary about your French . . .'

'I think she's rather flattering, but last night I found I had no difficulty talking in a group. And that's the real test, isn't it? My typing and shorthand are quite good, so the language might help me get a job that's a bit more interesting than the average.'

'I'm sure it will . . . What does Laura do, by the way?'

'She's training to be an interior decorator, working as assistant to one of the really top ones in Knightsbridge. I know she'll be good. She's got real flair. She's always loved anything to do with houses and furnishing. She says she wants to start her own business eventually. She's extremely efficient.'

He looked at her with his head on one side. 'I can't quite imagine the two of you . . . I must meet Laura when we're back in London.'

'Oh you will – you'll like her. She's very bouncy, great fun . . .' They smiled at each other. 'And she's going to be the career woman in the family. Although Mother is a writer . . .'

'Really?' Robin was interested. 'Should I know . . .?'

Kate shook her head. 'Probably not. Although her last book got very respectful reviews. She's a biographer . . . she discovers women, born in the last century, who have had useful and interesting lives – but who aren't much known. And digs up everything she can about them until she's got a good story, a piece of social history really. It's quite tricky because the famous ones have usually been "done" . . . We do tease her

35

about it, but she works away terribly hard – and she's getting recognition at last.'

'I'm impressed.'

He was starting to piece together an accurate picture of Kate's background. Her father a doctor in general practice, with artistic leanings; mother – writer and keen gardener. The twin daughters, identical, but with quite different personalities. A family house in the country, a small London flat which Kate and Laura obviously used a lot.

'We're very proud of her. You said that your father had sold his business and retired . . . do your parents live in Jersey all the time?'

'Yes they do. Although they travel quite a lot, cruises and that sort of thing. Dad's keen on golf and he plays whenever he gets the chance. And he's got a few cronies . . .'

'What about your mother?'

Robin flushed. He got on well with his father, admired his bluntness and enjoyed his open affection and his pride. He had done well by dint of hard work and good business sense. But his mother, whose big frame and fair colouring he had inherited, irritated him. He was also slightly ashamed of her; by the standards of the world in which he moved, she was provincial, limited, too quick to talk about money. And what were her interests? Apart from the hairdresser and obsessive house cleaning and a tendency to nag his father, particularly if he took an extra nightcap, he couldn't think of any. Unless it was her constant prying into his social life, hinting that it was about time he married 'well' – and presented them with some grandchildren. 'You know your father and I would gladly help out with a house and education and such like.' Money again; Robin wincing.

'She's more or less of a housewife,' he said hurriedly. 'Now what are you going to have next?'

Over their second cups of coffee, while they were still talking away as though they had known each other for months instead of not yet two days, Robin brought up the subject of tomorrow. Because Ina Berger, liking Robin on sight, had insisted over their aperitifs that Kate had been working too hard, that with this spell of wonderful weather and a friend visiting, she must take the rest of the week off to enjoy Paris. Not for nothing had she married off her own two daughters and welcomed two suitable daughters-in-law into the family.

Robin had blessed her silently.

'So what about tomorrow, Kate? Where will we go? What will we do?' It would only be Wednesday; the plane he must take late on Saturday seemed an eternity away. Beyond the intimate atmosphere of the restaurant lay the whole of Paris over which another limpid spring day would soon be dawning. To be enjoyed. Together.

Kate rested an elbow on the table, her chin in her hand.

'Let's think about it,' she said.

They kissed for the first time the next afternoon, sitting on the sweet new grass beneath blossoming cherry trees in the Bois de Boulogne. Robin's arms came round her and he pulled her down beside him – and it seemed the most natural thing in the world to lie there together, in that public place, quite unselfconscious, telling each other how happy and how lucky they were. It was something neither of them would ever have dreamt of doing in London, in Hyde Park.

'It was my cheek, coming over to you like that, I didn't even think . . . you must give me credit . . .' – hugging her, acutely aware of her fragility encircled by his physical strength.

'I do, I do . . .'

After a while, Kate opened her eyes and looked up beyond Robin's shoulder – he was covering her neck in kisses – and saw fragments of blue above the shimmering pink blossom. Trembling on a delicate branch, a thrush sang his heart out. The earth felt warm and dry.

'Do you believe in God, Robin . . .?'

'Mmmm . . . you smell wonderful . . . what is it?'

'Guerlain . . . but do you, Robin, believe in God?'

'No.'

He lifted his head. His hair had fallen over his forehead and his eyes were blue and guileless. He looked exactly like a small boy. Kate laughed and pushed back his hair.

'Laura doesn't either. Nor does Mother. Father and I do though. We go to church every Sunday.'

'You two can pray for the rest of us. Our souls are in your hands . . .'

'Silly . . .'

'You've developed freckles, a wavy line of them, on the top of your nose and across your cheeks . . .'

'I always do in the sun.'

'I love you, Kate . . .'

They went to the Flea Market and the Jeu de Paume and the Eiffel Tower; they explored the winding streets of Montmartre and saw the whole of Paris, lying below in the sun, from outside the Sacré Coeur. They held hands and exchanged kisses and talked and built up a short lifetime of shared memories. All in those few idyllic days. Robin watched carefully for any signs of Kate's tiredness – there were none. Since there was so much to see – and so little time – he insisted on spending a fortune on taxis. One night, they ate a superb meal in a famous restaurant; but mostly they wandered into bars and small cafés as they felt like it, sitting outside, starting to feel like natives.

Kate flitted in and out of the flat. She hardly saw the Bergers, although Ina, meeting her in the hall as she rushed out for dinner with Robin on Thursday evening, noted her shining eyes with approval.

'How pretty you are . . .' – in her red dress again, with a black shawl thrown round her shoulders. She had questioned Kate, lightly, about Robin's background and was quite satisfied as to his suitability . . . 'Enjoy the evening, my darling . . . have a wonderful time, *bon soir* . . .'

'Thank you. I will. Goodnight, dear Ina . . .'

The great door slamming behind her, Kate made her way down to the quay where she had arranged to meet Robin. He was there already, but because he was so engrossed in some prints hanging along the bookstall, he didn't see her. A few yards away, Kate stopped. She watched him. Very tall, he bent slightly to study the prints; he, too, had caught the sun and his face – although she was looking at him sideways – was tanned. She liked the way his hair grew at the back of his neck. He held the print up to the fading light to see it better.

38

Standing there, poised on the brink of love, Kate was surprised to feel a complexity of emotions: wonder, fear, joy, anguish. Not the simple uplifting happiness she had expected. It was nothing remotely like what she had felt for David, despite their years of youthful passion.

Robin straightened. He had evidently decided to buy the print. He spoke to the stallholder. Kate called out, 'Robin . . .'

He turned and saw her and held out his arms. 'Perfect timing . . . I've just bought us a present.'

'You're so extravagant,' she murmured. Each had an arm round the other.

'It's such a marvellous evening, darling Kate, the best we've had, look at that sky . . .' The vast expanse was streaked with pinks and mauves and lilacs and purples, the riotous explosion of colour merging around the edges into velvety midnight blue. 'Can we stroll for a bit, by the river . . .?' Hesitant, still, about her walking.

'Of course. Let's . . .'

They walked down the steps onto the wide quay. It was so calm; the trees were perfectly still. Barges slid across the darkening river. The waters lapped and lights came on. Across, on the promontory of the Ile de la Cité, a flautist was practising – playing the first few bars of a song over and over . . . *'The shadow of your smile . . .'* Stop. *'The shadow . . .'* Stop. *'The shadow of your smile when . . .'* Stop.

'I wish he'd get on with it,' said Kate, amused, slipping her arm through Robin's.

'Maddening . . . there it goes again . . .'

The notes floated sweetly through the dusk . . . *'The shadow of your smile when day is done . . .'* Stop.

'That's a bit better. It's a great song though.' He turned and folded his arms round her. Couples like themselves sauntered by; a woman walking a dog; there was a man sitting at the bottom of the steps patiently fishing. The traffic above was muted. They stood close to the river, watching as the sky turned richer and darker. Rapidly now, mist crept up over the bridges and the roofs, around the tall street lamps, giving a soft blue focus.

'Just the way it's supposed to,' Kate whispered. *'L'heure bleue . . .'*

'*L'heure bleue* . . .' Something stirred in Robin's memory but didn't surface. 'Translation, please,' Robin said against her hair. 'Twilight?' he asked hopefully.

'*Le crépuscule* . . . twilight. It is really. But I like the other better.'

'Such a romantic . . .' Robin held her tighter, feeling her slenderness against him, aroused. 'The hour of blue then?'

'Blue dusk.'

He saw her upturned face. Shadows all around them now. Her hands behind his neck pulling him down to her.

'Kate?'

'What?'

'Kate – I . . .'

All his being given up to that moment.

'*Now*. Your hotel. Let's go there,' she breathed.

He had known all along they would.

Chapter 6

He whisked her through the foyer and up in the old-fashioned birdcage lift. Neither spoke and Kate clutched his hand. Guests had left in search of cocktails and dinner and there was nobody much about. In the room, Robin switched on a lamp. The curtains were drawn and the bed had already been turned down for the night. The light threw soft shadows over the dark walls, the slightly shabby furniture and the large square, bleached white pillows on the bed.

'I like it,' Kate said immediately, looking round, nervous; putting down her shawl and her bag. 'It looks like a hotel bedroom in Paris should look . . .'

'It does, doesn't it?' That was exactly what Robin had thought when he had first seen it. Just the place for a romantic assignation. And now – he had Kate. His hands felt clammy. 'Although it's been rather lonely – until now. Come here.' He pulled her to him. 'Kate . . .'

He held her, tense, in his arms, kissing her cheek, moving his mouth down towards hers. Doing all the things he had done over and over in the past days. But the magical quality between them was unaccountably missing. Lost somewhere between the slamming taxi door – and *now*. The shadowy bedroom, muffled against the sounds of the great city, seemed alien. Neither had thought for a moment that this could happen – that they could suddenly feel like strangers again – not after they had fled up the steps from the river in a mutual surge of desire. Hailing a taxi. Clinging; hearts pounding; nothing mattering except the touch and the smell and the sight of each other . . . Kate shivered against him. After a while, Robin let her go, kissed her hand briefly and said, 'Let's

41

have a drink. I've got a bottle of pastis here and there's ice and glasses in the bar.'

While he did the drinks, Kate wandered round the room, peeping through the drawn curtains, examining the furnishings. She pushed up one of the big pillows and sat on the bed, leaning back against it. Robin handed her a glass and sat beside her and gave her the small etching he had just bought – essentially Paris, the Left Bank, where they had been strolling.

He watched while she examined it. She looked very graceful, her face warm in the lamplight, the red dress spilling across the white coverlet. His hands, he thought, could span her waist. Gradually, talking a little, touching, smiling and smiling at each other, they started to relax . . .

One of Kate's shoes fell to the floor. She bent forward to retrieve it, and as she did so, Robin's hand moved from her shoulder to her breast – and stayed there. They kissed lightly. Currents passed between them. She forgot the shoe, eased off the other, moved closer to him . . . Robin always believed that undoing the long line of tiny buttons on the red dress, between her breasts, gradually exposing her body to the waist – hands shaking, intensely excited – was the most erotic act of his life.

Kate stood and the dress rustled to the floor. The lamp was off; some light came through the curtains . . . slim as a reed, light as a feather, she lay beside him – now above him, now beneath. She had, as he had suspected, languorous arms and a long and narrow back. All of her skin was smooth as silk. He soared. But of the two, it was Kate who was instinctively knowing and giving, he – made clumsy with an excess of desire, out of control, too soon finished.

'Oh Kate . . .' – against her waist, breathing so hard, heart racing, as she cradled his head and kissed his face all over and soothed his body with her delicate touch. Love, she understood, had to be learned like everything else – and between them, it would be. She was certain of that.

'Robin . . .' – opening his mouth with her fingers, leaning down, her mouth there now too.

Paris glowed in the unseasonably warm night air – the velvety sky was a mass of stars. They had dinner in a small restaurant round the corner from the hotel which Robin had noted on one of his brisk early morning walks. Kate didn't eat much – but she looked very happy. They sat at a banquette, side by side, holding hands whenever they could. And for the first time they faced up to the future. He was trying, Robin told her quietly, to change his flight to Sunday so they would have an extra day. He'd know tomorrow. He had already fixed the hotel for another night. And what about Normandy? How long would she be there? Couldn't she cancel?

Kate shook her head. 'Not possible. I'll be there for a week or so. Ina and I are going on Wednesday to open the house – and Louis and some of the family are coming at the weekend . . .' Kate had been looking forward to visiting the old converted farmhouse surrounded by apple orchards which would be in blossom now. But Robin had changed everything . . .

'After that you'll come home? For good?'

'Yes. In about three weeks . . .'

'I might have made some changes by then.' His jaw, always square, looked even firmer. During his forays around Paris in between seeing Kate, he had decided to chuck the bank, never mind the name and the tradition. It wasn't for him, simple as that. Being away from it for a few days had given him a clearer vision. He had other ideas – and this was the time to explore them. He had hinted as much to Pierre when they met for a quick drink.

'I hope so, Robin . . .'

'Let me know the plane, what time you get to London. Will you? I'll meet you – or will Laura and your parents mind?'

'No.' Kate shook her head, her spirits leaping. 'No – I'll tell them.' She wasn't sure what, but she would. She had already decided to come clean about their chance meeting in the café. Once they knew him, they – and Laura – would think the pick-up funny. Her parents were like that. 'And can I have your address – at home?' It seemed absurd that for all their intimacy they knew so few practical things about each other.

'You won't get away without that.' Giving her hand a surreptitious squeeze. 'And the farm . . . can you find out the phone number there?' He sounded so serious, as though they were going to be separated for months, not just a few weeks. He hadn't said anything . . . but he must, he must surely mean . . . they would go on seeing each other . . . She had known, from the first day, that her feelings for Robin were utterly different to all she had felt during that too young, long-drawn-out affair with David . . . And what about Robin and *his* past? He was thirty-two, he had travelled widely, lived in the States . . . They had years ahead, perhaps a lifetime, to get to know all this.

'I'll ask Ina . . .

'And you'll look after yourself? Not do too much opening the house with Ina?'

Kate shook her head. 'She wouldn't let me . . . and I'm always well in the country.'

Robin picked up his glass. 'And there's someone I want to drink to, by the way – not us . . .' He was looking at her mischievously.

'Who's that?'

A waiter, standing by, trying to take some further order, took one look and gave up.

'Guess – no, that's not fair. Manou.'

'*Who?*' Kate felt a spasm of acute sexual jealousy. 'Oh that girl . . .'

Laughing at the droop in her voice, Robin said, 'My darling Kate, if it hadn't been for her, I wouldn't be here in Paris at all . . .'

This, Kate had to admit, was true. She relented – and picked up her glass. 'All right then.' Both laughing, clinking glasses, never taking their eyes off each other.

'To Manou,' Kate agreed.

'Manou . . . I'll have to thank her for you anyway. Always.'

Minutes later, Robin excused himself mysteriously. 'There's something I want to get. I've just remembered. I won't be long. Don't run away . . .'

The waiter watched, mystified, and shrugged his shoulders. All the English, he assumed, were mad.

Robin returned and slid into the seat beside Kate. He pushed a small, beautifully wrapped box into her hand. 'It's terribly

44

corny, something very small,' he told her. 'But I remembered something I'd seen – I don't know – in some shop . . . or an ad. And I had to get it. Tonight. Pure sentimentality . . .'

'Robin, you shouldn't have . . .' Intrigued, Kate pulled the ribbons. Not knowing quite what to expect, she undid the paper and held up an exquisite bottle of scent. 'Robin . . . but why on earth . . .?'

'It's because of what it's called – and you said you liked Guerlain.' For the first time since they met he looked – and sounded – embarrassed.

'L'heure Bleue . . . Oh Robin, that's perfect . . .'

'I thought it rang a bell – when we were by the river . . . and I remembered just now . . . twilight. . .'

'*Le crépuscule* . . .'

'But you said you liked the other name better. Remember?'

'I remember. The hour of blue . . . and it really was, wasn't it?'

She wrenched open the stopper and dabbed the musky, spicy scent on her wrists and held one up to him.

The waiter, dead on his feet, gave up.

Robin held her hand against his cheek. 'Blue dusk, you said.'

PART 2

Knyght's Wood

Chapter 7

Kate stumbled across Knyght's Wood on a wet and windy August afternoon. A Friday. Pushing through tangled, rain-soaked brambles with her stick she saw the house first – quite low, two old stone cottages knocked into one. Rundown, but somehow reassuring – settled comfortably into a crook under the rim of the downs, beneath a sheltering copse. She pressed on. The gate into the sizeable walled garden at one side of the house had been left open and was banging and creaking in the wind. There were remnants of an herbaceous border along the unkempt lawn. Beyond, among rough long grasses, sloping towards the valley, an old apple orchard. Even allowing for the grey and gusting weather, the place had a forlorn, deserted air.

Calling to Raffles, her mother's terrier, who was worrying away at the bracken, Kate started to tramp round the side of the property towards the impressive main gates. And it was then that she saw the 'FOR SALE' board, blown onto its side, stuck halfway into the hedge. On it, Kate immediately rec-ognized the name of a well-known local estate agent's. She stood, the huge raincape she was wearing dripping rivulets. All kinds of images and possibilities for the future flashed through her mind – but she always thought that it was the way daffodils would look in the orchard, in spring, which was what decided her. *Instantly.* First she smiled, then she laughed out loud.

'Come on, Raffles, you silly old thing . . .' she called affection-ately, 'There's no time to lose, we've got to be quick . . .' Always obedient – snuffling, bedraggled – Raffles trotted after her as she made her way back to the village where she had parked her car, no more than a five minutes' walk away. Using her stick on the rough path, she traipsed quite nimbly considering that she was heavily pregnant and wearing gumboots which were much too big.

'I'd better chain you in case you scamper off in search of a rabbit. Here . . .' Kate bent over, with some difficulty, and fastened the lead. Passing the attractive wrought-iron gates, she saw the name of the house. *Knyght's Wood.* With a 'y'. Kate liked it. Laura would pour scorn, without doubt, saying it was affected – that honestly, could anyone really imagine some medieval knight on horseback had come riding out of those admittedly pretty woods above . . .?

As a matter of fact, Kate could.

With Raffles panting at her heels, Kate loped round the corner into the village. It astonished her that she had never noticed the house – Knyght's Wood – before. For years, ever since she and Laura were small, they had passed through Laverton on their way to some of the family's favourite walks high up on the downs. It must be because the house was tucked into a small cul-de-sac lane, behind the row of shops and cottages and the pub on the corner, hidden from the main road. It wasn't more than five miles from her parents' house, which was on the edge of a much larger village. And it couldn't be more than a twenty-minute drive from the station and the London train – where she would be picking up Robin that evening. Laura too, if she could get away from work early enough to catch the same train.

They were all spending the weekend, the last holiday weekend of the summer, despite the disastrous weather, with her parents. Kate, delighted as always to be out of London, had driven down the day before and had expected to spend the day chatting and cooking with her mother. But after lunch, Felicity Holford – oceans-deep into research for a new book – had promised not to be too long, and disappeared into her study. Knowing that she was unlikely to emerge for several hours, Kate had marshalled Raffles, borrowed her mother's boots – and driven out into the country for a walk. Wind and rain never bothered her. But not wanting to go too far, she had stopped in Laverton and, largely through following Raffles's

50

enthusiastic gambols, happened upon the rain-battered bramble hedge – and Knyght's Wood beyond.

Knyght with a 'y'. What on earth would Robin think?

The bell clanged as she entered the cluttered general store-cum-post office. A stony-faced woman wearing an apron soon appeared behind the counter.

'I'm so sorry to bother you,' said Kate, 'but do you have a public telephone I could use? It's rather important.'

'Over there.' The woman pointed with her thumb. 'Help yourself, it's all the same to me.' She had immediately recognized Kate's condition and could also hear the frantic yelps of Raffles, who was tied up outside. Truculent at being disturbed from an afternoon shut-eye for nothing, she stomped back into the parlour.

Kate, relieved to have the shop to herself, went straight to the telephone and began scrabbling through a directory. Finding the number she wanted, she fumbled for change, dialled – and got through straight away.

'I'd like to make some enquiries about a property I've just seen,' she said distinctly, one eye on the counter, praying the woman – who looked forbidding – wouldn't come back. She didn't want to risk gossip going round the village like wildfire. Not yet. 'Yes, that's all right . . . I'll hold on . . .' She dropped more coins into the payphone – and waited. Raffles's yelps were growing more pathetic by the minute . . . Eventually, the person for whom she was doing the holding materialised. Kate asked several precise questions, made sure she had the name right, and fixed an appointment to view the property the following morning.

When she put the phone down, there was still no sign of the dour woman. So she had a stern look at Raffles who quietened, emptied the rest of the money out of her purse – and telephoned London.

'Mr Faraday, please . . . I see, but could you tell him that it's quite important, not urgent, just important . . . it's Mrs Faraday speaking . . .' Seconds ticked – and then she heard Robin,

'Kate? Darling, are you all right? Where are you?'

'I'm in Laverton – and I'm marvellous. Never better . . .'

'Now what are you up to . . .?' A bit suspicious – he could sense her excitement. 'And why all the way over in Laverton? You're not doing anything silly, are you? Are you alone?'

'Yes – yes, I am alone. With Raffles. But no, I'm not doing anything silly . . . Robin . . .'

'Well – what?'

A quick look round, her voice lowered. 'I think I've found us a house.'

'Hmm . . . in Laverton? Today?'

'Yes.'

'Just like that?'

'*Yes.*'

The wires zinged between them. They had been looking for a small and manageable country house – his parents' wedding present to them – ever since they got engaged. They hadn't been in a hurry, they had settled happily in Robin's place in London, and nothing they had looked at had seemed quite right. But now . . . Robin sighed. He knew his Kate – and he knew the steel that the genuinely frail physique belied.

'Well – what are we going to do about it?'

She told him – and he gave a huge burst of laughter. 'And Robin – could you get an earlier train? Please, just this once . . . do try to . . .' she pleaded. The woman had emerged and was looking at Kate quite pleasantly now. 'It's a holiday weekend when nothing much happens on Friday afternoon . . . If you hurry, you'll get the 4.15 – and I'll meet it . . .'

Robin looked out of the window and considered. London in a late summer rainstorm looked its dreariest. There wasn't much point in slogging along as one of three partners in a struggling new business if you couldn't occasionally do as you pleased . . . and as Kate said, nothing much was happening, businesswise. Unfortunately . . .

'All right . . . I'm off . . . but on one condition . . .'

'Which is . . .?' She sounded over the moon.

'Don't hang around in Laverton, not by yourself, not in this weather. Go straight back to your parents. Promise?' Over this he was stern.

'I promise.'

*

Before the train had quite stopped, one carriage door opened seconds before the rest. Robin jumped out, slammed the door behind him and began walking quickly up the platform. Kate, who often came down a day or so before him, always waited in the same place. He looked very urban in his dark grey suit, raincoat over one arm, swinging a briefcase. And handsome. His light brown hair was slicked down, neatly trimmed. A good colour, very clean-shaven. He was smiling, looking ahead expectantly.

Kate came hurtling at him the moment he passed the ticket barrier. Her pregnancy had been trouble-free; to her family and her doctor's intense relief, she had never looked, or felt, better in her life. Only her limp was quite seriously aggravated by the added weight which sometimes affected her balance. It did – slightly – then. Robin caught her as she tripped awkwardly against him.

'Darling . . .' Kissing her soundly – and after, holding her a bit away from him, looking at her hard. Both of them, even then, electrified at the sight and the touch of one another. 'Kate, you mustn't rush about like that, you nearly fell . . .'

'I wanted to get at you . . .'

'Kate . . .'

'Two days too long . . .'

Because of the holiday weekend, the station was particularly busy. Passengers carting luggage barged in and out, calling for taxis, hailing friends. The loudspeaker droned unintelligibly, engines hissed, whistles blew . . . Amidst the confusion, Kate and Robin stood quietly, their arms around each other. The baby heaved between them, straining against Kate's voluminous grey-and-white sprigged smock.

'Seven weeks to go before D-day,' Robin whispered somewhere near her ear.

'Better. Six and a half now . . .' – eyes closed, smiling, murmuring into his neck.

'I love you. And *you* – whoever you are – bumping around down there . . . now off we go . . .' His arm round her shoulders, they walked slowly towards the car – chatting about his day and wondering what time Laura would get down and whether she really had finally split up with Peter, her on-and-off 'steady'

53

for two years, as she said. Robin took the keys and helped Kate in. He took off his jacket and tie and tossed them in the back, rolled up his sleeves and slid into the driver's seat. Kate pulled an Indian cashmere shawl round her shoulders. It was chilly but the weather had cleared and the sky was a miraculous, but untrustworthy, blue. Robin started the engine – and turned to look at her. As he had learnt, her narrow face veered between pinched and plain – and loveliness. Now, her hair dark and shiny, cheeks a bit fuller, skin peachy and perfect – she glowed.

'Robin . . .' Kate began. 'Robin, I wonder . . . it's still quite early . . .'

'Don't tell me, darling,' he said, grinning; looking back over his shoulder, starting to inch out of the parking lot – a thousand times glad he had chucked the boring bloody office early. 'I already know. We're off to Laverton. Right?'

'It's got possibilities, certainly,' Robin said an hour later as they stood by the gates of Knyght's Wood, ankle-deep in the long and still soggy grass. They had trespassed freely, peering into windows, piecing together the number of rooms, guessing what led where. The place was empty – and looked as though it might have been for some time, Robin thought ominously. They both agreed that, as far as they could tell from the outside, it was about the size they needed. And it seemed to be in a fairly good condition. Robin had poked around the back and had a good look at the roof.

'A bit cottage-y though,' he commented. 'We'd have liked one decent room, wouldn't we?'

'Darling – it *is* a cottage – two cottages together. That's its charm . . .'

'Yes . . . well . . .' They started to walk, hand-in-hand, back down the drive to the gates. 'It looks like a hell of a lot of garden to keep up . . . the lawn, beds, all this . . .' He sounded uneasy, tempering Kate's enthusiasm.

'Oh but that's what I adore about it . . .' Kate turned to him, eyes brilliant. 'The walled garden and that border – it's still got some nice bits in it – and the orchard . . . just imagine, Robin, in spring . . . the daffodils . . .'

'A lot to look after, Kate . . . and I'm not much of a gardener, I warned you of that . . .'

'We'd manage . . .'

'And we're stuck to London in the week. We talked that through thoroughly before I left the bank. You know the sort of hours – and the entertaining – I've got to put in if we're to make a go of this business. *If* . . .' he finished gloomily.

'Oh darling, you will – you will.' Utterly believing, Kate clung to his arm. 'It's going to take time. You knew that. You've had a couple of slow weeks – and it's holiday time, people are still away. You're much too able and you've got far too many contacts for something – something big – not to click . . .'

Robin kissed her cheek. 'Bless you. I'm sure you're right – I hope so, at least. The fixed office expenditure is a tremendous drain while we're getting going. It's eating into our resources more than any of us had bargained for. I was reading through the accountant's break-down in the train – and I got into a bit of a gloom . . .'

'And then I dragged you here . . .'

'I came willingly . . . you know that . . . and yes . . .' He stopped and looked back at the house, liking the way a sudden shaft of golden evening sun lit the solid stone walls. 'Eighteenth century probably in origins . . . and I do think it has a lot of plusses. The price is right for one thing – and we can almost certainly get a bit knocked off. The property market is sluggish at the moment. And it's convenient, right in the village . . .'

'And close to Mother and Father, which both of us like. Don't we?'

'We certainly do.' He squeezed her arm. He had got on with John and Felicity Holford from the moment Kate had introduced him as the man who had, literally, picked her up in a café in Paris. Assured, utterly without pretentions, they had seen the amusing side as Kate knew they would – and liked Robin on sight. Their one and only concern was for their daughter's happiness. It had seemed almost a miracle that their shy, not very strong Kate, had gone off to France, blossomed – and come back oceans-deep in love with a thoroughly decent young man. Who clearly reciprocated.

It was the conventional, straight-laced Faradays who had to be told a carefully concocted story of their meeting. Some time later, Jim Faraday was let into the secret by Robin when they nipped out to the pub together on one of his solo visits to Jersey. He had seen the joke all right – and he liked and admired Kate. But Doris Faraday, who never bothered to disguise her disappointment at her son's choice – a skinny little thing with a limp, nice enough parents but no money to speak of, a bit of a let-down when you came to consider all the opportunities he'd had, all those schools etc etc. That Felicity Holford's father was a retired general and John Holford a fourth generation doctor cut no ice with her. *She* was never to know of the morning meeting at the Deux Magots.

'And lovely for the baby, darling . . . he-she can't only grow up in London, not knowing about trees and birds and plants and flowers.'

'I suppose not,' said Robin, who had done much the same in Birmingham and not felt in the least deprived. 'Anyhow, we'll have a good look round with the chap from the estate agent's tomorrow.'

Driving back to her parents' house, Robin suddenly noticed the boots Kate had put on just before they made their reconnaissance of Knyght's Wood.

'I do wish you'd stop wearing Felicity's boots,' he said – irritable as always when worried. 'They're miles too big and they're not fitted out for you . . .' He crashed the gears and swore. 'Why on earth don't you get a pair in London – if you must? You shouldn't wear them, Kate . . . particularly now . . . and when I think of you up there this afternoon, crashing around in them, all alone . . . what if you'd fallen?' He turned to her quickly, his face like thunder. Kate put her hand gently on is arm.

'I'm sorry,' she said contritely. 'I won't wear them again. I promise.'

Chapter 8

At precisely seven o'clock, John Holford entered his drawing-room and made straight for the drinks. It had been an exhausting day culminating in a difficult, unsatisfactory surgery – one or two nasty situations he could see looming; his experience had already told him what certain tests would reveal. He poured a moderate scotch, splashed some soda and threw himself into his usual armchair. His long legs stretched out, his face – handsome and fine-boned, which his daughters had inherited – almost as grey as his silvery hair.

Beginning to relax – where on earth is everyone, he thought? Felicity must be about, she always heard him come in, the car on the gravel drive . . . Kate was here, Robin too by now surely. And Laura? What train was she supposed to be catching? Even Raffles was nowhere to be seen . . .

He had been looking forward to having the three of them there this weekend. He had come to depend on Robin for some male company in the family; much as he adored his women, it was comforting to have another man about – even for him, the least sexist of males. Late night talks, long walks, the City point of view. A son-in-law who he liked and respected was a great bonus, particularly as he was so patently loving and caring of Kate – his darling Kate, whose well-being was never far from his consciousness. And the prospect of an imminent grandchild – especially, if he was entirely honest, Kate's child – moved him tremendously. Beneath his careful professional manner, he was a deeply emotional man.

He heard a door open and footsteps flying across the hall. 'Hello, my love, *there* you are . . .' Felicity rushed in, breathless and girlish as always, Raffles scuttling behind. She sat on the

arm of his chair, leaning over to kiss him . . .' Johnnie darling
. . . I did hear you . . .' – sounding penitent. 'But I was in the
kitchen dealing with dinner – something about to boil over . . .
And then I thought you'd gone off into the garden . . .' She
took in the scotch, as opposed to sherry, and concluded cor-
rectly that he had had a foul day.

'I was wondering where you all were . . .' Turning slightly
in his chair to see her better. She was wearing jeans and one
of his old navy guernsey sweaters. She must have done some
gardening after the rain stopped. She wore the oddest garments
– the girls were for ever trying to smarten her up – but
speaking for himself, he always loved the way she looked. He
did then. 'Has Robin got here yet?' – smiling up at her affectionately and holding onto her arm.

'Yes . . . Kate went to meet him, he got an earlier train
down . . .' She frowned. 'They've got something they want to
discuss with you . . .' Felicity Holford had a pretty and youthful
face, in which all the features were nicely rounded – cheeks,
brown eyes, slightly snub nose. Her hair curled naturally. Her
intense and artless enthusiasm for most people and things
concealed shrewd judgement, as John Holford was well aware.
Noticing the frown, he said cautiously, 'What kind of thing
would that be?'

'Nothing to worry about. I don't *think*. I'll let them tell you
themselves.' She walked over to the drinks and picked up a
bottle. 'I think I'll have a sherry . . . By the way, Laura phoned
– she's driving down after all and said she might be a bit late
and not to wait with dinner . . .'

'Oh dear . . . I do hope not . . .' John Holford was dismayed. He was about to open some good wine, he'd consult
Robin first if he could find him . . . he'd somehow counted
on them all being together that evening. 'Any particular
reason?'

'She didn't say, but Kate seems to think she's finally given
Peter the *coup de grâce*. Not that that need have anything to do
with it. I'm sure she'll be here soon – as long as the traffic isn't
too bad. . . We won't eat until after eight. Was it an awful day,
poor Johnnie?' she enquired sympathetically – already knowing that it had been.

'Pretty bad.' He leant his head back and closed his eyes. 'I'm not exactly looking forward to next week either . . .'

'Never mind, darling. You've got the whole weekend. You're not on call, are you?'

'Not until Monday night.' He looked over at her, feeling better already. If this bit of weather held, they could get in some tennis. Robin would enjoy that. 'And what about you, my love? Did you manage any writing?'

'Oh I did . . . three splendid pages, I really like them . . .' Bubbling away, eyes alight with enthusiasm. 'I feel as though I'm into it now. And Kate and I had a lovely rainy cooking morning, although I did rather desert her for the book this afternoon. Of course, I hoped she would rest . . . and although I'm trying not to get too excited about the baby, it is the most marvellous feeling, isn't it? All the things we ordered from John Lewis and Harrods have come and the baby's room is starting to look like a proper nursery Kate says . . .'

'Come here . . . you know I'm every bit as thrilled as you are . . . Gran and Grandpapa . . .'

Felicity brought her drink and perched back on the arm of his chair. He picked up her slightly grubby hand and kissed it.

'Oh Johnnie . . . and where *are* those two, Robin and Kate? I haven't seen them for ages . . . and I must go and make myself more respectable – I've been tidying up the poor roses after the storms – or the girls will be at me all night . . .'

Upstairs, in the big corner bedroom that Felicity had made over for them, Kate and Robin were stretched out on the bed – naked amidst a muddle of sheets, blankets and pale crocheted spread. The curtains were half closed against the brilliant, and so unexpected, flood of light. They had just made love – cautiously and inventively – and each was daring the other to be the first to stir.

'Robin . . . we must go down . . . I heard Pa. You go . . .' she pleaded. 'This would be a perfect time to tell him about Knyght's Wood – and see what he knows about Laverton. He's been so looking forward to you coming this weekend . . . and he's always in a bad mood – and tired – after a late surgery. The idea of the house would cheer him up.'

'The baby's moving around . . . look.' Robin raised his head.

'You're telling me . . . it's an acrobat . . . *ouch* . . .'

'You don't suppose we did anything we shouldn't have?'

'Of course not. It's in all the books – and I asked Pa . . .' Kate's openness with her parents never ceased to amaze him. Robin moved his hand lightly over the bulging outline of her stomach to her breasts. Enlarged and blue-veined, Kate hardly recognised them; they didn't seem to belong to her. She wasn't even sure she liked them – but Robin was mesmerised.

'Kate . . .'

'Darling . . .' She gently removed his hand. 'We'll be here all night . . .'

'That's fine with me.' Indistinct, his head lying where once her narrow waist had been. 'You get up first then . . .'

'All right. Mother's sure to be in the kitchen already. And I'll run the bath . . . I'll even scrub your back,' she offered hopefully.

Robin made a reluctant move and sighed. He sat up and reached for some clothes. 'OK – *if* you get in with me . . .'

'Not a good idea . . . Don't you think we'd all go right through the floor, the three of us?'

Twenty minutes later, Robin bounded down the stairs to the hall. He always enjoyed staying with the Holfords – very much more, he often thought guiltily, than he ever had with his own parents. The house was an Edwardian folly – difficult to heat and undistinguished to look at. It was also inconvenient – the dark back staircase led to a warren of what had once been maids' bedrooms and there was a nest of collapsing outbuildings beyond the kitchen. But the main rooms downstairs were large and well proportioned as were the principal bedrooms above. It had a pleasant garden with a hard tennis court. Kate and Laura had lived there all their lives.

Felicity Holford was a cheerfully haphazard housekeeper who worked on instinct rather than organisation. After spending one strained weekend with the Holfords, Doris Faraday had remarked, sniffing, that the whole place, particularly the baths, could have done with a right good clean. Robin knew there was some truth to this – and he also rather liked it. After being brought up in a house where his mother was forever plumping cushions and wiping imaginary rings from tables, relaxed domesticity was a welcome relief. And for all her slightly scatty ways, Felicity saw to it that the house was always attractive and comfortable. Most of the chintzy upholstery sagged a bit; oriental rugs covered the shabbiest parts of carpet. She believed in roaring fires at almost any time of the year and eccentric flower arrangements – always fresh – the larger the better. There were good reading lamps, strategically placed; reading was considered important in the family. Felicity was also a good cook – and meals with the Holfords were lengthy and enjoyable.

Raffles was chasing a large ball of fluff across the parquet hall floor – which badly needed a polish. After giving him a friendly kick, Robin went straight into the drawing-room.

'John, hello . . . how are you?' He grasped his father-in-law's shoulder, preventing him from getting up from the depths of the armchair where he was reading *The Times*. 'Kate will be down in a minute. Need a refill?'

'I think I do . . . help yourself too while you're at it. Good to see you, Robin – you managed to get off a bit early, Felicity said.'

'That's right. Inveigled by Kate – for a very specific reason which I'll tell you about . . .'

Robin settled with a drink in the chair opposite. He always found John Holford extremely easy to talk to – and consequently launched at once into the sudden saga of Knyght's Wood. John Holford's first comment, rather sharp – and with which Robin concurred – was: what on earth was Kate doing poking around Laverton by herself in the pouring rain for God's sake? Particularly at this stage of her pregnancy. Then, calming down, he said he thought that Laverton was considered a proper village, a community. A post office; some useful shops. A delightful church; very old, peeling frescoes. He couldn't quite place where Knyght's Wood was exactly.

'That's it's best point, really,' Robin interrupted. 'Kate's gone soft on the house on sight – as you'll soon realise. Frankly, my own feelings are rather more measured, not being a country-man perhaps. But the reason you don't know it is because it's tucked out of sight just behind the village. So it's private – and still round the corner from shops and the main road . . .'

'Sounds possible at least.' All the same, with Robin and his two partners just getting a new financial services business off the ground, the timing couldn't be ideal. He already knew that the business was slower than Robin had hoped – and that they had borrowed heavily from the bank. Perhaps this accounted for Felicity's frown. Or perhaps she was just nervous, as they both were, always, of Kate taking on – and trying to do – too much.

'You'll just have to see tomorrow, Robin – and take it from there. You might find the house is impossible. You'll want a survey, of course, if you decide to go on with it. Much land, is there?'

'Rather too much garden, I'd say.' Robin looked worried. 'Although Kate is very enthusiastic. She loves getting out of London – and with the baby coming I can understand this . . . weekends, the summer. Travelling is always difficult for her, she dreads it as you know, and having the baby and a place of our own all the year, near London, does make sense. Of course I like the idea of her being near you and Felicity if I'm not there, but frankly – I'd rather she didn't go getting too many ideas about managing the garden more-or-less single-handedly . . .'

'Quite.'

There was a relaxed silence between the two men. It was still light, and the room caught reflections from the last of the sun on the gilt frame of the large mirror over the fireplace and on the long french windows leading out onto the terrace. Newspapers and books and magazines lay about in piles. A large, silver-framed wedding photograph of Robin and Kate – two years old now – Kate swathed in white wild silk, had pride of place on the table beside the sofa.

'Look, Robin – I know that your father has most generously offered to buy you and Kate a house. I believe you thought you'd both prefer this than a larger place in London?'

Robin nodded – then grinned. 'Kate did, at least . . .' Because of this, she hadn't in the least minded moving into Robin's small, modern terraced house – and brightening it up charmingly.

'I know that. She's been bitten by her mother's gardening bug all right . . . But all the same, a move can't be coming – if indeed it is – at a good time for you. The business is going to take some nursing – and, frankly, luck. Felicity and I have a bit of capital between us. Laura is talking about starting up her own decorating outfit – and we'd be glad to help both of you out in a modest way. We have discussed this . . .'

'John – that's incredibly kind . . . I hope it won't come to that . . . you and Felicity look after Laura . . .'

'Well, if it's needed, the offer stands. Remember.'

'We'll give her a few minutes longer – Laura . . . that's all right, is it?' John Holford looked across at Felicity. She had changed into an old black velvet skirt and a gauzy, gold-embroidered black top which was once a sari. The material was beautiful, but the dressmaker hadn't got the neck quite right – and the sleeves were uneven lengths. After digging around at the bottom of her wardrobe, she had been unable to find both black pumps – so she had given up and put her everyday walking shoes back on. She was sitting on the sofa talking to Robin about her book, holding a glass of sherry – animated and very pretty. What Felicity wore never mattered very much.

John Holford looked at her. 'Ten more minutes, say, can we give her that . . .?'

'*Of course*, Johnnie, of course we can . . . it's the traffic I'm sure . . . as long as you're not starving any of you . . . Kate is turning the chicken down as low as possible and we've got a terrine to start with – so we can eat whenever we want . . .'

'We won't wait longer . . .' John Holford looked at his watch. He always got edgy when one of his daughters was driving – and late. And this was the start of one of the worst holiday weekends on the roads. He whistled to Raffles who came trotting over – all the while listening for the reassuring sound of Laura's car. And he looked very distinguished flung back in the deep armchair, stroking the little dog more for something to do than anything else. His lean good looks – the blue eyes and thick white-grey hair – were appreciated by many of the local female medical staff; and quite a few of his more susceptible patients. He was the senior partner in a large practice and the doctor by far the most in demand.

'So you see, Amelia Armstrong, poor love, really had nothing *whatsoever* to do,' Felicity was saying to Robin, charmingly intense. 'Maids saw to everything in the house, social life bored her – and to her *great* credit, she put the fortune she inherited, huge for that time and no taxes to speak of, into charitable trusts. She was *frightfully* intelligent, a bit of a blue stocking . . . I suppose if she'd lived now she would have been a civil servant or the headmistress of a school. Something clever and exceptional anyway. As it was, she set up these trusts, all to help women, all superbly administered by herself – and really did a great deal of good. None of which has *ever* been properly appreciated . . .'

'Until along came Felicity Holford, biographer, burrowing about in the public library looking for a subject,' her husband finished, pushing Raffles away.

They all laughed.

'Good for Felicity . . . I should think you've got an interesting story there,' Robin said. He was fascinated by his mother-in-law who seemed to break all the housewifely rules he was brought up with – and get away with it.

'Ah, *here* she is . . .' Before either of the others, John Holford's sharp ears picked up the sound he had been straining for – tyres crunching on the drive, the engine stopping. Laura. At last. He hid his relief which he realised was inordinate – and not unconnected with a recent ghastly road accident he had been called to. Felicity probably knew this. 'We'd better let Kate get to her first. Have you noticed, Robin, that when they haven't been together for a while, those two, they have to debrief each other before they can even talk to anyone else? They've been like that since they were small girls.'

'Johnnie's right,' Felicity agreed. 'It's part of their twinness . . . listen, there goes Kate . . .'

They heard her clumping out from the direction of the kitchen, opening the front door – and then shrieks and confusion, both talking at once. After a few minutes, they came into the drawing-room, hands clasped – although probably neither realised this. They were – and yet were not – so alike; tonight, their separateness contrasted starkly. For one thing Kate's pregnancy – and she was huge – accentuated her very thin extremities. Her arms looked like sticks beneath the puffed sleeves of her dress. Laura had a bigger build. Like Felicity's, her hair curled naturally – making her face seem broader than Kate's. Both girls had style. Being rather tall, clothes looked good on them. Kate, largely to compensate for her left side, chose simple, flowing lines. Laura went for dramatic make-up, the best hairdressers in London, and spectacular clothes – designer labels when she could afford them, cheap, racy fashion from the chain-stores when she couldn't. On good days, she looked dazzling. Today, as both her parents had realised immediately, was not one of them.

'Hello all ...' She left Kate and went on into the room. Kissed her mother, hugged her father, pecked Robin's cheek saying, 'A lovely large gin, please, brother-in-law mine. And easy on the tonic ...' Her voice was high and fluting, exactly like her mother's.

Felicity and John Holford spoke across each other.

'Was the traffic out of London terrible ...?'

'Darling – why on earth did you decide to drive ...?'

Laura was wearing a crumpled white linen suit with a very short, tight skirt. There was no sign of a blouse. No tights and high sling-back sandals. Her eyes were heavily outlined in black liner. Her father thought she looked distressingly tarty.

'And you certainly shouldn't drive in *those* things,' he said, pointing at the sandals.

'I didn't come from London, actually,' Laura said off-handedly, accepting a glass and ignoring her father. 'Thanks Robin ... a lifesaver ... so I missed the jams and the tail-backs ...'

'Then where ...?'

'Oh – near Marlborough ... some job in a house there went badly wrong, lots of screaming, the curtains were too frilly and the cushions hadn't turned up ... so I had to go and sort it out. Calm the old bag down. That sort of thing,' she said vaguely. 'Anyhow – here I am.' She took a gulp of her drink. 'Have I held up dinner?'

Kate was still standing quietly by the door. Her eyes never left Laura. All their lives she had held back – shy but composed, observant – while Laura pushed ahead, chatty, outgoing. Often over-confident. At school, at children's parties – and later, when they had guests of their own.

'Not impossibly – but long enough,' Robin told her cheerfully. 'Put that drink down and we can start. We've opened lots of good wine.'

'Come on Kate, we'll put everything on the table. Five minutes everyone . . .' Felicity took Kate's arm and they went off to the kitchen together. Laura caught sight of herself in a mirror and said, 'God, what a mess . . .' She fluffed out her hair with her fingers. She was pale and sallow. She looked, as her parents had already seen, jaded and extremely tired. Which was not like Laura at all. 'I'm going upstairs to have a wash. All right, Pa? Don't wait. I won't be long.'

'Looks a bit out-of-sorts, Laura, don't you think?' John Holford muttered to Robin, collecting glasses. They could hear Kate and Felicity taking things into the dining-room, laughing. Felicity's high voice carried.

'I do rather. She always burns the candle at both ends. Last week – or was it the week before – she went to some tremendous private party in the country . . . danced all night and then drove straight to work . . .'

'She always was a party girl . . . She seemed to have the verve and stamina for it . . .' Unlike my dearest Kate – he thought, but didn't say.

'Kate says she's broken up with Peter at last. He always seemed a lot keener than her and we thought she treated him very casually. Perhaps that's upset her . . .'

'I don't somehow think it's that,' John Holford said quietly.

He looked down the long refectory table with pleasure. He had been looking forward to this moment for days. A pity Laura had arrived in not very good form; a few days' rest and country air should put her to rights. Instead of gallavanting round the country, for a change, doing God knows what . . . This weekend was the last time they would all be together here before the birth of Kate's child. He raised his glass towards

Felicity, across the pale candles and the bowl of roses she had saved from the rain – 'Lovely to have the three of you with us . . . God bless . . .'

'Almost four of us now,' said Kate, giving her raffish smile, as they all lifted their glasses. Her long earrings swung.

'Quite right, Kate darling. We six – altogether,' John Holford amended. Felicity started passing the terrine and the hot toast round the table.

Robin, taking a liberal helping, turned to Kate. 'We're all geared up, aren't we darling? Did you tell Felicity that we now have a nursery . . .?'

'Yes – we're organised . . . D-day really is coming . . . at last . . . ' She faced it with relief. For the first time, she was starting to feel extremely uncomfortable. Watching Laura who had put on a skinny black cotton shift and a waterfall of green beads, she felt ungainly. Depressingly so. The pretty smocks which she had bought so happily at the beginning of the summer, when her pregnancy first started to show, seemed drab and boring. She knew she was limping very noticeably, despite Robin's reassurances. And everyone wanting her to rest and rest . . . wild horses wouldn't make her tell anyone, not even the doctor in London who was looking after her, but she had had bouts of excruciating pain in her hip this past week. Her *right* hip . . .

As though reading her mind, Laura said blithely, 'You must be longing for it – I honestly don't see how you could get any bigger, Katie-Kate, without popping . . . your tum must be getting all streaked and stretchy . . . horrid . . . I don't know how you stand it.' And while Kate looked at her, startled: 'Is there any reason this toast is so burnt, Mother?'

Felicity stared.

'Nonsense, Laura,' John Holford said briskly. 'Good brown bread, properly toasted, perfectly all right. Nothing burnt about it.' He helped himself to more terrine.

'Mine is,' Laura said stubbornly. '*Look* . . .' She held up a triangle between her fingers, nails brilliantly pink. Her mouth, now loaded with matching lipstick, quivered.

'Don't make such a fuss, Laura – for God's sake,' Robin said sharply. He hadn't at all cared for her remark to Kate. Although Kate was fiercely loyal – and they were, as twins, emotionally entwined in unfathomable ways – he privately thought Laura a very tough cookie indeed. She had her points; she was gutsy, he'd give her that. But there were times when she could be a right prima donna. As now. 'Here ...' He pushed the basket, in which the toast was folded in a napkin, over to her. 'Take another piece and hush up about it.'

'I am *not* making a fuss, I *don't* want another piece and mine *is* burnt. And I *won't* hush up, thank you, Robin.'

'As you will,' he answered pleasantly. But his chin was squared.

Felicity Holford jumped up, took the piece of toast from Laura's hand saying, 'Do behave yourself please, Laura,' and went out of the room.

'Good heavens, I seem to have made a scene.' Laura looked up and down the table. John Holford, unperturbed, went on eating his terrine. Robin poured more wine.

Only Kate saw that her eyes glittered; knew that she was close to tears. She said, very softly, 'Laura ... don't ... It's all right ...' Knowing, instinctively, that something important wasn't.

Then Felicity came back, clattering plates and setting a large casserole on the sideboard, gushing, 'Has Kate told you about the house she found today, Laura, in Laverton? They're going to see it tomorrow ...'

So the conversation turned safely to Laverton – and the awkwardness over Laura's toast passed off.

'How did you say it was spelt, Katie-Kate? Knyght with a "y"?' – Laura asked, leaning across the table, still sounding petulant.

'That's right. It's a romantic name. I rather like it ...'

'I think it's dreadful. That's the way it's spelt on old tombstones, in churches ...' Laura shivered, although it was a warm evening, and finished off her wine. She was only picking at her food; not really joining in the conversation, her mind clearly on other things.

Between the cheese and the raspberry fool, the telephone rang.

'It won't be for me. I'm almost certain,' John Holford said, looking at Felicity. In that house, the telephone was never taken lightly.

Robin pushed back his chair.

'No, I'll get it,' Felicity said, her hand on his shoulder. Laura followed her mother with her eyes as she left the room. Robin and John Holford began discussing tennis tomorrow afternoon.

'You must see Knyght's Wood, Laura, you really must.' Kate couldn't stop thinking about it. 'If we like it tomorrow, when the agent shows us round, we'll try and arrange to get you in over the weekend. The place is empty so it shouldn't be too difficult . . .'

'I'm not exactly sure of my plans – I may have to go off for a bit . . . But I'd like to, Katie-Kate, you know I would . . .'

Felicity had picked up the telephone in the study. 'Endfield 223 . . . Hello . . .'

'*Laura*, thank God it's you . . . can you talk?' A man's voice; not particularly young; urgent. Nobody, not even John or Kate, could tell them apart on the phone.

'I think you must want to speak to my daughter . . .'

'I beg your pardon,' – instantly formal, embarrassed – 'you sounded . . .'

'Yes, we do,' Felicity said evenly. 'If you hold on a moment I'll just go and get her . . .'

'I suppose it was a man?' John Holford enquired good-humouredly when Felicity sat down again. In her parents' experience, women rarely phoned Laura Holford.

'Yes.'

'What did he sound like?' Kate asked. She hadn't liked the look of Laura tonight, not one bit. Perhaps this was the interesting new man in her life; she had hinted at something of the sort when she told her about finishing with Peter.

'Older. In a bit of a state . . . he thought I was her. We'll get on with the pudding, shall we?'

Poor sod, Robin thought. The twins' closeness – and unlikeness – baffled him. As far as he was concerned, the best thing about Laura was her protectiveness of Kate. This, he

knew, was genuine. But as for her moral sense and habits . . .
He privately wished this older man, said by Felicity to be in a
bit of a state, the best of British luck.

'I expect I'll hear,' Kate said uneasily.

When Laura came back, after only a few minutes, she
looked transformed. They all saw this – only nobody commented. There were spots of colour high on her cheeks; her
eyes were brilliant. She ate the fool and told her mother how
absolutely delicious it was and insisted on clearing up and
making coffee.

Laura was like that, her mother thought helplessly.

Soon after dinner, John Holford ordered Kate to bed. His keen
professional eye hadn't missed the worsening limp and the
painful twinges. She was beginning to fade. After he had
watched her trail up the stairs, Robin telephoned his father.
He had decided to do this even before he had seen Knyght's
Wood. Kate, it was obvious, had fallen for the place; if it was
possible – she should have it. She was never extravagant or
irrational. Although it was, frankly, the worst possible time to
take on more financial responsibilities. His parents, it was
true, had offered substantial help towards a cottage as a
wedding present. But what Kate didn't know was that his
father had already guaranteed the new firm's considerable
loan from the bank. The three partners – James, Rupert and
himself – had raised what they could on their personal col-
lateral. His father's signature had done the rest and secured
them adequate capital to get started on. All this despite his
undisguised disappointment – echoed by Doris Faraday – that
he had left the high profile merchant bank.

Closeted in John Holford's study, he made the call to Jersey.

'You'll have to see what you can get them down to if you're
both set on it. Make an offer, a good way under, and let them
stew on it . . . it's empty you say, so they'll be looking for a
quick sale like as not . . .' – this was his father, all hard
common sense, talking. A bit rough; supportive; approachable.

In the background, he could hear his mother's rasping,
discontented comments. 'They'd better be sure there aren't
too many stairs or she'll be dropping the baby, Kate will. You

70

tell him, Jim . . .' Robin winced. 'And I don't know how the girl thinks she's going to do any gardening . . .'

'Pay no attention to your mother, lad. If you like it, both of you, you do as I say – and I'll keep my word. Tell Kate from me.'

Afterwards, Robin looked at his watch – it was still early – and pushed off out of the house. Kate would be in bed by now. He was aching for some air; a brisk couple of miles on country roads and across the fields would settle him down. He strode off down the drive . . . dismissing Knyght's Wood and tomorrow from his mind . . . trying not to think about Rupert's plans for the following spring. He had told him about them over a quick sandwich at lunch, when they were both feeling depressed over the fixed office expenditure. Come hell or high water, Rupert exploded, insolvency or no, in March he was off to Tibet for three weeks. Jill, his wife, was planning it. In fact, she was even keener than he . . . maps, books, guides were piling up round the house . . . neither of them could wait to kick off the dust. Robin then – and now – suppressed a bolt of envy. His days of travelling, genuine travelling, were over. No regrets. Or not many. Kate, with her delicacy and her candour, had given him joy he had never dreamed of. And he would join Rupert and Jill for a few days' skiing after Christmas. Kate had insisted on that. She would bring the baby down to her parents and let them dote . . . He vaulted a gate and started to tramp through open country. On the way back, he would inspect the tennis court after all that rain . . .

71

Chapter 9

Putting away plates and glasses in the cupboards of the big
old-fashioned kitchen, Laura watched Robin through the open
window as he tore off down the drive. Such physical opposites
they were, those two. You couldn't dream up a more dissimilar
pair on the face of it. Robin a skilled athlete with a yen for
esoteric travel; Kate – Laura knew so well – often battling
painfully to get through the day. Gentle; artistic. And yet they
were so good together, so supportive of each other. Look at the
way Kate had almost begged Robin to leave the bank – which
he hated – and start up in business in the City with just two
other people. He was certainly taking a risk; a lot less secure
financially. No one could say there wasn't a spark between
them. All the same, she sometimes wondered about Robin . . .

Kate must have gone straight to bed. When she had finished
with this lot, she would go up and have a chat – like they used
to, before Robin, before her marriage, before the coming baby
pushed its way into their natural intimacy. *Aunt Laura* . . .
Kate's baby, less than two months to go.

Working efficiently with an apron over her dress, Laura
hummed, over and over, a nostalgic show business tune which
she had danced to, with Nico, less than two weeks ago. In a
marquee set up in the formal country garden, gliding over the
smooth floor, tiny lights sparkling among the pink-and-white
beribboned decorations. Champagne flowing; so much going
on between them – Nico and her – on that floor crowded with
men in dinner jackets and bare-shouldered women. She *might*
tell Kate something – and again she might not.

Her parents were in the drawing-room, listening to music,
her father reading, her mother working away at her tapestry.

Laura was feeling happier in a feverish, light-headed way now that she had spoken to Nico; maddening that Mother had answered the phone and he had made the usual mistake over their voices. She already felt slightly guilty over her behaviour at dinner. Ashamed at what she had said to Kate – although she hardly needed protecting, not now, not with that feisty up-and-coming Robin hovering, jutting his chin out at her, telling her to hush up, not to make a fuss over the blasted toast. Even if she was . . . Bloody cheek.

It was she, not her parents, who had been stunned by a newly confident Kate returning to them from Paris – with Robin. Being told, coolly, over the phone from Normandy, not to meet her at the airport, that she was being met by a friend; she would explain everything when she saw them. Naturally enough, perhaps, Laura had felt ambivalent about Robin from the start – not that she could ever say why, even to herself. It was more intuition. Or imagination. Laura was also honest enough to think it might be underlying jealousy on her part. All the same, Kate being Kate, God help all of them if anything ever went wrong with *that* relationship.

She would, she decided, giving a final swipe to the sink, also lay the breakfast. Mother would be pleased . . .

When it was all done – sliding up the stairs past the drawing-room door – Laura went into Kate and Robin's bedroom after knocking briefly. Kate was already in the large bed, lying back against linen pillows, relaxed and rosy; a glossy art magazine beside her.

'*You* look comfortable . . .'

'Laura – I'm so glad you came . . . I was going to shout for you . . .' She sounded peaceful and drowsy.

'I was clearing up in the kitchen . . .' – Laura shut the door behind her – 'and I saw Robin go marching off . . .'

'Yes.'

'It's still not raining – I suppose he'll have a look at the tennis court. For tomorrow. He'll want a game. I wouldn't mind one either. I could do with some exercise, good for the figure.'

Laura plonked herself down on the old piano stool in front of the dressing-table. It was kidney-shaped, draped and frilled in yellow chintz. Chosen by Laura – who was constantly urging new carpets and wallpapers and curtains on her mother. Not to mention a decent, well-designed modern kitchen. She swivelled round, extended her arm, inspected her brilliant nails – and yawned extravagantly. 'So here we are, Katie-Kate . . .'

Perhaps it wasn't, after all, the time for confiding. Kate looked pretty done in. And nothing was quite as it used to be between them – they both recognized that. Also, she wasn't even sure she wanted to talk about Nico to anyone, even Kate; she was enjoying the loving secret, vibrant, deep inside her. Kate looked so cosy, and yet somehow so vulnerable, in her creamy cotton nightdress with lace at the neck. Her left shoulder was sagging, the arm lying inert on the sheet. Laura saw this.

'I hold him back,' Kate said softly. 'Robin. Don't you see?' There was nobody else in the world she could say this to. She had had some sudden loss of nerve that evening. She had been longing for Laura to come up.

After a pause, 'In what way?' – as if she didn't know.

'Well – the things he most enjoys. Skiing, travelling, the things I never can . . . They're very important to him, Laura.'

'I daresay. But he knew this long before he married you,' Laura said briskly. 'You both did. And now he's got a family, a business he's just started . . . he can't go on roaming the world forever like a student caught by the travel bug. Anyhow, he adores you . . .'

'Oh Laura . . .'

'Of course he does . . . Love at first sight and all that stuff. In Paris in the spring. Anyhow, what made you suddenly think about this holding him back – tonight?'

'I don't know. I looked at him after dinner, when I was feeling whacked, and I just knew that he wanted to be – over the hills and far away . . . kicking off the dust . . . something like that . . .' She smiled ruefully.

'Silly Kate. You're being fanciful. It's the baby I expect. He's an energetic man. All he needs is a good tramp round the countryside. Now tell me about Knyght's Wood with the dreadful "y" . . .' – amused about it, not angry and tense as she was before.

74

While Kate described the house – or what she had seen of it – and the garden and the way she pictured the orchard in spring, Laura spun the stool to face the dressing-table. Half listening to Kate's breathless preamble, she gave monosyllabic replies – 'Goodness . . . how lovely . . . mmmm . . .' – as she opened jars and sniffed; dabbed on scent; twisted up a lipstick. She loved getting her fingers into cosmetics of any sort; anything that was new or different or smelled nice. Poking about among Kate's things, the way she always did, she found a small leather case and took out a drop pearl and diamond earring.

'And there's room for a tennis court eventually – even a swimming-pool . . .' Kate was saying.

'Don't get your hopes up too high. There may be something dreadfully wrong . . . after all, the house is empty . . .'

Absent-mindedly, Laura glanced in the oval mirror. Her hair, fluffed wide and curly, made her face seem even narrower, all dark eyes and painted mouth. Chunky gold earrings, from Nico via Cartier, his first present, glinted. Over her right shoulder, Kate's reflection. She lay cocooned in her pregnancy, her mind full of Robin and the baby and the house that might soon be theirs. Miles beyond her reach . . .

Laura stood up. The black shift skimmed her curvy figure. She dangled Kate's earring towards the light.

'This is pretty, Katie-Kate. I thought so at dinner. They're delicate, like rain drops. They suit you.'

'Robin gave them to me last week. A good-luck-for-the-baby present. They're Victorian . . . he saw them in a shop window in the City . . . and bought them, just like that . . .'

'He spoils you . . . lucky Kate . . .'

'I suppose he does . . . he's terribly extravagant sometimes . . .'

'And *you* make him very happy,' Laura said generously. 'You were marvellous over his leaving the bank. And it's quite a name to turn one's back on. We know he had a future there. And he's comfortable with the way you've made the house in London, Katie-Kate, the way you do things . . . like Mother and Pa really. He fits in here – it's obvious. It must be bliss having *you* after being brought up by the dreaded Doris . . .'

They both laughed. Robin's disagreeable battle-axe of a mother was a recurring joke between them.

Laura put the earring back in its case. 'I think I just heard Pa's car go off . . . he never stops, does he? That's dedication for you.'

'It must be a patient he's worried about,' said Kate. 'He's not on call this weekend.'

'No?' Laura started moving about restlessly, pacing round the room. Distracted. She pulled aside the curtains and looked out onto the dark, humid summer night. Somewhere in the blackened trees an owl hooted. She wondered what Nico was doing, then, at that exact moment. Better perhaps that she didn't know . . .

She sighed and turned and came and sat on the bed, long bare legs in high heels crossed below the neat black hem. A bath had relaxed Kate and she looked floppy and happy – really rather lovely in a timeless maternal way, Laura thought, studying her. A modern Madonna in a Laura Ashley night-dress. Her hair was pushed back behind her ears and the odd sunny day had produced a line of light freckles over her nose. Laura glanced down at her own sleek, tanned arm – and began to stroke Kate's stomach, bulging beneath the bed-clothes.

'Nice old lump . . . nice baby . . . I'm sorry I was mean about it before, Katie-Kate.'

'It doesn't matter . . .' Kate smiled serenely. Nothing regis-tered much with her just then outside her immediate sphere – not even Laura. She, too, seemed distanced like the rest of the world; as though viewed from the wrong end of a telescope. 'But you seemed upset, at dinner, something was wrong . . . I did know.'

'Of course you did. Well – perhaps.'

'It wasn't anything to do with Peter, was it? I wondered if you were missing him after all.' Although, as Kate knew well, she had never been faithful to him for long. With Laura, it was safe to assume that any display of temperament was something to do with a man. Since she was fifteen or so, there had been a lot of them one way or another.

'Peter?' He was so totally erased from her mind and her

senses by Nico – in two short weeks – that she didn't immediately react. 'Oh Peter . . . no, nothing like that . . . not him.'

'Then what? The new man, the one you met at that grand dance?'

Laura stood up, arms crossed over her breasts, hugging herself, smiling down at Kate. 'Maybe. It doesn't matter. Another time, not now. You're tired. We both are. 'Night Katie-Kate.'

When John Holford went off – he had a patient in the hospital who hadn't been doing well after an operation – Felicity decided to go up and look in on her daughters. She didn't often have them together there any more and she thought she had heard them talking. She found Kate half asleep over her magazine, sat with her for a few minutes – then deftly removed the magazine and left. Laura now slept in a room at the back of the house, overlooking the vegetable garden, which had once been the girls' day nursery. Felicity knocked.

'It's me darling . . .'

'Oh Mother . . .' Laura opened the door. 'Come in . . . I've been with Kate . . .'

'I thought you had. I just looked in on her and she's practically asleep. Johnnie's gone off to see a patient . . . goodness, Laura, you're brown . . .' Laura had taken off her dress and was standing in a lacy black bra and pants and high-heeled sandals. The thick ropes of jade-green beads were still fastened round her neck.

'The people I was with last weekend had a swimming pool,' Laura said casually. 'And there was quite a bit of sun . . .' She certainly had no intention of telling her mother that Nico had whisked her off to the South of France in a client's private plane; and that they had spent three glorious sun-and-wine-splashed days in a villa high in the hills near Grasse.

'Really?' Felicity enquired politely, eyebrows raised. 'It poured here non-stop . . .' She glanced round. Any room Laura inhabited, even briefly, looked as though a bomb had been dropped in it. It did now. Clothes, underwear, make-up, tights, Tampax, brushes, sunglasses, scent, shoes, hairdryer, tennis shorts – all tumbled out of the two enormous squashy bags she travelled everywhere with and on to the carpet. The crumpled white suit she had arrived in was thrown haphazardly across a chair. She had just retrieved a scanty nightdress from one of the piles – and this was flung across the pillows on the bed. Even by Felicity's relaxed standards, Laura was mind-blowingly untidy. It never ceased to astonish her that out of this kind of chaos, her daughter rarely emerged looking anything other than stunning – and usually, even more surprising, pressed and groomed. She sighed – light years past reprimanding.

'She looks the picture of marital and maternal contentment, Kate does,' Laura said, removing her bra and slipping the nightgown over her head.

'She does, doesn't she? I only hope they won't be disappointed in the house tomorrow. She's set her heart on it . . .'

'So it seems,' Laura agreed, bored. She personally couldn't think of anything worse than being stuck down here in some gossipy village in a house called Knyght's Wood – with an infant. And Robin, no doubt, alone in London for most of the summer. She'd have a word with Katie-Kate about *that* some time. She stepped out of her pants and threw them towards the chair.

'Is the work going all right?' Felicity asked, automatically picking the pants up off the floor. 'You said you'd been decorating a country house, the one near Marlborough where you were today. I remember you told us something about it months ago. Was it an interesting job?'

'So-so. That particular job is finished now – bar the shouting.' Laura removed the necklace and began creaming off her make-up. In fact, she had spent less than an hour at the house that morning, calming the rich and difficult client who was displeased with almost everything the firm had done; delivering cushions for the drawing-room, the final touch, which looked instantly attractive when Laura flung them about. Privately, she agreed that the curtains didn't hang quite right; that considering the money that had been spent, it was a botched job all right. But, thick-skinned and confident, Laura had succeeded in charming her over coffee. If only, the client had said, seeing her off, if only Laura had been in charge all along . . . which made Laura think, as her small car shot off down the long driveway, that it was about time she set up something on her own. To give her more independence, for one thing . . .

She then met up with Nico, who was already waiting, at a country house hotel nearby. They had a long and anticipatory lunch – legs entwined under the table, Laura kicking off her shoes – and then spent the afternoon in bed. This was followed by their first explosive quarrel, after which, barely speaking, they had gone their very separate ways – Laura only just arriving in time for a strong gin before dinner. Looking, rather as she was feeling, distraught.

'That's all right then, darling . . .'

'I suppose so. But I'm getting pretty fed up with the job . . . I know as much as any of them there now . . . and I'm sick of being used to front it up when someone else makes the blinking mistakes. Now they always get me on the phone or ask me to go and have a word with so-and-so who's being impossible . . . I might start something on my own. This could be the right time to do it. I know I'd get the clients . . .'

'Then perhaps you should, if you feel that way.' Felicity shoved the white suit to one side and sat. She hadn't realised how tired she was. 'You know Pa and I would do whatever we could . . .'

Pa. Now he was well up in the art world. He was bound to know of Nico's gallery, just off Bond Street – even though the expensive nineteenth-century paintings he dealt in weren't his thing . . . Kate probably did too . . . everyone who dabbled in collecting knew *something* about Nico, had heard some story or other . . .

'Thanks Mother. I know that . . . I'm going to do some hard thinking. And I'm sorry about the scene and the toast. I was just feeling bloody-minded.'

'I think we all knew that, darling,' Felicity said tactfully. 'But you cleared up marvellously *and* laid the breakfast . . .'

And Nico had phoned. He had, he had, he had . . . God knows how – or where from exactly. He sounded terribly vague. But frantic to hear her, he said, frantic . . .

Her whole body tingled with the thought of him, melted by

79

her mother's openness, Laura got up, smiling, and came over and gave her a kiss. 'Conscience, Mother . . .'

Felicity never knew what made her ask the question; perhaps it was just Laura's closeness. But she said, apparently out of the blue, 'The man who phoned tonight . . . is he married?'

By then, Laura was on the floor, kneeling among her belongings, scrabbling around for a brush. She paused, looked up.

'Yes,' she said clearly, 'He is . . . very, as a matter of fact . . .'

'Oh darling . . .' Stricken, Felicity stared at her daughter. She looked so beautiful, crouched over that mess of womanly clutter. Childlike without her make-up; the image of Kate. She had a sudden urge to protect her.

'Do be careful, Laura, won't you . . .' – imploring, anxious. 'Don't do anything . . .'

'Don't worry, Mother. I can take care of myself . . .' And pulling a brush from a tangle of garments, 'I'm a big girl now, Mother. I know what I'm doing.'

'I hope so, Laura.'

At the bottom of the stairs, Felicity bumped into Robin. Preoccupied, she hadn't heard the front door close. He had come back from his lengthy walk looking refreshed.

'Hello there . . . have you been up talking to your girls? Keeping them in order? Kate ought to be fast asleep by now . . .' His eyes always puckered attractively at the corners.

'She is, I'm sure . . .' Felicity smiled back at him with relief. She was truly fond of Robin. After Laura's disconcerting response just now, he looked so reassuringly straightforward.

'That's good. We've got a big day tomorrow. I noticed John's car has gone . . .'

'He wanted to check on a patient. You know what a worrier he is. I expect I'll wait up for him . . .' She always did.

'Yes – well – bed for me too now . . .' He gave his mother-in-law a massive bear hug and took the stairs two at a time.

Felicity wandered about downstairs as the big old house settled itself for the night. Pipes rattled and gurgled. Upstairs, Robin had put on a radio for the late news. She let Raffles out . . . The dampness had brought out the heady scent of the roses in the beds along the terrace. Above, she heard Laura's window being flung open wide.

There was no possibility, none whatsoever, that Laura had acquired that golden bikini tan in this country. She must think she was extremely naïve to swallow that one. She picked up stray newspapers and a coffee cup someone had left on the hall table. Putting out most of the lights as she went, she took her bag of tapestry and went to the kitchen. Johnnie shouldn't be long now. She put on her glasses and sank into the corner of the ancient sofa. Her needle flew – stabbing in and out of the canvas – and her mind darted. Her father, the general. With all three of them down for the weekend, Kate – or Laura – must go over and see him in the nursing home. It wasn't far – and his life was getting lonelier and sadder. It wouldn't hurt any of them, not even Kate, Felicity thought in sudden irritation, to spend a little time cheering him up . . .

The moment John Holford walked in, Felicity knew that he was satisfied. The patient, whoever he or she was, was on the mend. He gave her a kiss as she was pushing the tapestry back into its bag and told her what she already knew. The crisis was past – he was much relieved. As he settled into his chair – they always talked for a bit, however late he was – Felicity poured a light whisky and water.

'Thanks, darling . . . everyone upstairs?'

'Ages ago. I went up to see the girls – and Robin had his walk.'

'Did you talk to Laura?'

'Yes.' She sat very close, on the edge of the sofa. She hadn't taken off her glasses and her brown eyes, a bit troubled, regarded him over the top of them.

'Say anything, did she?'

'He's married . . . the man I spoke to on the phone tonight. I asked her. "Very" she said.'

'I see . . .' He leant over and gave her his drink. She took a couple of sips and handed it back. 'What was your feeling – talking to her?'

'That it's serious, or going to be.'

Felicity was still sitting bolt upright. She had put on a bit of weight in the last couple of years, gently filling out her face. She had the healthy colour of one who spends a good deal of time out of doors. Except round her eyes, she had hardly any wrinkles. Her curly hair was shot with grey. John Holford thought, although no power in the world would make him say so, that she was prettier than either of her daughters.

Seeing that she was worried, he said, 'Now why did you think that?'

'I don't know . . . it was just – the way I thought she was . . . I hope she's not going to get herself into a mess, Johnnie.'

After a silence he said quietly, 'We really don't know very much about what goes on in her life, do we? Only what she chooses to tell us – which sounds more or less what one would expect of a young woman, on her own, about London. She's extremely attractive . . . good at her work. Daring as hell. She's got a decent flat . . .' It was the flat they had bought some years before with a legacy Felicity had inherited from her mother; using it themselves sometimes; knowing that it would do for Kate and Laura eventually. 'She comes down fairly often . . . we see her for an occasional dinner in town. On the whole, she's affectionate . . . But where she goes, who she sees, what she does – we don't know . . .' He drank.

'No . . . no we don't.' And there was, for example, that mysterious all-over-bronze skin of hers. She wouldn't bother Johnnie with that – now.

'Do you think she sleeps around a lot?' He shot the question at her – clipped, professional. It was a subject that they had mostly avoided through mutual tact.

'Yes I do . . . for whatever that's worth.'

John Holford shrugged. 'I've warned her. I've spoken to her directly and clinically. She knows the dangers as well – or almost as well – as I do myself. She seemed to be seeing Peter pretty regularly but I gather that's completely off now.'

'It is. What we need for her, Johnnie, is another Robin . . . I don't really mean that but . . .'

'I know exactly what you mean.'

'And she did also say tonight that she's bored with the job at Fairbrothers. She's got all this push – she's amazingly self-confident . . . and I do think that if she went off on her own as she's been talking about, it would give her direction. Responsibility. Channel her energies in a meaningful way.'

82

'That's a good point.'

'Will you talk to her about it? Seriously?'

'Of course. Tomorrow if I can . . . while Kate and Robin are out. That might be an opportunity to get her to myself.'

They sat there in the dark and silent house, both aware of the irony that it was Laura they were worried about all of a sudden; not Kate, whose dogged survival – and physical ups and downs – had caused them so much anguish over the years.

'Kate was tired tonight, Johnnie.'

'I saw that. I'm glad they've got that nice young doctor in London, Tony Martin – he was at Cambridge the same time as Robin. I get the feeling he understands Kate very well. And he'll look after the babe.'

'I hope she doesn't go wearing herself out over this house, Knyght's Wood . . .'

'She mustn't do that. Seriously. We can't be quite sure how she's going to cope, physically, with childbirth. I'm not suggesting that she stays in bed for the next six weeks or so. But she must take things very easily so she stays well. I'm going to have a word with Robin in any case. And she's got a first class gynaecologist looking after her. I'm sure he'll impress the same on them both.'

'They really are fixed on each other, those two, aren't they, Johnnie?'

John Holford set down his empty glass. 'So it seems, my love, so it seems. Although no doubt they'll have to weather a few storms in due course like the rest of us. That's the final test I suppose. Life – what it brings.' He sounded lightly ironic.

'Oh they will, Johnnie. I'm sure of it.' She sounded passionate. 'They're like us, aren't they?' John Holford laughed, stood up, held out his hand and pulled her to her feet. 'Aren't they, Johnnie?' she insisted.

'If they're lucky they are,' he said, holding her tight round the shoulders. He snapped out the last light and they went upstairs to bed.

Chapter 10

For Kate and Robin, settled back in their London life, the weeks crept by . . . Everyone except Kate was both surprised and relieved when she gave birth easily, with no complications whatsoever. *She* had never had the slightest doubt that she would.

She felt the first faint tell-tale twinges in her back soon after Robin arrived home, about seven, on a mild October evening. It was the day before the due date given by her doctor. Instantly recognising the signs, perfectly cool, she came into the sitting-room, now painted a soft terracotta with blue-and-cream splashed curtains. She told Robin, who was rustling about behind a newspaper, that he would have to forego his nightly gin, put on his coat again and get the car keys. She also told him not to worry.

The paper fluttered to the floor.

'Oh my darling – is this it?'

'This is it . . .'

'You're sure?' He had gone deathly pale.

'Absolutely . . .' – radiant. 'There are one or two things I've got to do . . .'

While Robin was absorbing this – which he did rather slowly – Kate telephoned her doctor, turned off the oven, and fetched a suitcase, which had been packed for weeks, from their bedroom. She paused by the door of the new nursery, looked in – and said a silent prayer. For a moment only she felt afraid. When she came down the stairs, a warm cashmere wrap flung round her, Robin met her at the bottom. He looked stunned and he hadn't put on his coat. But he was holding the car keys.

'Here, take this would you darling?' Kate handed him the case. 'I've spoken to Dr Roberts – he's meeting us at the hospital. And I think we ought to get a move-on.'

Robin blinked, swallowed, took her arm – and said nothing. The doctor was waiting when they got there. So too was their friend and general practitioner, Tony Martin. Although neither Kate nor Robin knew it at the time, Dr Martin had already put through a surreptitious call to John Holford.

Kate slogged through her labour, which progressed rapidly, with humour, stoicism, and – in the last stages – guts and a level head. Her weakened left side did not, as her father had feared, let her down. After no more than three hours, she was into the delivery room – a few whiffs, a lot of hard pushing – and just past eleven, Lucy was born. She weighed six and a half pounds.

Robin stayed with Kate throughout. By the time he was shown his daughter's face – red, just visible between folds of white shawl – he was upright, but barely in touch. Chalky white, he was pouring sweat. His face was impassive as a mask. Ever after, he had no recollection whatsoever of their drive to the hospital, where he parked the car, and who it was who whisked Kate away.

He went straight to the phone to give the good news to the Holfords. 'A girl,' he choked. 'Six and a half pounds. And Kate is fine.' John Holford, ecstatic, assured him that they would tell Laura – who was in New York – immediately. He would put in a call at once. This done, Robin rushed straight to the nearest lavatory where he was violently sick. Only then did he realise how desperately he had feared for Kate, and had done throughout her pregnancy. All the fervent protectiveness he had felt for her at the very first, in Paris, came back with her pains – and all but overwhelmed him. It didn't seem possible that her fragile body could go through all this. Something must be done ... grim-faced, he fought down his panic. Helpless, watching her ... his mouth almost too dry to utter words of love and encouragement.

But she had come through. Kate had coped miraculously; she was a survivor as she always said. He could breathe again – their world would go on after all. It was like being reborn, almost like that funny little wrinkled red thing who was, the doctor had informed him – briefly piercing his paroxysm of fear – his daughter. He washed his face, pulled himself together and made a second call, to Jersey.

When Robin brought Kate and Lucy home, five days later, Kate was wearing her normal clothes. Whatever weight she had put on with the baby slipped away. Even her waist had shrunk dramatically. The Holfords insisted that she had a young nanny to help with Lucy at the beginning. But she gained strength so quickly and was so exhilarated by the baby, that after a couple of weeks she decided she could manage on her own, with some daily help. Even her limp, which had been so exacerbated by the pregnancy, steadied. John Holford had been concerned that her general left-side weakness might hinder her looking after the baby; cause her to over-use her right arm and therefore tire easily. She had always compensated with her right side. He and Felicity slipped up and down to London regularly in the first days and weeks – and, relieved, saw that this was apparently not so. Tony Martin, often dropping in, kept an eye on the pair of them.

And Lucy was so obviously thriving – dark and pretty and particularly alert. She was also an easy baby, contented, rarely crying except when she was hungry; soon sleeping for long stretches at night. Robin, at first so wary, was beginning to carry her round and help with her.

Lucy was already three weeks old when Laura saw her for the first time. She had flown off to New York, on business, a couple of weeks before she was born. She had resigned from her job at the end of the summer – and was after a particular up-and-coming American wallpaper house, which she hoped to represent in this country. She was going solo – determinedly; putting together an interior design company, one which would also deal in residential property, for sale or rent, for foreign clients. Full of ideas now that she had made the break from staid and traditional Fairbrothers, bursting with confidence, she was feeling her way ahead . . . And a trip to the States, just then, seemed the right thing to do. Particularly piquant to disappear briefly, she thought, just as Nico had become so passionate about her . . .

She had expected to be in New York only for about a week. But she started having a marvellous time, seeing friends, making contacts, being invited all over the place – to the opera, a first night, parties, smart restaurants, to Connecticut at weekends. The pace and dazzle of New York, the social whirl she was caught up in, intoxicated her. She was meeting new people all the time – much taken by her looks and her style and her English appeal. 'And one thing leads to another, Katie-Kate, I can't afford not to follow up all the leads, not at this point . . .,' she said to Kate anxiously, in a long and expensive phone call just when the baby was due. 'You do understand, lovey, don't you?'

'Of course,' agreed Kate – who didn't. Laura's life was becoming more and more of a mystery to her; light years removed from her own increasing domesticity. Although she could somehow understand her instant attraction to New York; it would suit Laura's verve. But to think that they used to share everything . . . 'Wish me luck and come and say hello to whoever it is when you get back . . .'

And what kept Laura there in the end was – Nico Kirilov. Chasing her as extravagantly as she had thought, and hoped, he might. She knew he was in New York frequently; that he had a partnership in one of the big galleries. He turned up without warning. Being Nico, he had been offered the loan of a very fancy apartment, belonging to one of his clients, overlooking the East River. And Laura, after quickly deciding that Kate wouldn't need her in London anyway, had made elaborate excuses to all her new American friends, left the hotel in which she had rarely stayed – and moved in with him. For ten days they lived like lords, drunk on each other, New York there for the asking . . .

> I'll take Manhattan
> The Bronx and Staten
> Island too . . .

The piano tinkling in some smart and murky bar; ice-cold Martinis; hands entwined. Nico whispering suggestively,

87

nibbling her ear; on top form – which he by no means always was. He blamed his violent mood swings on his Russian background – 'too many dark ice-bound winters start to affect the genes,' he would say. But in the heady, vibrant New York air that autumn, with Laura, he scintillated. His arresting looks – grey-green eyes, colour washing over high cheekbones, shock of wiry hair – drew glances, even in the street. His acute intelligence and his curiosity made him a brilliant companion. He could charm. His background and education were impeccable.

And he knew his world, the art world, superbly. In New York, he played on this knowledge as on a violin: a sale to a museum in the Mid-West, another to a collector in California, yet another to an Ivy League college. He winkled two pictures he had been after, for European clients, for years – from the trustees of a family foundation in New Mexico. He named his price; they accepted. One after the other, like falling dominoes, the buying and the selling and the selling again – perfectly orchestrated. He was on a high. After many frustrating months, Nico Kirilov could do no wrong. And in between the heady trading of works of art, millions passing hands, he worshipped Laura – who adored him in return.

'*Autumn in New York . . .*'

They flew back together, first-class tickets organised by Nico – holding hands and drinking champagne all the way over. And the following afternoon, Laura drove her small car, furiously dodging the traffic, across London to Kate's.

'She's absolutely adorable, Katie-Kate,' Laura exclaimed, peering into the lace-draped cradle where her niece, Lucy, was sleeping on her back, tiny hands clenched, her face half turned. 'Dark like us . . . tiny features . . . and a mouth like a rosebud. Will it stay, do you suppose? . . . she's very pretty. Clever you – and Robin. Was it absolutely awful – having her?'

'Ghastly towards the end – but I was lucky, so they told me. It didn't go on very long. She was quick. Otherwise, I should think you'd just want to give up and die – the pain is awful. But you *do* forget . . . I have already . . .'

Laura inspected Kate closely. She had already watched her walking – and been satisfied. 'Pa said you came through it with flying colours. He was a bit worried about you, you know, before. Anyhow, you certainly don't look any different. Prettier perhaps . . .'

'I don't know about that.'

Lucy began to stir and wrinkle her face. Kate whispered, 'Let's go downstairs quickly and have a cup of tea and a good chat before she wakes and demands to be fed. She's very vocal over that as you'll hear.'

But Laura was right; Kate did look well. She had managed a nap that morning when the baby was sleeping; and her mother had looked after Lucy the other day so she could go out to buy some new clothes. After all those flower-sprigged smocks and shawls, she had hankered after something dark and slinky. She had come back laden with expensive shopping bags, feeling vindicated. One of her purchases was a straight black wool dress with long sleeves and a huge, soft cowl neck. She was wearing it now, sleeves pushed up, a thick black and silver belt round her newly-returned waist. Robin, she knew, would love it. She felt skinny and emphatically not pregnant. It was a glorious relief.

Going down the stairs she said, 'I just feel – happy . . . and lucky, and dotty about the baby . . . And it's wonderful to be a normal person again, not a great deformed mountain . . .' But she was determined not to go on and on about the baby and her self; she had decided that the moment Laura phoned. Domesticity of any kind never much interested Laura. So as they went into the kitchen and she put the kettle on she said over her shoulder, 'And *you* look terribly smart, Laura. What fabulous shoes . . . Do tell me – how did it all go in New York – really?'

'Great. I had a ball . . .' Kate thought she heard faint tones of an American accent . . . 'Friends – and all the people I had introductions to – were so hospitable. Everyone seemed to have tons of money. Autumn is the best time of year there . . . the weather was wonderful – warm days and blue skies and crisp at night. Everything starts again after the endless summer they have there – plays, the opera . . .'

'Oh I *am* glad . . .'

Laura carried the tray into the sitting-room and they sat,

drinking tea and eating biscuits while the light went and the room darkened around them. Without realizing it, they were back to the way they used to be, quite unselfconscious with each other. Chatting easily about their parents ... Laura's plans; the baby; and Robin and his business, Condicote Limited, which was still idling, on the verge of hooking several good deals but nothing quite coming through as they had hoped.

Laura leant back in a corner of the sofa. She was wearing a strictly-tailored suit and her hair had been cut very short. She pushed off her smart, claret-coloured shoes and tucked her legs beneath her, the way she always used to, saying, 'It's tough. Any new venture is. I'm sure I'll find that out too. Management buy-outs and mergers and acquisitions, the sort of thing Condicote is after, are a pretty esoteric area of the business world. They'll just have to sit it out until the breaks come ... and I bet they will. Robin's no fool, neither are James and Rupert ...' Then, speaking very fast, 'I was in New York with someone special, Katie-Kate – for the last ten days at least ...'

'I thought you might have been. Who is he?'

'He's called Nico Kirilov.'

'What – the man who's got the gallery – Nicolas Kirilov, in Cork Street?' Kate put her cup down with a clatter.

'That's right. Do you know him?'

'Only *of* him. And I've been to the gallery once or twice. He's very big time. Isn't he Russian?' So this was the new man; Mother had dropped a warning hint; she would tread carefully.

'Yes. Very. At least, his grandparents fled with his father and the family jewels soon after the revolution. Later, when they had settled in England, Alexander – his father – married a second cousin whose parents had also managed to escape somehow. So Nico is 100 per cent Russian on both sides. The Kirilovs were great aristocrats with a palace in St Petersburg and vast country estates. But all that ended in 1917 of course.'

'Oh *Laura* ...' She looked so sleek and sexy, perched in a corner of the chintzy sofa. So sure of herself. 'Is he the man you met last summer, at that dance you went to in the country?'

'Yes.'

'You were different after that . . .'

'Yes again, Katie-Kate.' She was smiling at her sister in the cosy half-light, sensing her doubts. Knowing that her expression, which she couldn't really see, was disapproving.

'He's married, Laura.'

'Indeed he is.' She sounded very matter-of-fact about it. 'With six children . . .'

'*Six?*' Kate gasped. '*Six?*'

'That's right. The Lady Arabella – that's his wife – is an earth-mother type. She's the daughter of a Scottish earl. Very beautiful, very gentle, very fat. Big shambolic house in the country. The children – also beautiful but I don't think fat – running wild. She has just turned the drawing-room into a kitchen. The soul of a home, she says it is. According to Nico. She bakes bread a lot. Wholemeal, naturally. Nico lives in Chelsea. Or New York. Or travels about the world. But he goes there quite often.' She leant over and put her cup down on a low table. 'I think he loves it. In small doses.'

'But Laura . . .' Kate was struggling to absorb what she was hearing. What on earth, she wondered irrelevantly, would all these half-Scottish, half-Russian children be like? 'Is he going to leave her – Arabella?'

'Good heavens no . . .'

'Then what . . . I mean, does she know that he has mistresses?'

'Yes, of course.'

'And that's what you are – one of those?'

'Not exactly. *The* mistress. Singular.'

After a crackling silence, Kate said simply, 'I see . . .'

Alert, she thought she could hear tiny, snuffly sounds coming from the nursery. Lucy would be getting hungry; her breasts were beginning to feel uncomfortable. Kate sighed. It was hard to tune into this sophisticated new life Laura was telling her about, now that her own world was bounded by Lucy's next feed and somehow getting a meal together for herself and Robin every evening . . . She felt unaccountably sad – for Laura. Even though she seemed so confident of everything. Their mother was worried about her too. And she

91

knew nothing, yet, of all this . . . Just as she asked, 'What's he like – Nico?' and Laura answered immediately, 'Brilliant – and exciting,' – Lucy started to wail.

'She must be starving . . .' Kate was already by the door. 'Come up with me . . .'

In the nursery, she switched on a lamp, picked up Lucy who was red in the face, frantically stuffing her fist in her mouth, and changed her. Laura watched, fascinated.

'She's so little, Katie-Kate . . .'

'But she's strong. Here. Take her while I get out of this dress, would you? Put a blanket over that suit first . . . like this – go on – she won't break . . .' Laura took her gingerly, holding her stiffly while Kate slipped out of her dress and put on a wrapper. The baby's mouth searched against the grey gabardine of Laura's arm. 'Ready now . . .' Kate took her and settled in a low chair and started to nurse her. 'There she goes . . .' She looked up at Laura. 'There's another chair over there . . . push away whatever's on it and bring it over . . .'

Glancing at her watch – thinking that it was time she got home and changed for the evening with Nico – Laura was, nevertheless, a little moved at the sight of Kate and Lucy. She did feel a sudden stab of – not envy exactly – but regret. It was a lovely sight, the two of them – Kate's expression of tenderness, Lucy's fist waving – sitting in the old nursing chair, their grandmother's, haloed in soft lamplight.

They chatted about this and that. Nico was not mentioned again. As Kate shifted Lucy to her left side, propping her elbow on the arm of the chair, she said suddenly, 'I completely forgot to tell you . . . Laura, we're moving into Knyght's Wood. This Saturday . . .'

'Goodness Katie-Kate, that's quick.' In her excitement over Nico and New York, her head full of ideas for the business, she had completely forgotten about that new house of theirs. She had only seen it from the outside – and thought it rather a lot for Kate and Robin to take on. At least, as a second home. And Laura knew about houses. But Kate had been set on it from the beginning. A good deal more so than Robin, in Laura's opinion. His father had kept to his word and bought it – and they had paid considerably less than the asking price once he took over the bargaining. 'You haven't done anything to it, have you?'

'Not a thing. It's perfectly sound. We've got together the basics – and Mother has rounded up some bits and pieces she doesn't want at home. A few things from Grandfather's house . . . Robin is very stern. We can't do anything more for the moment, not until the business gets going. They're over-extended at the bank which is worrying him a lot.' A shadow passed across Kate's face as she bent over Lucy. 'Not one penny more on Knyght's Wood, he says. So for the moment, we'll just camp there when we feel like it . . .'

'That's lovely then,' Laura said without enthusiasm. 'Lucky old you . . .' Personally, she had thought from the beginning that they should stick to one home and get a bigger place in London. This house, although you couldn't swing a cat, would fetch a bomb today. She hoped that Kate wasn't going to overdo the garden bit. Or spend too much time there without Robin. She knew all about Robin's wanderlust and his need to test himself to the limit physically. She never believed he had got that quite out of his system. He wouldn't fancy spending all his precious time away from the office in a cottage in Laverton.

'And only at weekends,' Kate said quickly. She and Laura still had their uncanny knack of reading each other's minds. 'And Robin is going skiiing with Rupert and Jill after Christmas for a few days. You know how keen he is – and everyone says he's amazingly good. So Lucy and I will stay at Knyght's Wood and see lots of Mother and Pa.'

'They'll love that. And what about carpets and curtains? Did you buy the whole lot?'

Kate nodded, holding Lucy expertly over her shoulder and rubbing her back. 'Everything. It's shabby – but it's plain, and we can certainly live with it for the time being.' With secret pleasure, she remembered the bulbs – daffodils and narcissi – she had bought and hidden from Robin in a box under the hall table. 'Good girl, Lucy,' she said, as the baby brought up air and dribble. 'I think you've had enough now . . .'

Laura did some quick thinking. She wasn't meeting Nico until late tonight. He had lots of paperwork to catch up on in the gallery in connection with his recent selling triumphs. And they were starting to hang a new exhibition. She didn't have to rush. And she was feeling nicely soothed being here with Kate and the baby. She really was a sweet little thing . . .

'Can I have her again, Katie-Kate? Come to Laura, Lucy . . .' She took her with more confidence this time, giving her a finger to curl her tiny hand round; relaxed, enjoying her. 'I think she's going to look like us, don't you – not the Faradays? The same eyes . . . it's a funny feeling, isn't it? A bit eerie . . .' She sounded pleased.

Kate was putting her dress back on. 'It is rather. But lovely to think of new life, another generation, going on . . . no, I don't see her like Robin either . . .'

'She's very alert. Looking around everywhere as though she knows the score already. Aren't you, Lucy?' Laura wiggled her hand up and down.

'Pa is convinced she's a genius. He claims you can always tell, with experience, even though no doctor will admit it. He says she's exceptionally observant.'

'You wouldn't call him biased by any chance . . .'

Kate laughed, fastening her belt. 'You could say that. He dotes . . . even more than Ma. He always was an old softie . . . Laura, you can stay until Robin gets back, can't you? He's going to try and leave the office early and he'll be terribly disappointed not to see you . . .'

When Robin arrived, it was Laura, with Lucy held snugly over her shoulder, who met him at the door.

'Laura,' Robin shouted, warmly embracing both her and his daughter at the same time. 'How marvellous . . . I hoped I'd catch you. In fact, I couldn't get away from the workplace soon enough. How's New York these days?' Hugging her again, looking very debonair in his dark suit. Exuding good health and energy. 'It's done you a power of good . . . you look terrific – and what do you think of your niece here?' His light brown hair bent towards Lucy's dark crown.

Laughing and talking, his arm still round Laura, they went into the sitting-room. Kate had drawn the curtains and put on all the lights. There was a huge vase of pale chrysanthemums in the corner. The room was colourful and pretty and comfortable. Kate came in from the kitchen with the ice bucket.

'New dress, darling?' Robin asked, kissing her. 'I like it. Very sexy. And we don't want you in the family way again just yet, do we?'

Kate blushed. 'Sex maniac . . . what sort of day was it?'

'Don't ask,' he replied cheerfully. 'Drink, anyone?'

Then he started quizzing Laura about New York – did she get an exclusive on those decorating lines, whatever they were? Had she decided how to get Laura Holford Ltd off the ground yet? Did she do any travelling – manage to get away from Manhattan for a bit? Eyeing her over his glass and wondering exactly what – and who – she had been up to over there all these weeks. She was certainly looking very pleased with herself. And she was a stunning girl, no doubt about that. Her face made up to the nines, of course – which he hated. But her legs were fantastic . . .

'Property first, Robin,' – grinning cheekily, flinging those legs seductively across each other, one shoe dangling. 'That's where I'm starting, that's going to be my base. A cheap flat on the edge of a good neighbourhood, do it up, sell it quickly . . . I'll raise enough on my own flat for this. And Mother and Pa have offered to chip in. If I'm lucky – and the timing is right – I'll be able to cover my costs and have enough left over to get into a specialist decorating business. That's where the exclusive American lines come in. I might consider letting the flat . . . I'll combine property and decorating. They're a natural together. And I want to make money. Quickly.'

'Ho-ho, heard that one before – but you could well pull it off. Any ideas where you might buy?'

'I got on to the estate agent's this morning. I'm viewing twelve properties tomorrow – all reasonably priced, all needing tarting up . . .'

'Quick work.' She was a sparky girl all right. Like Kate – but in a very different way – full of determination. He didn't doubt she would carve out some career niche for herself.

'I thought it was time you left Fairbrothers,' Kate said, impressed. 'Mother and Pa did too. Much too stuffy for you . . .'

'But I learnt a lot, Katie-Kate,' Laura said quickly. 'I got the know-how – and I made the contacts ...'

After one drink – and a toast to Lucy who was lying peacefully asleep in a blanket on the sofa – Laura said that she must be off. She lingered for a moment, quite tenderly, over the drowsy baby. Then she wished Kate and Robin good luck for Knyght's Wood that weekend; she would be down to see it soon. On the way out Kate suggested that she came for supper one night next week.

'Lovely, Katie-Kate ... I'd adore that ... give me a ring when you get back from the country ...' Nonchalant as ever. Not giving much away. Where, for example, was she off to? Kate wondered ... Through the front door in a cloud of expensive scent, those high heels clattering.

Kate and Robin watched her zoom off towards the West End – and as soon as the door was closed, Kate said, 'Oh Robin, I've got masses to tell you ... Laura told me a bit about the new boyfriend ...'

'That's interesting ...'

'Well, I don't know ...' One look at her face which was noticeably less vivacious than when the three of them had been together, moments before, put Robin on guard. He thought she looked suddenly drained. Laura was inclined to do this to her at the best of times.

'Listen,' he said quietly, his hands on her shoulders. 'I'll pop Lucy back upstairs and join you in the kitchen. Then you can tell me everything. All right?'

Over cold lamb from the night before, and a good salad, Kate told Robin what she had learned of Nico Kirilov from Laura. Robin, now in his shirtsleeves, listened attentively. He got up and poured them the remains of a bottle of wine.

'What else?'

'Nothing very much ...'

'Is she going to live with him?'

'I certainly didn't get that impression. "Heavens, no," she said when I asked if he was going to leave his wife. She sounded very definite about that. She didn't say much about him that was personal – just that he was exciting – and brilliant. But she's crazy about him. I could tell. And she sounded so . . . so assured. As though she knew exactly what she was doing. And felt it was right . . .'

'Six kids,' Robin said gloomily. 'I've heard of him of course. And the gallery. I suppose I could find out a bit more about him if I tried . . .'

'I wish you would, Robin.' She looked worried.

'Darling . . .' His hand grasped her across the table. 'Don't worry so. Please. It's not good for you. Laura – and I know you don't like my saying this – is tough. Quite a hard number. I expect she finds Kirilov exotic – the Russian background sounds romantic. And he's extremely successful. And you've always said she's not the domestic type . . . She's got her head screwed on, I'm sure she knows what she's getting into . . .'

'I wonder . . .' Chin on her hand, Kate gazed across the kitchen. 'I really wonder this time . . .'

'A penny for your thoughts,' Robin teased, pouring himself the last of the wine. 'Or are you debating how many hours Lucy will let us get tonight?'

Kate shook her head, tucking a strand of hair behind her ear as she always did when her mind was miles away. She said dreamily. 'I wasn't thinking about Lucy at all . . . I was thinking about Knyght's Wood. I hadn't meant to tell you, but I bought masses of bulbs this morning – and I know just how they're going to look in the orchard, round the old apple trees . . .'

Chapter 11

Next spring, as a cold and windy March dissolved in gentle sunshine, the daffodils burst into flower and glowed and nodded among the long wild grasses in the orchard at Knyght's Wood.

Exactly how Kate had imagined.

Most were planted by Felicity Holford. Kate had made a start that first weekend they spent at the house; but there was so much to do, unpacking boxes and looking after Lucy – and she was physically much more tired than she realised – that she only got in an hour's gardening on the Sunday morning while Lucy was asleep and Robin was putting up shelves. So her mother came over during the week and finished the planting.

Although they rarely used it for more than two or three days at a time, they settled into Knyght's Wood surprisingly easily. The dour woman from the general store turned out to be a transplanted Scot with a kind heart that belied her gruff exterior. Soothed and charmed by Kate, aware that she badly needed a helping hand with the house, Mrs Bundy agreed to clean one morning a week. She and 'Bundy' – which was how she always referred to her husband, who was rarely seen – would also keep an eye on the place when they weren't there. That first wet afternoon when Kate came bursting into the shop, Mrs Bundy had seen her hugely pregnant – and limping badly. Now, her frailty, and the good and pretty baby, appealed to her caring nature. Mrs Bundy was needed – she asked no more.

Robin was practical and good with his hands, a trait he had inherited from his father. And Kate was sure of her taste – and her priorities. On the whole, they agreed over these; ambitious plans, like a new kitchen, belonged in the future. In those early weeks and months, Robin worked off much of his energy – as well as the frustrations of business which he was learning to put up with – decorating the house. The living-room was painted white, brightening the long, low room and enhancing the dark beams and the huge fireplace. The wide chimney-breast, the original part of the house which had been a bakery, pushed up through the room above, adding character.

Lucy's room was transformed by pale primrose paint and gleaming white woodwork. The main bedroom, which stretched over the length of the house, had a sloping ceiling and windows which looked out right across the village to the bottom of the valley and the lazy, winding river which drew passionate fishermen like a magnet. Kate chose green-and-white patterned wallpaper – and Robin rose to the challenge. After a particularly disappointing week when Condicote so nearly, and yet didn't, land a potentially lucrative client, Robin took Friday off, and drove Kate and Lucy down to Knyght's Wood. Rolls of wallpaper were wedged on the back seat of the car next to Lucy's carrycot. The moment they arrived, Robin put on his oldest jeans and prepared to attack the bedroom. Every now and again, between feeding Lucy and starting to weed bits of the garden, Kate looked in to help with the cutting and measuring and to bring cups of coffee. And verbal encouragement. His intelligence and perseverence paid off. He worked non-stop, with absolute precision, for most of the weekend. By the time they returned to London, the bedroom was a bower of greenery.

The following Monday morning, Robin set off for work with a renewed passion to succeed. And he did. With icy aplomb he reopened the negotiations which had failed the week before and insisted on a final meeting. After working half the night, he then presented an altered expansion and takeover scheme. It was slightly less favourable to Condicote – but in small, important ways more attractive to the client. Robin was forceful, fluent and persuasive. He won them round – and by the end of the week an agreement had been signed. Robin, James and Rupert cracked a celebratory bottle of champagne together. It was their first breakthrough, coming at a time when they had all begun to question whether it ever would.

To Robin and Kate it was, and always would be, 'the wallpaper contract'; a private joke which lingered on . . .

They had very little furniture. They invested in a solid pine table and chairs for the kitchen, which was big and square and looked out onto the small walled garden which was a jungle of weeds and wild, overgrown raspberry canes. The living-room had a sofa, long discarded, from the Holfords' attic – and a few odd chairs and tables which had once been in Kate and Laura's bedroom. John Holford, foraging in a country house auction, as he sometimes did, had bought them a large oriental carpet of faded reds and blues. The dining-room was completely bare. In a burst of optimism, soon after the signing of that first invaluable contract, Robin painted the front door a brilliant yellow.

The Sunday after Easter, on a day of sunshine and breezes and spring flowers, Lucy was christened at a brief ceremony after the morning service in the village church. They now shared a vicar with three other small parishes, and services were held every other Sunday morning. Kate never missed. Lucy was looked after either by Robin or, if he was fishing or off on some hike, by Felicity Holford. Kate had also joined the rota of women who did the flowers. She had done them, with her mother's help, the day before the christening and the font was wreathed in golden forsythia.

It was a small gathering – the Holfords and the Faradays; Ina and Louis Berger, over from France for the occasion at Kate's urging; Felicity Holford's father, the General; Lisa, an old schoolfriend of Kate's. Tony Martin, their doctor, had hoped to come but had been delayed in London. Kate was disappointed because she wanted to introduce him to Lisa, a lawyer with a London firm – and, like Tony, unmarried. She had been trying to get the two of them together for months. Tony would drive down later, to the house, if he could . . .

And finally, Laura and Nico Kirilov.

They arrived in Nico's sleek and expensive car just as Kate and Robin – Lucy in Kate's arms – were going into the church. Everyone else was already inside. Laura and Nico came charging up the path behind them. Kate turned.

100

'Laura – you're only just in time . . .' She stopped. She had never seen Laura like that before; switched on like a lamp. Looking a knock-out in a pencil-slim black-and-white checked suit and a strange grey feather boa wound round her neck, floating over her shoulder; brilliantly happy. Introducing Nico, not bothering to lower her high, breathy voice although the organ was already playing inside the church.

'This is Nico Kirilov, Katie-Kate. And this is Robin. And my adorable about-to-be goddaughter. We made a late start and simply *flew* down . . .' Laughing, her head thrown back, her hair set in stylised curls. 'Frankly, I never thought we'd make it . . .'

'You underestimate my driving ability. How do you do Kate? I've been longing to get a glimpse of you – and *so* deliciously pretty . . .'

Robin glared.

Excitable, Kate thought, meeting those intense grey-green eyes. That's what he looks – excitable. His colouring, everything about him too vivid. Speaking in that same exaggerated way Laura had taken to. She smiled and murmured as he and Robin shook hands, and walked on into the church holding Lucy in her cascade of ivory ruffles and lace, grateful for Robin's steadying arm.

The walls of the church were white-washed and had, as John Holford remembered, decorative frescoes around the altar. The small gathering stood in a semi-circle around the font. Kate kept her eyes glued on Lucy, in the vicar's arms . . . *Be good, Lucy, be good*, Kate willed her daughter silently. Just before the end, Lucy did start to yell. She had been interested and aware – but she had had enough. Her wails echoed off the walls, tears ran down her face; legs under the delicate silk kicked away. But beneath the screeching the final Blessing was already being said and suddenly it was over and Kate gathered her up and calmed her down. Everyone crowding round, smiling, relieved. Thanks and laughter and a general move towards the door which was thrown open to the sunshine.

Kate and Robin stayed back for a few minutes talking to the vicar in the porch. The others stood in small groups up and down the path, chatting, admiring the setting of the church which was just outside the village, surrounded by blossoming cherry trees. The grass in the graveyard was newly mown; many of the oldest tombstones had settled crookedly and were encrusted with mosses. John Holford, who noticed such things, bent to decipher dates and names from the past, all but obliterated by time and weathering. In the far corner, beside the grey stone wall, were the plain mounds of the newly buried.

It was Doris and Jim Faraday who started briskly back to Knyght's Wood. Jim Faraday pushed open the gates, leaving them wide, and they began to trudge up the drive. Robin had trimmed back the verge where primroses nestled round the edges. But the rest of the garden was still wild and unkempt, everything badly in need of cutting back. The sun made the walls of the old cottage honey-coloured and the bright yellow door was cheerful. Fresh cotton curtains hung at the open bedroom windows upstairs. The beech copse behind, below the crest of the downs, was already a filigree of pale greens . . . Although there was so much still to be done, the place had lost its air of neglect which had first struck Kate the summer before. It was beginning to look cared for.

'I've said it before and I'll say it again,' Doris Faraday asserted in strident tones. 'What they needed was a decent bungalow. All on one floor and easy to keep. Not all this with the stairs and a daft big garden to be looking after. They'll learn . . .'

Robin, with his fresh colouring and athletic build, looked very much like his mother. And she was a handsome woman with a good bearing; a strong personality – accustomed to making herself felt. She dressed expensively and conservatively, with never a lacquered hair out of place; as obsessive about her appearance as she was about her home. While every cushion and chair had to be exactly chosen, so also did her outfits. 'Doris mixed-and-matched,' Laura called her unkindly.

'It's what they wanted, Doris – and that's what we said we'd give them when they first got engaged. It took a while for them to find it – but they knew their own minds.' Jim Faraday was a good four inches shorter than his wife but in no way intimidated by her. 'It may not be to your liking, but you'll do well to keep your opinions to yourself.' Firm and pleasant was the way to deal with Doris when she was in a bristling mood. Dapper in a dark suit and a stiff white collar, he walked with his hands behind his back, his eyes darting about, taking in the state of the garden and shrewdly working out the cost and the labour of putting it into shape. Privately, he was inclined to agree with Doris. And it wasn't as if they would be living there all that much. Robin's work was in London. Although he did see that Kate wasn't going to be up to much travelling, especially now with the baby . . . pity, that, when the boy was so keen on it. He'd been travel-mad ever since he was a youngster. And as he got older, he took it very seriously indeed. You only had to read one of those long articles he got published – the silk routes from the East or some such thing – to realise that.

'All that lawn,' Doris sniffed. 'And who's going to keep those borders weeded I'd like to know . . .' No weed had ever lasted long in hers. 'And I thought Kate was limping badly, myself, whatever Robin says about her being better after the baby . . . Look, Jim, that must be the woman that comes in to help . . .'

The yellow door had been opened and Mrs Bundy stood inside, wiping her hands on her apron. Catching sight of the approaching Faradays, she pulled the door to and vanished. Jim Faraday turned and looked back down the drive. There was still no sign of the others behind.

'Well, now, there's no point us hanging about outside like this – we might as well go in and find that Mrs what's-'er name and see if we can do anything useful . . . they'll be along in a minute, I daresay.'

Kate insisted on carrying Lucy home. Although the church was no more than a few hundred yards from Knyght's Wood, it was slightly uphill – and the day was warm. By the time she and Robin stepped into the hall, she was exhausted. Robin rushed straight off to sort out the drinks. Doris, coming out of the kitchen, saw Kate standing with Lucy, her face very flushed and her left arm hanging. Lucy gave a huge yawn –

and started to fret. Even Doris Faraday, who had never been keen on babies, softened. She was a capable woman who had helped her husband in the business in their early days. She could turn her hand to anything.

'Here, love, let me take her . . .' She scooped Lucy expertly from Kate. 'That coat's a lot too warm for the day . . . you go and take it off and tidy yourself up. Don't you worry . . . I'll look after the baby . . .'

'Thanks, Doris. I'm sure she needs changing – Mrs Bundy is going to give her her bottle . . . and don't let her dribble on your suit, she's teething like mad . . .'

'We'll be all right. Now off you go . . .' Gratefully, Kate escaped upstairs. She was hot and slightly giddy; she hadn't realised how nervous Lucy's christening would make her, even though the church was becoming so familiar – a bit of an emotional sanctuary, although Robin would laugh if she told him. Except for one outburst at the end, Lucy had behaved very calmly. Kate took off her coat and shoes and went into the bathroom. First, she massaged her left arm from the shoulder down. Relieved of the weight of the baby it felt easier. She didn't think she would need to take anything; it was a mild ache, not a throbbing pain . . . After a minute or two, she splashed her face and held her wrists under the cool running water from the tap. Out of the window, she could see the others, strung out along the path from the gates to the house now, dawdling, enjoying the warmth, looking at the spectacular view across the valley.

And there they were – Laura with Nico Kirilov. Absorbed in the ceremony, she had forgotten all about them. Laura was shading her eyes with her hand in the bright sunlight; Nico – you couldn't miss him, not even from the back, with that shock of black hair – one arm round her, the other pointing something out in the distance.

Today was the first time either she or her parents had set eyes on him, although they all knew Laura had been seeing him constantly since last summer. Laura had only told them that he was coming last night, that he was driving her down from London. 'And we'll just say that he's separated, Katie-Kate . . . that sounds respectable enough, doesn't it?' Peals of laughter from Laura on the other end of the phone while Kate could find no possible reply except '*Is he?*' – which seemed unwise. With Laura she could always tell. So she warned her mother, who made no comment except 'I see . . .'

She turned from the window, dried her hands, and went back into the bedroom to find a more comfortable pair of shoes and brush her hair.

In the kitchen, Robin and his father had quickly decided that they should get the champagne started outside. 'We could all do with one, speaking for myself,' Jim Faraday said reasonably. 'There's nothing to touch it for a morning drink and a bit of an occasion. Got a napkin handy, have you?' He and Robin always worked well together. Using whatever glasses he could find, ones that they had brought from London and borrowed from the Holfords', Robin efficiently opened several bottles and filled up two trays. He and his father took them out through the front door and started going down the line of guests.

Felicity Holford was standing with her father and Ina Berger, discussing whether or not camellias would weather in tubs by the front door as Kate wanted. John Holford was fiddling with his camera, determined that the christening of his first grand-child should be recorded. Robin's two partners and their wives were discussing the recent adventures of Rupert and Jill in Tibet. Louis Berger was wholeheartedly admiring the English countryside on a rare good day. And lastly, Laura and Nico, apart from the rest, whispering and laughing together as though they were alone. In fact, Robin had to say, 'Champagne, Laura?' twice before he got the attention of either.

Doris Faraday and Lisa were still upstairs with Lucy. Kate had not reappeared. Mrs Bundy was warming up the food for the fork luncheon which Felicity Holford had made at home and brought over that morning. A huge christening cake, decorated with pink and white icing, was on a stand in the centre of the kitchen table. It turned out that Mrs Bundy, who was full of surprises, was an expert pastrycook. This was, she said, 'Sommat for the bairn from me an' Bundy.'

'Oh Mrs Bundy . . . you're an angel,' Kate had cried, mean-ing it, determined not to let on that she had known about it, through Robin, all along. Mrs Bundy had sworn him to secrecy. Robin, looking round for Kate, left his father manning the bottles and went upstairs to find her. She was sitting at her dressing-table spraying on scent. She had combed her hair – which turned under just above her ears – and put on lipstick. Her diamond earrings caught the sun and added to the slight shimmer of her burgundy silk dress.

'All right, darling?' Robin sounded anxious. As so often, he had been wondering if she really was; he knew the walk back from the church tired her – and she had insisted on carrying Lucy in all her cascading finery of ribbons and lace.

'Yes.' A few minutes on her own, in peace and quiet, had restored her. The hectic flush on her cheeks had disappeared. And a change of shoes helped. Her left arm, which had begun to ache quite badly, was recovering. 'Yes I am – really . . .'

'Thank goodness . . .' looking at her carefully, as he had learnt to. 'Here . . .' handing her a glass of champagne. 'Well deserved . . . everyone's very happy down there – Dad's coping . . .'

'And your mother is looking after Lucy. She's marvellously practical, I'm so grateful.' Kate took a sip of champagne. 'Heaven, just what I needed . . . Lisa, being a dedicated bachelor girl, is terrified of Lucy. And on the whole, she was very good during the whole performance, wasn't she?'

'A trooper. Very gutsy. And beautiful. Just like her Mum.'

'*Robin* . . . chauvinist . . . Oh – I was suitably surprised by the cake – which is magnificent. Have you seen it? Mrs B. almost smiled. What a treasure that woman is . . .'

'Darling . . .' – kneeling beside her, kissing her neck, sniffing the scent and her body; touching her soft skin. His large, capable hand holding her slender wrist. Kate put down her glass and drew him to her.

'I love you Kate' – muffled behind the curve of her ear.

'I know. Me too . . . *you* . . .'

'I wish they'd all go home . . .'

'They will . . . but we've got to feed them first.' She leant her cheek against his hair. 'Darling – what do you make of Nico?'

'Strange. Definitely a wild man . . . not that I've spoken to him much . . .' His hand moved up from her waist. 'Kate . . .'

A warm, tingling sensation shot swiftly down her body; she drew in her breath. Felicity Holford's laugh floated up from the garden through the open windows. They could hear Ina Berger's attractive French accent exclaiming 'How pre-e-tty' it all looked.

'We must go down to them . . .' – from Kate. It was almost a whisper.

'Not sure I can . . . *now* . . .'

'Tonight, darling . . .'

After half an hour or so of convivial champagne – guests wandering in and out of the cottage, everyone, except for Laura and Nico, meeting everyone else – Kate and her mother decided it was time to call them into the kitchen to lunch. Kate was now looking bright and beautiful, her wide smile glowing; chatting away; manoeuvring Ina Berger into a corner for a special word. Doris Faraday had seen that Lucy was taken out of her christening robe, fed, and put down in her cot upstairs. Just to be sure, she had popped her head round the door a few minutes later. Lucy was already peacefully asleep.

In the midday warmth, Doris had shed her emerald wool coat to reveal an exactly matching silk shirt. Holding out her glass to Robin for a refill she loosened up and started moving among the guests, beginning to enjoy herself. She liked a good party. The garden did have possibilities once they got it tidied up a bit, even *she* allowed that. And little Lucy was a duck. Louis Berger, when they were introduced by Robin, inclined his head courteously towards her . . .

Kate, coaxing everyone into the kitchen, handed a plate to her mother-in-law. 'Begin, Doris, please . . . and thank you so much for helping with Lucy . . . here, you too Louis . . .'

'Try some of this, Jill, why don't you?' John Holford had abandoned his camera for the time being and was offering red wine. 'There are some chairs in the sitting-room – and Robin has dragged various tables and a bench or two out into the garden if you're feeling brave . . .'

Later, Robin took Jill and Rupert Cook on a tour of the garden and the orchard. Through an intriguing ad in the *Sunday*

Times, the Cooks had just bought a dilapidated farmhouse in Provence which they hoped, over the years, to restore. 'As soon as we saw it we realized why the price was so reasonable,' Rupert said, laughing, as they strolled beneath the old apple trees. 'The roof had literally caved in – and so had most of the walls. The centre part, around the kitchen, is habitable though. And the food is marvellous, although it's miles from civilisation . . .'

'Any chance you and Kate could drive out for a week this summer?' Jill enquired. 'We're having to do some of the work ourselves to economise – and an extra pair of hands . . .'

There was an awkward silence. Already that year, Robin had skied with them, mostly off piste, exhilarated to the point of fervour by the speed and the nerve and the blinding whiteness. They were all three expert skiers. But unspoken between them suddenly was the knowledge that Kate would not be comfortable, or even safe, in the rough Provençal terrain. And the intense summer heat.

After a pause, Robin said lightly, 'I shouldn't think we'd manage it this year, not with the baby and so forth . . . Let's go back and I'll show you the plans Kate has for the rest of the garden . . .'

Laura and Nico made no move to join the party. Topping up their glasses, Robin told them that lunch was ready. But neither followed him. They were still standing in the drive – very close, laughing, almost out of control, Robin thought – when Felicity Holford went out to get them.

'Do come and eat,' she called out, approaching them rather formally. 'It's all on the kitchen table . . . if you don't come soon, I'm afraid there will be nothing left.'

'I'm so sorry, Mrs Holford, we must be more sociable,' Nico agreed, whirling round, smiling at her spectacularly. 'And it's so *awfully* good of you to welcome me like this on such a private family occasion.'

'Laura only phoned last night to tell us you were coming,' Felicity replied coldly. 'We were quite surprised. The dining-room is still minus furniture, so people are sitting about wherever they can find a chair. Do take Mr Kirilov in, Laura.'

'I will, Mother, I will,' Laura cried gaily – at the same time giving her a sharp look. 'And it's Nico, Mother – never Nicolas – just Nico . . .'

'I see. Well, then, take Nico in, would you?'

As she watched them disappear through the yellow front door Felicity Holford thought: separated . . . I wonder if his wife knows about it. Somehow, she thought not.

Laura and Nico ate ravenously standing up in the kitchen. They scraped out the remains of the huge casseroles, but discarded the salad as being too oily and wilted. Mrs Bundy, still wearing her long white apron and looking at them both with disapproval, had just finished cooking another pot of hot noodles. Nico wolfed them down exclaiming through a mouthful how 'absolutely, marvellously divine' they were. He seized on a bottle of John Holford's claret. Mrs Bundy, only half charmed by such over-elaborate praise, thought what a pity it was that this Miss Laura couldn't look a bit more ladylike and find herself a decent husband like Mr Faraday.

While they were eating, they missed the christening cake being cut and the toasts to Lucy and her parents. Although they could hear the laughter and the cheers in the sitting-room, they didn't participate. Neither of them, not even Laura, seemed in the least connected to this family party they were attending. When they had finished, they wandered into the drawing-room where they found John Holford sitting alone, still messing about with his camera. He had taken another roll of film during the cake-cutting ceremony.

'Oh there you are Laura,' he said, looking up. 'We wondered where you'd got to. Do come in both of you. Sit somewhere if you can find a chair . . . the others seem to have disappeared into the garden.'

'Sorry we missed the christening cake, Pa.' Laura picked up an empty plate lying on the floor. 'Stay with Pa, Nico, and I'll go and find us some of Mrs B.'s cake . . .'

John Holford put down his camera and smiled at his daughter. Despite his good looks, Laura thought he seemed tired. He must have been called out a lot in the night recently. His hair was more silver than grey now and his blue eyes lacked their usual good-humoured glint.

'Off you go. I'm sure Mrs Bundy can manage that.' And turning to Nico, 'Laura tells me that you're running the gallery now. I remember going into it once, some years ago. An exhibition of Victorian sporting pictures, I think. Very fine – very expensive. And I believe your father was there then.'

'That's right. He would have been. He still comes in at least twice a week ... doesn't trust the rest of us to get along without him.' Nico, who was lounging in a deep, old-fashioned armchair, slung his long legs one over the other and pushed back his thick black hair. He blinked rapidly. 'We're all passionate about pictures – our kind, at least. It's in the blood so to speak. And they saved us, in a way. My grandfather was the great collector, and he managed to get some of his collection out both before and after the revolution. Thank God for them. Otherwise, the family was penniless. It was decided to sell a few immediately and pick up some more, cheaply, with the proceeds ... And that was the beginning of the Kirilov Gallery.'

'I think I did know something of the sort,' John Holford replied. 'I collect myself in a modest sort of way – modern English, keep an eye on the sales. An occasional extravagance at one of the galleries. That sort of thing. Not that I've much time for it at the moment.'

'I know. Laura told me. With me, it's a *passion* as well as a job. I see it as a sort of highly specialised game ...' He laughed wildly. 'It is, you know ... And as luck would have it, our stuff is becoming very fashionable again. You could hardly give them away when my grandfather began in London. Nobody wanted that sort of thing. He had a hell of a job unloading any to start with. He was such a dilettante, an aesthete – brought up as a complete aristocrat with no business sense whatsoever.'

'It can't have been easy for him. He was a refugee after all with a family to support. His world crashed around him.'

'That's right.' Nico did not appear to be listening. Then he said suddenly, 'You must come and have a look round the gallery one day – let me know when you're coming and we'll go out for lunch somewhere. My club is handy, around the corner.'

'Thank you. I should enjoy that.' John Holford had been

watching Nico attentively. He noticed that he fidgeted a lot; and that he spoke fast and often in jerks. Beneath the conventionally good manners, he thought he detected arrogance. Not surprising, perhaps, given his background and education. And his very obvious success as an international art dealer. 'I hope to have a bit more time in the future. I'm thinking of easing my way out of my practice, letting the younger partners carry some of the load . . .'

'But wouldn't you miss it? Laura says you're absolutely dedicated . . . And one must do what one's *passionate* about – surely?' He turned sharply towards John Holford, his eyes glittering.

'Oh – I don't know . . .' John Holford smiled easily. 'The fishing round here is excellent, as I expect you know . . . my wife and I enjoy a bit of lazy travelling, driving through France, say. Or Italy. And I could look at a few more pictures. Yes, I can think of a lot of pleasant ways of spending retirement – or semi-retirement.'

'We're simply *lunatic* about whatever we do, we Kirilovs, we have to be. Otherwise we don't do it. My grandfather was, both my parents – and they were second cousins. In fact, my great-grandfather broke his neck in some specially designed sled in St Petersburg, racing across the Neva when it was frozen, trying to break the record. Alas, it was his neck he broke, not the record . . . and he died instantly.'

'How sad – and reckless. How old was he?'

'Quite young, I should think. My grandfather inherited – and then had to flee after the revolution.' He sounded utterly disinterested. 'But *I'm* like that. With me, it's paintings mostly, the thrill of the chase in tracking them down, matching them up with the right buyer – I'm really quite insane about it. But then, I am over everything – everything I really want . . .'

Laura came back with two small bits of christening cake and handed him one.

'No more plates – here you are. Fingers or nothing. Now why did I hear you telling Pa you were insane, Nico? Not that I don't sometimes agree . . .' She sat on the arm of her father's chair, swinging a silky leg, cramming the rich cake into her mouth; the feather boa still wound round her neck.

111

'Not *a* lunatic, Laura my angel. Just lunatic generally. Take my new passion – flying. I'm learning, I've just started . . .'

'Oh yes?' John Holford enquired politely.

Nico brushed the crumbs away from his mouth and stood up abruptly – his elbow on the mantelpiece, one hand thrust in his pocket – looking down at them; his eyes, which were slightly slanted, mesmerising. His normal high colour accentuated his prominent cheek-bones. A remarkable-looking man by any standards, John Holford thought uneasily. He must be in his early forties, he decided, looking rather younger.

'I'm ecstatic about it – flying – aren't I, Laura? I think I must get a plane. Definitely. It combines it all – speed, height, skill, nerve . . . all the petty restrictions somewhere far, far below . . .'

'Not quite all, I hope,' John Holford remarked drily. 'There must surely be rules of the sky – rather like driving a car I imagine.'

Nico ignored this – if indeed he heard it at all.

'I'm going to fly Laura to the moon. We might even find a star to sit on, mightn't we, my darling?' Devouring her with his strange eyes.

'Not before you have obtained a licence and a certain amount of experience, I trust,' John Holford said steadily.

Nico dragged his gaze away from Laura and gave him a dazzling smile.

'But naturally not . . .'

'Nico always talks like that, Pa – don't pay any attention. He's a bit of a madman . . .'

But John Holford continued, 'And remember Icarus . . .'

'Pa, you're so learned – who on earth was he?' Smiling, Laura put her arm affectionately round her father's shoulders. But he had spoken directly to Nico who threw back his head and roared with laughter.

'That's a good one. Back to my school-days. I must remember that. Greek mythology. Icarus, Laura, flew from Crete on waxen wings and passed too close to the sun, which melted them . . . And that did for him. Down he plunged into the icy wine-dark sea. Exit Icarus. But not me, Dr Holford, I can assure you of that . . .' Still the eyes glittered – with merriment now.

Laura shivered and said, 'What an awful thought . . . falling and falling like that, knowing you were going down, spinning out of control, and then the sea . . .'

'Stop it, Laura. You're being silly,' Nico said, suddenly cold and sharp. There was a silence. Then John Holford got up and said he thought it was time he saw what everyone was doing with themselves. When he had ambled off, Nico said, his voice like a whiplash, 'Don't talk like that. Ever. And this Katie-Kate nonsense whenever you mention your sister. It's ridiculous. You're grown-ups now, not little girls.'

Laura went on swinging her leg for a few minutes. Then she said coolly, 'Perhaps. I'll compromise. That's what life's about, isn't it? Katie only, then. Will you be all right on your own for a bit? I want to go and find her and see the baby . . .'

In the hall, she bumped into her mother.

Felicity Holford looked flustered. 'I was just coming to find you, Laura. Grandfather is leaving, his taxi is by the gate. The Bergers have already left for London . . . Come and say good-bye, would you? He's been complaining he's hardly seen you today.'

'Of course I will.'

While they were walking down to where the General stood, leaning on his stick – Kate, Robin and John Holford surrounding him – Felicity said crossly, 'I think your hair looks terrible like that, Laura, all wild and over-curled. They're not curls, they're tangles. It needs a good brush.'

Laura laughed. 'My hairdresser would kill you. It cost a fortune.'

'Pointless waste,' Felicity snapped. 'And that ridiculous, mangy, feathery thing you've got round your neck . . .'

Laura laughed again; she could hardly stop that day. Even Nico's sudden spitefulness didn't faze her. 'Poor Mother, what a trial I am to you . . .'

After they had helped the General into the taxi and waved him off, John Holford said to Robin, 'I thought young Tony Martin was supposed to be coming? Your friend – the doctor. I

113

took rather a liking to him the last time we met. And I like to think he looks after Kate and Lucy . . .'

'He was meant to be here – you're right. But he did say he wasn't sure when he would be able to get away. He might still turn up . . .' Then he excused himself and walked over to where James, Rupert and his father – all now in their shirt-sleeves – were talking earnestly. Definitely business by the long looks on their faces, Robin thought as he joined them.

The partners' wives, plus Doris and Lisa, were prowling round the garden, swapping suggestions as to what should be done to it – and where. Rose bushes, some flowering shrubs, nothing that needed too much care. It had been such a happy family gathering; it was the first warm weather of the spring. Even Doris Faraday was enjoying herself; laying down the law quite forcibly to the much younger women who were too well mannered to contradict. Seeing they were all chatting happily, Felicity Holford decided to go back to the kitchen to see about tea. Mrs Bundy, good friend that she had become, was still there – putting out cups and saucers now, the kettle boiling away. Laura saw Kate going upstairs and followed her. Nico, she noticed, was still in the sitting-room, now absorbed in some book he had taken off the shelves. Perhaps Pa would join him. They seemed to get on in a funny sort of way.

'Can I have a peep at Lucy?' she called up to Kate.

'Of course. I expect she's awake. We'll bring her down. And come and look at the new curtains in our bedroom – matching the wallpaper. I don't think you've seen them, have you?' But after they had been inspected and admired, it was impossible for them not to mention Nico. They did – simultaneously.

Dropping the curtain, her back to the window, Laura began, 'Nico, I don't expect you approve . . .' – while Kate had already begun, 'He's amazing-looking, Nico, I quite see . . .'

Then they both laughed and clung together, eyes very bright, all disharmony swept away, as close and as knowing of each other as they had ever been.

'Laura – it's just that I'm afraid for you . . .'

'Don't be. It's what I want. *He* is.'

'But his wife – he *hasn't* left her, has he?'

114

'Arabella? No – and never will do. Or not for a long time yet . . .' They drew apart. Laura folded her arms and Kate sat on the edge of the bed.

'But what about you, Laura?' she asked quietly. 'He won't make you happy . . .'

'I think he will, Katie. He does. A lot of the time. He's terrifically exciting. We have a marvellous time together.'

Katie?

'So you . . . share him? With Arabella and the children? You don't mind that?'

It was all quite incomprehensible to her. She could hear Lucy starting to make noises in her cot in the next room. How *could* Laura? How was it possible . . .? No real home. No child. Didn't she care?

'I seem not to. He goes there quite a lot – to the country. Arabella hardly ever comes to town. It's not her style – I told you, she's an earth mother. He's fond of the children, rather erratically. But then, that's Nico. He's dreadfully temperamental.' She shrugged. 'It's the way he is . . .'

'It's a sort of deal then,' Kate said slowly.

'Yes it is. Exactly. But then all relationships are – in their individual way . . . aren't they?'

'Are they? Perhaps . . . I hadn't thought of it like that . . .'

Robin and me . . .?

'No, I don't expect you had,' Laura said briskly. 'But in our case, with Nico and me, it has to be. We see each other during the week whenever we want. Except for some times in the school holidays. We travel together. And there's no one else. Only Arabella. Wife and mistress.' The corner of her mouth turned up. 'I suppose you could say that we're all true to each other – in our fashion,' she said ruefully.

'There is that,' Kate agreed.

'Oh – and one other thing . . .'

'What's that?'

'Financial independence. Mine. I'm not a drain on Nico in that way – and never will be. That's *my* pride. The flat I bought last year and did up, in the wrong part of Notting Hill, has sold. And well. I meant to tell you last night when I rang but I was a bit nervous about Nico coming today, to be honest. Anyhow, I'm paying back Mother and Pa what they lent, and I'll still have enough to give me a small income. The flat was ours, yours and mine, and Pa insisted on dividing its capital when you got married. So you had a bit of your own – and I had somewhere to live . . .'

'What about those American decorating lines, the wallpapers and fabrics, you wanted to bring over?'

'I'm coming to them. Now that I've turned that flat around, I'm going to concentrate on them. I've got masses of contacts. I know I'll make a go of it. I might even hire an assistant part-time to do the legwork once I've got it started up. I don't want to be tied down to a constant job. I want to be free to travel. With Nico.'

'Presumably he pays for all that, the travelling?'

'*That* – certainly. And I'm an asset. Believe me . . . he's in the big time with his painting is Nico.' Laughing again, twirling round in her very high-heeled shoes. 'Wining and dining the clients, the museum curators. Dressing up for the big evening sales. Being entertained. Wife? Girlfriend? No questions asked, nobody cares. Good upper-class English lass. The right accent. Not bad-looking. Sexy figure. Goes down a treat in Tulsa and Tokyo, Katie. Even in the highest reaches of New York society. So-called.'

Katie?

'I'll bet it does.' Kate was laughing now despite herself. 'You always were the fearless extrovert. But how are you going to explain all this to Mother and Pa? Mother's looking extremely anxious, by the way . . .'

'She certainly is. I *had* noticed. Nico and Pa seemed all right together. They're both extremely bright. I think Pa might understand – have an inkling of what it's all about . . .'

Whatever that may be, thought Kate.

'Are you off again somewhere soon?' she asked.

'Yes, as it happens, we are. Europe this time – Paris and Geneva and Milan. And back by Friday when Nico has his next flying lesson. He's potty about it – he'll have his licence soon.'

'I hope he's careful . . .'

'Being careful is not one of Nico's characteristics, Katie . . . Thank God . . .'

Katie again.

She turned to the mirror and began winding the feather boa round and round her neck, tying it down the front of her suit in a loose knot.

'Where on earth did you get that feathery muffler thing?' Kate asked, slightly irritated. She had noticed it on and off all day. Who could fail to? 'You seem absolutely devoted to it. I can't think why. Your suit is divine – and it ruins the look of it.'

'Yes? Oh, I'm mad about it. You'll never guess where it came from. Try . . .' She was into Kate's cosmetics by then, rubbing on some blusher with her fingers, investigating a tube of mascara . . .

'A trunk in somebody's attic I should think.'

'Right,' Laura shouted triumphantly, leaning towards the mirror, flicking on mascara. 'Or nearly right. In a charity shop. War on Want or something.'

'It wasn't very hard to guess,' Kate replied sarcastically, getting up and going towards the door. Lucy had started to cry in earnest. 'I must go and get her – we'll bring her down and let her be sociable for a bit.'

'Coming,' said Laura.

Chapter 12

Carrying Lucy carefully down the steep stairs, Laura a step or two behind, Kate saw Tony Martin standing at the door with Robin.

'*Tony* . . . you've got here at last. I'm *so* pleased . . . we really missed you.'

He was the only unmarried partner in the medical practice and frequently found himself standing in for some family event or other. Although he and Robin had been friends for years, since his marriage to Kate they had become much closer, the three of them. Tony often dropped in for supper with them in the kitchen in London. And Robin had had several off-the-record chats with him about Kate's condition. He respected Tony's judgement both as a man and a doctor.

'Kate's right. We did. But somehow I thought you'd manage to get here in the end . . .' Robin was looking flushed and jovial after a couple of days in the country, away from his desk and all the nagging concern over Condicote. He put his hand on Tony's shoulder. 'Come along in. There's plenty of champagne left.'

'I'm terribly sorry . . . I had to cover for one of the partners at the last moment,' he explained to Kate. 'Hi there, Lucy . . . I hear you behaved yourself reasonably well at your first public airing.'

'She was a very good girl. Tony – you know my sister, Laura, don't you?' But Laura, waving, was already slipping past them into the sitting-room.

'Of course. Only I have to look hard at both of you to realise you're identical . . .'

'Everyone does. Nowadays, most people think we're sisters,

118

not twins. Wouldn't you like a cup of tea and some christening cake? You and Robin can get to the drink later.'

'That sounds wonderful . . .' – automatically giving her leg a quick look as he and Robin followed her into the kitchen. Mrs Bundy had gone at last, but a substantial tea was now spread on the kitchen table.

'What a marvellous sight,' Tony exclaimed. 'An honest-to-goodness old-fashioned tea. You don't see that much now, do you?'

'Our Mrs Bundy believes in fortifying food. Robin – take Lucy out to one of the Grans, would you? They've been longing for her to wake up. And keep the shawl round her . . .' – handing her over, gurgling, to her father. 'I'll get Tony some tea. And do tell everyone he's here . . . and don't forget Lisa,' she called after him.

'Lisa? Who's Lisa?' Tony enquired.

'I'll tell you in a minute.' She brought over the teapot while Tony sat at the kitchen table. He had a thin, dark face, and he often looked tense and drawn for a youngish man. He took his work with extreme seriousness. But now, away from London, with friends, and without onerous responsibility for a few hours, he relaxed.

'All right if I start, is it? I had some nasty cases thrown at me last night and this morning. I can't honestly remember when I last had a square meal.'

'Of course.' Kate poured the tea. 'Mrs B. is convinced we're on the brink of starvation. If the whole thing isn't demolished, she'll be mortally offended.'

'I certainly wouldn't want to do that,' Tony said, reaching for a couple of scones.

'Whoever is still here will have to help themselves. Lisa too.' Kate handed him a cup. 'Sugar? Now Lisa, Tony, is one of my oldest and dearest friends. I've been wanting to get you two together for years, but the timing never worked out. She's very athletic and very bright. She always got me tactfully out of *any* kind of sport at school. She's now a lawyer with one of the big City firms. Not married. Robin says she's bound to have a successful career. According to him, young, attractive women solicitors are all the rage just now.'

Tony laughed. 'Now Kate – you wouldn't be matchmaking by any chance, would you?' Kate sat down opposite him. She didn't look as thin today as she really was. Frankly, although he had not admitted this even to Robin, Tony had been amazed at how easily she had sailed through pregnancy and childbirth and now looked after Lucy. And he fancied her father had felt the same anxiety. Mercifully – they were both wrong.

'Matchmaking?' Kate asked, her eyebrows raised quizzically. 'After all these weekends when you've been left coping with the practice because of one of your partners' wife or child? And knowing Lisa as I do? I should certainly say I am . . . And why on earth not?'

In twos and threes, everyone, including Lisa, drifted into the kitchen. Lucy was brought in by Doris Faraday and put in her play-pen in the corner, the subject of considerable attention. Leaving her mother to cope, Kate went off to find Laura and Nico. She half suspected that they might already have left, without even saying good-bye. Mother, she knew, was furious. Or perhaps just worried about Laura, turning up with this strange and undoubtedly married man. At an intimate family gathering, their first at Knyght's Wood. With no explanation – except to her, briefly, when they were alone upstairs. She knew that Felicity found Laura's determined, cold secrecy about her private life deeply hurtful. She was a warm, giving mother; to be excluded from the emotional life of one of her children was unbearable to her. Having a child of her own, even though Lucy was so young, had given Kate a sympathetic insight into their mother's endearing, although often irritating, personality.

Thinking that they were still outside, Kate was about to step into the garden when she heard soft music coming from behind the closed dining-room door. The room was empty – one of their projects for the immediate future. Everyone else was now crowded into the kitchen. So it must be Laura and Nico. Hesitating, she stood for a moment outside the door. She could hear a tango playing, very softly, 'Dum de dum, de dum-dum-dum . . .' They must have taken a portable radio in there.

120

She turned the handle very quietly and opened the door a few inches. The music met her, louder. 'De dum . . . de dum, de dum, de dum . . . dum, dum . . .' They were standing cheek to cheek, close as possible, dancing; arms, hands clasped, rigidly extended in a parody of an old-style tango. In perfect time, they took a long step forward, Laura's short skirt clinging to her thigh; dark, gleaming leg and polished shoe. The boa floating behind her back . . . 'De dum, de dum, de dum . . .' They executed a lightning swivel turn. Nico's hair had fallen forward onto his forehead.

They hadn't seen her. Over Laura's shoulder she glimpsed Nico's face – totally absorbed, eyes staring hypnotically. As she closed the door soundlessly, she saw an open bottle of champagne and two glasses on the floor.

There was no way she could intrude; they were utterly lost in some world of their own. So she sighed and went back to the kitchen where she was pleased to see Tony and Lisa talking away at the table. She went straight to Robin's side and was absurdly reassured when he immediately put his arm round her and drew her into the conversation he was having with Jill.

'Darling Felicity, you're being unusually silent.' John Holford reached for his wife's hand as they drove home sometime later. 'What is it?' As if he didn't know . . . 'It was a delightful christening, our granddaughter is enchanting . . . a very happy family day. Kate – with lots of help from you and Mrs Bundy – managed nicely. Robin is a thoroughly good chap – and he can't help having dear old Doris for a mother . . .' But even that didn't raise a smile. Felicity went on looking out of the window, her hand listless beneath his; she who was always so quick and responsive. John Holford sighed. 'All right. Out with it. Laura . . .'

'But it's *awful*, Johnnie,' she erupted, turning to him, her cheeks flaming. 'That man, Nico. I know he's married . . . Kate more-or-less admitted that he's *not* separated from his wife when I asked her straight out just now. She sort of hedged – you know how protective of each other they've always been those two . . . And Laura barely talked to me – *really* talked –

121

all day. She just clung to that – *person* . . . and giggled. Even my father remarked on it. Rude and exclusive the pair of them. I was absolutely fuming.' He suspected she was on the verge of tears. 'But I can't help it, Johnnie, I can't. She's so beautiful and talented . . . to throw herself away on a man like that . . . he's years older than she is and he looked so – *odd*. No manners at all that I could see,' she went on frostily. 'I saw them eating in the kitchen like a couple of peasants. Pouring wine down their gullets, at least he was. Mrs Bundy was horrified.'

'Mrs Bundy has narrow views, my love.'

'Mrs Bundy is a very sound woman,' Felicity snapped. 'And he's got young children too. Kate did admit that when I tackled her just before we left. Although she swore she didn't know any details. Which she probably does. And I'm pretty sure, by the way, that he's the man who rang up last summer and thought I was her, the night before Kate and Robin settled on the house.'

'Very likely.'

'Well what did *you* make of him, Johnnie? You're the only person he deigned to talk to. When Laura was upstairs with Kate and the baby I saw him lying with his feet on the sofa reading a book – as though he owned the place.'

'He does tend to give that impression.' He drove in silence for a bit.

John Holford thought carefully. This was Felicity at her most intense. Like Kate, he knew that Laura's emotional defection from the family since she had taken up with Kirilov had shaken Felicity badly. She interpreted her daughter's coolness as a rebuff. She was a brave woman – not a general's daughter for nothing. She could face most things, but not coldness from someone she loved.

'Kirilov? Frankly, I did find him interesting,' he said cautiously. 'I couldn't help but be somewhat fascinated by the gallery. You know that. He's got a good mind, I should say. I know he's got a brilliant reputation as a dealer who is honest – and who knows his business through and through. You don't get that for nothing, even by inheritance. So much for his work. I also thought he was amusing, bright and articulate.

But he showed, I must be honest, other aspects of his personality which slightly disturbed me . . .'

'Such as?'

'I thought he seemed more than a touch manic. And I mean that clinically. Decidedly egocentric – quite as though the world revolved around him. And I should be surprised if there wasn't a darker, depressive side to all that euphoria. The way he spoke about his new passion for flying tipped me off.'

Felicity said nothing but turned and looked out through the window at the new green hedgerows rushing past. After a while, she said quietly, 'Do you think it's this sort of wildness – I sensed it too – that Laura finds so attractive about him?'

'Partly . . . yes, I suppose I do. Larger-than-life, up-and-down personalities can exert a deadly fascination.'

As they turned into the driveway of the house, Felicity said decisively, 'I'm going to phone Laura and ask her to meet me for lunch one day next week. I'll try and get her later tonight. I'm her mother. At least I can do *that.*'

'Darling Felicity – I think it's an excellent idea. For both of you.'

But he also didn't think she would learn much more about Laura's association with Nico Kirilov.

When everyone had gone and Lucy was bathed and fed and tucked in her cot, Robin and Kate slipped out of the back door to the path which led up into the ancient beech copse above the house – the true Knyght's Wood. The spring evening had turned chilly; after changing into comfortable old clothes, they had both put on warm jackets. Twigs crackled beneath their feet as they climbed. Kate clung to Robin's arm; although he did not know it, when she came walking in the woods alone, she invariably brought a stick.

'It was a lovely day, Robin, but I'm glad it's over.'

'It all went well. Everyone enjoyed it – and Lucy was good as gold. Mrs B. was a marvel. Not too tired?'

Kate shook her head. 'I hardly ever am when I'm enjoying myself – and I seem to have a lot more energy these days, despite looking after Lucy . . .'

The delicate new leaves spread a green canopy above them,

123

while last year's made a russet carpet on the ground. Night was creeping on, softening the red-streaked sky and making the woods mysterious. Somewhere above them, an animal rustled and rooted in the undergrowth among gnarled and mossy roots.

They stopped and looked down. The solid old stone cottage looked safe and cosy with its bright lights gleaming. Faint rising mist mingled with the smoke from the fire Robin had lit in the sitting-room. Beyond, the straggling houses in the main road of Laverton; the low, square church tower. And just visible through the twilight, the wooded valley where the river ran below. Robin put both his arms around her.

'Knyght's Wood – all ours,' he gloated. 'And all because you came here for a walk last summer.'

Kate laughed. 'It was raining and blowing a gale. And I brought Raffles. And you were all furious with me because I was about to have Lucy . . .'

'We were. Only because we love you. And anyhow, you were right – whatever my misgivings. We've begun to make it into a home. It really felt like one today.'

'And it looked so neglected before, poor place. So desperately unloved. Your father was marvellous the way he kept his word. Despite everything he's done financially for Condicote. And I don't think they really approve of Knyght's Wood – your mother certainly doesn't.'

'Oh, I think they've come round to it. They see it suits us – and our life.' Meaning – as they both knew – that they wouldn't be travelling much from now on; not even going on holidays abroad; that the country life suited Kate. And that Robin, for all his youthful fantasies of foreign travel, was content that it should be so.

'Robin,' – she twisted her arms around his neck. 'Robin – thank you, thank you so much . . .'

After they had cleared up in the kitchen, they took mugs of coffee and sat on the fluffy white rug in front of the fire. There were no lamps on in the room, just the warm firelight glow. Robin had looked in on Lucy who was sleeping peacefully.

'Mother is terribly upset about Laura – being with Nico

Kirilov,' Kate said, leaning against Robin's solid shoulder. 'She forced me to admit that he's married – neither of us mentioned the bogus separation. And that he has children. But I managed not to tell her how many . . .' She sighed. 'I don't know what to think. What should we?'

'Nothing much. It's Laura's business, darling. Although I can't honestly say that I took to him.'

'Neither did I. He's so full of himself. You can tell. And Laura could have been a bit friendlier all round . . . and more helpful.'

'Your mother thinks she's throwing herself away on him. I'm sure of that.'

'So do I,' Kate said quickly. 'That's exactly what I think. He'll never leave Arabella, his wife – Laura told me. She accepts it. And I don't see how she can be happy living a life like that.'

'You can't judge, darling. It's *her* life – not yours. But it doesn't seem very satisfactory from any point of view. I've no doubt she realizes that from time to time – or will do – rather painfully.'

They stared silently into the fire.

And why 'Katie' all of a sudden, Kate was thinking. Were they too old for 'Katie-Kate' which Laura had always called her privately within the family? 'Kate' she had been on more formal occasions; but never, never 'Katie'. Why now? Today? Was it – possibly – something to do with Nico Kirilov?

Robin leant back comfortably on his elbow, stretching his legs out to the fire. 'Tony seemed to be getting on very well with Lisa,' he said, breaking in on her thoughts. 'He took her phone number and said he'd get in touch in London – suggested the four of us went out one evening. So your plotting might have worked after all,' he teased gently. He knew she had long had her eye on Tony for Lisa. She thought Lisa's bounce and optimism would balance Tony's too serious outlook.

'I'm so glad, how marvellous,' Kate said, genuinely excited. 'I told Tony I was matchmaking . . . and he laughed. But it's time he settled down. When he's on his own for too long I'm sure he broods.' In the rush of goodbyes, everyone leaving at the same time, she had forgotten all about them, just waved them off with the rest. 'I've always thought they would get on, those two . . . and everyone has to meet someone *somewhere* . . .'

But the moment she said it, she clapped her hand over her mouth. She knew at once what she'd let herself in for. Robin threw back his head and started to laugh and Kate blushed deeply. She had left herself wide open on that one.

'They certainly do,' Robin agreed, still shaking with laughter. 'Even if it's two tables away at the Deux Magots. On the Boulevard St Germain. In Paris.'

'*Beast.*' Kate began to laugh with him. 'You always bring that up. And it wasn't a pick-up – it was just romantic. And it was spring . . . We've always agreed we would have met somewhere. Sometime. Through somebody.'

'Our way was better.' He reached up and kissed her hot cheek.

'*Yes* . . .' Her hand on his shoulder; touching his hair. Still smiling, looking down at him. '*Oh yes* . . . I had a private chat with Ina this morning. She always says she hadn't an inkling I was making it up when I said I had bumped into someone I knew slightly at home – she thought I was much too shy and well mannered to let myself be accosted by a complete stranger . . .'

'And then march him smartly off on to a bateau mouche . . .'

'And then let him kiss her under a tree, lying on the grass in the Bois de Boulogne . . .'

'*The shadow of your smile* . . .' Kate hummed. His hand found hers.

'And go back with him – *quelle horreur* – to his hotel bedroom . . . I love you. Come here.' He pulled her down beside him. Her left leg, so thin it looked as though any weight would snap it, stuck out at an awkward angle. The exquisite tenderness he felt for her, always inextricably bound up with sexual desire, surged powerfully.

Now she lay quiet on the soft rug; the fire leapt. Robin above her – arms, shoulders, neck, so massive in contrast to her fine-boned delicacy. Slim hips, shoulder blades, thin,

126

attenuated arms . . . Kissing her temple, her mouth; pushing back the silky hair; electrically aware of her blow-away slenderness beneath him. Clothes pulled off and scattered. Kate's back a long white curve; her dark hair parting at the nape. This, he always had to kiss.

'Here, Kate, here . . . I want to make love to you here.'

She touched him everywhere; silver-fingered, open-mouthed, rhythmically moving. Whispering her private words . . .

'Oh *yes* . . .'

A long while after, arms around each other, they trailed upstairs. One by one, all the lights in the cottage went out. The orange embers of the fire faded. Towards dawn, a light wind sprang up, ruffling the sweet new leaves in the Knyght's Wood above – where the only other sound was a vixen shrieking for her young.

PART 3

Camelot

Chapter 13

After dropping nine-year-old Lucy off at her dancing class on a cold afternoon late in November, Kate decided to walk home, not wait for the bus as she usually did. A pallid sun was trying to break through the haze. It wasn't far – and the exercise would do her good. A friend whose child was in the same class was picking both children up by car. And besides, there were one or two things she needed in the local shops which she could get on her way. Including candles. And she needed these particularly because she and Robin were having a dinner party later in the week for new American clients who were to be introduced to Rupert and Jill. They would be working largely with Rupert whom they had not yet met. It was important for Condicote, which was just beginning to get on its feet, that it went well; this was a valuable connection that needed to be well and truly cemented through pleasant social channels.

And Kate had turned out to be a surprisingly skilled hostess – organised, quite unfussed, knowing how to strike just the right note of agreeable informality. People liked her, too. Although she could never be described as outgoing, she had natural warmth. Her voice was soft and pleasing. She also had the knack of making whoever she was speaking to seem the only person in the world who mattered to her at that moment.

Robin had come to rely quite heavily on her social back-up in his business life. He only wished that she would make the effort to travel with him more. But although her health had remained fairly good over the years, she rarely did. And there was Lucy to be considered. Apart from working trips, Robin skied regularly with Rupert and Jill each winter and occasionally dashed off on brief, strenuous walking tours with other friends, mostly from his university days. Kate never minded – in fact, she encouraged him – because her heart was given to Knyght's Wood. She hardly counted the small London house as 'home'. They spent every possible weekend there – and she and Lucy a good part of the summer too. Over this, Kate was firm. The house and the garden, both improving little by little every season, were her passion.

She had already planned the food for Friday night with Libby, a young trained cook who occasionally came in to help when they had guests, as she would this week. Kate had also decided on the plants and flowers which would give the house the countrified air which she loved. She would get the candles today, leaving one thing less to think about later.

It was while she was poring over boxes of them, in carefully graded colours, that Kate first began to feel faint. She put out her hand and steadied herself; closed her eyes for a minute. The world stilled and righted. Slowly and deliberately, she took her purse out of her shoulder-bag, bought the candles and watched while they were being wrapped. Outside again in the cold, clear air, she felt perfectly all right. So she crossed the street to the greengrocers where she was an almost daily customer.

'Some parsley please, Kev,' she said to one of the two boys, sons of the owner, who she had known since they were youngsters and came to help out after school – and who now ran the place while their father did the buying. 'Lovely day, isn't it?'

'Better make the most of it,' Kev said cheerfully. 'Snow or sleet tomorrow they say. Winter's come early . . . This enough then?'

Kate looked. She thought of the party on Friday night. 'A bit more, I think. Another handful. Thanks.'

Glad that there wasn't a queue, as there usually was, she wondered what else she ought to get while the going was good. She spied some juicy pink Florida grapefruits and put out her hand to pick one up . . .

The next thing she knew she was sitting on a rickety chair in the back of the shop, a firm hand pressing her head down on her knees, and the reassuring Cockney voice of Kev's father saying, 'There, luv, you just stay like that a bit. Come over all queer you did. You'll be right as rain in a tick. One of the boys'll walk you 'ome . . .'

Through laced fingers Kate could see cabbage leaves trodden into the grubby floor. A rock station on the radio shouted advertising jingles. Cautiously, she raised her head and sat up straight.

'I'm terribly sorry . . . I don't know what . . .'

'Nah . . . listen, my missus done jus' the same in 'er time. Feelin' more like yerself are yer?'

'I think so, Fred. Yes – yes I am.' Her bag, she saw, was on the makeshift desk by the telephone; beside it, the carrier with the candles in it. It looked a bit battered. They must be smashed to smithereens, must have keeled over with her. Or whatever it was she had done. 'I'm terribly sorry . . .' she began again weakly.

'Don't you worry about nothin'.' Fred walked round and gave her a keen look. He scratched his head. 'You's a bit pale-like, Mrs Faraday. Don't want us to give your 'ubby a call do you? No trouble it ain't, no trouble at all.'

Kate shook her head quickly. 'No, honestly, Fred. Thanks all the same. I'll be quite all right. And I must get home – a friend is dropping Lucy back and there's no one there.' She stood gingerly and retrieved her bag and the candles. Fred looked pointedly at her left foot.

'Can't 'ave you goin' on yer own. 'Ere, Kev . . .' he called out to the front of the shop. 'When you finished servin', come on back 'ere and take Mrs Faraday 'ome, there's a good lad.'

Kev picked the keys out of her bag, opened the front door, and deposited her – and her parsley – in the kitchen with all the lights blazing. Then he went back off to the shop, whistling cheerfully.

As soon as she had taken off her coat she made herself a cup of tea and sat with it at the kitchen table. She glanced at the clock. Lucy would be home in twenty minutes. She sat very still listening to the clock – tick, tick, ticking away . . . There was no doubt about it, even here, in her own kitchen with all

133

her familiar things round her, she was still feeling most peculiar. She took a sip of hot tea . . . and immediately rushed to the downstairs cloakroom where she was quickly and painlessly sick. Lifting her head from the washbasin, she looked at herself in the mirror – lank hair, dull eyes, cheeks suddenly and hectically flushed. Of course. She knew. Without any doubt at all. After seven frustrating years of trying and almost losing hope – although none of the doctors could find any reason . . . a baby.

And that was the beginning of Guy.

'What's wrong Mummy? You look – *funny* . . .' Dawdling over her tea, Lucy, head to one side, considered her mother. At nine, those dark eyes missed nothing. She was slight and pretty, very like her mother and Laura at that age. 'It's like seeing oneself all over again, isn't it?' Laura invariably said at some point when she came to see them; almost wistfully, Kate sometimes thought. Kate wasn't so sure. Had either of them, ever, been quite so assured? Also privately, she thought Lucy was cleverer than both she and Laura put together. She had a razor-sharp memory, she never had to be told anything more than once. An early talker, she now sometimes used quite complicated words which left Kate gasping. At school, she was streets ahead of the others, already reading everything she could get her hands on and doing difficult maths. The headmistress had told both her and Robin that she needed all the mental stimulation she could get; otherwise, she predicted, she would get quickly bored with formal learning. That was always a danger with very bright children.

And here she was, confidently telling Kate that she looked – *funny*. Now of all times. The little witch . . .

'Don't be silly, Lucy,' Kate said faintly. 'Eat up and get ready for your bath. And then you can watch your TV programme.'

'Well, *I* think you look funny,' Lucy said, pouring herself more juice. 'You don't look the same as you did when you left me at dancing class. Or this morning at breakfast.'

Uncanny child. Kate's relationship with her daughter was a slightly uneasy one. She wondered sometimes why she was so watchful; never quite felt she knew what was going on inside that little head of hers. She didn't, if she was honest, always feel comfortable with her. She didn't then.

'I did feel a bit peculiar this afternoon,' Kate said, smiling cheerily – or so she hoped – at the dark eyes regarding her over the rim of a glass. 'But I'm absolutely fine now. Have you finished? Is that all you want?'

'I knew I was right,' Lucy said, putting down her glass, wiping her mouth with the back of her hand and slipping off her chair.

Kate was in the kitchen pretending to do something about supper and Lucy was in the sitting-room, one eye on the television, the other on her book, when they heard Robin's signature ring on the doorbell. Lucy uncurled herself with lightning speed and ran into the hall to open the door. A dark angel in a long pink dressing-gown and slippers, hair pulled back in a pink band, confronted Robin. She had the cherubic look and sweet smell of a well-brought-up, recently bathed child.

'Hi Lucy . . .' He dropped his briefcase and swept her up in a hug, pleased to see that bathtime was evidently over so that he and Kate could immediately settle down with a drink, which he needed. New clients were all very well but they expected a lot of attention on top of everything else. At least, these ones did.

In the kitchen, stirring home-made soup which she had fished out of the freezer, Kate heard Lucy say in her high, clear voice, already so like Laura's and her mother's, 'Mummy feels peculiar, Daddy. And she looks funny. Ask her. Go on.'

He went straight into the kitchen, put his arms around Kate and kissed her neck. 'All right, darling, are you?'

Kate turned – and he saw that she was not. The ethereal beauty, so dependent on her state of health and her emotions, had vanished. She smiled at him wanly.

'Medium.'

'Lucy said . . .'

'I had a bit of a turn at Jones's. They were terribly sweet and kind. Kev saw me home . . .' She had hoped not to tell him.

'When was this?'

'This afternoon. While Lucy was having her dancing lesson.'

'I wish someone had told me.' He looked grave. Kate noticed that he hadn't yet taken off his overcoat.

'There was no need.' Her skin was pale and so were her lips. 'Honestly . . .' He took both her hands, which were icy-cold, in his – and began to chafe them.

'Darling, perhaps we ought to get you into bed, phone Tony . . .'

She shook her head. Then, 'This soup smells awful. I hope it's all right.' If possible, she had gone a shade paler. 'If I go on smelling it I'll be sick. Again.'

'*Again?*'

'Yes. I made myself a cup of tea after Kev left and then I had to make a dash . . .'

'Kate – you don't think . . .' He was holding her hands right under his chin now, his blue eyes – tired at the end of the day, sunk in lines – looking straight into hers.

As the months and years went by with no sign of another child, they had begun to accept that they were lucky at least to have Lucy.

'Yes, Robin,' Kate said. 'Yes – I do.' And she burst into tears, her shoulders shaking convulsively against his chest. Holding her tightly, looking over her head, Robin saw Lucy standing in the kitchen doorway, watching, one finger in her mouth. He had no doubt at all that she had heard, and taken in, every word. 'B-E-D,' he mouthed at her firmly. 'Go on . . . I'll come and read a story . . . OK?'

Lucy turned and fled upstairs as Kate sobbed on uncontrollably – and Robin, starting to stifle in his coat in the warm kitchen, felt more than ever in need of a good scotch.

'It's only a few days, darling. You can't possibly be sure.'

'I am,' Kate said dully.

They were in the sitting-room, Robin on his second large whisky, trying to keep his mind off a particularly worrying problem in the office. He had warmed the soup himself, eaten it in the kitchen standing up – and pronounced it very good

136

indeed. Once she had calmed down, Kate had managed a piece of toast and some soda water. Lucy had long since been read to and tucked into bed – by Robin, Kate calling 'goodnight' up the stairs. She really couldn't face Lucy again that day.

'In that case, you must go and see Tony. Tomorrow. I really insist – particularly as you're feeling so rotten . . .' With Kate, Robin thought wearily, no physical chance could be taken. As he well knew, any cold could end in bronchitis, the least strain result in the kind of exhaustion that required days in bed, although her health had been good for the past couple of years. He couldn't remember when he had last seen her looking so unwell. More than thin – emaciated. Perhaps it was something else altogether, perhaps she was coming down with flu or a stomach virus – despite her certainty.

'All right. I will.' Kate made an effort and smiled over at him. 'Sorry to be such a bore and a nuisance . . .'

'Darling – don't be silly. But you've got to be careful . . .' He frowned and put down his glass. More than ten years of sweating it out with Condicote had taken their toll. He was into his forties now, watched his weight and grabbed whatever exercise he could – tennis, squash, walking, disciplined running. His physique was as good as it had ever been. But there was a lot of grey in his hair and his face was lined, particularly around the eyes. He often looked drained – as he did that night. There wasn't much sign of the dynamic, good-humoured enthusiasm which was essentially Robin. Kate saw this – and was pained.

'What I mean is – the dinner-party. On Friday. I could easily put them off, or we could take them out. If you're not feeling up to it . . .'

Kate got up and knelt beside his chair. For the first time that evening she sounded like herself.

'Don't you dare. We'll have them here. I'll be fine by then. And I've got Libby coming.' She put his hand to her cheek. 'Did you find out if both the American chaps are bringing their wives?'

'Only one of them is. That's definite. Then there's us – and Rupert and Jill . . .' The third partner, James, was away with his wife in Japan – also scouting for business.

'Seven altogether. We'll be a woman short. I tell you what, I'll try and get Laura. She's marvellous at chatting away. And she looks very glamorous . . .'

'All right. But we certainly don't want Nico. Not at any price,' Robin said quickly. All the family's meetings with him over the years had been uneasy. Laura now had the sense to keep them apart whenever possible.

'No indeed,' Kate agreed. 'But I think he's down in the country with Arabella, having one of his collapses . . .' Several times a year, he disappeared back to the bosom of his family for extended stays – suffering bouts of severe depression, they assumed. At least, that was John Holford's assessment of the situation. Every time this happened, Kate and her mother had long telephone conversations, telling each other hopefully that this must be the end; that surely Laura wouldn't put up with this tiresome man, and a relationship leading nowhere, any longer. But each time, back Nico bounced to the beautiful, waiting Laura – and off they would go on some fabulous yacht in the Aegean or to spend a month in New York or to a sale in Geneva. Laura radiant and insouciant; giving little away – even to Kate. Seeming as much in love with him as ever. Year after year after year . . . It was fair to say that if she hadn't broken her mother's heart, she had certainly given it a good dent.

'Christ, how does that poor woman Arabella stand it? Let alone Laura . . . For God's sake be sure he's out of town or we'll be landed with him . . .' On the rare occasions they met, Robin found it hard to be civil to Nico – who reciprocated. They had disliked each other almost on sight. And Robin shared Kate's bafflement at the way Laura chose to live.

'I am – quite sure. I spoke to Laura yesterday. She said she was alone – and I know what *that* means – and she sounded a bit down.'

'Try her for Friday then. It's a good idea. And Kate . . .'

'What?'

'If it is – what you think – a child . . .'

Life and colour came suddenly to the pale, upturned face. Her smile reached her eyes and made them shine. She looked – almost – beautiful. Certainly quite different to the woman he had come upon earlier stirring frozen soup in the kitchen. For the first time, the thrill of it caught them both.

'Wouldn't it –' Kate said passionately. 'Oh wouldn't it be *wonderful?*'

Tony squeezed Kate in for a brief, late appointment the next day. It was too early to be sure, he told her briskly, but it seemed reasonable to assume she was pregnant. He told her to be sensible, not overdo things, and make an appointment for a month hence with her gynaecologist. His briskness concealed his concern that she and Robin should not be disappointed. No one knew better than he how much they wanted another child. They were lucky last time, with Lucy; but Kate's health was always a question-mark and he was too fond of both of them to watch anything go seriously wrong.

'Love to Lisa,' Kate called back as she left. 'And a kiss for my godson . . . bye.'

And that marriage, Kate reflected with satisfaction as she drove home, really was my doing. My one and only piece of successful matchmaking. Because after meeting at Lucy's christening, Lisa and Tony had been inseparable, announced their engagement and married within months. Lisa had continued to work, taking only a few weeks off to have their two children. Emma was now three and Daniel six months.

'Steady,' Kate said aloud as she let herself into the house, 'steady . . .' But Tony had said her supposition was 'reasonable'. A quiver of joy shot through her. She would phone Robin, quickly, at the office before collecting Lucy who was playing with a friend next door.

'Who have you got coming then?' Laura enquired cautiously when Kate managed to get hold of her much later that evening. She sounded at her lowest ebb, her voice, for once, dragging; and she was probably wondering, Kate guessed, what attractive and eligible man she and Robin were wanting to introduce her to. Although after several such failures during the early part of her relationship with Nico, they had given up – 'for the duration' as Robin put it.

'I told you – Rupert and Jill and an American couple – and

the other American who's in the same business, only his wife isn't with him. So we're a woman short and besides, I'd love to see you . . . Wear one of your jazzy dresses and all the make-up. And you're such a help with people, Laura,' Kate flattered.

'I suppose I *could* come,' Laura said ungraciously. 'What time?'

'About eight. Libby's doing the cooking. It's really so that the Americans can meet Rupert in surroundings that are more relaxed than the office. And Robin says the connection is terribly important for Condicote.'

'God, what a terrific company wife you've turned into, Katie . . . little dinner in the lovely home . . . smoothing the way for the office deals . . .' It wasn't funny, it was flat and petulant.

Kate ignored this and said, 'Nico's still away, is he?'

'Yes.'

After a tiny silence Kate went on, 'I thought so. Even more reason for you not to stay on your own . . .'

But Laura was lofty and defensive. 'Actually, I'm tremendously busy. I've been working in the gallery for the past two weeks.'

Living with Nico, at least for the professional part of his life, Laura had become extremely knowledgeable about his genre of art. She even came out with information and judgements that surprised her father. She was also a shrewd business woman. She had bought and sold on at a profit at least three small West End flats. And although she always protested that she was up to her eyes in debt at the bank, Robin thought otherwise. The association she had formed with an American company producing a superb range of wallpapers was flourishing too. She had retained the sole UK rights, and discriminating decorators were using them more and more. She had a small office near Covent Garden and a part-time assistant to keep the business ticking over when she was away. This arrangement worked particularly well as she and Nico were in the States at least three or four times a year. This meant that she stayed in close touch with her American contacts, editing their new lines for what she thought would appeal in London.

'Working in the Kirilov Gallery? Doing what?' Kate asked.

'Oh – this and that.' Evasive as ever over her private life.

'The past few months have been rather slow. But we've got a show coming on early in December which is a tremendous buying time. It's a good one too, lots of fine sporting pictures. As we depend on overseas clients, the catalogue is terribly important. And I've been doing some work on that.'

'Clever you ... Nico will be back, I suppose, before the opening?'

'Probably.' Kate actually heard her taking a deep breath before she said, 'Providing Arabella has had the baby by then.'

The baby? Arabella? Was she hearing right? The impossible Nico's – presumably. Kate was so totally flabbergasted that she could hardly speak. She was also angry.

'*Arabella*? But – but ... they've already got six, haven't they? And it doesn't sound very appropriate ... Anyhow, isn't she too old?' she asked brutally.

What she meant was: How dare this bloody man take anything he chose from both wife and mistress – and get away with it? Really, it was too monstrous ... And Laura, silly idiot, apparently putting up with even this final humiliation.

'She's forty-two, I think. The youngest is eight – and she got broody. Arabella's like that. She adores children, children and food. And cooking.' She sounded quite neutral, almost indifferent. She might have been talking about any old acquaintance – not her longtime lover's wife.

'I see,' Kate said coldly – furious both for, and at, her sister. 'Well, we'll see you tomorrow then.'

When she went back to Robin who was immersed in watching a late-night news programme she simply said, 'I got hold of Laura. She's coming tomorrow night. Without Nico of course.'

'Oh – is she?' – hardly listening. 'That's good. This is terribly interesting ...' He pulled her down and they sat together on the sofa, Robin engrossed in the analysis of some new economic crisis.

She must be mad, Kate was thinking. Laura – over this, I just don't understand her at all. Her perverse love for Nico – perhaps. But not this.

For some reason, she didn't want Arabella's baby to intrude

on the close and happy evening she and Robin were spending together after her initial visit to Tony. She would tell him – perhaps – tomorrow.

Chapter 14

But she didn't. Robin bolted out of the house while Kate was still upstairs arguing with Lucy about which shoes she should wear to school. And what with last-minute bits of shopping, seeing that the house was immaculate, arranging the flowers and fetching Lucy from school, there wasn't time even to think about it. She didn't want to, either. Over Arabella and Nico's latest child, she felt shame for Laura – even with Robin.

Before he got back from the office on Friday, she started to feel sick again. The smell, and even the sight, of food made her queasy. After seeing that Libby had the cooking well under control in the kitchen, she fled upstairs. Thank heaven, she had laid the table that morning. She had to get through the evening appearing to be a charming hostess, *she had to*. Everything else was banished from her mind.

Nerves and willpower alone kept her going over a bad hour during which she changed into her good black dress, did her face, carefully brushed her hair and put on the pearls which the Faradays had given her for her last birthday. Her left arm and shoulder hurt badly. This, too, she kept from Robin.

'I'm so glad we can get them together at home tonight, darling,' he said, putting on a crisp, clean shirt. 'And everyone always enjoys having dinner here. Clever Kate.'

Sitting at her dressing-table, dreadfully pale, she watched him in the mirror as he paced about their room – fixing studs; grimacing as he tied his tie; bending over to get shoes out of his wardrobe. Exuding masculinity and confidence. Let it be a boy, she prayed. A boy who looks just like Robin . . . Then I'll put up with anything. She swallowed – and felt more like retching.

143

'I enjoy it,' she said bravely. 'You know I do. And having Libby makes all the difference. She's so good with Lucy too.'

'Feeling all right? Not sick or faint or anything?' Robin looked over at her as he tied his laces. Kate had just applied wings of terracotta blusher to her cheeks.

'Fine.' She smiled back at him. 'Absolutely fine . . . isn't that a taxi?' They both heard the engine shuddering outside the front door. 'They won't get here early, will they?' Kate asked, alarmed. 'It must be Laura then.'

It was. Just the sound of her voice, known for ever, reassured Kate. She had always depended on Laura for confidence. Robin opened the door and shouted out that they would be down in a minute.

'She's all right, she's encountered Lucy,' he said to Kate. 'They get on so well, those two, don't they?'

Lucy was sitting, ready for bed, on the bottom stair. Laura, exotically dressed in shocking pink, sat beside her. They were deep in conversation. Neither of them moved, so Kate and Robin stepped awkwardly round them into the hall.

'Laura's going to take me to the Science Museum in the Christmas holidays,' Lucy informed them. 'We're going to spend the whole day there and have lunch. That's right, isn't it, Laura?' Their voices were so alike it was laughable. Lucy looked at her aunt sideways. From the first, although none of the family approved, Laura had resolutely refused to allow Lucy to call her 'Aunt'. 'All the steps and the walking are a lot for Mum. So it's better if I go with Laura, isn't it?'

Kate, said lightly, 'Yes, I expect it is. How nice of Laura . . . Lucy, you've got crumbs round your mouth. You haven't been eating all Libby's cheese straws, have you?'

'Only one,' lied Lucy who had systematically denuded each of the small dishes Libby had set out in the sitting-room, carefully removing several straws which she thought wouldn't be missed from the bottom of each. 'It was yummy.' Hugging her knees, she stared innocently up at her mother.

'Can I help at all?' Laura asked without enthusiasm. She recrossed her legs; she was wearing black spotted tights and very high black suede pumps. 'I did look into the kitchen and

Libby said everything was fine – so Lucy and I had a good natter. Didn't we Luce?'

'Mmm ...' Lucy moved closer to Laura, the woolly dressing-gown nestling up to the shimmering silk. She hardly ever does that to me, Kate thought with a slight stab, turning away.

She said, 'I think it's all done. I'll just go and see Libby – and then Robin can make us all a good drink. You can have a lemonade with us, Lucy, if you promise to go straight upstairs when you've said hello to the guests – and no fussing . . .'

'OK,' Lucy agreed. 'And can I have more – I mean another – cheese straw. Please?'

'Just one. Then shake everyone's hand when they come – good manners, Lucy please – and then off you go.'

'But I can still read in bed for a bit, can't I?'

'Of course you can, don't be silly,' said Laura, giving her an affectionate nudge.

Sitting at the head of the pretty oval table, Robin easily dominated the room which was small and intimate even though they had extended it into the garden by building on a conservatory. He threw back his head, laughing at a remark made by one of their guests, passing bread, spearing butter. Calling across the table, somehow dispelling any awkwardness, making everyone feel at ease. Robin was good at this.

Jill and the American wife, Betsy, sat on his left and right; opposite, Kate turned politely to Bill, Betsy's husband. She had been sipping soda water while the others had their drinks and was feeling slightly less deathly. 'How long are you in London?' she was asking. 'I expect you've seen all the galleries and the theatres that we hardly ever manage . . .' He had. But she and Robin had been invited to a private view of an exhibition at the Tate Gallery – so that provided a basis for conversation. Kate's rather shy, confidential manner had a way of drawing people out. She spoke quietly, so in a crowded room people often had to bend towards her to hear what she was saying. As Bill did now. And she was looking very appealing, graceful in the tucked and draped black silk dress. Long, loose sleeves camouflaged her left side which still ached dully. Bill, a prominent Wallstreeter, who had been talking tough management terms with Robin all afternoon, started to relax. The Faradays did things nicely, he could see. Modest – but a bit of style. Good silver ... he'd been dragged to the silver vaults enough times by Betsy to know that ... And this, he was thinking as Kate smiled at him and raised her soup spoon, this is one very classy lady.

All round the table, the talk was lively. Robin poured wine, still talking away, as Libby cleared the first course. Everyone, even Kate who had managed most of her soup, was enjoying themselves. Candlelight flickered – and seating eight at the table, everyone close and yet able to talk across the centrepiece of white lilies, encouraged intimacy. Kate had painted the main part of the room a glowing ruby red which gave a warm and flattering light and showed off the few good pictures her father had helped her buy.

Laura was giving her undivided attention to the other American male present – who was called Jake. He and Bill were partners in the same Wall Street securities firm which was on the verge of signing an important contract with Condicote. The final details were still being thrashed out. Robin, always cautious, still felt it could go either way ... But Jake, clearly, was having fun that evening. He had unexpectedly revealed to Laura over a neat vodka before dinner that he was recently divorced. Intrigued, Kate had overheard this and kept throwing them hopeful glances. Laura, too, appeared animated. And Kate thought she looked extremely pretty. The dramatic make-up, which she could never wear, perfectly suited Laura's slightly theatrical air. Her hair was soft and curly, pushed back from her ears to show huge gold earrings encrusted with tiny diamonds, daringly modern in design – and given to her by Nico that summer. Their tenth anniversary – 'as it were', he had said, nonchalantly producing the leather box from his pocket. Now, she threw back her head, laughing at something Jake told her, showing off the lovely line of her throat. The bright pink silk cocktail dress only just covered her shoulders.

'That's a very cute little girl you have – Lucy,' Bill told Kate. 'We always hear how well mannered English kids are – and you certainly seem to have one ... Our two boys, teenagers now, were little monsters at her age.'

'She was on her best behaviour tonight. Bribery,' Kate said, smiling attractively. The wine, frequently replenished by Robin, was loosening all their tongues a little.

'I guess all parents do a bit of that ... Now listen, Kate' – confidingly – 'we have a great place out on the island, in Easthampton, where we spend summers. We love having friends visit. Ask Betsy. We're right on the ocean, terrific beaches ... you ought to get Robin to bring you and Lucy out next summer ... No, really, I mean it ... And particularly since we're going to be in business together, Condicote and ourselves. And I think we should drink to the success of that, by the way.' He raised his glass and moved slightly closer to Kate.

'You're so kind,' Kate murmured, smiling directly at him. 'And I've never been to the States ... Robin did mention it ...'

And thinking, elated: so it was going through; it was all right; Condicote *had* got the contract. The iron-clad agreement that could lead to so much. Robin had been afraid that when it came right down the wire those last, difficult details could scupper the whole thing. He'd seen it happen often enough. Some triviality, apparently innocuous, suddenly blown up. Good vibes turned sour and suspicious. All the work and the planning – everything – down the drain. Kate had heard it all since they were married – often in the dead hours of the morning, when sleep wouldn't come and when everything seemed blackest. But not this time. The Americans – these Americans at least – had come through. And they were big fish, one of the most respected names on Wall Street. With the changes that were rumoured to be coming to the London Stock Exchange too in a few years – who knew where the association might end?

She felt strong and well. She looked across at Robin and he caught her eye and winked. She smiled back at him as he turned to Jill on his left. He looked flushed and healthy; his chin stuck out a mile. Love welled and stuck in her throat.

'I mean it, Kate.' Bill looked towards his wife who was saying something to Jill, leaning forward to speak across

147

Robin. A pretty woman, perfectly groomed, her straight brown hair cut in a fringe. 'We'll talk about it with Betsy after dinner . . .'

Laura had discovered that she and Jake had a mutual acquaintance in New York, a wealthy, rather overblown hostess who fancied herself as a patron of the arts. They both thought she was rather a joke. Helping himself to Libby's vegetables, Jake told an amusing story he had recently heard about her pretentiousness. Laura laughed again, picking up her glass. She was enjoying herself. She liked Americans on principle – they were rarely stuffy she found – and this one was attractive in an Ivy League sort of way. His good head of prematurely grey hair made his face look incredibly young. Decent button-down shirt and tie. Tall. Nicely ironic. He had a bit of style, she thought. Fiddling with one of her earrings, she decided not to move her leg that his had just pressed against – quite subtly.

Around Kate, the conversation changed and became general: politics, someone's exotic holiday, hearsay concerning a notorious Royal marriage. Robin came round again with the wine, touching Kate's shoulder. And looking at Laura, flirting with Jake, truly dazzling now she was interested and amused, Kate remembered Arabella. Playing about with the succulent, just-pink lamb which she was only pretending to eat she wondered: Has she had the baby yet? Laura might – and might not – tell her. And what about Nico? She stabbed the meat furiously with her fork. Playing the proud father? Holding Arabella's hand? If only Laura would come to her senses and stop destroying her life. Was this nice Jake, whom Robin had said several times he liked very much, another opportunity she was blind to?

The party broke up some time after midnight, the front door opening onto the clear and frosty night. There were thanks and laughter and promises to meet again – soon. All the good feelings of warmth and satisfaction which a successful dinner-party creates.

Laura and Jake, who had been whispering on one side, went off together. Kate and Robin heard them race across the road, whistling for an empty taxi . . .

148

Much later, in bed, feeling well and happy and loving, Kate told Robin about Nico and Arabella and the seventh child.

'The man's a cad. And a creep. Whatever you say, I feel sorry for Arabella. She can't really like being down there in the country with all those children – Nico turning up when he feels like it – knowing he lives with Laura the rest of the time. She can't. It's not normal.'

'Laura says she's not. Normal. Arabella that is.'

'As for Laura . . . but she looked marvellous tonight, didn't she? She certainly made an impression on Jake. He seemed to be having a great time.'

'Everyone did.'

Robin hugged her. Her body so slender under the silk nightdress; bones so delicate he sometimes wondered they didn't snap.

'I knew they would. I told you. It's your knack. Darling – why are your feet so bloody cold?'

'Bad circulation. Have I really got a knack? For small parties like that?' Sounding pleased.

'You really have. And neither you, nor it, was lost on Bill and Jake tonight. Or Betsy. That I can tell you. Tonight sealed it. We'll sign tomorrow.' He sounded, for once, utterly confident. 'The sky's the limit after that . . .'

'Like Bill said?'

'Like Bill said . . .' Then, very softly, lips moving down her neck, 'You felt rotten didn't you – before they came?'

'I didn't think you knew. I hoped not. But then I got better. I'm not much liking food just now.' They were both afraid to speak of what might be a pregnancy – wanting it, both of them, so much.

'You're a brave woman, Kate' – meaning it, absolutely serious; his hands sliding upwards. 'I love you. I thought so tonight, at dinner.' In the darkness, she smiled at her own secret recollection – Robin's chin, his jaunty air. The way he looked – handsome and confident. The catch in her throat . . .

'Me too. Goodnight, my love. Go to sleep.'

But he couldn't – he was far too excited about the future – keyed up, his mind going round and round. And Kate wouldn't. So they made love slowly, and with unwearying tenderness, until it was almost dawn.

149

Chapter 15

Kate's second pregnancy was confirmed early in December. But thrilled as they were – Robin and Kate and both sets of grandparents – it was difficult from the beginning. Not in the least like Lucy. Kate felt wretchedly ill and listless, couldn't eat – and had soon lost an alarming amount of weight. Particularly as the baby was so desperately wanted, neither Tony nor the gynaecologist could offer any but the most banal explanations. The first three months were often trying. Kate was not physically robust – and just because she had had barely a qualm having Lucy meant nothing. All pregnancies were different; nothing seemed to be wrong; she must take life a day at a time . . . it was only a matter of weeks before she would start feeling her old self. Or so they hoped.

Then a few days before Christmas, Kate passed out cold. Her mother was in town doing some last-minute shopping and had dropped in to see her on her way home about lunchtime. Calling out from the kitchen where she had dumped her parcels after Kate let her in, she got no reply. She found Kate lying at the bottom of the stairs in a crumpled heap. Tony came as quickly as he could and firmly ruled out Knyght's Wood for Christmas. John Holford, now semi-retired, arrived later in the day – and agreed. Kate was feeling weak as a kitten and didn't care – not even, then, about Knyght's Wood. Almost everything was too much of an effort. So for the first time since they had acquired the house, the Christmas holidays would be spent in London.

Lucy was told this by Felicity Holford when she came skipping home from playing with her friend Lucinda next door. Her dark hair was held back in a yellow Alice band and her cheeks were rosy from the wintry air. She looked, her grand-

mother thought, an absolute picture . . . suddenly remember-
ing the twins as little girls, her heart missed a beat. Her
mother, Felicity said soothingly, hadn't been well again. Dr
Martin had come during the afternoon. And with the baby
coming, he said that she must stay put and be quiet. And that
meant no travelling for the time being.

Lucy – who always seemed to know everything that was
going on in an often maddening way, the adults thought –
had asked about the baby straight out, weeks ago. She had
heard them talking – and had noticed Kate's sickness from the
very beginning. So many of her friends at school had young
brothers and sisters; it seemed a perfectly normal happening
to her. So, when asked, after a brief hesitation Kate had said
yes – a brother or a sister, in the middle of the summer, they'd
keep it a secret for the moment – and wasn't it exciting? Lucy
had taken it in a very matter-of-fact way – not showing much
excitement, or even interest. It seemed such a long way off . . .

'Are we staying here then? Oh goody-good, Gran,' Lucy
said, throwing coat, gloves and muffler on the floor. 'That's a
bit of luck. Silly old Knyght's Wood is so boring. What's there
to eat?' . . .

Hearing that Kate was feeling badly under the weather, Doris
Faraday went into action. She had little confidence in Felicity
Holford – whom she considered suspiciously arty – coping
with a family Christmas. If this next grandchild was to be born
at all, they were needed – in London – as soon as possible. So
Jim, who had been hoping for some cheery outings to his local
pub with golfing pals over the festive season, went reluctantly
off to deal with plane tickets and reservations while his wife
wrote out lists and started packing.

Kate, languishing in bed for much of the time, could have
wept with relief at the sight of her – something she had not
previously considered possible. After one look at Kate, skinny
and sallow, Doris abandoned her mink coat, hat and muffler,
rolled up her sleeves and went straight down to the kitchen.
She put on an overall and rummaged through cupboards
muttering darkly about how young women these days didn't
seem to be bothered over keeping a good stock in the larder.

151

'Sickly,' she said triumphantly to Jim who was trailing behind her feeling both daft and out of place. 'Sickly she is – Kate. I always said so, mind you. She'll be lucky to carry this one from the looks of her . . .'

By the evening Doris Faraday had the household totally under her control. And during the busy, difficult run up to Christmas it stayed that way. Kate, who had at most a couple of hours each day when she didn't feel violently sick, was content that it should be so.

The Holfords – and Laura – came for Christmas Day. Kate and her father took Lucy to church in the morning. Lucy fidgeted or read the book she had squirrelled away in her pocket throughout the service. And walking home, linking arms with her father as Lucy ran ahead, Kate told him laughingly that she feared Lucy had inherited Robin's agnostic tendencies.

'We two are the only real believers in the family, my darling,' John Holford agreed. 'We may as well face it. Your mother always says she's a foul-weather Christian – she only needs faith to prop her up when things go wrong . . .'

'Robin won't even go that far. Neither will Laura.'

'On the whole, I think we're the lucky ones,' he replied, giving her arm an encouraging squeeze. 'Full-time, part of our lives. It's there all the time, isn't it?'

When they got back to the house, they were met by Felicity Holford, looking pretty and festive in a red-and-black checked dress, and gesturing towards the kitchen.

'Doris is steaming ahead in there,' she murmured, amused. 'I realised I wasn't wanted and beat a hasty retreat. Robin and Jim are tucking into the champagne in the sitting-room . . . so let's leave her to it . . .'

Laura arrived while they were opening presents – each one ceremoniously picked from under the tree by Lucy.

'It's Laura,' she squealed when the doorbell rang, running off to open the door and fling herself at her aunt. 'Laura, Laura . . . why are you so late?' they heard her shriek. 'Come on, you're missing everything . . .'

'I fancy our young Miss is going to have her nose put out of joint by the new arrival,' Doris commented smugly, sipping her drink, her face red and shiny from the hot kitchen.

'Nonsense, Doris,' said Jim. 'She's a good lass, Lucy is, not spoilt. And she's not a baby any longer, not by a long shot. She'll be old enough to enjoy a baby brother or sister.'

'I doubt it,' said Felicity Holford, adding, surprisingly, 'I absolutely agree with Doris. I don't think she'll like being ousted one bit.'

'Darling, don't cross bridges . . .' her husband teased her fondly.

'I mean it, Johnnie,' she said seriously. 'Yes, I'd love some more, Robin dear. Kate darling, go and see what Laura and Lucy are giggling about in the hall . . .'

Kate, who was starting to feel queasy again from the smells of roasting turkey, did as she was told. Lucy rushed past her back into the sitting-room – eyes sparkling as she piled yet more presents, brought by Laura, under the tree.

'Merry Christmas, Katie,' Laura called as she saw her – unfurling herself from her silver-grey wool coat. 'Lucy tells me you've been to church to pray for the sinners in the family – and that Grannie Faraday is in charge of all the cooking . . .' She glanced at herself in the mirror and fluffed out her hair with her hands. 'Mmmm . . . smells delicious . . .' She gave Kate a peck on the cheek. 'Feeling a bit better are you?'

Kate, who was long used to the 'Katie' by now – and absolutely certain that it had been initiated by Nico on the day of Lucy's christening – pecked her back.

'On and off.' She pulled a face. 'Food is still my worst thing – and there's this huge lunch to be got through some-how.'

'Oh cheer up. Don't look so down-in-the-mouth,' Laura told her gaily. 'I'm dying for Lucy to open my present. Hope she likes it.'

'She always loves anything you give her, Laura.'

'Does she?' Laura looked pleased. Watching her, Kate blinked. Something was up with her. She could tell. But what? She always spent Christmas with them – Nico, it was pre-sumed, performing his dutiful father rôle. So there was nothing new in that. But she sensed something . . . For one thing, she looked happier. She would sniff it out, whatever it was, if she possibly could. They went back into the sitting-room

153

together in time to hear John Holford saying, above loud laughter, 'My dear Doris, it's what I've wanted all my life ...' – and holding up a red flannel night shirt.

When Kate did get Laura to herself, it was much later in the day. The weather had turned freezing, so their parents had already left, before the driving became too bad. Robin and his father had disappeared for a walk long ago. To be followed by a pub, Doris suspected. Robin had found being stuck in the small crowded house all day stifling. Even Knyght's Wood, he had thought gloomily – for he had never taken to it as passionately as Kate – was preferable. A lot roomier; decent walks; the possibility of a shoot.

But here – cooped up, eating and drinking too much – he was feeling decidedly out-of-sorts. Their bedroom, too, had started to depress him. With Kate – poor darling – lounging about it so much it had begun to take on the air of a sick room. He hated that. So he marched his father off on a longer and more rugged walk than he had bargained for.

Lucy went to show off her new acquisitions to Lucinda – and Doris collapsed in front of the television. Kate and Laura escaped upstairs to the bedroom where Kate immediately curled up on the bed, wrapped in an old shawl which she had clung to since childhood.

'You mustn't spoil Lucy so,' Kate scolded. Laura had given her a tiny Victorian gold brooch in the shape of a horseshoe, dotted in seed pearls. 'For luck, Luce,' she had told her when she opened it, awe-struck. Nobody else called Lucy 'Luce.' Only Laura. 'What are you going to do when she's older?'

'It wasn't expensive – and she liked it.' Laura shrugged. 'You can't give Lucy childish presents any more. She's much too bright. By the way,' she said suddenly, 'Arabella had a girl. Two weeks ago. Did I tell you?'

'No.' As if she thought she had ...

'Guess what they're calling her.'

'I really couldn't.' Or care, Kate thought frostily.

'Jasmine Lavender Rose.'

'Go on,' Kate gasped despite herself.

'True. All the others are wildly Russian ... Natasha,

154

Anastasia . . . that sort of thing. There's even a Boris. Imagine having a son called Boris . . .'

'Boris Kirilov . . .' Kate was starting to giggle. '*Boris* . . . but at least they do go together somehow . . .'

She was right. Laura was happier; altogether more light-hearted than usual. For years, over these family holidays she had tended to brood. But not today. She had been bright and amusing during the interminable lunch – even made Robin laugh . . .

'I suppose they do. But she was fed up with having everything Russian foisted on her so she decided to name this one after what she liked best in her garden.'

'I see – well, good for Arabella,' Kate said. Laura, kneeling, joined Kate on the wide bed. Just this once, not secretive and defensive over Nico. And now that the ice was broken between them, Kate asked, 'Did Nico come back to London? After the flowery child was born?'

'No he didn't. Not once. Not even for the Christmas show – which did extremely well. Mostly thanks to me. The sod.' But she didn't sound as though she minded all that much.

'Oh . . .'

'The fact is, we've had an almighty row, Katie. A humdinger. We've had them before – but not like this . . .' Kate had a mental picture of a depressed Nico surrounded by disorderly children of all ages, including a shrieking infant, in the drawing-room-cum-kitchen; Arabella – beautiful, calm and fat – presiding over the chaos. Meanwhile, Laura was expected to organise the gallery and cool her heels alone in London. Small wonder they had one of their famous rows.

'I'm not surprised.'

'But it wasn't what you're thinking – Nico staying on in the country. Not this time.'

'Oh . . .' Kate said again, deflated.

This recent and most bitter row had been conducted on the telephone between Laura's flat and the public phone at the pub in the Kirilovs' West Country village. It had ended with Laura slamming down the receiver at her end – and Nico, in a passionate rage, attempting to rip the entire phone out of the wall at his. Laura had heard the heavings before hanging up –

and guessed what was happening. She imagined the locals were used to his temperament by now.

'Perhaps he's decided he wants to stay there for good?' Kate asked hopefully.

'Not bloody likely. She drives him mad with all her cooking and nesting and general madness when he's on an "up" . . .' Kate opened her mouth and wisely closed it again. 'No, it's turning out to be something quite different this time.' She smiled seductively. 'I've got another man. I think it could be serious. Nico knows – and he doesn't like it.'

Kate sat bolt upright against the wall of pillows – her private world these days.

'Laura – who?'

'As a matter of fact – it's Jake.'

'You mean – the nice American Jake? Who you met here?'

'Yes, indeed.'

'Well, I *never* . . .' Kate was astonished. He was an attractive man; Robin liked him a lot. It was true that he and Laura had seemed to get on well – and they had left the party together. But after these years with Nico, they had all lost hope. 'Oh Laura, I'm so pleased . . . You are a dark horse . . . Why didn't you say?' Her pleasure was obvious.

'I wasn't sure at first. I don't think I am quite – still. I started out wanting to punish Nico. You can imagine why, we won't go into that . . . And then I started to like Jake.'

'He's very likeable. I know he's gone down well with every-one at Condicote. When have you been seeing him?'

'Practically all the time. He's been over here working since last month.'

'Of course, with Rupert.'

'Exactly. We went off to a nightclub after we left here . . . lunch the next day . . . then dinner. All the nice touches – flowers, champagne. And one thing led to another . . .'

'Laura . . .' Kate put her hands on her shoulders. She hadn't been wrong about her happiness after all. Even her face looked softer. 'I'm so thrilled. I can't wait to tell Robin.'

'But only tell Robin, for the moment. I don't want to get Mother and Pa all excited – not yet. Let's postpone the wedding bells . . . You know, you're looking better, Katie.

156

Honestly. It's the first time today you don't look like a washed-out ghost.'

'It's your good news . . . Where is he now – Jake?'

'In New York. He's got one daughter, Lisa, who lives with her mother. She's about Lucy's age. He's taking her off to Vermont for a few days after Christmas.'

'Robin had no idea Jake was divorced. You know that.'

'He let it drop when we were chatting . . . He's fun, Katie. He's dependable, he always does what he says. He's good company . . . he does sweet and thoughtful things . . . and he's easy to have around . . .'

Both thought briefly of Nico. From this description, they could hardly be less alike.

'We must meet him again. Bring him for supper. When is he coming over?'

'For New Year's Eve – if he possibly can. And then I expect I'll go over to New York soon. I have to go on business anyhow. And he wants me to meet Lisa . . .'

'Now that's what I call a really good Christmas present,' Kate said – with her liveliest smile.

157

Chapter 16

In February, soon after the final deed of association between the old Wall Street firm of Morton Paine & Moore and Condicote Ltd had at last been signed, Robin went skiing with Rupert and Jill. Kate saw him off, smiling bravely, wincing inwardly at his obvious exhilaration as he stowed his skis on top of Rupert's car and slung his gear in the boot. His face wiped clear of worry for once, handsome and boyish in a polo-necked sweater and bulky ski jacket. They were driving out. Rupert had rented a chalet for a month in the French Alps, but he and Robin were flying home after two weeks. Jill was staying on, with friends, until Rupert came back out for a long weekend to fetch her.

'We'll be losing a couple of days in the car – so it's hardly worth my going unless it's for two weeks. You don't mind, darling, do you?' Robin had asked Kate not long before on a grey Saturday afternoon when they were at Knyght's Wood, in front of a blazing fire. Kate, head bent, was working away at a tapestry. 'You'll be all right? You're sure?' Robin insisted, standing over her. In the past, his skiing or walking trips without her had never been for more than a week, usually only for a few days. But this, as he said, seemed only sensible.

'Of course I will . . .' – chilled; her heart plummeting. Numbed by what she perceived – at that moment – to be her own physical inadequacy. 'But – but why ever not? Laura can come and stay. Or Mother. I'll be fine – really.' Braced, she put down the tapestry and raised her face to his.

'A work-out on the slopes is exactly what I need just now, Kate – I'm aching for it. I can almost smell the air, feel the crunch of snow, sun so brilliant it hurts the eyes . . . God, the speed, the freedom . . . out of this world – literally . . .' He started pacing up and down the room. He had been badly on edge for weeks now. Even their joy at her pregnancy had been tempered by this wretched, debilitating nausea she was still suffering almost continually. Kate's eyes followed him anxiously.

'You've had such a difficult few months, Robin. You've worked so hard. And you've brought it off – the first part at least. The right American link. I do know how much you need a change from the office grind . . .' She did. But behind the calm words, fear lurked as it always did when she lost him to the active life he craved. And which she could never share. Automatically, she glanced down at her left shoe – turned over slightly as it often was, the leg and ankle noticeably thinner than the other.

'And you'll have Lucy.' He stopped his pacing and looked down at her again. 'It's a rotten time to leave you, Kate.'

'I don't mind,' she said steadily, meeting his eyes. 'I told you. It's silly not to take advantage of Rupert and Jill's chalet. I'm over the first three months – and by the time you come back I should be feeling fine again. Remember how I was with Lucy? Never better . . . and Tony swears not many women go on feeling sick . . .'

It happened that Felicity Holford, who was in the middle of editing a book, needed to be in London anyway. So she left 'Johnnie' with a packed refrigerator and stayed the first three nights, dashing off to her publishers each morning. On the fourth day, John Holford came and collected her – and took Kate, Lucy, Felicity and Laura out for an early supper at a local Italian restaurant. Kate polished off a large plate of spaghetti and drank a glass of red wine. She was feeling a bit better at last, she said – sounding surprised. Her father looked at her sharply.

'You're not to stay alone in any event,' he told her. 'We promised Robin. I know Laura has moved in, but if she has to go for any reason before Robin gets back, let us know. I mean that, Kate.'

The next day she started to bleed. Laura, who was in the house at the time, tried to stay calmer than she felt – and

159

rushed to the telephone. Tony Martin came, followed by the gynaecologist who he had phoned from the surgery. Tony waited until he had examined Kate. It was a threatened miscarriage, no cause for undue alarm, bed-rest essential. He was breezy and professional and totally non-committal. Laura, who had just returned from New York and had no business pending which she couldn't handle on the phone or through her assistant, took charge. As Kate lay in bed looking frightened, she went downstairs with Tony when he left a little later. They whispered by the door. Better not to inform Robin, Tony thought. He would worry desperately, feel he ought to return – and there was nothing he could do. They would see how she went ... And both he and Mr Roberts thought she had a better than fifty/fifty chance of keeping the child. Slightly shaken, Laura shushed Lucy who was singing in the bath at the top of her voice and went in to face Kate.

With terrible slowness – so Kate thought – the days passed. The grey February light dulled even the pretty chintz of the bedroom. She lay so still, hardly daring to breathe, willing whoever it was in there to hold on and grow strong ... every day, every hour counted ...

Lucy, meanwhile, unaware that anything serious might be amiss – and used to her mother's uncertain health – was enchanted at having Laura to herself so much. Listening to the pair of them chattering away in the kitchen downstairs, sounding so alike and chirping like birds, Kate thought she had never heard Lucy so talkative. Usually, she was rather quiet and reticent. Kate and Robin put this down to her being an only child, so often with grown-ups. But now Kate felt an unaccountable wave of sadness; if only Lucy was as open with her as she seemed to be with Laura. But perhaps she was imagining it – having Laura to look after her was a novelty. So Kate sighed and wondered if the skiing was good and looked down at the bump of her stomach, trying to believe that this summer – please God, fingers crossed – there would be an infant in the house again.

The bleeding, which had never been serious, stopped. Daring to hope, Kate sat up and took notice of the world again. Reluctant sunshine pierced the gloom and slanted across her

160

bed. Tony dropped in on his way home, said he thought the upset had calmed down – and looked quite pleased with her. She could get up the next day for a few hours, a bit longer the day after, and so on. Back to her normal existence.

'It's like the old days,' Kate said, the first evening she was allowed downstairs. Robin was due home two days later – and although he had phoned several times, they had all agreed to say nothing to him about the scare. 'I mean, before I got married. When we shared the flat together . . .'

'I was thinking just the same thing today,' Laura agreed, helping herself to a large vodka. 'And I had never realised keeping a house and looking after a child took so much time. Or energy.'

'I don't know what I'd have done without you this past week,' Kate said. 'Mother would have had to come . . . and she gets so scatty and muddled these days. All she thinks about is Pa and her writing and a bit of gardening. It must have been quite a strain for her when we were young, don't you think?'

'Perhaps.' Laura curled up on the sofa opposite with her drink. 'But she got the essentials of mothering right. She's warm and intuitive – that seems to be what's needed . . . more important than all the pernickety details . . .'

Am I, Kate wondered uneasily, warm and intuitive? With Lucy? Or just fussy? Easy to say when you weren't in the thick of it – like Laura. When Kate stayed strained and not very talkative, Laura began telling her about her time in New York. With the fright over the baby, and Lucy and the house to be dealt with, they hadn't got down to much chat. Anyhow, New York had been the greatest possible fun, lots of laughs, full of interest. Although she didn't say so to Kate, a lot more low-keyed than her frenetic trips there with Nico. Jake took her everywhere – skiiing in Vermont, the theatre, parties. They spent a weekend with his parents outside Boston. She met – and liked – his friends. Lisa was a delightful child, very affection-ate, and Jake and his former wife, who was a buyer for one of the major department stores, seemed to have a friendly and rational relationship. As for Jake, like her he was hesitant about getting too serious. They liked each other enormously, enjoyed each other's company – and were both content to leave it at that for the moment.

'What about Nico then?' Kate asked.

Silence. Laura drank her vodka and stared into the fire.

'Is he out of your life for good?' Kate persisted.

'I don't know, Katie. I just don't know . . .' Then, wrenching herself suddenly round: '*Somebody* is walking about upstairs,' she said loudly. 'Now I wonder who on earth that could be . . .' Banisters creaked and they heard a scurrying sound. 'That naughty child of yours . . . she was up there listening, I'll bet . . .' Laura unwound her legs, in very tight blue jeans, and went to the door. 'Back to bed, Luce. Or there'll be no treat after school tomorrow,' she ordered sternly. A door shut softly – and there was silence. 'She was sitting on the stairs, listening to every word, the little minx. She doesn't miss much, that Lucy . . .' Laura topped up her drink from the vodka bottle.

'Mother thinks she's like you as a child,' Kate said, smiling wanly. 'You know – confident.'

'Perhaps.' Laura considered her twin sister. She wished she didn't look so peaky. Pale little face; long grey housecoat with lace at the neck and wrists. Dark hair hanging straight – narrow wrists and hands resting limp in her lap. When pregnant with Lucy she had been quite different from the start – positively sparkling; more vibrant than they had ever seen her before . . . Laura thought momentarily of Robin – cutting through the white slopes in graceful swathes, leaning his body into that crisp, exhilarating air; the chalet at night when they were all still high on the dizzying speed and the blinding whiteness; good food, a lot of laughter; wine flowing . . . She took a mouthful of vodka, gulped, and squared her shoulders.

'Poor love,' she said. 'You do need cheering up. And I've got something funny to tell you. About Arabella as a matter of fact . . .'

'*Arabella?*'

'That's right . . . Nico, as I'm sure you can imagine, has been growling and sulking in the background recently. Because of Jake of course. Vanity outraged, licking his wounds between manic outbursts . . . everything about him always *is* extravagant . . . Anyhow, the night after I got back from New York, he rang me at the flat . . . all sweet reasonableness, the perfect gent . . . simply wanted me to have dinner with him . . .'

'Just dinner?'

'Yes. Just dinner.'

'So you did?'

'So I did. He was unnervingly well-behaved, madly attentive – and really he never is except if he's play-acting – hand-kissing, opening doors with a flourish. We went to the Savoy . . . and he kept it up marvellously. All my "treachery" as he calls it – i.e. Jake – as though it had never been . . . along with the screaming tirades down the phone at all hours, scenes in the street outside the flat . . . throwing roses up at the sitting-room window on one occasion . . .'

'Good heavens Laura,' Kate murmured, impressed.

'All part of his wide Russian soul, as he calls it . . . but as I say, none of this was on view that particular night. He set out to charm and amuse – and I must say he did.'

'But what about Arabella? That you said was so funny?'

'I'm just coming to that . . . Well, you know she cooks non-stop, don't you? Apart from her trail of children, it's her *raison d'être* . . .'

'I think you told me that . . . and I know she's fat. I saw her photograph in one of the glossies not long ago . . . Lady Arabella Kirilov in her garden somewhere. I thought she looked beautiful – the most lovely face . . .'

'Fat as butter,' Laura said crisply. 'Fatter. Since the last baby she's taken to walking leaning on a stick, so one of the girls in the gallery told me when I went there to remove some of my belongings. When did you see the picture anyhow?' Laura asked.

'A few months ago . . .' She had come across it while thumbing through magazines in the hairdressers – and decided on the spot to ignore it. This was well before Jake came on the scene, when both she and her mother considered Nico and everything to do with him taboo. 'I can't remember exactly. She was wearing a sort of smock, surrounded by a great tangled mass of herbs and roses. Anyhow, do go on . . .'

163

Laura looked at her suspiciously but said, 'The food thing with Arabella is completely neurotic. I've heard that – apart from Nico. She simply can't stop cooking. Or eating, for that matter. She has been known to get up in the middle of the night and make huge pots of stew and casseroled pigeons and *coq au vin* . . .'

'But what on earth does she do with it all? Surely she and the children can't eat it all?'

'Of course not – although Arabella tries. That's the point. The reason she had the drawing-room made into the kitchen was so that all down one side – and apparently it's an enormous room – she could have a bank of deep freezes . . .'

'*A bank of deep freezes . . .?*'

Kate leant forward, her chin resting on her hand. Her eyes at least had come to life. That's more like it, Laura thought, knocking back her vodka.

'Just so. I can't remember how many cubic feet of space altogether – but Nico did tell me – and it's enough to feed an army . . . Then the other day, disaster struck.'

'How?' Kate was starting to smile.

'In a word – electricity. It's an old house and the wiring is hopeless and one night there was a violent explosion and half the circuits blew . . .'

'Including the deep freezes . . .'

'Of course. And when the electrician finally turned up, he said it wasn't safe to repair any of it . . . the whole house has to be rewired which might take weeks . . .'

'And what about poor Arabella's food?' Kate gasped – genuinely amused and absorbed now, eyes glued to Laura's face.

'I'll tell you . . . Nico had one of his mad, inspired ideas. While Arabella was upstairs with the baby, quite late, when it was dark, he marshalled the children and torches and gardening tools . . . and in the field at the bottom of the property they dug a huge trench . . .'

'Don't . . .,' Kate giggled, her white face washed with colour. '*Don't* . . . they didn't . . .'

'Of course they did. They had to do something with it or it would go bad and start to smell. Even after all the digging it took hours . . . the children traipsed back and forth across the

164

lawn with dripping plastic boxes of stew and soft fruit and ice cream . . .'

'And casseroled pigeons . . .' – tears were rolling down Kate's face now and her shoulders were shaking.

'And whole carcasses,' Laura shouted. 'And game from Arabella's parents' place in Scotland . . . and semi-frozen half lambs . . .' She was laughing and hiccuping, the drink jiggling wildly in her glass. And Kate looked better than she had seen her for months – young and happy and suddenly pretty.

'Poor, poor Arabella,' Kate said, smoothing the laughter-tears away from her eyes and collapsing back in the chair. 'Was she absolutely devastated – when she knew that they had literally buried all her lovely, lovely food?'

'Apparently not. The rewiring is almost finished and she has all that empty freezer space to fill. Nico says she contemplates it with bliss . . . but we had a hilarious dinner – in a bizarre sort of way. The waiters must have thought we were out of our minds, we laughed so much. Look,' she said suddenly, 'speaking of food, you've had practically nothing to eat all day. Shall I make us some eggs?'

'I think I'd like that . . .'

While they were eating in the kitchen Kate, still looking her old self, said, 'What happened that night, with Nico, after dinner at the Savoy? Or shouldn't I ask?'

'We went back to the flat. He stayed.'

After a while, Kate asked thoughtfully, 'Do you think you'll ever be quite free of him, Laura?'

'Perhaps. And perhaps not . . .'

Still feeling unwell for a good part of each day, Kate battled on through the spring and into the early summer. Even the simplest chores in running the house and looking after Lucy were an effort for her. Despite repeated assurances from the doctors that 'some pregnancies are like this', that everything appeared normal, her listlessness depressed her. The slightest upset – usually to do with Lucy – brought her close to tears; although she refused to give in, except privately, and presented a reasonably composed front to Robin.

By the time July came – and Kate had sometimes felt that it

never would – it was clear that the baby was a lot larger than Lucy had been. Noting this, as well as her pelvis which had gradually become misshapen through her uneven walk, Mr Roberts informed her, brooking no argument whatsoever, that he had decided on a Caesarean.

When told, her father, looking concerned, nodded and put his arm round her. 'It's for the best, my darling. Roberts is a sound man. You're not too upset about it, are you?'

Kate shook her head and bit her lip. Mr Roberts had also told both her and Robin, forcibly, that this baby must be the last.

'I suppose I ought to get my bag packed,' she said, 'just in case . . .'

Guy was born on a dull July morning – eight and a half pounds, red in the face and with Robin's wide shoulders. Still dopey from the anaesthetic, Kate smiled and dozed through a succession of brief family visits. Robin – noisy, pressing champagne on all and sundry – over the moon with pride and happiness; her parents – loving and slightly anxious; the Faradays all broad smiles – even Doris won over to Kate at last, now that she had produced a lusty son, the image of her own.

Robin, happily neglecting the office for once, picked Lucy up from school and brought her to the hospital to see Kate and her brother. In a rush of affection, Kate, still weak, thought how pretty she looked in her crisp pink cotton frock, her hair tied back in a bow – nearly ten, already more young lady than child. The baby, snuffling a bit, was in a bassinet beside her bed.

'Look, Lucy darling, here he is at last . . .' Watching, Kate could feel tears . . . Robin put his arm around her. Lucy, hands clasped behind her back, stared down at Guy's tiny face, peeping out of the blue cotton blanket, still red and puckered.

'So *that*'s what he looks like. I expect he'll cry a lot, don't you?' Ignoring her parents and her brother, she skipped over to where she had spied a box of chocolates among the stiff florists' arrangements. 'Lucinda's sister bawled the place down when she was little . . . can I have one?'

'All right, darling . . . he's sweet, isn't he? We're going to call him Guy . . .' Kate looked up at Robin who put his other arm around her and kissed her. He thought she looked soft and pretty, much younger than her age, in the pearly pink nightdress.

'I know. Granny Faraday told me.' Lucy bit into a chocolate, made a face, and took another. 'Has Laura been yet?'

'She's coming this evening,' Robin said. 'She's terribly thrilled, Kate darling, sent her love . . . she's got masses of work on but she'll pop in to see you later . . .'

Laura, still tantalisingly enmeshed between Nico and Jake, had decided to concentrate on her work – and lower the emotional temperature of her love life. She had an aptitude for business – and she enjoyed the cut and thrust of dealing. In addition to her property ventures, she had added several lines and new patterns to her wallpaper collection and now had one of the most exclusive small selections in London. Recently, she had taken a small shop in a mews near Oxford Street where the public, as well as interior decorators, could come and browse. If it went well, she hoped to expand into fabrics and unusual objects for the house.

'You're sure she'll come? Oh she must . . .' As always when something important happened in her life, Kate longed for her.

'I'll ring her again soon if you like,' Robin said reassuringly.

'You won't be coming home for a bit, you two, will you?' Lucy asked hopefully, mouth full of a chewy chocolate. She sidled over to the crib and stared expressionlessly down at her newborn brother.

'That depends,' Kate said, slightly taken aback.

'It's up to the doctor. Entirely,' Robin said crisply.

Laura sashayed in sometime after seven. Robin and the Faradays had gone out for dinner, taking Lucy.

'Well done, clever you . . . I'm only going to stay for a few minutes . . .' She kissed Kate and peered down at Guy.

'They all think he's just like Robin,' Kate said, warming at the sight of her. 'Come back here . . .' She patted the bed beside her.

'Hmmm . . . not sure. Perhaps . . . not like us, certainly . . .' She opened the blanket gently. 'Look at that dear little hand,

167

all curled,' she smiled, melting. 'He's absolutely adorable . . .' She sounded almost wistful. 'There, you see, all those dreary months were worth it . . .' Then she sat on the bed and scrutinised Kate.

'Are you all right? Was it hell?'

Kate shook her head and smiled a bit groggily. 'Not at all. Not this way. But I'm starting to feel it now . . . Mr Roberts said it takes a bit longer to recover completely . . . but I'll soon be up and about . . .'

'Mother and Pa are insisting on your having a nurse for the baby for a while.'

'I know. I can't tell you how grateful I am . . . and Doris is staying on for a week too. It'll be a very full house.'

'Never mind. And I can take Lucy off your hands sometimes if you like – in the school holidays. She can come to the shop and we'll put her to work.'

'That would be marvellous, Laura. School finishes next week – and she gets terribly bored without it. Robin brought her in to see us. I must say, she didn't seem particularly excited.'

'Give her time, Katie.'

'I suppose so . . .'

Laura got up off the bed and went over to the dressing-table where the vases were placed, side by side, like soldiers. She read out, and commented on, the cards.

'Do you want a drink?' Kate asked from her pillows. 'Robin left a bottle here somewhere . . .' She looked around vaguely. Laura shook her head.

'No thanks, Katie. I'm not staying long. It's not good for you. You must get lots of rest while you're here. Make the most of it.' She walked round the foot of the bed and again looked down at Guy who was beginning to stir and fret. 'He's a poppet, he really is. All male. You'd never mistake that face and head for a little girl, would you?' Kate leant over and looked at him with her. Already, only hours old, he was totally familiar.

'He's a boy all right . . . Lucy looked quite different. Remember? She had such a pretty little face.'

168

'Young Guy will be a handsome lad too. You wait . . .' She tucked the shawl around him – he had stopped squirming and was sound asleep again. Straightening, flicking invisible fluff from her short, tight skirt, she said, 'I'm off, Katie. No long chats. I promised Robin. I'll come and see you both tomorrow. I'm whacked too.' She looked it. There were dark circles under her eyes and the heavy make-up looked garish. 'Getting the shop-cum-showroom going is never-ending . . . And Jake is ringing later. He's got his parents' house on Cape Cod for the whole of September – they're coming to Europe – and he's twisting my arm to go over for a couple of weeks . . .'

'You should, Laura. You're crazy not to . . . everyone loves the Cape – and September is the best time. And you have such a good time with Jake. He's so – well – *personable* . . .' A shadow passed over Kate's face. 'I suppose it's still because of . . .'

'*Don't* Katie . . .' She turned abruptly.

'All right. Off you go then. You'll come tomorrow? Please?'

'Promise . . .' She took her car keys out of the neat little shoulder-bag.

'Laura?'

'What?'

'All today, on and off, I've been thinking about Arabella Kirilov . . .'

'What on earth for?' Laura was astonished.

'It made me laugh, the things you told me about her . . . when I was feeling so sick and hopeless . . . cheered me up . . .'

'Oh *that* . . .'

Kate lay back on the pillows, smiling, dark hair tousled. She was still light-headed with happiness – and relief. Still slightly woozy; feeling as though her body didn't quite belong to her. The door opened and a nurse poked her head round, gave them both a disapproving look, and vanished, clicking the door smartly shut.

'Poor Arabella,' Kate said.

'I wouldn't say that at all.' Laura's fluting voice came over with a hard edge. She had her hand on the doorknob; very svelte in her dark linen suit and gold jewellery. 'I think she gets exactly what she wants out of life. *Exactly.*'

After behaving perfectly well for the first few days of his life, once he was home Guy promptly mistook night for day and vice versa. He wasn't happy about either. Walking the floor with him one misty 4.00 a.m., Robin, at his wits' end, decided that he must think he was living in Australia. As Lucy had predicted, he yelled often – and loudly. 'Colicky,' the nurse said sternly. 'And *none* of my babies ever was that . . .' She then left for what she said was a previous commitment as soon as she decently could – and no replacement could be found. After some weeks, Kate and Robin agreed that they had forgotten what it was like to have an unbroken night's sleep. Perhaps because she was so continuously tired, Kate suffered bouts of weeping depression which she had never had after Lucy's birth.

During all this domestic upheaval Lucy, who had suddenly sprouted legs that seemed to start in her armpits, walked round the house with her fingers stuck in her ears, humming loudly. She now went almost everywhere on her own. As she said, raising her eyes towards Guy's room, 'It's so much more peaceful without *him* . . .'

Then at three months, the screaming suddenly ceased. Guy had made peace with himself and the world. His innate good humour asserted itself once and for all. Tiptoeing into his room one afternoon, Kate found him unexpectedly awake. He was lying on his back in his cot, looking at the door as though waiting for her to appear. His smile beamed at her – and went straight to her heart. Where it stayed.

Chapter 17

Later, much later, Kate came to visualise the period of Guy's infancy and early childhood as the golden part of their lives – quite separate from all that went before and after. For her, everything about that time had an aura . . . Guy's first steps in the field dotted with wild flowers; Robin's huge business success; Lucy's academic cleverness. Her own confidence, contentment and widening interests. Robin wanting to give her the moon as he then could . . . it seemed, in those years, as though everything they touched went effortlessly right for them all.

Greece. Early in the summer following Guy's birth, Robin insisted on a holiday together, right away. He knew she hated travelling, but this was exceptional. They had had a difficult couple of years – the trying pregnancy and birth, the strain of guiding the continual upward push of Condicote. They would get away, forget about everything; flee to the sun, just the two of them. Guy was such a happy baby, no trouble at all. Even his teeth popped up without any fuss. He rarely cried. He was a picture to look at – roly-poly, blue-eyed, with wisps of fair, curly hair. The previously disapproving nurse was hauled back, and immediately fell under his angelic spell. John and Felicity Holford would move in and keep an eye on the house – and Lucy. The mere fact that John Holford, now fully retired, was willing to forsake his study and burgeoning June garden for two weeks in London testified to his grandson's charm.

So Robin and Kate found themselves alone, for the first time for years, in a plain white villa which Robin had rented through a friend, on an island in the Aegean. It was the idyllic spot of almost anyone's imaginings. The house was bare and cool, overlooking rocks lapped by azure seas. A small village; fishing boats that came and went. No tourists there. That special light – so brilliant, yet soft-hued. And after the initial strangeness of being without children, home and office – the entirety of both their worlds – they gave themselves up completely to all this.

They spent most mornings dipping in and out of the water – wonderful therapy for Kate, as John Holford had remarked before they left. And she had never felt, or looked, better. As she removed the top of her bikini, spreading it out to dry along the rocks, Robin, watching with a lazy sexual interest, swore daily that she had put on weight – something unheard of for her. Her skin, inclined to olive, tanned evenly. She always wore a wide-brimmed straw hat or twisted a colourful bandana round her head. The clothes she had pulled together so hastily, but still with her distinctive touch, suited both her and the surroundings: white cotton trousers and T-shirts in purple or yellow or black. Big round sunglasses; espadrilles or sandals.

Later, when the sun scorched, they sat on the shady terrace drinking ouzo and spitting out the stones of delicious green olives . . . Robin showing no sign of his usual restlessness, hardly wanting to move from that magical spot any more than Kate did.

In the afternoons, after the live-in cook had produced a simple lunch of salad, some Greek dish or other and plenty of retsina, they made love. And slept. Waking when the first shadows crept up to the long white curtains, just moving at the open window. It was during one of these hours of limbo, surfacing from a half sleep, that Kate called Robin – who was looking out at the darkening sea – back to bed. She told him what she wanted.

'Kate . . .' – amused, tender. And excited – it was a word he had never heard her use before. He came to her and she touched him; instantly aroused – both of them.

'Here . . .'

But it was her way this time – one she hadn't dreamt she ever new. Altering forever the sexual balance between them; introducing the piquancy of shock and delight and, finally, amazing laughter.

That evening, they walked down to the village's single taverna for dinner. Sometime during the meal – they were totally absorbed in each other, hands touching constantly – Robin said that the beads she was wearing looked pretty. And he smiled, his eyes crinkling – very blue – reminding her instantly of Guy – who was never far from her thoughts in any case.

But that night, they wouldn't phone home to speak to Lucy or her parents. Not even to ask about Guy. She smiled dreamily into the glass she was holding; under the rickety table, Robin touched her thigh, so smooth and bronzed. She looked up.

Robin my love, Oh Robin my love . . .

Just after his first birthday, late in July, Guy started to walk. Kate and the children had moved down to Knyght's Wood for the summer and one sunny afternoon, when Lucy was spending the day with her parents, she took Guy out into the open country on the other side of Laverton. She carried him through the gate and into a field of high grasses and wild flowers and plopped him down. For weeks, he had been letting go for one step, two steps, and tumbling, bottom in the air. He stood there swaying, turning round to Kate, smiling delightedly.

'Off you go, Guy, off you go . . .' She gave him a slight push. And go he did – veering into the grass nearly up to his waist, a sturdy little blonde boy in his miniature blue jeans and striped sweater; chubby arms outstretched to catch the white butterfly that hovered just ahead . . . Then he fell headlong – and Kate, only feet behind, laughed and scooped him up and cuddled him and held him high in the air. Back in the house, still holding him against her good hip, she made two breathless phone calls – one to Robin's office, the other to her parents. 'Just wait until you hear this,' she began . . .

'I'm going to get in the car and drive straight down,' Robin said. He then cancelled a pre-arranged phone call to New York – and left the office.

In the autumn, Lucy started at a new school. She shot straight to the top of the class – and stayed there. The following summer, Kate, Robin and Laura watched her collect two

173

prizes at Speech Day, walking up to the stage looking very composed. She still read everything she could lay her hands on, often simultaneously watching television. She was popular. Groups and clubs and a clutch of 'best friends' – including Lucinda – took up Saturday mornings and much of her spare time. As far as she could, she ignored her brother at home. But there were times, like the day he staggered across the kitchen and wordlessly put his arms around her when she came in from school, when even Lucy couldn't resist his guileless affection. She picked him up and took him upstairs with her to • her room where he sat on the floor with a crayon and paper, making large round circles – concentrating hard, his tongue stuck out – imitating her as she did her homework.

And it was around this time, just as Guy was starting to grasp at words and put them together, that the miracle of Condicote occurred. All Robin's dogged work with their New York associates paid off in the end. Because in the mayhem that followed the deregulation of the New York Stock Exchange, Morton Paine & Moore had merged with a larger broker/merchant banking firm to become the hugely powerful Morton, Paine, Pearson, Black. With a similar change soon about to happen in London, the decision was taken to buy into the UK side of the market. Several small, go-ahead firms like Condicote were approached. But because of the ties they had forged over several years with the old Morton Paine & Moore, Condicote had the edge. So all their dreams and calculations – Robin's in particular – came true. Condicote was bought out by Morton, Paine, Pearson, Black – all three partners retained on generous contracts; all three becoming wealthy men, practically overnight.

'I was right, you see, from the beginning,' Kate told Robin smugly. 'I knew you hated that bank the first day I met you. I could see you'd never be happy unless you were in charge . . .'

'You were right – over that,' Robin teased, dropping a kiss on the back of her neck, as he always wanted to. 'Even then, even when I picked you up on the Boulevard St Germain . . .'

'*Don't say that* . . .'

The announcement was accompanied by just recognisable

photographs of Robin – clean-cut, jaw clenched manfully, hair sharply parted. The financial journalists, grovelling, all suggested that it was he – sussing out the market for management buy-outs and anticipating the growing need, both personal and corporate, for sophisticated financial advice – who had led the Condicote team to this triumph. *The Times* said outright that Robin Faraday had for some years been marked out as one of the City's up-and-coming men – and this proved it. They went on to say that they hoped his talents would continue to be marketed creatively, not swallowed up behind the façade of a giant financial corporation.

Jim Faraday, who let it be known that he had never failed to put his money where his mouth was in backing Condicote, was pleased as punch. Robin told Kate with a good deal of satisfaction, 'The future's secure now for you and Lucy – and Guy,' his voice softening at his son's name. Because this child had a hold on their emotions in a way Lucy never had. Even as a small child, she had been self-contained. Sure of herself; precocious. She had never easily shown affection. They were proud of her – sometimes Kate felt almost in awe of her – and they loved her, of course. But with Guy clambering all over bestowing wet kisses; tumbling, picking himself up saying 'Whoops', still smiling, they had no resistance at all.

Eager to communicate because he was so naturally friendly, he picked up language early. He climbed on everything; he adored cars and he was fascinated by other children. His favourite grown-up, after his parents, was his grandfather, John Holford. The devotion was mutual. Kate believed secretly that it was from her father that he had inherited his wonderfully even temperament. As long as his day followed the routine he expected, he was happy. It was things like broken biscuits and mixed-up toys that produced mild tantrums. Guy loved orderliness.

At three, he developed a passion for red rubber boots. For weeks, he wore these wherever he went, indoors and out, rain and shine. His inquisitiveness wore Kate out. A million questions formed – and his mind raced ahead of them. 'What happens to the sea?' 'Where does it end?' 'What makes waves?' – this after they had spent a freezing Easter weekend in Jersey, staying at a hotel near the Faradays. Three mornings a week, then, he went off to a playgroup, where he spent hours building with blocks in a corner with his special friend. Although Guy believed that everybody was his friend. 'Will you come to my house for lunch?' he enquired politely of a pretty young woman when he and Kate were standing waiting for the lights to change on their way home from school one day. Kate thought, terrified, that he would undoubtedly go off anywhere with anyone who asked him. He had no sense of danger.

With Guy no longer a baby, Kate had time for herself again. She took a course in horticulture and one morning a week she attended art class. A local hostel for foreign girls, in London to learn English, provided an endless stream of baby-sitters. Laura, approving of Kate's venturing outside her home, encouraged her. She had become every inch the smart business-woman, always wearing sharp suits and carrying a slim brief-case under her arm. Her tiny showroom-cum-shop had become a byword in rarified chic. She had thrown out all the light, airy wallpapers she started with; now, everything in the shop was dark and rich and vibrant. Her signature colours were burgundy, navy, pewter, deepest green, old gold – and black, black, black. So also were the astoundingly expensive personal gifts like small boxes and cushions and frames which she also stocked. Kate privately thought the whole place was ridiculous – but *Vogue* devoted two whole pages to photograph-ing Laura there, in several poses, draped over various pieces of guilded furniture. And the customers, from New York and Paris and Milan and every corner of the globe, flocked.

She and Lucy were still very close. Laura had taken her to Spain for a week one spring holiday and Kate often heard her whispering and giggling into the phone – and knew instinc-tively that it was Laura she was speaking to. But Laura had remained the bachelor girl-about-town. She still saw Jake either in London or New York. Much of his work was still with what had been Condicote, so Kate knew when he was in London from Robin. And she also knew, from various off-hand remarks Laura made, that she was still close to Nico Kirilov ... But since Guy's birth and her obsession with her *outré* shop, she had remained aloof and breezy. She came and went as she chose, answerable to no one; she worked tirelessly at getting her shop's image right and played her emotional cards close to her chest.

Occasionally, Kate thought she sounded hard. There was an edge to her voice, close to bitterness, which was something new. No confidences were given – but Kate, entranced by Guy, absorbed in her own lovely life, hadn't asked for any. It was Felicity Holford who remarked to Laura crisply that if she wanted a family she was leaving things a bit late – the twins were now well into their thirties. But Laura only shrugged and remarked 'To each her own, Mother dear . . .'

Imperceptibly, after the sale of Condicote, Kate and Robin's life changed gear – into considerable affluence. Thanks to the Faradays' generosity, their married life had always been financially secure. Educational trust funds were set up for both the children. But now, most material things were within their grasp. They dined out often and went to the opera, which they both loved, as a matter of course. Kate chose the clothes which became her and which Robin liked her to wear – soft skirts and cashmere sweaters for the day; draped Jean Muir dresses, perfectly disguising her left arm, at night.

Often, he bought her presents for no reason; he had always been generous, even in the early years of their marriage when Condicote was struggling. But now, he went out of his way to find a particularly fine pair of earrings or a bracelet; or to bid for a picture that he knew she admired at one of the auction houses.

'Robin's been at it again I see,' Laura would say crossly, seizing and examining her wrist or catching sight of a new painting. She had sharp eyes and missed nothing material. 'Goodness, what a spoiled lady you're getting these days . . .'

Robin was often away now – on business in New York or the Far East. And he skiied regularly twice each winter, sometimes still with Rupert and Jill, sometimes going off on his own. He went to China with a business delegation for three weeks. Kate went with him once to New York but she came back exhausted, not liking the noise and speed of the place – all the things that Robin and Laura had assured her were so

177

exhilarating. And when Robin was away, she had Guy now – not just Lucy who in any case, young as she was, went her own way. And with whom Kate was still not entirely at ease. But Guy was always companionable. Like Kate, he loved the freedom of Knyght's Wood where he could run in the orchard, climb trees and go for walks in the woods above. When they were there together, alone, the two of them never ran out of things to do or places to explore. Whereas Lucy had always found the country boring, her life centred on her London school-friends. The cry: 'When are we going back to London?' was one of her first whole sentences.

Mrs Bundy still did the house and helped with the cooking. Through the church, which she attended regularly, Kate had met local people and got the feel of village life. And with the financial means and her vastly increased knowledge, she was preoccupied with making the garden at Knyght's Wood beautiful. There was always something new to consider – changing a bed or trying out a particular plant. Finding her gardening feet, a source of great joy, she wanted exuberance – colour tumbling over walls, apparently artless wildness. It was, Robin told her laughingly when they were walking round in the sweet dusk of a summer evening, her romantic nature asserting itself . . .

Her father had found her a reliable local gardener, Peters, who took pride in the place. In summer, the herbaceous border was superb – colourful but restrained, full of depth contrast. Delphiniums and lupins, peonies and pinks, sweet williams and snapdragons. Tall, deep-scented lilies. Between the three of them – the gardener, Kate and her father – a new seating area had been designed, riotous with honeysuckle and climbing roses and a billowing lavender border. The painted wooden furniture was placed on a base of Portland stone at the exact point where the eye looked through a gap in the trees, beyond the village, right down to the winding river. They grew all their own vegetables and soft fruit. Kate was pondering a conservatory or a gazebo. Or perhaps, Robin suggested, a summerhouse . . .

So when Robin went off crewing on a boat in the Caribbean for three weeks, Kate took his absence in her stride. His yen for adventure was an integral part of his nature; Kate had long since accepted that – had done so years ago in the Luxembourg Gardens . . . 'Travelling to odd corners of the world,' he had said. 'The wilder the better . . .' She could picture him doing so – even then. And he had been preoccupied lately; vague and evasive when she asked him about the office. It had all become so big now, not like the old Condicote days. A break like this would do him good.

And there was no question of her going, they had never even discussed it . . . Her limp was more pronounced every year now – she knew that and she knew that it was progressive. Her left arm, too, was noticeably weaker. She tired more quickly. Her father had taken her to a Harley Street specialist soon after Guy was born. Her condition, of which she was so well aware, had been carefully and kindly explained to her. It was expected that her good right hip would eventually be affected; there was a brief discussion of therapy and a possible operation. But all this was in the future. She could cope easily with her life as it was. She simply hoped that nothing in it would change.

While Robin was crewing on the boat, lapping up the sunshine, Kate and Guy came down to Knyght's Wood. It was April, the school holidays, and Lucy had gone off to France for a week on a school trip. Kate, guilty at the thought of a whole week alone at Knyght's Wood with Guy, had fussed inordinately before she left. She had insisted on phoning the Bergers and arranging for Lucy to spend part of a day with them. They had grandchildren now of the same age; and Ina had always enjoyed young people around her. Lucy, who liked the Bergers, seemed moderately pleased.

One cold, windy afternoon, when the early blossoms were blowing a blizzard, John Holford left Felicity struggling with a chapter and drove over. He could never resist an hour or so with Guy; his eyes, Kate always noticed, lit up at the sight of him. Guy had run on ahead as he and Kate were walking slowly down to the orchard, pointing out clumps of primroses and discussing the planting for the summer. Startled, they heard Guy shrieking, 'Grandpa, Grandpa . . . look . . . it's a snake and I hate it, hate it . . .' He came flying up the path towards them, cheeks red, eyes wide with horror. He flung himself on his grandfather. 'Come and see, come on ...' – tugging urgently at John Holford's hand. 'Quickly, quickly ...'

'All right, old chap, I will. Now calm down ...'

Smiling, Kate watched them go off together – hand in hand. Her father, silver-haired and handsome still – bending down to listen, rapt. Guy, trotting along beside him, jeans tucked into his boots, looking up at him, talking a mile a minute. The fierce wind from behind blew her hair flat onto her face and she put her hands in the pockets of her old sheepskin jacket and hugged it round her. What a lovely sight they made ... Surely it could only have been a grass snake, nothing dangerous. She wished that Robin could have been there with her to see them. But he'll be home next week, she thought happily. Wednesday – or was it Thursday?

The September after Guy was five, he started school all day – in a small private school ten minutes' walk from the house. He had been chattering about it for weeks; this was a 'proper' school, he told everyone, not for 'babies' like the one he had just left. He had a school uniform of short grey trousers, blue blazer and blue and red tie. Kate admitted to a pang when he was shorn of his fair curls. With his hair cut short, darker and neatly parted, he looked ridiculously like Robin.

They both took him on his first day. He left them with hardly a backward glance, running towards a group of children in his class, wearing his shiny new shoes and carrying a satchel that looked enormous. Robin, glancing at his watch – he was already late for a meeting – went on to the office, and Kate walked home alone.

In the early part of the winter, quite unexpectedly, she and Robin bumped into Laura and Nico at the theatre. Neither Kate nor Robin had seen Nico for more than a year. Sensibly, Laura kept Nico in one compartment of her life; her family in another. It was Kate who spotted them as they walked to the bar in the interval. Laura had her back turned and at first, she thought she must have made a mistake. They looked such an unexceptional pair – at least Nico did. And Kate had always thought of Nico Kirilov as such a handsome and virile man,

180

sweeping Laura off her feet – as indeed he had done. She had never forgotten coming upon them dancing alone in the dining-room at Lucy's christening, lost to everyone else in the world except each other.

Nico had aged noticeably – those long bouts of emotional illness which Laura sometimes hinted at had taken their toll. His hair was quite grey and his face was drawn. Laura flicked something off his shoulder and slipped her arm through his. They might have been any ordinary married couple, out for the evening. Laura was dressed, as she usually was these days, in starkest black. She had on large glasses, the first time Kate had seen her in them, and very little make-up. Kate thought she looked decidedly plain. She nudged Robin.

'Look – over there . . . it's Laura and Nico . . .'

'Where? Is it really? Oh my God, I think you're right. Laura wearing glasses, is she . . .? They're bound to see us. Shall we go over and ask them to have a drink?'

'We'd better . . .'

While Robin and Nico were shouldering their way, quite amicably, to the bar, Kate and Laura talked as best they could in the middle of the crowded lobby.

'I hardly recognised Nico, Laura . . .'

'You haven't seem him for a year or so . . .'

'No – well, he's changed a lot . . .'

'He looks older, you mean?'

'Yes.'

Instinctively, they looked over to where Robin and Nico had reached the seething bar. Robin, taller than most, still fresh-faced, had dealt with the payment and was holding a drink in each hand above the heads of people still waiting in the queue. Nico, also carrying two drinks, was following.

'Jake was over the other day, Katie . . .'

'I know. Robin said – and I wondered if you'd be seeing him. Is he still besotted?'

Laura smiled ruefully. 'You could say that . . . in fact, he delivered an ultimatum. Marry him and go and live in New York – or it's all over.'

'You'd have a good life, Laura,' Kate said carefully. And so she would. Surely by now she had had enough of running

181

around London, fêted for her strange little shop which was really just a shrine to the avant-garde taste she had developed? 'You love New York, you know you do – Jake is a super person – and you're not getting . . .'

'*Any younger*,' Laura finished, laughing. 'Quite. And you've noticed the glasses . . . I'm blind as a bat these days. It happened quite suddenly. But I get enough of the ageing single woman line from Mother, thank you. Anyhow,' she said quietly, 'I told him no. Very firm I was. I've wavered a lot – but not any longer. He's a great chap, but he's not for me.'

Robin and Nico, only feet away, were deep in conversation. Nico had become suddenly animated, gesticulating, his eyes blazing, more the way Kate remembered him from the past.

'So it's Nico?'

'Yes, yes it is. And I've got the oddest feeling somehow that we'll end up together. We don't even have spectacular rows any more . . . Let's go and rescue our drinks before Nico spills the lot, shall we? He's in full flood on something or other . . . How's Luce? And tell me how Guy has settled in his big new school . . .'

'He loves it . . .' As always, Kate's face brightened at the mention of his name. 'He can't wait to get there in the mornings. But Lucy is a bit of a trial these days – the standard moody teenager . . .'

That Christmas, the whole family came to Knyght's Wood. The previous summer, they had completed a major extension – renovated the kitchen, enlarged the dining-room and built on two more bedrooms and a bathroom. Although they had been careful to retain its period charm, Knyght's Wood was now a substantial home. There would be plenty of room for the Faradays who were coming over from Jersey. Jim Faraday had had a mild stroke and Kate was anxious that he spend a comfortable few days with them. Mrs Bundy, as she always did, had provided a hefty Christmas fruit-cake, lavishly iced. Mr Bundy had cut down and brought over the tree as a present and Kate and Guy got out all the old lights and ornaments, saved and added to through the years, and decorated it until there was hardly a bare branch to be seen.

While they were doing this – Guy flushed with excitement, standing on tiptoe – Kate was determinedly ignoring Lucy's baleful adolescent presence upstairs. Always touchy, over the past months she had become a full-blown, often sullen, teenager. Neither Robin nor Kate could communicate with her. Almost any remonstration ended in a row – with Lucy storming out of the room . . . Only Laura occasionally had her confidence.

Now, Knyght's Wood literally shook to powerful rock music on the hi-fi in her room. She was fifteen, long-legged and reedslim and more off-hand and moody than ever. Copying Laura – or so Kate suspected – she dressed in strange black garments almost exclusively. Robin gave her a modest allowance – and Kate felt helpless to exert any influence. She had done exceptionally well in her exams last summer and was nagging to be sent to a coeducational boarding school, with a fashionable reputation, which wasn't very far from Laverton. Robin, who thought Lucy needed treating with a very firm hand, had already told her: 'No, Lucy, nothing doing. Sorry. Your London school is excellent – and you've done very well there. I can't see any point in changing now . . . none at all.' – and, as Lucy glowered and fumed, had gone straight on reading his paper. He refused point-blank to reopen the subject. All they needed, he told Kate, was Lucy thrown together – more-or-less unsupervised – with a group of adolescent boys.

Kate wasn't so sure. Although she sometimes wondered, guiltily, if *she* wouldn't be happier with Lucy packed off and out of the way for a good deal of the time. The secretiveness and the door-banging were getting her down. There were never any complaints about her schoolwork; but what she and her pals got up to out of school, Kate shuddered to think. She knew perfectly well that she smoked, although never when Robin was around. Her attempts at discipline were, she knew, feeble. Lucy undoubtedly thought so too. And Robin was so often away or overworked or unwinding from a demanding business trip. She had never found Lucy receptive. Lately, there had been very little give-and-take between them. Lucy had brains and a strong personality; her negative, brooding presence could quickly cast a blight on the household. She wondered what Laura thought ... she wasn't even sure that they were still particularly friendly. Lucy regarded all adults with suspicion. Anyhow, she would sound her out over Christmas and see if she had any ideas about the different school; or what could be done to make her happier with her life.

Boom, thud, boom, thud, boom, thud, boom ... Lucy's amplifiers, at full throttle, were right above their heads. The glistening baubles on the Christmas tree trembled. Just as Kate thought her nerves would snap, it was Guy – loved by both Kate and Lucy, the one genuine bridge between them – who volunteered to go up and tell Lucy that the music was much too loud and, possibly, disturbing the village too; Kate having wondered aloud what the people in the nearby row of cottages could be thinking about it.

'I'll go, I don't mind,' Guy said equably, trudging off. 'You know how she is, Mummy ... she just sits there all curled up with her legs over the chair and twiddles her hair. And Granny Faraday will have a fit if she has that noise going on all Christmas, so Lucy might as well stop it now ...' And off he went.

Kate, on her knees in front of the tree where she and Guy had been piling presents, started clearing up extra lights and bits of tinsel. After a few minutes, the deafening thump quietened and stopped. She could hear her children's voices – Guy's high-pitched and childish, Lucy's fluting, like her mother's and Laura's. They went on and on ... Guy was having a pleasant conversation with Lucy, something that she and Robin despaired of. Soon, they were laughing – and she hadn't heard Lucy laugh openly for months. Kate closed her eyes, sighed with relief, and said a silent, grateful prayer for Guy.

Laura arrived down from London just before lunch on Christmas Day in a new dark blue BMW. She spent much of the day dodging both her mother and Doris Faraday. After disliking each other for years – Doris considering Felicity Holford 'stuck-up and odd', Felicity finding Doris Faraday 'frankly, a bore' – the two grandmothers had at last become friends. As they both realised, they had nothing in common except the family – but it was enough. Particularly after Guy's birth.

Felicity Holford had also come to use her as a sounding board for her continuing disapproval of Laura's personal life. And Doris Faraday – tut-tutting and thinking Laura a right baggage, and getting on a bit too now – sympathised. It was high time she stopped racketing around, put paid to this nasty association with a married man, and settled down. In her opinion, John and Felicity Holford were right to be worried about her. Accustomed to speaking her mind, she was just waiting for the opportunity. So far, Laura had eluded her.

'Ma Faraday has a wild look in her eye,' Laura told Kate while they were clearing up in the kitchen after lunch. Guy, pushing his new bike, had gone out for a walk with Robin and his two grandfathers; Felicity Holford and Doris Faraday were sitting speaking in whispers in front of the sitting-room fire. 'She can't wait to have a go at me – *help* . . .'

Kate laughed and threw her a clean cloth.

'She says it's time you were 'settled'. Do some work and stay in here with me and you'll be safe. As long as she doesn't get you on your own in a dark corner . . . Tell me, what do you think of Lucy these days?'

'Luce? Well – it's a tricky stage, isn't it? She not very forthcoming even with me. She hardly said a word at lunch. Just glowered. Do you want me to have a go at her?'

'Would you, Laura? She's always loved you. I'm nowhere compared to you with her – never have been,' Kate said ruefully. 'She's dead set on going to this boarding school, Yarnston – and Robin won't hear of it. You know how forceful Lucy is when she's got the bit between her teeth. Personally, I'm not sure . . .' She sighed. 'It might be better to get her away, off on her own. We've heard excellent reports of the school – and this is important because she's clever. She would walk over any teacher she didn't respect. An old friend of Robin's has a child there who's very happy . . . Robin thinks it's just because they have boys there that Lucy's so keen . . .'

'That's not a bad reason,' Laura said briskly, putting away a pile of plates in the cupboard. 'I'll see if she opens up a bit to me. Isn't she going to Paris to stay with the Bergers soon?'

'That's right, on the 28th.' She turned from the sink to face Laura, hands dripping, pushing her hair out of her eyes with her arm. Laura thought she looked tired – not to be wondered with all this family festivity to be coped with. 'Ina offered and we thought it would be something interesting for her until school starts again. Her French is already good. And Ina is such a dear, clever woman. She might be able to help Lucy with whatever it is she's going through,' Kate said hopefully.

Laura shook her head.

'I doubt it. It's just growing up, Katie. And I think it's harder than when we were her age – not so many rules these days. Don't you remember how Mother and Pa fussed when *you* went off to Paris to the Bergers for all that time? And we were a lot older than Lucy is . . .'

'And look what happened to me there . . .'

They laughed.

'I tell you what, Katie . . . if she wants to, Lucy can come back with me, today. You've got quite enough on your hands here. But she'll have to behave – no sulking. And I'll put her to work. We're marking things down for the sale and she can help . . . then she can go straight off to Paris . . .'

'Oh Laura, would you? Do ask her . . . I'm sure you'll find her skulking in her room. She shuts herself up there for hours on end.'

Chapter 18

When she could bear to look back, in a time of terrible bleakness, Kate would think that it was during that damp, grey English winter – the winter after they had all spent Christmas at Knyght's Wood – that their luck began to run out. And yet, ironically, she was still so happy then . . .

Waiting with a group of mothers to pick up Guy from school was always a highpoint of her day. She warmed to the sight of him coming down the steps – clutching something he had made, tie askew, socks around his ankles. But there was so much else to fill her day that she was for ever looking at her watch, hurrying, rushing out to the car or waiting impatiently for a bus that wouldn't come . . . Encouraged by Robin and her father, she combed the galleries and was starting to acquire some good paintings. Full of ideas for the garden in the coming spring and summer she searched through the colourful gardening catalogues. Lucy was always a bit of a worry; but she was more talkative these days and working diligently towards the next set of exams. Laura and the Bergers had done her a lot of good, and Laura had promised to take her off somewhere during the Easter holidays, perhaps to France. Mercifully, she seemed to have dropped her boarding school mania for the present.

And although she felt herself at heart a countrywoman, Kate was making the most of London then: concerts, a matinée with a friend, the galleries. With taste and money, she dressed beautifully. Even Laura grudgingly admitted that she never wore a garment that didn't look exactly right – both for her and for wherever she happened to be. And she and Robin went out endlessly to theatres and restaurants, Henley and Glyndebourne in the summer. They often had London friends or business acquaintances of Robin's to spend the weekends at Knyght's Wood. Kate had forgotten what it was like to feel shy and uncertain. People were always telling her, in those days, how well she looked; she could feel herself blossoming like a well tended plant. And that winter, for once, she didn't have a single cold.

Also looking back, one afternoon in particular stood out in her mind. It must have been mid January as she was rushing back from an art class. When she got off the bus, the sky was faintly pink. She thought: the days are lengthening, it's the first time I've noticed. There was a bucket of daffodils stuck among the fruit in front of the Jones's shop – and she popped in and bought a couple of bunches, calling out to Kev not to bother to wrap them, she was going straight home. And when she rounded the corner, Guy was at the window, still wearing his school blazer, cramming something in his mouth, waiting for her. She remembered that too, her eyes closing and her heart dropping like a stone.

After January – February.

There was the dinner-party in Bryanston Square on a Saturday night. That, too, was vivid in her mind. It was the first weekend Robin had been home for a month . . . He had taken to dashing off on quick ski trips, leaving the office for the airport at midday on Friday, getting back at noon on Monday. He had been angling to take Guy. Next year, they both agreed, next year when he's six.

And it was while they were driving towards Bryanston Square that Robin said abruptly, apparently out of the blue, 'There's something I've been meaning to tell you, Kate . . . I'm fed up with the job. Sick and tired of it. All the fun's gone out of it. As a matter of fact, I'm thinking of packing it in . . .' He spoke rapidly.

'*Robin* . . .' Jerked out of her cocoon of complacency, Kate turned towards him. He was looking straight ahead, driving the powerful car swiftly through the glistening streets. 'But you couldn't . . . I mean, it's all going so successfully. And Big Bang – deregulation or whatever it is – is about to happen – it's all go . . . You're too important to the firm. And besides, when they bought Condicote out you signed a contract . . .'

'I could make an arrangement . . .' He zoomed, too fast, along a broad crescent. 'There are ways . . .'

'But – but what would you *do?*'

'Other things, something quite different perhaps . . .' He hadn't even glanced towards her. His jaw was squared. 'But you're right. It's all a pipe dream, wishful thinking . . .'

As he backed the car into a parking space, he caught the bewilderment on her face. He laughed, suddenly relaxed.

'Don't worry, darling. I'm only thinking aloud. Forget I ever said it. All right?' He gave her a quick kiss on the cheek. 'Put it down to an attack of middle-age blues . . .'

And she did forget – for a very long time . . .

Old friends had invited them to dinner. It was an evening which began with effervescent gaiety and gradually settled into the mellow intimacy of a good dinner-party. There were ten people, seated at a rectangular table; and everyone seemed to have some interest, or acquaintance, in common.

Towards the end of the meal, their host stood and offered a brief toast to one of the couples who had just married. And after the fuss had subsided, Robin – looking diagonally across at Kate – asked the woman on his left, the recent bride, how she had met her husband. It turned out to be very conventional – one expansive Sunday lunch at her cousin's house . . . Robin then described to the table at large, briefly and amusingly, how he had seen Kate sitting two tables away from him in the café on the Left Bank, made up some fatuous excuse to do with a Michelin guide – and got up and joined her.

Everyone, including Kate, laughed.

'A marvellous story – but it can't be true surely?' their hostess asked Kate from the head of the table. 'It's like a book or a film – not real life . . .'

'It's *just* how it happened,' Kate said charmingly, smiling, earrings glinting.

As they walked back to the drawing-room after dinner, Kate

189

passed Robin, very close. Their hands touched – and they exchanged quick, knowing smiles. They would make love tonight . . . Then they attached themselves to different groups while coffee was poured. Kate found herself sitting beside the fireplace, Robin's old partner, Rupert, standing next to her. Robin was talking to his wife at the far end of the room.

'You've heard about our Miss America in the office, I expect,' Rupert said, looking down at her, holding a coffee cup. 'We're all tickled pink . . .'

Which was how, Kate would remember one day, BJ Carson first entered her life.

'I don't believe so. Should I know?' Her head tilted upwards.

'Oh – hasn't Robin told you? The New York office has sent her over here for a year to learn our marketplace . . . She's extremely bright, a graduate of the Harvard Business School and all that. A law degree too. They're grooming her for high places. This year is more of a learning holiday. They don't want to lose her at head office in New York. They've even provided her with a rented flat in Knightsbridge, very ritzy . . .'

'I see . . .' Kate put her coffee cup on a low table. 'No, I don't think Robin has mentioned her . . .'

'I'm extremely surprised, Kate.' Rupert looked it; he also appeared slightly taken aback. 'As a matter of fact, we all tease him about her unmercifully. She's taken rather a shine to Robin – insists on sitting in on his meetings and so forth. She's not backward about coming forward, either. She makes her point – and they're always devastatingly good ones – in this husky Southern drawl. She comes from North Carolina. Actually, she's a very bubbly girl – and great fun . . .'

Kate laughed.

'How intriguing. I must ask Robin. What's she called? Scarlett O'Hara?'

'Nothing so romantic. BJ Carson . . . God knows what the initials stand for. Americans do that with names sometimes, don't they? But BJ's an absolutely gorgeous girl – big and blonde and beautiful. Extremely tall. Great clothes. And very forceful – not to mention tough. The accent is deceiving . . .'

Kate laughed. She had the faintest intimation that Rupert was needling her.

'How very amusing.' She held out her cup for more coffee –
and deftly changed the subject.

Key in the ignition, Robin turned to Kate. He said urgently,
'Let's go straight down to the country – to Knyght's Wood . . .'

'What – now?' Kate said stupidly. It was nothing he had
ever suggested before. And it was she, not Robin, who really
loved the place. So why . . . ? All evening there had been
something in his manner that had puzzled her.

'Yes. Now. Please, Kate darling.' His hand on her thigh.

'But it's so late Robin . . . and the children . . .'

'You worry about them too much . . . they're all right.
Monique's with them and she's very responsible . . .' This was
true. She was the best part-time, live-in help they had ever
had; over from France to live with a family and attend classes
for part of every day. Guy adored her – and Lucy practised her
French on her relentlessly. She was handy round the house
too. And pleasant. They all liked her.

'Yes – but Guy's not a hundred per cent. I've been worried
about him . . .' Guy had had a particularly nasty ear infection
which was followed by a fluey cold and had been under the
weather for a couple of weeks now. Tony Martin had seen him
several times. He had finished a long course of antibiotics, but
he still looked peaky – and was off school. 'Give him a couple
more days at home,' Tony had said seriously. 'Watch him,
Kate – and see how he goes . . .'

'He was better today,' Robin countered. 'When we went for
a jog in the park, he was quite bright. A bit of air did him
good . . . We can phone Monique on our way. And Lucy must
have got back from her party hours ago.' This party, plus the
tail end of Guy's cold, was why they had stayed in London that
weekend. The dinner, which they had both enjoyed, had only
been arranged a couple of days before. 'Say yes, darling –
please . . .'

And so she did.

They slid out of London – it was well after midnight and
there was very little traffic – and started belting down the
motorway. An almost full moon shone silkily. Monique, when
phoned, had reported all well at home. Guy had spent the

191

evening playing with his toy soldiers. He insisted that he was going to ride his bike in the park next day. He had eaten a huge dinner. Lucy had been dropped home from the party, right on time, by the parents of a friend. Monique had already locked up – and was off to bed herself.

'He'll miss us in the morning – Guy will.' Kate imagined him flying into their room in his blue striped pyjamas, hair tousled, still half asleep; diving into the bed between them . . .

'We'll see him soon . . .' He felt for her hand. 'I want you to myself tonight . . .'

'I know . . .'

Robin said nothing – but the speedometer leapt, pushing eighty. It would be the first time, or almost so, that they had been alone since Greece. Something quickened in Kate. She was already given up to the intimacy of being alone with Robin in the enclosed darkness. Towns, houses, petrol stations flashing by. She sighed – these days there was always the children, the garden, domestic chores. She hated travelling – and Robin was always on the go.

A couple of miles from Laverton, when they had left the motorway and were snaking through narrow country roads, Kate said, 'What's all this about a beautiful young American woman in the office then? Brainy too . . . BJ someone . . . Have I got a rival?' She gave him a seductive sideways smile, watching his profile in the dashboard glow.

'Don't be ridiculous . . . What on earth do you mean ?' he said sharply, braking before a curve.

'Rupert told me. Tonight – after dinner. He said she was after you . . . or implied so . . .' – mischievous, utterly confident. Not so much as a glimmer of uncertainty in her head.

'Absurd. Rupert has a big mouth. He always did have.'

He's touchy, Kate thought – touchy. Overdoing the work, as usual.

And that was the end of that.

They were there – home. Through the village and round the corner and easing into the gates of Knyght's Wood. Up the drive, past the ghostly shrubs . . . Robin fished the key out from under the flowerpot. They went straight upstairs.

Without any preliminaries, Robin threw off his clothes and

flung back the bedspread. He grasped her wrist. Her dress landed on a chair and she found one of her earrings the next morning embedded in the rug. He made love to her roughly, almost violently. Kate froze. Words like 'stop', 'please wait', 'don't ...' came to her lips – but were not uttered. She gave up. He slept almost immediately. Kate lay there – shivering and cold and shocked, her mind blank. After a while, she got up, washed her face and put on a warm flannel nightgown. When she crept back to bed, Robin hadn't moved. He was snoring. She lay awake through the still hours – until at last, when the birds began to chorus, she fell into an unquiet sleep.

She slept on until after ten. When she woke – to lemony sunshine and a heartbreakingly lovely thrush's song – Robin wasn't there. She could smell fresh coffee. Soon Robin appeared, pushing the door open with a tray, clumsily feeling his way across the sunny room. He banged the tray down on the dressing-table and came and sat by her on the bed. He was fully dressed in his old corduroys and red sweater. His hair had fallen over his forehead. He looked for all the world like Guy when he had done something naughty – and been found out. He picked up her hand and held it against his cheek.

'Forgive me?'
Kate nodded.
'The coffee smells good.'
'Truly forgiven?' He wouldn't release her hand.
'Truly.'
What she wanted to ask but didn't was – *why?*

Kate skipped church. They went for a gentle stroll and had lunch at the pub. In the afternoon they poked around the desolate garden – and discussed a summerhouse seriously. When they phoned Monique, she reported that she had just come back from taking Guy and his bike to the park and he was tearing round the house with a model plane they had just put together. He was eating better than he had done for a couple of weeks. Even Kate was reassured. There was no reason for him not to go back to school on Monday; Tony

Martin had agreed that he should. And he was begging to go . . . Lucy was stuck in her room doing a difficult homework project – apparently to loud music. When Robin suggested staying over and driving up early tomorrow morning Kate – lulled as she always was by the peace of the country – agreed.

The Holfords came over in the early evening. They were planning a leisurely stay in Tuscany this spring, and brought maps and guidebooks with them. Robin and John Holford pored over them at the dining-room table while Kate and her mother went out into the garden and made idle suggestions about a summerhouse. Felicity thought Kate looked well – and said so. 'Oh and did you know that the Kirilovs really are getting a divorce at last?' she asked as they walked back up the sloping lawn to the house. 'I had lunch with Laura in London last week – and she mentioned it very casually. It's definite, she said. I had the feeling that questions would not be welcome . . . I have learnt *some* things . . . Did she tell you?'

'No,' Kate said. She stopped, surprised. 'No – Laura hasn't said anything. You know we met them at the theatre not long ago . . . We both thought Nico looked – well, much older. Do you suppose that means . . .'

'That they'll get married? I honestly don't know, Kate darling . . .' She linked her arm through Kate's. Her voice was as light as a young girl's. 'Even I have come to accept, at last, that Laura has to live her life the way she sees it – and there's absolutely nothing I can do about it. Let's ask Robin to get us a sherry . . .'

'You're sure Guy's well enough to go back to school tomorrow?' John Holford said quietly to Kate. Robin and Felicity were involved with the map of Tuscany. 'He had a serious ear infection – and I don't care for ear infections, never have, dangerous things. Very nasty. And then a lingering cold, you say. I know he's finished the medication – and Tony's looking after him – but it might be wise to give him a few more days away from a classroom of coughs and sneezes.' He looked worried, tapping his finger on the table. 'Particularly at this time of year . . .'

'When Tony checked his ear he said to watch him – but he thought a couple more days at home would be enough. He hasn't had a temperature all week and his cold has almost cleared up. He's so much better, Pa . . . Monique had him out again today. And he's eating properly. Now he's back to normal he gets so bored at home.'

'Very well, my darling. You know best.'

They let the fire go out, collected up the papers and went to bed early. Robin made up in tenderness, many times over, all he had lacked the night before. Kissing and kissing the nape of her neck, he found – or said he did – her first grey hairs. And it was Kate – warm and loved and happy – who fell asleep first that night.

Chapter 19

In the morning, early enough to avoid the worst traffic, they set off back to London. It was another bright winter's day. In what she would come to think of as a different life, Kate would marvel at how carefree they were that morning, purring along in the expensive car; talking on and off; listening to the news on the radio. They had both agreed, sometime during those long, lost hours in bed the night before, that they must make the effort to spend more time alone together. And now, Kate had nothing more pressing on her mind than plans for the summerhouse. That, too, she would find incredible – that something like a summerhouse could ever have been of the least importance to her.

She dropped Robin off at a convenient underground and made her way home via the local shops. It was nearly eleven when she unlocked the door and went into the narrow hall, carrying the shopping bags. There was nobody in. The cleaning lady never came on Mondays and Monique would be off at her English classes. The phone rang immediately. Kate answered. It was the nurse from Guy's school.

'Guy's not himself at all today, Mrs Faraday . . . He's got a bit of a temperature and he's quite flushed. He's coughing too. I've got him in my room with me. I think you should come and fetch him and take him home . . .' She sounded cautious. 'Pity, since it's his first day back . . .'

'I'll be there in a few minutes. Tell Guy I'm coming, would you?' And Kate went straight back out again, fur jacket over her country jeans, leaving the shopping on the hall floor.

Guy was sprawled at a table, one hand holding his head. He

glared at Kate quite balefully when she came in. He didn't run to her as she expected.

'I don't see why I've got to go home when I've just come back.' He sounded tearful. Kate saw at once that his cheeks were unnaturally red – and his eyes looked heavy.

'Poor old love . . . it *is* bad luck,' Kate said sympathetically, touching his forehead. Guy jerked away from her and made no move to get up. Kate and the nurse exchanged glances over his head. 'We thought you were all better, didn't we? Monique did too. But I'm sure Nurse is right – I'll take you home and pop you into bed. Have you got your coat?'

'It's here, Mrs Faraday,' the nurse said quickly. 'And his scarf. And gloves. Come along now Guy . . .'

Reluctantly, he stood up – looking cross and sullen – and allowed himself to be bundled into his things.

'I want to bring my books – and my writing things. I *said* so . . . and I'm not going home without them. I'm *not* . . .' With Guy, everything had to be exact. 'I want the red writing book, the one we're doing now . . .'

Kate thought he was going to start crying. Nurse was right; he wasn't at all like himself. She remembered what her father had said the night before and a spasm of anxiety gripped her.

'The teacher – Mrs Smith – brought these.' There was a small pile of school-books on the table. 'These are the ones you're to take, aren't they Guy?'

Guy nodded and sniffed and rubbed his eyes with the back of his hand.

'Right then,' Kate said briskly. 'Let's put them in your satchel – and we're off . . .'

On the school steps, Kate holding Guy's hand – he was drooping against her, kicking at the ground with his shoe – the nurse said, worried, 'I do think he ought to be seen by a doctor, Mrs Faraday. It's possible that the ear infection hasn't quite cleared up. He's always such a sunny little lad.'

'I know. You're right – he's not himself. I'll get in touch with the doctor as soon as we get home . . .' They walked down the steps to the car, Kate half dragging Guy. There was a cutting wind despite the bright sun – and he began to cough drily. Beside the car, Kate pulled his scarf higher, round his ears. 'Thank you so much, Nurse . . . goodbye . . .'

'Let me know how he's getting along. Goodbye, Guy. I hope you'll be feeling lots better soon. I'll go and tell Mrs Smith that you've gone home . . .' she called, shivering in the doorway, waving to them as Kate drove off. Guy, who had insisted on sitting in the back, hunched up in his grey coat, ignored her.

Once they were home, Kate put Guy straight to bed. He coughed frequently – and his nose was running. He was fractious and whiney. He didn't want *anything*, he told her . . . he just wanted to be left at school with his friends. It wasn't fair. And they were going on an expedition walk that afternoon to look for special plants. But after Kate had tucked him in, as she left the room, she saw him turn over on his side – his thumb in his mouth, clutching his bear – and shut his eyes.

She phoned the surgery, quickly explaining Guy's recent illness and apparent relapse. She was genuinely worried now. 'I really must speak to Dr Martin,' she said, quite breathless. 'Will you tell him . . .' The receptionist cut across her. Dr Martin was with a patient, she would see he got the message and he would phone back when he could. Her number please . . .

Kate wandered about the house, clasping and unclasping her hands. She wanted to phone Robin – but she should speak to Tony Martin first and keep the line clear. Whenever she looked in on Guy he seemed to be asleep. Once or twice he muttered and tossed restlessly. Kate felt his forehead repeatedly. He was hot to the touch – but his face looked drained and pale.

Tony Martin rang back in about an hour. He was crisp, even with Kate. He was under a lot of pressure, one of his partners was off with flu, and yes, there was an unpleasant bug around causing a lot of problems. He listened carefully to her description of Guy. Was he complaining of anything in particular? Earache? Headache? Stiff neck? Had he vomited?

'No – no, nothing like that. No more problem with the ear. He had a slight temperature when I picked him up at school. I haven't taken it since – he's been sleeping, on and off, although he's cross at being home. He's just very irritable, not like himself. Nurse, at school, said the same. I'd like you to see him, Tony. As soon as possible.'

'All right. Of course.' He knew Kate understood illness; he had caught the anxiety in her voice. A touch of panic. 'Look, I'll be round as soon as I've finished the afternoon surgery . . . between four and five. See you then.'

Calmer, Kate went back up to Guy's room. He was awake.

'I feel sick,' he said. 'And my head hurts – all over.' Seconds later, he vomited. Kate cleaned him up and changed his pyjamas and popped him back in bed. He closed his eyes and seemed to go off into a doze. Putting towels to soak in the bathroom, Kate heard Monique come in downstairs. Her classes finished about midday. Guy was lying quietly, so she went down to the kitchen.

'It's Guy,' she told Monique, tense. 'He's ill again, I'm afraid. The nurse rang from school and I went and fetched him. He's got a bit of a temperature – and he's just been sick . . .'

Monique looked stricken.

'Oh Mrs Faraday . . . I am so sorry, the poor little boy. This morning he was perfectly all right. He could not wait to go to school . . . you can ask Lucy . . .' She had gone white. 'I would never have taken him if I had thought . . .'

Kate touched her shoulder. All in grey with her long dark hair hanging limply, she looked waif-like. Thick glasses gave her a studious air.

'Monique, *of course* you wouldn't have,' Kate said warmly. 'We all thought he was perfectly fine, completely recovered. He was on Saturday. But I'm afraid he isn't over that bad ear yet.' Monique was still standing staring at her, clutching her big shabby black shoulder-bag. 'Look, why don't you make us both a cup of coffee . . .' Kate looked distractedly at her watch. 'It's lunchtime. Have a sandwich, you must. I bought masses of groceries on my way back. I don't feel very hungry . . . I've spoken to Dr Martin and he's coming later this afternoon.' Kate thought of something. 'I'm going to phone my father. Then I'll look in on Guy . . . but do make that coffee. I could do with a cup – you too, Monique . . .'

When Kate rang, her parents' daily cleaner answered. The doctor had taken Mrs Holford out for a bit of lunch, what a

199

shame, she had barely missed them, they hadn't been gone long. Somewhere out in the country, she thought.

'Tilly,' Kate said clearly, 'will you tell my father that Guy isn't well again. I fetched him from school, the nurse phoned . . .'

Tilly said Oh dear, she hoped it wasn't serious, they did go through phases when they seemed to pick everything up, poor mites, didn't they . . .

'Will you tell him that he's got a temperature, he's very grizzly . . . he's been sick and he says his head hurts . . . Will you tell him, Tilly? And ask him to ring? . . . Yes, yes I've spoken to our doctor . . . No, I'll try not to worry . . . Thanks Tilly . . . 'Bye . . .'

Kate then thought again of phoning Robin but decided to wait until later. She was almost certain that he had said he had a business lunch. There was no point in alarming him unnecessarily. Guy was still asleep and seemed peaceful, so Kate went into the kitchen where the practical Monique had coffee percolating and a plate of sandwiches neatly cut. She had retrieved the shopping bags from the hall and put everything away. She was such a sensible young woman; it was a comfort to have her there, Kate thought, seeing the cups and the plates on the table.

Once she sat down, Kate found that she was hungrier than she realised – and they both tucked in. Kate was still half listening for Guy – but they chatted about the weekend.

Monique, who took her English lessons seriously, was pleased with her progress she said. Now that she had had something to eat – and was no longer on her own in the house with her sick child – Kate felt stronger. Sleep must be best for Guy now. Robin would have finished lunch, be back in the office . . .

She left Monique to clear up and deal with the window cleaner who had arrived, as ever, at the most inconvenient time possible. Kate told her to tell him to come back tomorrow if he could. She was about to pick up the phone when she heard Guy upstairs – screaming. She and Monique reached his bedside simultaneously.

'The light . . . it's hurting my eyes . . . make it go away, make

200

it . . .' Kate held him tight in her arms, soothing and rocking him. Suddenly desperate; fighting down waves of terror.

'Guy, lovey, it's daytime, there's no light on . . .'

'There is, there is – and it hurts . . . make it go away . . .' He was frantically clinging to her, his head buried in her neck, sobbing now. *'Please,'* he said piteously, *'Please make it go . . . I can't bear it, I can't . . .'*

Monique sprang to the window and drew the curtains, cutting out the wintry, early afternoon sun. The small room darkened – and Guy's sobs gradually subsided. When he was quiet and relaxed against her, Kate put him gently back under the bedclothes. Monique drew the covers up. The little face, turned sideways on the pillow, was ghostly-white and frighteningly still. Eyes shut tight with bluish lids. Instinctively, Kate and Monique looked at each other above him – bending over, grave. Their faces were only inches apart.

Monique mouthed, 'Madame . . . do you think . . . the hospital?'

After a moment – and another look at Guy – Kate shook her head. Two thoughts hammered: *Tony . . . Robin . . .*

She whispered to Monique, 'Stay with him . . . I must get the doctor – *at once* . . . and phone his father . . .'

Monique nodded.

Kate flew down to the hall. Forcing down panic, she spoke calmly to Tony's nurse, demanded to speak to the doctor, had his assurance that he would come immediately. She then phoned Robin's office, shouted at his secretary, heard Robin's voice . . . She had no idea, ever, what he said – telling her something, repeating it forcibly. He was telling her to take Guy straight to the hospital; Kate, in her paralysis of fear, did not hear this. Then the secretary again, saying quietly that Mr Faraday was on his way home.

Guy was as she had left him, he hadn't moved at all, with Monique beside him – her face as white as the bedclothes.

Kate crouched by his head.

'He's coming, he's coming . . . the doctor . . .' she whispered across to Monique. Almost croaked, her mouth was so dry. A little later – there was no sense of time any more – Guy opened his eyes and smiled straight at her. He looked exactly as he

201

always did – and Kate went weak with relief. She could feel the tears running down her cheeks. Her face was beside his.

'Guy, Guy, it's all right, darling. Dr Martin will be here in a minute ...' Monique moved in closer. 'I'm with you ... Mum's here ... and Daddy's coming home ... and Lucy will be back from school soon ... Monique's here ...' Coaxing; soothing.

'The snake, Mum, don't you see ...'

'There's no snake, Guy ...' – smiling back at him – Oh so joyfully – smoothing his sticky fair hair from his forehead. 'I promise, I promise ...'

'But there is, you silly billy Mum ...' he said, clearly and happily, still looking straight at her from the pillow. 'And Grandpa says it might get caught in the wheels of my bike ...' He laughed.

'Guy, Guy ...' He was looking through her; not really seeing her at all.

Kate went icy. Relief, so momentary, evaporated. He was delirious. He sighed and closed his eyes again and seemed to fall at once into a deep, unnatural sleep.

When the front doorbell rang, Monique raced to get it. Tony Martin, bag in hand, found Kate kneeling by the bed. Her cheek was next to Guy's on the pillow, her arms over him. He had to move her quite forcibly to get to Guy.

While he was examining him, Monique put her hand on Kate's arm. 'I should wait downstairs perhaps, for Lucy ...?'

'Thanks, Monique.' Kate flashed her a look of gratitude.

Tony Martin straightened. He looked grim.

'Where's the nearest phone?'

'In our bedroom – across the hall.'

He strode the few steps and left Kate, still crouched over Guy – an animal at bay, protecting her young. Robin found her like that when he crashed into the house, took the stairs in a couple of strides and burst into the room.

'Kate?' He looked down at Guy, stiff and motionless on the pillow beneath her encircling arms. 'Kate?'

She couldn't – wouldn't – answer. She stared at him – white, dumb. Her throat parched with fear.

'Tony . . .?'

'In our room,' she whispered, 'Phoning . . . Robin, what are we going to do?'

He knelt beside her, one arm round her shoulder, the other across Guy's small, still body.

They both heard Tony say, 'Yes – yes I need an ambulance.' He gave the name and address. 'And make it quick . . . Thanks.'

He came back into the room and looked from Robin to Kate – and down to Guy's still head.

'Tony . . . *What* . . .?'

Robin's face was agonised. Tony stared at him, his eyes boring . . .

'I'm afraid it's meningitis . . . I'm sorry . . . I hope we've got it in time.' He sounded clipped. 'Everything that can be done will be . . .' He pushed Kate aside and pulled open his bag. Out came a syringe, a phial . . . Deftly, he pulled aside the sheet, rolled up Guy's pyjamas . . . He muttered, 'We can't wait. Every second counts . . . I'm going to take him to the hospital myself . . . Bring my case, will you?'

Folding Guy gently in his blankets, he picked him up and started out of the room and down the stairs. Robin took Kate's arm and they followed.

Guy slipped into a coma and never regained consciousness. He died early the following morning in St George's Hospital of pneumococcal meningitis.

The next hours and days were a jumbled blurr to Kate. Nothing seemed to happen in sequence. Friends came and went; her parents reaching out to her – always weeping; Laura dependable, relentlessly practical. Doris and Jim Faraday, suddenly grown old and pathetic. Robin, tight-lipped, dealing with the horrors that must still be faced – the death certificate, the announcement in the papers, the funeral. Kate never slept because she was afraid of the waking agony. She dozed a bit at odd times – at the kitchen table or curled in an armchair in the sitting-room. Tony Martin pressed pills on her and she nodded and promised – and pushed them away somewhere, untouched. A lot of the time she wandered around the house clasping and unclasping her hands. She couldn't answer the simplest question. Through the long nights they lay in bed, not talking or touching much. Stunned by incomprehensible loss and the appalling shock; the ground gone from beneath their feet. Whenever she saw Robin during the day, he had a glass of whisky in his hand. Kate thought, looking at what was going on around her as though from a long, long way away, that everything was very quiet. Even voices seemed hushed.

Out of this miasma of grief – the unthinkable – a few images, of haunting clarity, slipped over and over through her mind . . .

There was Lucy, watching in horror – wide-eyed, hand over her mouth, Monique's arms around her – as Tony Martin carried Guy down the stairs and out through the hall.

The pitiless light of the hospital corridor in the early hours, Tony Martin walking towards them – worn, defeated – to tell them what they already knew. Within an hour of arriving at the hospital, they had been warned to fear the worst.

Robin driving home through that misty grey morning; she sitting in the back with her father. He had received her message and phoned just as the ambulance, which had not been needed, pulled away from the house – and had driven straight to the hospital. Some time during those excruciating hours of waiting, someone – a nurse? Robin? – had found her a rug. She had been shaking uncontrollably. In the back of the car, her father held it round her.

In the house, John Holford had immediately poured three brandies. He drained his at a gulp. Neither she nor Robin could touch it.

It must have been quite soon after that – it was still dark – that she and Robin sat on Guy's dishevelled bed. She had no recollection of how they got there. It was exactly as it was when he had been taken from there, in Tony Martin's arms, hours before. The room was full of his five-year-old's paraphernalia – toys and books and games. Woolly animals. It was stuffy and still smelt, very faintly, of Guy's vomit. They sat side by side, clinging to each other, and for the first and only time wept together for their child. As the room lightened, the blurred lump on the floor turned into Guy's eyeless bear, dropped in the panicky rush to the hospital.

Kate had one final image – which would not go. The day before the funeral she came upon Robin sitting on an upright chair in their bedroom. He was staring into space, red-eyed. He said quietly to himself, 'It should never have happened, it should never have happened . . .' As Kate edged back into the shadowy landing, she heard him say it a third time.

She fled blindly.

After a simple service, Guy was buried in the churchyard at Laverton, beside the old grey stone wall, beneath the row of cherry trees.

It was after the funeral, standing in the hall at Knyght's Wood in the fading light of a bitter winter's day, that Kate told Robin that she was not coming back to London with him and Lucy. Her parents had already left. She could hear the car running outside; Lucy had slipped out and was curled on the back seat.

'But Kate – Kate you must . . .' Robin stared at her – wretched, both of them drained to the last ounce. 'You can't stay here alone. I can't leave you here – and what about Lucy?'

'Laura is going to stay with you and Lucy for a bit. I've already asked her. She can have Monique's room now that she's left . . .' Her mouth was set.

'Kate . . .' He took her by the arm. He seemed bewildered. 'Kate – why is this . . .?'

She was too numbed and too tired to think straight enough to answer. But her reasons included the memory of Tony Martin carrying Guy down the stairs in his arms and of Guy's happy childish voice echoing through the house – and in her head. None of these could she bear. Most of all, it was a primitive instinct for survival. At Knyght's Wood, she believed, she might . . .

'I'm going to stay here, Robin, and see how I go . . .'

'I don't like it,' Robin said forcefully. 'Not for you, not for Lucy, not for me. We must deal with – this – together. There's

205

Lucy, my work ... for God's sake, Kate, please don't do this ...'

'I must,' she countered, obstinate. Nothing he could say would move her. 'And you and Lucy will be back here in two days ...'

Eventually, he gave up.

Kate stood listening until the sound of the car had died away.

PART 4

An After-Life

Chapter 20

One spring morning, some months later, Kate was standing in the kitchen at Knyght's Wood – doing nothing, thinking about making a cup of coffee – when there was a rap on the window. She looked up, startled. Mrs Bundy wasn't coming that morning – and anyhow, she always let herself in. Through the panes she saw a smiling woman's face – topped with wild reddish hair. Kate didn't think she recognised her. She walked slowly across the kitchen, her hand pressing on her hip. She opened the door.

'I *do* hope it's not terribly inconvenient my just arriving on your back doorstep like this . . .' the interloper said disarmingly. She was wearing a knitted coat in every colour of the rainbow which looked as though it had been made by hand. She was a large woman with an ample figure, and was carrying an armful of forsythia – interspersed with spring flowers. 'I should have telephoned first, I'm so sorry. I'm dreadfully impulsive, always have been . . .' She had an infectious smile and very light blue eyes; Kate thought she liked the look of her. 'I'm Margot Sinclair . . . We – my son and I – moved into Thrush Cottage last summer . . .'

Somewhere at the back of Kate's mind, which was still working with painful slowness, she remembered having been told something about newcomers to the village, something newsworthy . . . but she couldn't remember what . . .

'Do come in,' Kate said, blinking. 'Please. I did hear Thrush Cottage had changed hands.'

'I'll stay for a minute . . .' She looked at her shrewdly. 'But not for long . . . I really don't mean to intrude . . .'

'I was going to make a cup of coffee in any case,' Kate said, shutting the door behind her and walking carefully back into the kitchen. 'Won't you join me?'

'I'd love to. How very kind . . .' Margot Sinclair glanced round the spectacular designer kitchen – thinking it looked exactly like an illustration from one of the glossiest decorating magazines. 'Heavens, Thrush Cottage isn't the least like this, not grand at all .... We haven't even got bannisters going up our precarious stone stairs yet . . .'

Kate, filling the kettle, smiled wanly.

'We only did all this last year . . . it was very basic before . . .' She pushed thin strands of hair back from her face. 'I've walked past your cottage hundreds of times . . . I've always admired it. It's one of the oldest in the village, isn't it? And it hasn't been mucked about with.'

'I liked that about it,' Margot admitted. 'Sebastian – he's my son – did too. It's really what finally decided us.'

Kate measured coffee and took two mugs from a cupboard. 'I think you'll enjoy Laverton . . .' Her voice trailed off. She couldn't yet manage even minimal social contact.

Margot Sinclair saw that. She held her armful of flowers towards Kate and said simply, 'I came this morning because I wanted to say how sad I am – about your little boy. I used to see him in the village last summer . . . I loved seeing him, he reminded me of Sebastian at that age. This morning I went out into the garden and picked all these flowers and I suddenly had the urge to come here . . .'

Kate nodded. 'Thank you,' she whispered. 'They're so lovely . . .' She looked around helplessly.

'If you tell me where you keep the vases, I can stick them in one for you,' Margot said gently. Kate pointed to a shelf and Margot inspected the row. 'This one should do, it's big and white and plain . . . I think you should sit down Kate, I can call you Kate can't I? . . . and let me make the coffee . . .'

Kate didn't protest but sat silently, her hands spread on the table, watching. Margot Sinclair's direct and unselfconscious manner reassured her. She poked about – finding spoons, getting milk out of the refrigerator. Curiously, Kate took some slight comfort from this stranger. She liked the matter-of-fact way she spoke; she even liked the sound of her voice.

'I've seen you in church,' Margot said. 'Sebastian and I usually go when he's down. I've wanted to come up to you then, but you always seemed to be surrounded . . .'

'It's because I help with the flowers . . . I'm glad you came this morning,' Kate told her truthfully. 'I haven't been getting on very well . . .' She had hardly eaten a thing for weeks; she was more than thin – almost skeletal. Her white, high-necked jumper was belted at the waist – narrower than ever now – over a long, grey corduroy skirt. Her cheekbones protruded sharply. She was drained of colour; there were fine new lines on her face.

'I wouldn't expect that you have,' Margot said steadily. 'Could you manage a biscuit?'

Kate shook her head.

When they were both sitting at the table holding mugs of coffee, the large vase of sweet-smelling flowers beside them, Margo said, 'Sebastian was about the same age as your little boy when Simon, his father, died. He had cancer, there was no hope. They couldn't even operate . . . So I always remember Sebastian very vividly, the way he was then . . . It was the moment in my life when time stopped for me . . . for a while, at least.'

Kate thought: *time stopped* . . . yes, that's it. Exactly. It has for me. Guy's voice; the warmth of his body clinging; the moments of unbearable desolation . . .

'How awful for you,' she said, putting down her coffee. 'Is he your only child – Sebastian?'

'Yes he is . . . It was quite a struggle from time to time bringing him up – and me working. But we've ended up good friends, so it was all worth it. He's not married so we spend quite a lot of time together.' She was still wearing her remarkable coat. Her hair, although slightly unkempt, curled exuberantly. She had wonderful skin. Close on sixty, she was still a handsome woman. 'He'll be spending most of the summer here as a matter of fact. He told me not long ago that I was his best friend – and I was *extremely* pleased . . .' Her wide mouth curved upwards.

While she was talking, Kate had put her hand deep into her skirt pocket. She brought out a dog-eared envelope and handed it to Margot.

211

'Read this. Please. I'd like you to . . .'

Margot took a large piece of lined paper out of the envelope, held it well away from her and peered. It was a short, simple letter written by Guy's teacher and signed by all the children in the class. Along the bottom was an uneven row of X's. Margot folded it and handed it back to Kate. She said nothing.

'He went back to school that day,' Kate said shakily. 'He had – been ill. Robin – my husband – and I were down here for two nights . . . If I'd been there and not sent him back, it *might* have made a difference, it *might* . . .'

The clock ticked-tocked on the dresser and a dog barked somewhere.

'You really mustn't torture yourself like that, you know,' Margot said seriously, after a while. 'It won't help . . .' Kate just shrugged. 'Is your husband here with you? And your daughter . . . I saw her quite a lot last year, in and out of the shops.'

'No, they're in London. We've always lived there, you see, except for weekends and holidays. Robin works there . . . he's in the City . . . Lucy is fifteen, at school.'

'Who's looking after them?'

'In the house? Laura – my sister – is. She comes and goes . . . and there's a daily. They come down every weekend. Lucy was here for the Easter holidays. I won't go back there.'

'But surely . . .'

'I won't,' Kate said stubbornly. 'I won't ever. I thought I might in time. But now I know I won't . . . I've told Robin.'

The school run . . . 'Mummy, Mummy . . .'; his toys; his friends . . . Impossible there . . . impossible . . .

'You want to live here, in Laverton? All the time?'

'Yes . . . It's bearable here, sometimes – what happened to Guy. My parents live quite near and one or both of them comes over every day . . . and I have the garden . . . I love that.'

'What about Lucy?'

'She wants to do her last two years at a boarding school. She's been after that for some time.'

'And your husband?' Margot asked quietly. Kate didn't answer. 'Surely it would be too long a journey for him to do

212

every day – and I expect he works endless hours. They do in the City these days I'm told.'

After a silence Kate said, 'He blames me. For Guy. For not doing – perhaps – everything I could. Or soon enough.' She tugged obsessively at the collar of her sweater. Her face was blank. 'We don't talk much any more.'

Margot thought: *shellshocked . . . she's the walking wounded . . .* Her heart went out to her. She had seemed a tragic figure, limping ahead of her into the kitchen – thin as a rail, grief-stricken. Possibly in physical pain also, Margot suspected.

'Has he said so?'

'Not yet.'

Senseless guilt, thought Margot, over a tragic fact of life. Today, a healthy child was taken for granted . . . Warning bells sounded *vis-à-vis* the husband too – and she had always heard in the village that the Faradays were such an attractive and happy couple. She finished her coffee and smiled across at Kate – who smiled back. Margot Sinclair's buoyancy and optimism were hard to resist.

'Tell you what,' she said cheerfully. 'It's a nice morning, quite mild . . . Why don't you put your coat on and walk back to Thrush Cottage with me? Then you can see the inside of it too, such as it is. Stay for lunch . . . I've got masses of delicious pâté – and we can pick up some fresh bread on our way . . . Do say yes . . .'

Much to her surprise, Kate did.

Laura phoned after seven. John Holford, who had spent the afternoon at Knyght's Wood, had just left. They had walked down to the church together and sat there quietly for a while – as Kate did most days. It was the nearest she came to peace; it was, as her father said, 'this thing called faith' . . . But today, he had looked so haggard that even Kate had noticed. It was the first thing she said to Laura.

'Poor Pa . . . and I know he's thinking – wishing . . .' Laura stopped – and changed the subject. 'Robin's not back yet but I thought I'd ring anyway. He's working the most absurd hours. Are you all right, Katie?'

'Better . . . I had a better day. A new neighbour came over

and took me back to her house for lunch. I liked her a lot. She's called Margot Sinclair.'

'Margot Sinclair? The actress?'

'I don't know, she didn't say ... we just talked about things ... She's started a handknit business in London, and she's in the middle of moving it down here ... But her voice sounds as though she could have been an actress.'

'I think she still is, mostly in radio plays ... but you know who her son is, don't you?'

'Sebastian. She talked about him quite a bit too.'

'*Sebastian Sinclair* ... Doesn't it ring a bell? Come on Katie – *think*. He's being spoken of as the new Richard Burton – without the booze and the temperament. You've probably seen him on stage at the National ... and you certainly saw him in *Hunter's Island*.'

'Oh God ... yes, of course. Margot must think I'm a complete ignoramus ...' So *that* was the village gossip she had vaguely heard, but failed to place that morning. The photograph of him in Margot's cluttered living-cum-workroom had looked familiar too.

'And I just read the other day that he's finishing off a television play – and then later in the year he's going out to Hollywood ...'

'Of course, I'll tell Margo I've clicked when I see her again ... Laura?'

'What?'

'I'm so grateful – to you – for keeping everything going for me there. You know that ...'

'I do know. But you'll have to come back, Katie. You can't walk out on your life. Not even now – after Guy. Sooner or later, you've got to come to terms with it. Here. I mean that.'

'Not yet.'

Kate heard her sigh. Then Laura said, 'Robin and Lucy will be down on the 5.30 on Friday. Robin told me to tell you. He'll phone when he comes in. And Lucy, by the way, broke down last night, poor child ...'

'Was she bad? I should have been there, shouldn't I?' All through the holidays, she had mooned about – pale and withdrawn. The thought of her instilled wild panic – and guilt – in Kate.

Laura ignored the question. 'She's been keeping everything bottled up, but perhaps she's easier now . . . anyhow, you'll all be together over the weekend . . . And she's revived the boarding school issue. That's something you really must talk about – all three of you. Robin seems to be coming round to it.'

He doesn't care, Kate mouthed silently as the withering bleakness – which had been mostly kept at bay since that morning – overpowered her and dragged her to the depths. *We neither of us care – about anything.*

'Laura – can't you come down with them on Friday? Please?'

This suddenly seemed very important to Kate.

'Not this weekend. Nico's in town and we've got plans to make. I'll tell you about these when I see you . . . But I'll come soon – perhaps I'll drive down for the day next week . . . And Katie, will you think about what I said? About coming back to London and going on? You've had the time you needed at Knyght's Wood. It is very, very important that you do . . .'

'Oh Laura . . .'

When Laura hung up, saying that she was cooking something for herself and Lucy – adding 'and for Robin if he turns up,' Kate sat where she was in the darkened room. She sat there, without moving, for an hour. Perhaps more. Then she went upstairs, swallowed two of Tony Martin's sleeping pills, turned off the phone, and curled up – still in her clothes – on the edge of the bed.

Late on Friday night, Robin stood staring out of the sitting-room window at Knyght's Wood. Lucy, who had barely said a word all evening, had long since sneaked off up to her room. She hadn't shown much more than bored politeness when Kate told them, at supper, about her meeting with Margot Sinclair, mother of the actor/film star Sebastian. Robin, almost equally disinterested, thought he had read in an interview that Sebastian Sinclair had bought a house down here somewhere.

'I think you should come back to London with us on Sunday, Kate,' he said now – expressionlessly, his back still towards her. 'I'm *asking* you to . . .'

215

'I can't,' Kate said in a small voice from beside the fire. 'I can't.'

'Laura has – cleared the room. Disposed of all his things.' He went on staring out across the garden which was luminous with moonlight.

'She's been wonderful, Laura has . . .'

'She has been . . . and still is. She's in and out of the house all the time. But she's got to get on with her own life.' Kate didn't answer and Robin, turning abruptly, went to pour himself a drink. Holding the decanter, he looked over to her. 'We must too, Kate . . . get on with ours. It's been weeks now – months. I've been patient. But Lucy needs you – and so do I.'

He looked worn and exhausted – and a bit crumpled. He had thrown himself into his work harder than ever; he had been at his desk well before eight that morning. And he's aged, Kate thought; the old zest has gone. I suppose we both have – suddenly. She found many silver strands when she brushed her hair now.

'Please Robin – darling, please understand,' she said desperately. 'Give me time . . . I can't think ahead. I can't bear the thought of going back there . . . to the house. For you and Lucy – I *must* survive, I must. I think I will if I can stay on here . . .'

'It's the church, that's it – isn't it? You're there all the time, putting flowers on his – *grave* . . .' He said it angrily, as though the very word disgusted him. 'You and your father, the pair of you. It's morbid, Kate,' he shouted. 'That's what it is – morbid . . .'

He tossed back his drink and strode out of the room. Kate heard the back door bang shut. She waited for a few minutes and then went upstairs and knocked at Lucy's bedroom.

'Yes?'

Kate opened the door. The television was on in the corner, very low; but Lucy, lying on the bed, her head propped on her hand, didn't seem to be watching it.

'All right, are you darling? I wondered . . . I thought I'd come and see you and have a chat. Dad's gone out for a walk.'

'I know,' said Lucy looking away. 'I heard.'

Kate felt for a chair and sat down. This offhand, nearly-grown-up child daunted her. But she said clearly, 'He thinks I

216

should come back to London – but I'm going to stay here, at least for the moment . . . do you mind very much?'

Lucy looked at her sideways. 'It's up to you,' she said coldly, flinging one long, elegant black leg over the other.

Kate flinched. 'I'm afraid I'm being selfish – to both of you. I'm thinking of myself at your and your father's expense. We are all suffering . . . and I can't bear you to be unhappy, Lucy,' she said quietly.

'I don't suppose any of us is particularly happy about anything just now, do you?' – Lucy countered, very cool. 'How could we be?'

'No.' Kate bowed her head. The too quiet house, which shrieked of Guy's loss, settled round them. 'But I wanted to tell you that – how much I care about what you're going through now – all the same.' She longed to touch her but was afraid of being rebuffed.

Lucy jerked restlessly on the bed. The room was in semi-darkness. A nearly full moon was visible through the window. Yearning, Kate looked up and glimpsed Lucy's face. It was white against the dark hair which she was now wearing in a frizzy mass. Kate wondered if she was sleeping properly.

'I'm thinking about boarding school again anyway,' Lucy said, evading the subject. 'I'm fed up with this all-girls stuff . . . I don't think I can face a year and a half more of it until college. Last week I spoke to old Bidders' – the formidable headmistress of her present school. 'It was a good time because she's feeling sorry for me, naturally . . .' She stared up at the shadowy ceiling. 'Because of my grades, she thinks I've got a good chance of getting into Yarnston for next autumn. There are always one or two last minute drop-outs. They'll give me a good write up – and I'd rather enjoy having an interview. So I've decided to go for it. Bidders had a talk with them on the phone. She's getting the entrance forms – and she'll send them on to you and Dad.'

'So that's that,' Kate said wearily to Robin, recounting the conversation later when they were in bed.

'She said much the same to me . . . and I can see a change would make sense for her now. Particularly . . .' – his voice rough with sarcasm – 'particularly since as a family we no longer appear to be living under the same roof . . .'

Kate's heart contracted at this. 'I think so too. And it will give her a goal, something to aim for. An interest to take her mind off everything else . . . she's full of pain, poor child . . .'

As they were themselves. Neither of them could sleep – and they both knew it. They could hear the wind gusting up the valley, through the village, and tearing into the Knyght's Wood – where it pushed at the carpet of last year's dead leaves . . . rustling and dragging. An owl screeched, fell silent – and screeched again.

No more than hundreds of yards away was the darkened churchyard . . .

Nothing lasts, Kate thought bitterly – not love, not grief . . .

'The Lord is my shepherd; I shall not want. He maketh me to lie down in green pastures . . .'

Weeks before, they had stood and murmured those words in the dank church – stunned, eyes averted from what they could not bear – Guy's coffin, smothered in bright flowers. She and Robin, Lucy, her parents, Laura, the Faradays . . . friends from London, locals from the village behind them. Tony Martin – desperately worn – with Lisa . . . After, at the graveside, Kate had thought over and over: the blossom will be out soon, the blossom will be out soon . . . Recited in her head like a litany. Anything to blunt the reality of what was happening; of facing that dreadful gash in the sodden green turf . . .

It was then that she saw her father as an old man for the first time; bent, without strength, leaning on her mother for support.

The semi-circle of unsmiling faces . . . Robin's red-rimmed eyes; she, clutching Lucy's hand . . . An icy wind billowing the vicar's robes . . .

Guy, Kate mouthed silently, lying there in mounting agony, keeping her eyes shut very tight . . . Oh Guy . . . Fighting down his voice, his ways, his touch; his beloved presence without which she didn't think – she really didn't – that she could live at all . . .

The blob on the floor of his room which as it grew light turned out to be his shabby old bear . . .

In despair she turned – and Robin's arms came round her.

'Kate . . .' his voice breaking . . . When they were both quiet, he reached, as he always did, for the nape of her neck. 'There's nothing left of you,' he muttered, his hand sliding down past her waist.

There isn't much, Kate thought bleakly, that's true – opening her eyes wide and clinging to him with icy fingers.

They kissed and touched; but there was no passion between them that night. And little comfort.

After a while, Robin flung himself away from her, lying with his hands behind his head, staring at the shaft of hard, bright moonlight. He spoke into the silence. 'You should have got him to Tony earlier, taken him straight to the hospital . . . I begged you to – when you phoned the office . . . that day.'

So that was what he had been shouting – she too crazed with fear to hear.

Now, the words were said. They had been festering between them ever since.

Even then, Kate felt for his pain.

It was he who had so uncharacteristically insisted on them driving down to Knyght's Wood that fatal – last – weekend.

She did not say this. Summoning her last reserves of strength, she pleaded, 'Please Robin – darling – don't torture yourself. Or me. Perhaps I was wrong, but a child – any child – has bouts of ill health. Infections, colds . . . This – was different. But it happens, and it happened to us. There seems to be no reason – and yet, I do believe in some Divine presence, wider than our understanding. Beyond questioning. I must have some faith, Robin . . .'

'Ah, good old God,' he said bitterly, 'The bottom line . . .' He turned onto his side, pulling the covers up to his face and falling quickly into a heavy sleep. While Kate, appalled – tears pouring down her cheeks, soaking the pillow – went on thinking: *What is happening to us? What?* Over and over – until it was dawn. Before six, she got up, pulled on a dressing-gown and went downstairs. She had not slept at all.

Robin's black mood persisted the next day. He and Kate were polite but cool to each other; both deathly tired. Kate decided not to go to church. Robin walked round and round the garden while she cooked the lunch. Lucy, to Kate's surprise, was unusually cheerful and made herself useful. She did the vegetables efficiently, washed up and laid the table. She told Kate, sounding adult and concerned, that she had lost much too much weight and that it was time she started eating. 'Laura thinks so too,' she added.

'I will do, darling,' Kate said, pushing the potatoes round the hissing roast. 'It's just that . . .' She stopped.

'Poor Mum . . .'

Lucy put her arm round her. Kate could have wept; instead, she nodded and squeezed her back.

After lunch, Robin announced that he had a full briefcase to be gone through before tomorrow – and he needed to spend at least two hours at his desk. 'It's all hands on deck in the office at the moment with Big Bang coming off in October . . .' He looked dreadful. He had drunk two whiskys before lunch, something she had never known him do. So without protest, Kate looked up the trains and drove him, with Lucy, to the station late in the afternoon. She hadn't long returned when the phone rang. Expecting it to be one of her parents, she was pleasantly surprised to hear Margot Sinclair's voice.

'Kate? I'm ringing at the last moment . . .' Her son, Sebastian, had come down unexpectedly, and they would be delighted if she and her husband – Lucy too if she felt like it – could come over for a drink.

Kate thanked her – and explained that they had just left for London. 'Another time please, Margot,' she said. 'We would all enjoy that.'

'Does that mean you're alone there?'

'Well – yes . . .'

'In that case, come straight over. At once. Just as you are . . . I'd love Sebastian to meet you . . .'

Pausing only to put on a wide, grey suede belt and her comforting old sheepskin jacket, Kate left the house.

Chapter 21

Sebastian Sinclair resembled his mother only in his red hair and beautifully modulated voice. Otherwise, he seemed quite different – tall, extremely thin, and reassuringly shy.

'Hello,' he said, opening the car door for Kate when she had parked by the side of Thrush Cottage, 'I'm Sebastian . . . Do come in . . . We're so glad you could come . . .' He smiled hesitantly and held out his hand and his hair flopped onto his forehead.

'She's so kind, your mother,' Kate said as he followed her up the path to the cottage. She was limping badly; it was always worse when she was tired – as she was then. 'I think she's extraordinary.' She was too close to grief – and too weary – to bother with pleasantries. 'I feel better when I'm with her. Or I did last week . . .'

'I agree,' Sebastian said, behind her. 'I do too. It's a talent she has – for making people feel better.'

Margot had heard the car and was standing in the doorway – swathed in a cerise knitted outfit, hair in a curly halo and with a dazzling smile.

'Hello, Kate . . .' – she put her arm round her. 'Good – you and Sebastian have met . . . Come in . . . We've got a blazing fire going, although I'm afraid it's a bit smokey, trouble with the chimney which I must get seen to . . .'

Inside, Kate found herself – as when Margot had brought her there for lunch – in the middle of a parrot's cage of muddle and colour. Margot was setting up her small business of individually designed, hand-knitted sweaters in Thrush Cottage. She already had outlets in several London shops. It was partly because she wanted more space – and, she hoped,

221

competent outworkers – that she had moved to Laverton from her tiny London flat. Sebastian could use the cottage whenever he wanted; so it had been a joint financial venture, she told Kate. The ground floor was entirely given over to a sitting-room and kitchen. Stone steps led up to the first floor where there was a bathroom and three bedrooms. One bedroom was Sebastian's private territory; the rest of the cottage was devoted to Margot and her knitting. This was self-evident, as every surface was draped with brightly coloured sleeves and fronts and ribbings, all draped at crazy angles. Baskets were crammed with different coloured yarns and knitting needles, and free-form designs on sheets of paper were pinned haphazardly from the mantelpiece. Two or three finished sweaters swung on hangers in unexpected places – like the standard lamp and the top of the curtains.

It was astonishing to Kate that out of this agreeable chaos, such beautiful and expensive garments did finally emerge. Margot's own wardrobe was proof of this. She knitted prac-tically everything she wore and, although she was a big woman, the flamboyant colours and outlandish designs suited her personality. She was her own best advertisement.

'Sit here, Kate,' she told her, gathering up an armful of sleeves from the sofa. 'You look exhausted – and cold. Warm your hands by the fire . . . and Sebastian will get us a drink. You look as though you could do with one. I'll just stack these upstairs while I still remember what they belong to . . .' And off she went in her floppy boots up the curving stone stairs.

Sebastian stood in front of the fire. Kate, huddled in the corner of the sofa, looked up at him curiously. Brown cor-duroys and an old navy jersey. He didn't seem at all like his mother – and yet . . . she sensed that he had some of her warmth . . .

'What can I get you to drink, Kate?' He smiled apologetically and gestured round the room with both arms. 'It's a bit of a shambles, here, I'm afraid . . . but you know about that, you've been here before . . .'

'It's a nice shambles,' Kate said, looking about vaguely. Something in her relaxed – and started to thaw. She sat back against the squashy cushions. 'Don't you think so?'

'In small doses – yes.' He ran his hand through his fine hair. He looked very young; Kate thought he was in his early thirties. He had fair skin which suddenly flushed a hectic pink. Kate didn't think he seemed at all what she would expect of a rising theatrical star – which she now knew him to be. 'But please – what about a drink?'

'Yes, a drink *would* be nice. Gin perhaps?' – Kate, who never drank spirits, asked experimentally.

'Of course. Tonic? Ice? Lemon?'

Kate nodded. 'Not too strong or I'll keel over . . .'

When Sebastian handed her the glass he said quietly, 'Mother told me about your son – Guy. I am – so very sorry . . .' He drew up a stool and sat quite near her, dropping his hands between his knees. The tables being covered with Margot's stuff, he put his drink down on the wide hearth. Like his mother, he was unselfconscious about expressing his feelings. And his voice was marvellous – crystal clear and lightly shaded. He was looking at her closely. 'Something happening like that – there is nothing meaningful to say . . .'

'No.'

'Will you be all right?' he asked gently.

Kate looked down at her drink, noticing as she did so that her nails were bitten and ragged and the long grey skirt, which she had worn for days and days, was decidedly grubby.

'I don't know.'

'Mother wants you to stay here – during the weeks, when your husband is in town. She doesn't think you should be in the house by yourself . . .'

'Doesn't she?' Kate smiled at him. 'There, you see, she is a kind person . . . she hardly knows me . . .'

'But she cares.'

'Oh she does,' Kate almost shouted, leaning forward. 'It's extraordinary – but I know that . . .'

'*What* do I do?' demanded Margot, flip-flopping back down the ancient stairs. 'Or are you talking about someone else?' She picked her way through the room and sat in the armchair on the far side of the fire. The cat, who had been prowling the room, jumped up and settled on the arm of her chair.

'I was telling Kate that you don't like her being alone

223

during the weeks, Margot,' Sebastian said, swivelling round on the stool. 'That's right, isn't it?'

'It is indeed. I know your parents live close . . . but do think about staying here, Kate, in the week.' The cat majestically raized his head so that she could tickle the white fur of his chin. 'The spare room is tiny – and full of all my clutter . . .' Sebastian shot Kate an amused look – which she returned. 'But it's warm and comfortable. And you'd have company. Will you remember?'

'I will, I will . . . thank you, Margot,' Kate agreed. The drink, the heat from the fire and the cosy cushions were making her sleepy. Thrush Cottage seemed agreeably removed from the painful rest of the world.

'Good,' Margot said briskly. 'I was going to mention it to your husband, Robin, too . . . Sebastian, get me a whisky, would you? And chuck another log on the fire . . .'

The three of them sat talking while the light faded; neither Margot nor Sebastian made any move to turn on a lamp. The huge fire leapt and flickered, encompassing them in its warm glow. Margot's strong hand stroked rhythmically; the cat purred – and slept. Sebastian and his mother spoke casually about his plans . . . the play for television was almost finished. He didn't know whether he was pleased with it or not . . . They didn't need him tomorrow which was why he had come down for the night . . . There were only a couple more days' shooting . . . After that, there was the possibility of a play early next year . . . He wanted to explore that – and a few other things that might, or might not, materialise . . . Then he was taking a couple of months off – he didn't have to be in California until late August – so he would be at the cottage quite a bit during the summer, he thought.

Kate half listened. She didn't say much. She was enjoying just being with them. She hadn't felt so peaceful for ages, not since that other life, before, as Margot put it, 'time stopped' . . . Later, when they were finishing off their second drinks, Margot stretched lazily and said not to move, either of them, but she was going to see about food. She had fresh eggs and good ham – and off she went to the kitchen.

Kate and Sebastian went on staring mesmerically into the

fire. The cat gave them a hostile look, uncurled himself, and stalked out after Margot.

Kate said dreamily, 'It was only when I told Laura, my sister, about meeting your mother that it all came back to me – how famous you are . . .'

'I wouldn't say that . . .'

He turned away from the fire, towards her, half amused, half embarrassed.

'Oh but you are . . . Or will be. Have you always wanted to be an actor?'

'Always. It's in the blood, perhaps. My father was a playwright – did you know?' Kate shook her head. 'Margot got regular work on stage, often in long runs, when I was a kid. A bit of film work. She still does radio plays from time to time – although she's increasingly involved in all this . . .' He indicated the half-finished pieces of knitwear in the surrounding darkness. 'And when I broke it to her that I wanted to go to drama school she was really pleased. She understood. She's been marvellously supportive too – as you may imagine.'

'And it's lovely for her that you're doing so well.'

'I've been lucky,' he said, going on looking at her. 'Very lucky . . . I don't think one can say any more than that . . .'

Kate stared back at the flames licking about the shifting logs; ash, white hot, crumbling through the iron grate; sparks shooting.

'I wonder what Guy would have been,' she said slowly, 'when *he* grew up . . .'

Sebastian, who hadn't taken his eyes off her face for some time, put out his hand and grasped hers.

'I think you *mustn't* wonder that,' he said quietly. 'At least, not yet. Perhaps never . . . What about your daughter – Lucy?'

'She's clever . . .' Kate dragged her gaze from the fire and looked at Sebastian. She liked him leaning towards her; liked his clean, sure grasp. 'She's good at everything – languages, English, the sciences. And she's a hard worker too . . . She'll definitely go to university. Cambridge perhaps, like Robin.'

She thought: they'll be back in the house by now . . . Robin working, a glass by his side. Lucy on the phone to friends. Upstairs, the empty room . . . 'Laura has disposed of all – his

225

things,' he had said . . . Days, weeks, months passing – soon, it would be years.

'Does Lucy look like you?'

'I think she does, rather. But she's much more like my twin sister really. They're alike temperamentally. It seems to make a difference, even though we're identical.'

They hadn't moved when Margot came back carrying a tray with three plates.

'A picnic tonight . . . ham omelettes and hunks of bread . . . forks and napkins are here too . . . Pass everything round, would you Sebastian? And a glass of wine would be nice.'

Over supper, still in darkness apart from the glowing fire, they spoke of Margot's business. She told them why she had finally decided to make the break from London.'My head – and my designs – are clearer and easier here, away from the cramped flat and the tiny workroom. I'm surrounded by ordinary, non-fashion people who help me see what the public wants to wear. This is terribly important . . . and I'd like to expand. I've been looking at an old barn which is for sale on the other side of Laverton. It would make a marvellous headquarters-cum-showroom for the future.'

Kate asked her if she knew Laura's shop – which of course she did.

'You must meet her,' Kate said. 'I think she's got a bit stale with it. It's so terribly – well, exclusive. All those dark colours which everyone – *Vogue* editors at least – think are so terribly chic. But I'm sure you would find her interesting.'

'I'd like that,' Margot said, holding up her glass to Sebastian. 'I'd like that very much. She's not married, is she?'

'No. She's been more-or-less living with Nico Kirilov for years now. The gallery owner. The family was very disapproving, my parents particularly. He's gone on being married and has lots of children. I suppose some of them must be grown-up now . . . Anyhow, Laura seems happy enough and we've all accepted it. And she's been marvellous since . . .'

'Oh I know,' Margot cut in swiftly. 'You said. She's keeping an eye on Robin and Lucy in London.'

226

'That's right. She's coming to spend the day with me next week. We must fix up a meeting.'

Sebastian made mugs of coffee – and soon Kate heard the grandfather clock by the stairs chime ten. Kate looked startled. What if Robin, or her parents, had tried to phone?

'I must be off. I'd no idea it was so late. Thank you for the evening – both of you – I've loved it . . .'

When she got to her feet, helped by Sebastian, she swayed visibly.

'I'll take you home,' Sebastian said quickly. He grasped her arm. 'Right, Margot?'

'Of course,' his mother agreed. 'My car keys are lying about somewhere. You can walk over and get your car any time tomorrow, Kate. You look all in, bless you.'

Kate was too exhausted – by her chronic sleeplessness, the food and drink, the fire, the good company – to protest. In fact, she felt relieved.

By the door, putting on her coat, Margot asked, 'Is that what you came in? You'll be cold after this heat. Here – wrap this round you.' And she produced a knitted woollen shawl in shades of peacock blue and wrapped it round Kate's shoulders. 'Off you go . . . give me a ring tomorrow. Sebastian is going back to London early, so I'll be all alone.'

'Thanks, Margot.'

Kate kissed her on both cheeks and went off down the path with Sebastian holding onto her arm – while Margot watched from the lighted doorway.

Knyght's Wood was in darkness – it had been daylight when Kate left and she had never expected to stay so long. Sebastian insisted on coming into the house with her. In the hall, she switched on a lamp and went quickly into the living-room where she did the same. She had been sitting for a long time on Margot's sofa; pains like hot wires were shooting from her hip.

'What an attractive house . . .' Sebastian looked around, taking in the pictures and the good furniture. A huge vase of blossoms just coming into bud. Expensive, polished chintz curtains.

227

'Yes,' Kate agreed, oddly impersonal. As though it had nothing to do with her. 'Yes – it is, isn't it?' She caught sight of her desk in the corner, piled with letters which had yet to be answered. 'And it was a lovely evening – thank you both so much for it.'

Sebastian, who hadn't bothered with a coat over his rough navy jersey, came up to her and put his hands on her shoulders.

'I don't like leaving you here, by yourself. It's so quiet . . . lonely . . .' For the first time he looked, and sounded, awkward. His face was ruddy; his hair fell, lank, almost to his eyes. Margot's must have been just that colour when she was younger. And for all his actor's training and his superb voice, he was shy after all – just as she had thought the moment she met him by the car. She lifted her face to his.

'I'll be all right. I'm used to it. Please don't worry . . .' For some reason, Kate knew that he did. 'Laura's coming this week, and my parents, and Robin and Lucy on Friday . . .'

He seemed not to have heard. He touched her cheek with his fingers.

'You are a beautiful woman,' he said – and bent and kissed her gently on the lips.

When the house returned to stillness after the sound of Margot's old banger had died away, Kate walked over and stood in front of a mirror. One hand at her throat she looked at her face above the slash of blue-green shawl. Neat features; no make-up; fine hair dusted at the sides with grey; faint lines across the forehead now; dark smudges under the eyes.

'You are Kate Faraday,' she told herself aloud. 'You are happily married to Robin – whom you have loved forever. You are Lucy's mother . . .' Her eyes closed briefly. 'And you're not far off forty, what's more . . .'

She went on looking at her image until her senses had stopped their extraordinary confusion – then she switched off all the lights and went up to bed.

That night, for the first time, she had a vividly remembered dream – which would become recurrent . . .

She was running as fast as she could, light as air, no vestige of a limp . . . there was a young man striding ahead of her. She could only see his back, she thought he was tall and fairish, and she was positive that he was Guy – grown up. She called out to him again and again . . . there was something she was holding – a sweater? a scarf? – which belonged to him, which he had to have, which it was desperately important that she gave to him. Imperative. She held it out, whatever it was, trying to reach him, willing him to turn round . . . but he would not, he strode on and on – just beyond her reach. 'Guy,' she called out, frantic, 'Guy . . .'

She woke at once, sweating and shivering, recalling the seconds of the dream with absolute clarity. The clock beside the bed showed 3.00 a.m. She calmed, and slept peacefully until morning.

Chapter 22

Two days after Kate spent the evening with Margot and Sebastian, May slipped in. It was warm and sunny – the countryside come magically alive with flowers and blossoms and delicate greenery.

It was to be Kate's best week since Guy's death.

Mrs Bundy, stomping into the kitchen, eyed Kate as she unwound her scarf – she was essentially cautious over the weather was Mrs Bundy – and breathed a sigh of relief. The grubby white sweater and long, dragging skirt – which Mrs Bundy had been itching to get her hands on to wash, and which Kate wore like a ritual, day after day – had disappeared. Instead, Kate had put on a grey-and-white striped dress and a sleeveless grey cardigan. She had also, Mrs Bundy noted, glancing at her surreptitiously again as she filled the kettle, washed her hair and managed some lipstick. Now that was more like it. She couldn't go on wasting away to nothing over the loss of that bairn, light of her life though he had been. Not that there weren't times when she and Bundy both believed that to be her intention. She had Lucy, Mr Faraday – devotion itself, the home, the family . . . Although poor Dr Holford was taking it terrible hard, she'd heard.

'What a marvellous day,' Kate said, opening the window and looking out, breathing in the sweet air. 'And it's supposed to stay for the week, it said on the radio. Too bad it was so cold over the weekend when Mr Faraday and Lucy were down.'

'Ne'er cast a clout . . . you know what they say . . . and quite right too,' Mrs Bundy said darkly as she tied herself into her apron.

'I'd love a piece of toast,' Kate said, craning to look at her budding azaleas.

'Right you are then,' – another good sign. Mrs Bundy bustled about – warming the teapot, cutting a loaf, opening and shutting drawers and cupboards. If she was lucky, she'd get into the poor little boy's room this week. Mrs Faraday hadn't let her near it so far. Although she'd removed every other trace of him she possibly could. His coats, his boots by the back porch . . . and a nasty turn it had given her too. She knew for a fact – she'd seen her – that Mrs Faraday sat there alone, hour after hour some days, in that old rocking chair Guy was always so attached to. Staring into space. Downright unhealthy if you asked her. She wanted nothing moved in his room, she'd said, not even dusted. Yet she wouldn't so much as set foot in the house in London, where the bairn had been taken to the hospital from. Miss Laura was living there for the moment; but that couldn't go on. She'd have to put her mind to it and go on back, Mrs Faraday would. It wasn't right, leaving Lucy like that – not to mention her husband. There'd be trouble if she didn't. Bundy thought as much too.

'Will ye have some of my marmalade then?' Mrs Bundy asked as Kate shut the window and came to the table.

'Thanks . . .'

While Kate was eating, Mrs Bundy said cannily, 'There's a whole lot of things we're needing from the shops – cleaning stuff, coffee – and we're out of light bulbs . . .'

'I'll make a list,' Kate said. 'I was planning to go out in any case.'

'Were ye now,' Mrs Bundy's eyes narrowed. 'Well, then, I'll be seeing about the bairn's room this morning. It's time it had a good clean in there . . . and I'll be helping ye get some of his things together, when ye feel ready for it too. It canna all be left . . .' Mrs Bundy's sympathy combined with the soft Scottish accent had their effect. Kate looked straight at her.

'Yes, Mrs Bundy,' she said. 'Yes. I know. We will do it – soon.'

Laverton was a lively village which still retained a few small independent shops in the High Street. Kate, shopping basket

231

slung over her arm, was just leaving the bakery when she bumped into Margot Sinclair.

'*Kate*,' – with her warm, ready smile and the bright, clean colours she always wore, Margot Sinclair radiated good feeling.

Kate was in the middle of thanking her for the impromptu supper, when she broke in with, 'You are better, aren't you? I could see it at once. Oh Kate – I am so glad . . .' She put her hand lightly on her arm.

'Yes, yes I am,' Kate said, realising that she felt it. The mist through which she had been viewing everyone and everything seemed to be clearing. Her mind was functioning more sharply even over trivial domestic matters. Both of them moving out of the way of other shoppers, Margot told her that she had just spoken to Sebastian. 'He's hating London in this glorious bit of weather . . . they're shooting ahead of schedule . . . and he's coming down again on Thursday. I particularly want him to see this barn I'm thinking of. I've spoken to my bank manager and decided I can take the plunge and put in a low offer. I do want Sebastian to see it first. Any chance you could come over with us, Kate – Thursday afternoon or Friday?'

'I'd love that, Margot.'

'Good. I'll let you know as soon as I've fixed a time with the agents and Sebastian. Oh – and you really charmed *him*, by the way . . .'

Doing her rounds, Kate met several other people she knew. She found, to her amazement, that she was suddenly talking about Guy; thanking this one for her sympathy note, another for a beautiful plant she had sent to the house. When she got home, later than she expected, Mrs Bundy had done her two hours and left. Dumping her shopping on the kitchen table, Kate saw that her corduroy skirt and sweater had been washed by Mrs Bundy – and laid out to dry. Deliberately, she went straight upstairs and saw, as she had expected, that the door of Guy's room was open. It had been dusted, polished and vacuumed. Toys had been collected and put in the corner; games and books stacked on a shelf. The old rocking chair had been moved nearer the window, the bed cover tucked in neatly. Everything in it was the same – and yet it was inde-finably altered. It was no longer a room which belonged to a child who lived there. Expressionless, Kate left the door still open and went slowly back downstairs.

In the cheerful kitchen, which was now splashed with sunshine, she put away the shopping. It was nearly one o'clock. She made herself a sandwich and poured a glass of cider. In ways she didn't understand, bridges had been crossed that morning. Sitting at the table, Kate opened the newspaper she had just bought, the first for months, and started to read. She glanced at her watch. She would do some gardening that afternoon.

Robin telephoned just after two. He sounded ragged, she could tell at once.

'It's about Lucy,' he said. His voice was hard. He was angry – with her. She could tell that too. 'She's got an interview at Yarnston. We heard this morning. Because of her academic record, it looks as though they'll give her a place in September. Anyhow – she wants to do it . . .'

'I think it's a good thing for her. I'm pleased. The school has an excellent reputation. And she's enthusiastic.'

'At the moment. Let's hope it lasts . . .' a bitter edge; she could hear voices in the background. 'She'll miss all her London friends . . . Anyhow, they want to see her on Thursday morning. Laura's offered to drive her down.'

Laura has. And I haven't even been asked. Kate could feel her own attitude hardening.

'I see. Well, they can come on here for lunch. It isn't far. Laura was coming for the day this week anyway.'

'As you like.' *As I like* . . . 'You've chosen not to live with us in London so we have to make the best arrangements we can.'

Kate's anger flared.

'In other words,' she said coldly, looking out on the sunny spring garden, mentioning the unmentionable, 'as a mother I have been found wanting – again.'

'I really can't talk now,' he said impatiently. 'And it's out of the question my taking a day off this week. As a matter of fact, I'm in the middle of a meeting right now.' Equally ungiving.

233

Kate thought she heard an American voice – a woman's, with a distinctive drawl. Whoever it was must have been standing close to Robin's desk.

'I'll speak to them later. It's the most wonderful day down here. Too bad you're missing it.' Kate had changed into jeans and an old shirt of Robin's. 'I'm going to do some gardening.'

'You were out this morning, I tried to get you . . .' He still sounded aggrieved. 'I missed Mrs Bundy too.'

'I was shopping in the village.'

'Yes – well, I've got to go. I'm wanted. I'm in a meeting. I told you.' Kate definitely heard that American voice again. Louder; a bit husky. '*It just has to be Sunday. I'm going to get you people to make a decision on this one. Right now. OK Robin?*' This was followed by a throaty laugh mixed in with other voices.

Kate heard it all quite clearly.

'Goodbye,' she said. 'I'll talk to Lucy later this afternoon when she gets back from school.' And she put down the phone.

Kate had one eye on the clock and the other on the new potatoes boiling gently on the stove when she heard Laura's car come purring up the drive. She got to Lucy first.

'Lucy – darling, how did you get on?' She hugged her. 'I've been wondering all morning.'

'Fine,' Lucy said coolly, disentangling herself. 'I rather enjoyed it.' She was looking neat and appropriate in a pleated skirt and blouse, a sweater tied round her neck. 'Laura'll tell you. When is lunch? I'm starving.' And she walked towards the kitchen.

'Hi Katie, here we are . . .' – Laura uncoiled herself from the car. She gave Kate a peck on the cheek. 'It seemed easier for me to take her to Yarnston and come on here with her. I'd intended coming to see you anyway.'

'I suppose so . . . Come in and have a quick drink and then we'll eat. Lucy says she's hungry.'

'It was a long morning.' Laura slipped her arm through Kate's. 'We were shown all round the school, of course. And the house is beautiful . . . It looked all right, very impressive in parts. The kids looked a bit wild . . .'

234

'Whatever do you mean?' Kate stopped and stared at her.

'Well – free, then. These schools have changed out of all recognition since our day. No uniforms, boys and girls together, you could hardly tell the teachers from the pupils. The place has always had the reputation for being way out and arty.'

'But it's academic too. All the teachers at her school in London recommended it. Lucy must have good teaching. She deserves it.'

'Oh, she will. But it's only recently that it's improved so much academically, isn't it? Now it's an "in" school for the middle classes who can afford it. Anyhow, Lucy saw the headmaster for half an hour or so and I spoke to him after. Acting in *loco parentis*, of course. He was impressed all right. She's a clever girl is Lucy. Loads of confidence, never batted an eyelid. I think she liked the challenge. He's going to write to you and Robin – and I should think they would be delighted to have her . . . Look, I'm dying for a gin – we'll tell you all about it at lunch.'

Their discussion of the school ended in Kate saying firmly, 'If you do decide to go there, Lucy, I'll certainly go over and look round myself. And your father must too.' Laura was simply out of touch with schools, Kate decided, quite dismissing her negative impressions of Yarnston.

'OK,' said Lucy indifferently. 'Do I have time to go to the village before we go back to London, Laura? There are some things I want to get. And I won't be coming down the next weekend, Mother. I'm going to stay with Lucinda.'

When Lucy had gone off – humming and looking pleased with herself – Kate and Laura decided to have coffee outside. The continuing warmth had brought on the flowers and shrubs. The birds called cheekily. From the terrace, the garden looked like a spring bower.

'How marvellous this is,' Laura said, shutting her eyes and lifting her face to the sun.

'It's the first time we've sat out this year,' Kate said flatly, pouring. Laura shot her a quick look sideways. She had noticed at once that Kate seemed much more natural today.

235

Over lunch, talking about the school with Lucy, she had been controlled and sensible. For the first time since Guy's death, she had lost the frightening blankness of a sleepwalker. And that God-awful skirt and grubby sweater had disappeared; Laura fancied that Mrs Bundy may have had a hand in that.

'Let's make the most of it . . . thanks . . .' Laura took her coffee. Uncanny at reading Kate's mind, she knew that it had also suddenly struck her acutely that this was the first spring and summer without Guy. So her next question did not surprise her.

'Did you give all Guy's things to charity?' Kate asked carefully.

'Yes.'

'Including his bike?'

'Yes – that too.' Laura touched Kate's hand. 'It was the best thing. It had to be done.'

'Oh – I know. Thanks Laura.' Kate squeezed her hand back. 'What would I do without you?'

Steering the conversation into safer waters Laura said casually, 'By the way, Nico and Arabella's divorce will be through in a couple of months. After all this time. Amazing, isn't it?'

'I think Mother said . . .' Kate frowned. Her memory had developed gaping holes recently; she had been so totally taken over by grief. 'Or did you tell me?'

'I'm telling you now. It's all over and done with. Arabella is staying on in the house with the younger children – and Nico is living in London. The children were what it was all about for Arabella, so she's been very reasonable. And Nico seems to be much calmer these days, less in need of obsessive mothering. Which he won't get from me.'

'Will you get married, you and Nico?'

'Oh yes . . . we'll never get away from each other now.' She tipped back her head and laughed. 'There's never been anyone else for either of us, not for years. And we've always been faithful – in our way . . .' Laura sounded more contented than Kate had ever known her. And Kate thought she looked marvellous; thin as a rail, perfectly groomed, in her chic black and white outfit. The headmaster of Yarnston must have been bowled over. That Nico, soon to be her brother-in-law, seemed to have the knack of falling on his feet where women were concerned.

'I'm so glad, Laura.' Impulsively, Kate leant forward and kissed her. Laura looked surprised and happy. 'Do Mother and Pa know yet?'

'Mother asked, of course. She's never been exactly tactful in hiding her disapproval of Nico . . . But yes, they do know now – and say they're pleased.'

'What about the children? They must be quite grown up by now.'

'Yes, they are. Boris is a nice lad and he's helping out in the gallery and showing promise. The others come and go . . . they've had such an odd life with the potty Arabella that Nico and I must seem very ordinary to them. And one thing really does please me.'

'What's that?'

'Nico has promised to give up flying. He got hooked on it soon after we met – and it's been a serious bone of contention. I'm always nervous when he's flying. I daresay he's an excellent pilot – he's brilliant in whatever he does – but he takes risks. This plane has caused endless trouble. So he's promised – just a couple more trips and he's selling it. And that's that.'

'Thank heavens . . . and what about the shop?'

Laura turned and held out her cup for more coffee.

'Frankly, I'm bored stiff with it. I feel it's gone about as far as it can go. I'm thinking of ways I can decently – and profitably – get out of it. From now on, I want to be able to go off with Nico without wondering what's about to go wrong when I'm away. Because something invariably does . . .' She turned her head and looked directly at Kate. 'And what about you, Katie? It's time, you know – that you got on with your life too. With Robin.'

Kate looked away.

'I don't want to run before I can walk,' she said obscurely.

'Now what's that supposed to mean?'

'I'm feeling better . . . here . . . about Guy. Easier. I can't look beyond that just now.'

She always had been the stubborn one.

237

'Katie,' Laura said gently. 'I think you should. I think you must.'

Kate wouldn't look at her.

Laura thought: we'll have to do something about that greying hair. And get her back to looking herself. The pink cotton skirt and sweater was an improvement, certainly. But *she* couldn't keep her eye on the house in London for ever; Kate must accept this as Robin did. With boarding school in sight for Lucy, he was already talking about selling it, getting a small flat somewhere in central London.

Laura sighed. She had learnt years ago never to cast stones. But did Kate know, or suspect, anything at all? Surely . . .

'*Why* must I?' Laura was caught off guard by the harshness in Kate's voice. '*Why* must I come back?' she repeated, staring. Laura blinked. She decided the time had come to deliver a careful paragraph or two on family togetherness, which she had, as it happened, rehearsed in her head in the car that morning. She took a deep breath.

'Look Katie,' she began. 'It can't be wise . . .' But Kate's look veered away; her face suddenly brightened. Following her glance, Laura saw a tall, very thin, red-haired young man approach across the lawn. Kate jumped up.

Laura heard her say as she went quickly towards him, one hand outstretched, 'Sebastian, what a lovely surprise. Margot told me you'd be down later this week . . . do come and meet my sister, Laura . . .'

What Laura had been going to tell Kate – circumspectly of course – was that unless she started to take up the threads of her life in London with Robin very soon, it might be too late.

She got up and followed Kate down the shallow steps to the lawn. There were daisies scattered across the grass; clouds of forsythia billowed across the old stone wall. Kate had done well with Knyght's Wood, Laura thought irrelevantly. She stood behind her, as she chatted away to Sebastian Sinclair, waiting for her to turn round. He was still, she noticed, holding onto Kate's hand. And it suddenly occurred to Laura, that perhaps it already was too late. For Robin – and for her.

Robin drove down late on Friday night. He was exhausted he

said, looking it, and he'd had dinner before he left. He poured himself a scotch, picked up the sheaf of papers he had brought and went straight upstairs.

In bed, wide-awake, watching the shadows on the ceiling, Kate said, 'I had a better week after all, Robin. Perhaps it was the fine weather – and the spring. I don't know ... but everything began to come into focus again. For the first time. Since Guy.' She ran her fingers caressingly down his back. He was lying on his side in the semi-darkness, away from her.

'Good,' he said.

He did not turn towards her.

'The Sinclairs want us to come for lunch tomorrow,' Kate told him at breakfast the next morning. 'They're charming people – I'm sure you'd like them. Sebastian is so natural – you'd never think he was already such a successful actor. I said I'd ask you when you got down and let them know. So is it all right?'

Robin glanced up from the paper he was still reading. He still looked weary – his faced lined, his eyes clouded. It hurt Kate to see him like this; she felt helpless.

'Out of the question I'm afraid.' He held out his coffee cup.

'But why, Robin? They're neighbours, they've been so kind to me. They took me with them on Friday to see a sort of converted barn Margot is thinking of buying. She needs more space for her knitwear business. I thought you might enjoy seeing it too ...'

'I've just told you, Kate, it's out of the question. I've got to go back to London first thing tomorrow. I meant to tell you last night only I was so dog-tired. We're having a whole day's seminar on the new high tech equipment which is piling into the office at a frightening rate – and alarming cost. It all goes into immediate operation in October – and we can't afford mistakes. We discussed it – and Sunday seemed to make the most sense. So everyone is coming in, including the experts. Sorry. Any more milk?'

'In the refrigerator.'

He got up and took it out.

Robin's business was a mystery to Kate these days. He was

239

rarely forthcoming about it. This was as much as he had told her for months.

'You go,' he said casually. 'To those people for lunch – the Sinclairs. Please. Just because you've decided to stick yourself down here, there's no reason for you not to have friends, is there?'

He returned to his paper – and Kate didn't reply.

Complaining that he was in desperate need of exercise, Robin telephoned friends who had a hard tennis court and arranged a game for later that morning. After lunch, he took the car up on the Downs and went for a long tramp. On his way back, he dropped in briefly on the Holfords. Kate did some shopping and messed about the house and garden. Late in the afternoon, she walked over to Thrush Cottage. She came upon Sebastian wrestling with the hedge, brandishing shears, high rubber boots caked with mud. His usual heavy sweater was stuck with twigs and old leaves. From the state of his clothes and his face, which was covered in grime and sweat, Kate guessed he had been savagely attacking the garden all day. It needed it.

'You look busy, Sebastian,' Kate called out, laughing aloud at the sight of him. 'Who's winning – you or the garden?'

'Kate . . . it's you . . .' He squinted at her in the sunlight, dragging a muddy sleeve across his forehead. 'Not a bad question.' He looked embarrassed. 'I suspect I've probably made everything worse. But it's exhilarating stuff isn't it? Come in and give your advice. I'm a hopeless townie . . . Margot just wants everything to look beautiful instantly – with no work . . .'

Kate, who had brought her stick as she often did these days when she ventured any distance, joined him in the small, umkempt garden. She saw at once that it had possibilities.

'It could be charming,' she said. 'Those bushes will have to go . . . and the border needs re-stocking. That's a marvellous old apple tree you've got . . .' Walking round, they scrutinised every inch with both of them making suggestions and frequently disagreeing in a friendly way.

'I thought you didn't know anything about gardens,' Kate mocked. 'An actor, living in London . . .'

'I'm a beginner. But I like it. It makes a marvellous change from learning lines and sweating out auditions. Sitting by the phone and willing it to ring. What a way to live – pleading to be allowed to prance round the stage pretending to be someone else.' He sounded depressed.

'Sebastian . . . I know it's a risky business, but you're making your name. Finishing the play for television, a film in Holly-wood next. You must be turning away work all the time.'

'So I am. Of a sort. And you're right, I've been lucky. I always say so. But you know that play Margot and I were talking about the other night? I'd really like a chance at that next year. It's something to get the teeth into. I thought I had it. But I spoke to my agent this morning – and so far, the great man who has written the thing hasn't asked for my services. And we thought he was so keen. To talk it over and get me to do a reading at least.'

He sounded so despairing that Kate tactfully led the conver-sation back to the garden at Thrush Cottage – and Sebastian cheered up. She also promised to go with him to the local nursery sometime next week – to get bedding plants, some new rose bushes. And advice.

'By the way, Margot is closeted with the estate agent in his office. She's determined to go after that barn. I'm glad. It's terrific, isn't it?'

'It could be wonderful.' It had been disastrously converted to a house at some stage. But enough of the original features were still left – the high vaulted roof and dark beams. 'Once its simplicity is restored, it would be ideal for Margot's purposes. Obviously, the cottage is too small and there's no room for a shop or showroom.'

'That's what she says. And she's really digging in with the business. Her enthusiasm is one of the nicest things about Margot. Ever since we all saw it together on Friday she's been doing sums on the backs of envelopes. That's how Margot arranges her finances, always has. But actually, she's quite shrewd.' Sebastian looked down at Kate. She was standing close beside him, inspecting the climbing roses by the small dining-room window. 'Kate . . .'

'What?' She peered more closely at the climber. 'I think this will be pretty in the summer, I believe I remember seeing it one year, a mass of creamy flowers . . .'

'*Kate* . . .' His magical voice low and intimate. It was an instrument he could do anything with. She turned. Instinctively her lips parted. She had coloured slightly. 'If I weren't in this piggishly disgusting state, I would be strongly inclined to kiss you again.'

'*Sebastian* . . .'

He caught her hands in his, dirty though they were – and held them.

'Where is he – Robin?'

'He went out. He needed exercise he said. I expect he's gone for an endless walk.'

'And left you alone – as you've been all week.'

'I don't mind,' Kate said defensively.

'What about lunch then? Tomorrow?'

'Robin has to go back to London,' she said quickly. 'They're having a try-out of the computers for Big Bang. It seems odd, but he says Sunday is the only day it can be managed.'

'Poor devil. That makes me feel that an actor's life has its blessings after all – despite the racked nerves and the uncertainties. But you'll come, won't you?'

Kate looked down at the grubby hands which still gripped hers. Then back up at Sebastian. He was a marvellous colour from all the fresh air and the last of the sun had turned his hair carrotty red. She laughed. She felt on an instant something she hadn't for a very long time – young and free; that everything was possible; gay.

'Of course I will,' she said wholeheartedly. 'Of course I will . . .'

'Where on earth have you been?' Robin asked when she let herself in through the back door. Talking to Sebastian, she hadn't realised how late it was. Being outdoors had invigorated her; she looked well. Robin, who was unlacing his walking boots, looked up.

'I went over to the Sinclairs,' she said serenely, slipping off her coat. 'To tell them that you wouldn't be able to manage lunch tomorrow. They're redoing the garden at Thrush

Cottage, so we talked over some ideas about planting.' As he hadn't met either of them, Kate saw no point in mentioning that Margot had not been there.

'It's quite a way – and a rough path.' He had seen her stick. 'I do wish you'd be more sensible,' he said crossly. 'You don't always do as much as you could to help yourself, you know.'

This struck a sensitive nerve in Kate.

'Did you have a nice afternoon?' she enquired, steeling herself against him. 'I suppose you saw my parents . . .'

'Only for a few minutes. Felicity was stuck in the garden. John has aged . . .'

'We all have,' Kate said quietly.

During that long, sad evening in the unnaturally still and childless house, they didn't talk much. After dinner, Robin put aside his book and told Kate quickly and bluntly that if Lucy was accepted at Yarnston he would put the house on the market and look out for a small flat in the West End. 'It's all we need now – the house is too big, it's expensive to run – and as you have persistently declined to live there . . .' Kate bowed her head. 'You surely can't object?'

Kate looked up at him.

'Don't bully me, Robin,' she said.

'For God's sake, Kate . . .' He wrenched himself out of the chair and stood with his back to her, hands gripping the mantelpiece. He took a deep breath and went on, very deliberately, 'I have kept going the only way I know. Routine – work – getting through one day at a time. I have tried to be patient. Nothing can ever be the same for either of us again. We both know that. But we've got to go on and my work and my life are in London. Not here. You seem not to have understood that . . .'

'I do, Robin, I do . . . but I had to get away from that house. I couldn't have borne Guy's loss – not there . . .'

'I understand that. I have, as I said, been patient. But it's nearly four months now since – since . . .'

'Since what, Robin? Go on, say it . . .' Kate leant forward. She could see his face in the mirror above – reddened, deeply lined, anguished.

243

*It should never have happened, it should never have happened . . .
you should have got him to Tony earlier . . . taken him straight to
the hospital . . .*

'Say it, Robin,' she shouted in suddenly fury. 'Say it . . .
Since *when?*'

She, too, knew how to inflict pain.

He turned to her – shocked, vulnerable. He said through lips
stiff with grief, 'Since – Guy – died.'

'Repeat that, Robin, repeat that . . .' She was pitiless.

He did.

Kate dropped her head onto her knees and burst into wild
sobs. He did not touch her. He left the house immediately –
doors banging, gravel crunching. Kate slept in Lucy's room
that night. Sometime towards midnight she heard Robin using
the phone. She pulled the duvet up round her ears. The
upstairs telephone jangled lightly as he replaced the receiver.
Next morning, when she got down, there was a note on the
kitchen table saying that he had already left for London.

An excited call from Lucy later in the week announced her
acceptance at Yarnston. 'I'm so glad, darling,' Kate told her.
'Well done . . . I'll meet you off the 5.30 on Friday – and we'll
have a celebration.' Lucy had taken to enjoying champagne
on special occasions – and she would see there was a bottle in
the refrigerator.

Laura, phoning later, seemed equally pleased. 'But I hope
she likes Yarnston after all this,' she added. 'I wasn't all that
taken with it myself. It thought it seemed a bit creepy, but I
didn't want to put Lucy off . . .' She was leaving the next day
for New York with Nico – a quick trip for an exciting auction.
And this was – possibly – the last time they would go there as
an unmarried couple.

'Laura, how marvellous . . . is the divorce really through
then?'

'At last. We'll have to make some wedding plans. That
should make Mother happy.' She sounded on top of the world.
'Speaking of plans, have you got any yourself – for coming
back to London?'

'Well – no . . .'

244

'I think you're wrong there, Katie.'

The following morning there was a letter from Robin, the first part typed by his secretary, the last hastily scrawled by him. Lucy had decided on Yarnston and as of that day, he had put the house on the market and instructed the same agents to find a suitable two-bedroom flat somewhere central. He mentioned one or two squares. His father had had a suspected second stroke and he was flying to Jersey to see him the following weekend. He did not suggest that she came with him and made no mention of when he was next coming down to Knyght's Wood. Kate replied at once, more memo than letter, saying that of course she agreed about selling the house – and looking for a small flat. She was sorry, she wrote, to hear about his father. She would give his mother a ring that evening. She signed the note simply 'K'.

As she was about to post it, the enormity of what was happening to their lives struck her like a physical blow. She stood stock still, thinking hard, for a few moments. Then she slipped the letter through the post box.

They had not exchanged a word since the scene after dinner the previous Saturday night.

Chapter 23

At least once a week, Kate's parents spent the day with her at Knyght's Wood. Felicity Holford was devoting more and more time to her garden these days. The continuity of her plants and flowers soothed her and the hard work helped her sleep at night. The proposed book she had discussed with her editor so hopefully towards the end of last year had come to nothing. Felicity doubted that it ever would. Just turned seventy, she had more on her mind, and all of it burdensome, than ever before. John Holford's continuing depression following Guy's death worried her terribly. They were off to Italy soon for an extended stay as they had planned on earlier. She hoped, desperately, that the change and the interest would begin to pull him back from his edge of despair; from the hours spent alone, doing nothing, in his study, which was the reversal of a lifetime of meaningful activity. Her one solace was that at last, it seemed as though Laura was going to settle down harmoniously with Nico Kirilov. But Kate and her Robin? All Felicity's keen antennae were aroused in that direction . . .

One afternoon, Kate and her father walked down to the church. The simple headstone they had ordered for Guy's grave would soon be ready. And it seemed to comfort John Holford – Kate noticed this particularly – to see the churchyard well tended. If the weather was fine, he would linger, strolling up and down the paths or sitting quietly in the church.

'It's Lucy's half-term, next weekend, isn't it?' her father asked. 'So you'll have company in the house for a few days. Er – Robin up to his eyes in it at work, is he?' He looked at her keenly, taking her arm as they crossed the village street and started down the narrow lane to the church. Kate had an obscure feeling that her mother had put him up to asking the question.

'You're right – he is rather,' Kate replied easily. She had been half expecting this. 'And he's been to see his father for two weekends running. The second stroke badly affected Jim's left side – and his speech. They're very worried about him. He's in hospital now, but Doris is having the house altered downstairs so that she can manage him at home with a nurse. Lucy and I will go over to see them later in the summer.'

'Poor chap. Terrible for him – and hard on Doris too.'

'She's a strong woman, and she's coping well, Robin says . . .' Kate then quickly changed the subject to their Italian holiday. She couldn't be sure, but she didn't think her father sensed anything amiss. She hoped not. They had both suffered enough at Guy's death; the situation between her and Robin was too raw and intimate even to be hinted at. It was one of several aspects of her life that made no sense at all to Kate at the moment.

Because she had not seen Robin since he left very early that Sunday morning, while she was still asleep in Lucy's room, and they had had only two short, formal telephone conversations from his office.

When they got back to the house, Felicity asked, 'What about a summerhouse, Kate? Last winter, you were so keen on it . . .' She looked achingly at her daughter to whom she could bring so little comfort. She, more than her husband, had divined deeper emotional confusion. She suspected that Robin was avoiding Knyght's Wood even at weekends now. And she wondered – and worried – why. This was the first serious concern about their daughters which Felicity had not shared with her husband.

'A summerhouse? Yes of course, we were planning for it, weren't we?' Kate laughed in a way that Felicity didn't care for. 'What an age ago it seems. Another life almost. No, we won't get one now. I can't think why it ever seemed important . . .' Listening, Felicity thought she caught a note of despair – which made her hurt more. 'I'm not even doing much with the garden . . .'

This was true. The gardener kept it reasonably tidy, but Kate had worked in it very little that year. One reason was her hip. The pain had been so bad lately that it frequently woke her during the night. When her father came back from Italy, she intended telling him this. She was certain that she ought to make another appointment with the specialist in Harley Street.

Then, 'It's exciting about Laura and Nico, isn't it, Mother? Laura seems so contented . . .'

'Oh yes, I'm absolutely thrilled for her . . . I never thought I would be – but I am.' Felicity's eyes brightened. 'We had dinner with them in London a couple of weeks ago, just before they went off to the States, and they seemed so happy together. He's such an interesting man – to be fair – and he seems to have calmed down a lot, Pa thought. It's sad about the children and the divorce, but there we are . . . When we get back from Italy, we'll make plans for the wedding. In the autumn, I think. Very quietly in London – and a family lunch after. After all these years, imagine . . . It's still nothing we would ever have expected for Laura – it's a funny old life, isn't it? You can just never tell . . .'

'No,' Kate agreed. 'You can't, can you?'

As they were leaving, Kate took her father to one side and asked him whether he thought the local hospital could use Guy's games and toys in the children's ward. 'Mrs Bundy and I have sorted them all out – and I'd like to have his room here cleared now,' Kate said quietly. 'It would be nice to think of them being used and enjoyed again.' Instinctively, they leant together.

When he could, John Holford said, 'I'm sure this can be arranged. I'll have a word with the staff there.'

'Thanks, Pa.'

'And Kate – it's time you thought about London again, my darling.' He grasped her shoulder. 'You can't go on living here alone. It's not right. He's a good man, your Robin. Remember that, will you?'

Kate felt tears stinging her eyelids. She nodded.

'I will, Pa, I will.'

When she came to Knyght's Wood for the half-term holiday,

Kate took Lucy over to Thrush Cottage. Sebastian was doing an important audition in London – 'The play he's been driving himself – and me – mad about looks like coming through for the spring,' Margot told them at the door. 'But once this is over, he'll be down for the rest of the summer . . . Hello, Lucy, lovely to meet you at last . . . Come in and look at all the samples. Excuse the mess, but I'm getting a collection together.' She turned to Kate and kissed her on both cheeks. 'Kate, love, where on earth have you been hiding yourself? I've got masses to tell you, all exciting . . . Sebastian and I came over to find you last week but you weren't home . . .'

'I've been helping my parents get themselves organized, Margot,' Kate told her evasively. 'They've gone off to Italy for two months . . . which meant the house had to be shut up and Raffles taken to the kennels . . .' This was partly true; Kate had spent several days packing, cancelling newspapers and dealing with the indoor plants. Both her parents seemed to Kate to be slightly out of touch; more than once she had wondered how they would cope with the driving and the unknown villa awaiting them in Tuscany. But she had also, since her bitter words with Robin, avoided any social contact, even with the Sinclairs.

'Heavens,' Lucy was saying, looking around Margot's sitting-room in astonishment. 'I've never seen anything like it . . .' Knitted garments, in every colour – some plain, some with striking designs – hung from every possible ledge. The haphazard piles of knitted pieces came magically together in an Aladdin's cave of smart designer knitwear. 'Wherever do they all come from?'

'Faithful knitters I've had for years in and around London – and one or two new ones I've managed to inveigle down here . . .'

'But who does all the designs?'

Lucy fingered a black sweater with a starburst of brilliant fuchsia across the front.

'Oh, I do that,' Margot told her. 'I've been doing it for knitting patterns for years. Knitting myself too.'

'Laura – my aunt – would be fascinated,' Lucy said, impressed. 'She adores anything creative. Have you met her?'

249

'Not yet. But I know her shop ... I've even bought one of those wickedly expensive and heavenly smelling candles that she imports from France. Look, Kate, since it's a sunny day let's sit outside and have a decent cup of tea ... I've been working on the catalogue all day ... I'm longing to tell you everything that's happened. It's been such an exciting time ... Lucy – you come with me and we'll put everything on a tray. Go out and sit, Kate. We'll be with you in a few minutes ...'

So Kate sat in one of the chairs placed round the wooden table beneath the old apple tree. Sunshine filtered through. Climbing roses smothered the side of the old cottage, curving round the window sills, milky petals spilling onto the path. It was very peaceful; bees humming and pausing and humming again. Here and there a bright splash of flowers. She could hear Lucy and Margot chattering away in the kitchen like old friends. Margot, Kate thought amused, had made another of her instant conquests.

She heard a burst of laughter from Margot; Lucy replying – high and clear; china clattering. She realised with a start that she was listening for another voice, Sebastian's. Although it was warm and sheltered where she was sitting, Kate shivered and pulled her cardigan tightly round her.

They came out with mugs of tea on a tray and a plate of homemade biscuits. Margot came first, bending her head at the low doorway, pleasingly eccentric in her white trousers and a large Mexican poncho. Lucy followed, also dipping beneath the lintel. She was taller than Margot, Kate noticed, and slim as a reed, in her usual creased cotton skirt and T-shirt and wide leather belt. Her hair was still short and frizzy and she wore delicate silver earrings. Her looks were striking rather than pretty. Kate sometimes despaired of her using her allowance on more becoming clothes. Perhaps Margot, with her sense of colour and design, could bring some gentle influence to bear.

'Have you heard about the old barn, Mother?' Lucy asked. 'The one on the road north from Laverton – where we used to go for walks?' She handed her a biscuit while Margot poured. 'It's going to be a showroom – for all those sweaters and things ... I think it's amazing ...'

'So you've actually bought it, Margot?' Kate said, taking the tea. 'Sebastian said he thought you were determined . . . and you certainly haven't wasted any time . . .'

'I couldn't afford to do that,' Margot replied crisply. 'It's all systems go. I simply had to have a headquarters for the business. It's far too big now to be coped with at Thrush Cottage, it's been building very rapidly this past year. So the moment I got the barn I took the painter we used here over – and *he* brought a carpenter and an electrician . . . and we worked out the simplest and cheapest way to get it into shape. Good lighting and whitewashed walls and the floors sanded down and polished. With a bit of luck, it should be ready in a month or two.'

'Margot – that's wonderful . . .'

'I think so, too. I'm very enthusiastic – I've been telling Lucy . . . I've been in touch with my London outlets, plus a few shops round here, and all sorts of buyers throughout the country. And abroad. Several buying agencies in Europe are showing interest – and I might have landed a couple of browsers from the States. But if my one-off production line is to work at all, I've got to get the orders straight – sooner rather than later. Then I can parcel the work out to my knitters – and oversee it all myself. If the quality isn't up to standard or we don't deliver on time – the business is dead. No second chances.'

'So – are you having some sort of an opening then?' Lucy asked hopefully.

'Of course we are . . . at the beginning of September, before Sebastian goes to Los Angeles. A fashion show combined with a blast of a party . . .' Margot sat back in her chair; her smile dazzled. Her hair looked more gold than grey in the sun and heavy ropes of blue beads hung round her splendid neck. 'Tea for you, Lucy? I've got my three models I've used for years coming down from London . . . and once I get the catalogue together it can go off to the printer. You'll be there, both of you, now won't you?'

Kate and Lucy looked at each other.

'I'm sure . . .' Kate began.

'Oh we will, of course we will,' Lucy finished. 'We're not

going anywhere this summer, are we Mother? Only to Jersey for a few days . . . and Yarnston doesn't start until later in September . . .'

'That's marvellous,' Margot said. 'Sebastian is in charge of organising the party . . . and we'll put you both to work. I've got my eye on you, Kate, to help with the orders.'

'Margot, you know I'll do anything I can . . . I'd be happy to . . .'

'And I can do the invitations for you, Margot, if you like. I'm not bad at calligraphy, am I Mother?'

'You're very good, Lucy,' Kate agreed. She could never remember Lucy being enthusiastic about anything around Knyght's Wood before.

'Excellent. Do them you shall,' Margot told her.

They sat on in the sunny cottage garden, swapping ideas and making suggestions – laughing a lot – until Kate said reluctantly that she was sure it was time they made a move to go home. 'We've been here for hours – and you've got work to do, Margot . . .'

Just then, the phone rang. Margot went inside to answer it. She came out minutes later to say that it was Sebastian. The reading had gone well and he had a meeting with the playwright to talk about the part tomorrow. It wasn't in the bag by any means, but he was hopeful.

'And I'm not going to let you go without a drink . . . Take the things in, would you Lucy, and I'll get us a glass of lovely cold white wine.'

Walking back to Knyght's Wood as the sun set, Lucy asked Kate, 'What's Sebastian Sinclair like then? He doesn't look like his mother . . . I wasn't keen on him in *Hunter's Island* although most of my friends thought he was divine. He looked wet, I thought.'

It occurred to Kate that this was what Lucy thought about her too.

'Oh he's not,' she said quickly. 'He's charming. He's got the most wonderful voice . . .'

'Well, obviously. He would have. He's a trained actor after all,' Lucy replied crossly.

'I suppose so, although he sounds completely natural . . . He's got his mother's red hair – and her nice manner. I think he's a bit shy underneath.'

'Margot's great,' Lucy said decisively. 'She's absolutely great.'

'I thought you'd like her.'

They walked on through the village in silence. Kate was thinking: I'm glad Lucy got on with Margot. And she sounded quite enthusiastic about the business and the opening party. Perhaps Margot will take her in hand a bit and give her something to do. Lucy can do anything she sets her mind to. And it looked as though Margot could do with all the help she could get.

Privately, Kate had been dreading the long summer holidays ahead with Lucy – often alone and mostly bored – hanging round the house. She had already asked her several times if she had any plans or wanted to go off somewhere with friends; Lucy had simply said, 'Don't think so, no.' And refused to be drawn any further. And it was the time of year, with Guy running in and out of the house, that she had come to look forward to most . . . Now, she wondered, panic-stricken, how she would get through the hours and days and weeks of it . . .

'Dad coming down is he – this weekend?' Lucy asked non-chalantly as they walked up the drive. The grass had been cut that day. Long golden shadows fingered the smooth green. Roses scented the air. The herbaceous border, set against the weathered old wall, was a picture in soft blues, creams and whites. Kate thought of Guy, rounding the corner in his muddy boots, calling out to her to come and see something, running straight into her arms . . .

When she didn't answer, Lucy said, 'You're thinking about Guy, aren't you?'

Kate started.

'Yes – yes I was. I'm sorry, darling, you said something . . . I didn't hear . . .'

'Do you often – think about Guy? Or all the time?'

'It's always there,' she said faintly, rubbing her hip. 'I suppose it always will be . . . What about you, Lucy?' She fixed anxiously on Lucy's inscrutable face. She would take the burden of that pain from her – if only she could.

253

'I don't know – sometimes it seems unreal, as though it couldn't have happened. Not to *us*. Some days are all right. And then I remember something silly about him. And I go to pieces.' Kate started to put her arm round her, but Lucy moved away. Kate blinked and swallowed. They were by the back door now, Lucy fishing out the key from behind the big tub of geraniums. 'Your hair needs cutting, by the way . . .' Lucy pushed open the door. 'It's too long and all wispy round the sides . . .'

'Oh . . .'

'I noticed today, at Margot's.'

'I'd rather forgotten about it . . . I'll get one of the girls at the hairdressers in the village to do it.'

'I could cut it for you, if you like.' Lucy offered, hitching herself onto the table and picking up the local newspaper. 'I cut Lucinda's hair last weekend. Her mother nearly fainted when she saw . . .' She flipped the pages.

'Perhaps – we'll see . . . You asked about Dad, didn't you? Whether he was coming down . . .?' Kate went on cautiously. 'I'm not absolutely sure but I expect so. He didn't say anything about it, did he?'

'Nope.'

The next day, Saturday, walking home with some shopping late in the morning, she heard, '*Kate.*'

She would know that voice, at any time, anywhere in the world. She spun round.

'Sebastian . . .' He was only yards behind her – his arms folded, smiling with some of his mother's radiance. She had never seen him except in old country clothes before. He was wearing a cream-coloured suit, loose fitting, with wide shoulders. It looked exactly right on a young man with his lanky build and red hair. Kate also registered instantly that it was nothing Robin would ever own. 'Where on earth have you sprung from? I thought . . .'

'London. I took the early train down. Here – let me have that . . .' He grabbed her shopping basket and took her elbow. 'I'll walk back to Knyght's Wood with you. I was going to drop in anyhow.' And as he steered her across the busy main street, 'I got the part, Kate. I got it . . .' He sounded as exultant as he looked. 'The old man liked my interpretation – and he made up his mind immediately. So it's mine. Make or break . . . it's a terrifying thought . . .'

As soon as they were back on the pavement, Kate stopped and looked at him. His excitement had communicated itself to her. She felt tremulous – and a bit breathless.

'Sebastian, that's wonderful . . . congratulations . . . you must be ecstatic . . .'

'I am. You know it was what I wanted more than anything.'

'I know, I know.'

They stood smiling at each other while Saturday morning shoppers sauntered round them. Half recognising Sebastian, who was beginning to be talked about in the district, there were a few curious stares.

'We'd better get a move on . . . we're holding things up rather . . .' He guided her up towards the house, walking slowly as he knew she must.

'You'll be brilliant, Sebastian . . . He must be sure or he wouldn't have chosen you.'

'It's an awful responsibility . . . You'll have to come to the first night and bring me luck. You're the first person to know apart from my agent and Margot. It's a long way off – but you will come, won't you?' Kate didn't answer. 'Please Kate . . . we're a superstitious lot, we actors,' he pressed.

'Perhaps.'

'That's better . . . Margot was going to give you a ring but I said I'd drop in on you instead. We're having a sort of party tonight, more of a spur-of-the-moment picnic really . . . a celebration for my good luck combined with a kick-off for Margot's business. She's got some of her knitters coming with their families . . . two London buyers plus one who's over from the States, an old friend of hers, who's coming for the weekend. Some local shopkeepers Margot has her eye on. My agent. A couple of London friends . . .'

'It sounds a lot of people . . .'

'Oh, Margot loves organising things like this. And they always work. It's going to be a moveable feast beginning early

255

with drinks in the garden – then a cold buffet supper – and going on as late as possible. One of my friends is bringing his guitar . . . and the weather is marvellous . . .'

'I don't know, Sebastian . . . Robin . . . and Lucy . . .'

'Margot said particularly that she wanted Lucy,' he said quickly. 'She took to her in a big way. And of course,' he added courteously, 'if your husband is here, we'd love to have him. Is he?' Eyebrows barely raised.

Kate shook her head.

'And I'm not sure . . .' She stopped. 'Your mother was so kind to Lucy when I brought her over . . .'

'She adored her . . . in that case, you'll come? Both of you? You give up?'

'Oh *yes* . . . And why don't you come in and meet Lucy now?' They were already at the bottom of the drive. 'And let's have a cold beer. It's hot suddenly – and I feel like it.'

'Good idea.'

Kate called all through the house; but as Lucy was nowhere to be found, they took their glasses outside to the terrace.

'I can't think where she's got to, she'll turn up,' Kate said.

Sebastian squinted down at the garden, riotously colourful in the sunshine. Through the trees, at the bottom of the valley, the river snaked and glittered. 'It's lovely here, Kate, so peaceful . . .' He tipped back his head and closed his eyes. He had already undone his collar and loosened his tie.

'Yes – I think so. I always have . . .'

After a few moments, eyes still closed, Sebastian said, 'You've cut your hair . . .'

'Yes.' Kate laughed, pleased – and surprised – that he had noticed. 'Lucy did it with my nail scissors last night. She said it needed it. I'd forgotten – really – about things like hair.'

'You mustn't.'

'No.'

She glanced down at her long denim skirt and the specially constructed canvas shoes which she wore every summer. She would have to look something out to wear to Margot's party. It was months, nearly four and a half now, since she had done anything other than get dressed, putting on the same clothes, over and over again, without a thought. She waited for the familiar tide of anguish and bitter regret – which, strangely, did not come.

They could hear the distant traffic sounds of the village. A bee nosed around the table – and buzzed off. As Sebastian leant forward, intending to pick up his glass, his hand touched Kate's. He raised it briefly to his lips and went on holding it lightly.

'Dearest Kate – are you a little healed?' he asked softly.

Kate considered the question seriously.

'Sometimes. I am now . . . at this moment.' And looking away. 'I get on with things – but there's nothing much left inside. Unreal – that's what Lucy said last night. About Guy. And it does seem unreal, that it had to happen to us.' She looked back at him. 'But what I can't bear is the – *if only, what if . . .*'

She couldn't bear it then; her face contorted.

'Getting Guy to the hospital earlier?' he asked quietly. Margot had already told him this.

She nodded.

'Isn't it unlikely that it would have made a difference? In any case, you could not possibly have known . . . or been expected to. As if you wouldn't, ever, have done everything you could.'

'Robin doesn't think so . . .' – her mouth tightening. And she could have added: I can't even talk to him about it – Robin – not naturally, not like this . . . not at all any more . . .

'Have pity . . .' Speaking so low – and yet distinct.

'*He* hasn't got very much,' she said.

After that they sat silently. When he had finished the beer, Sebastian looked at his watch, got up and said he had to be off. He must relieve Margot with the cooking chores. He was sorry he had missed Lucy, but he would see her tonight. And there was no question of them walking over; he would pick them up around 6.30 and bring them home – whenever that may be.

Lucy strolled into the kitchen some time after 2.30. She had met some kids who lived locally who she had known when she was small, she said, and they had sat around having a good natter. They seemed to have the lowdown on Yarnston

257

all right, she told Kate as she opened the refrigerator and began poking around.

'What did they say about it – Yarnston?' Kate was curious.

'Oh – this and that . . .'

'*What?*' Kate asked, exasperated. Lucy's evasiveness could be so maddening. She made a mental note to phone for an appointment with the headmaster on Monday morning. Robin had been quite wrong sending Lucy off for her interview with Laura in that high-handed manner he seemed to have adopted. Arms folded, she watched with growing irritation as Lucy stuck her finger into various plastic containers and began opening a sealed packet.

'Don't do that, Lucy,' she said sharply. 'Take what you want and leave the rest alone.'

Lucy looked round at her, mildly surprised.

'OK.' She took some ham and butter and made for the bread-box.

'Well, what did they say? About Yarnston?'

'Oh that . . . they all said the same thing, really: don't go there, mate . . . Apparently, it's a pretty rum set-up.'

Somewhat shocked, Kate decided not to pursue this. Spiteful local gossip, no doubt. The acceptance had already been posted. Robin had done this from London. So instead, she decided to spring tonight's party on Lucy – before she started her usual awkwardness about plans she had made. To her surprise, Lucy seemed pleased. 'Sebastian is going to pick us up about 6.30. He insisted . . . drinks in the garden and a buffet supper. It's in honour of a part Sebastian has just got – and Margot's business. Some of her knitters are coming – and friends of Sebastian's from London.'

'Sounds fun,' Lucy said briefly, licking mustard off her knife. 'Lucky I got your hair into shape last night, isn't it?'

Kate spent the afternoon in the garden, watering and weeding and deadheading roses. All the time her ears were strained for the phone – which would not ring. Surely Robin was coming down this weekend; he knew Lucy was here. He had been to Jersey two weekends running, she knew this from speaking to Doris Faraday. Ought she to phone – at least to ask . . .?

258

Should she? Was she being fair? Several times, walking through the hall, she so nearly dialled that familiar number; or if he was in the office, which was entirely possible, she could get him there.

Each time, something stopped her. Stubbornness? Pride? Hurt? A mixture of all three?

At five o'clock, she put on the kettle and made a cup of tea. Lucy had disappeared again. She would go upstairs and rummage around in the cupboards for something to wear. They mustn't keep Sebastian waiting. And if Robin did come, he would find the key in the usual place.

Chapter 24

And this was what he did.

Sebastian brought Kate home around half past ten. The party, as Sebastian promised, had gone splendidly, with unlikely combinations of people mixing well; moving in and out of the cottage and garden, enjoying the good, simple food and the cold wine. It was a warm night and Sebastian, who was used to pitching in theatrically, had rigged up white fairy lights in the bushes and the old apple tree. The party was still in full swing when he looked over at Kate and knew instinctively that she had had enough. He quietly disengaged himself and went over and whispered something to her. Kate looked at him gratefully, nodded, and they slipped away. One of his friends was beginning to strum on a guitar . . . it would all go on for a long while yet. Lucy was enjoying herself; he would see that she got home safely. Kate was pleasantly tired for a change, so they drove the half mile to Knyght's Wood in the companionable silence she found so effortless with Sebastian.

Kate saw Robin silhouetted against the light from the front door – which was wide open. After all, she was weak with relief at the sight of him. Everything and everyone else wiped instantly from her mind. She went quickly, blindly, towards him, 'Robin . . . Robin . . . you're here . . .' Only then did she remember Sebastian, behind her, still holding the car door. When she introduced them, she thought, for one ghastly second, that Robin was going to ignore Sebastian's friendly, outstretched hand. But he took it, nodded curtly and turned to Kate.

'Where on earth were you?' he asked coldly. 'And Lucy . . .'

'We've been to the Sinclairs . . . Margot and Sebastian kindly asked us to a party they're giving. Lucy is still there . . .'

'She's having a great time. The night is still young – and I've promised faithfully to see she gets home safely,' Sebastian said pleasantly. 'That's all right, I hope?' He looked quizzically from Robin to Kate and back to Robin.

'It's so kind of you, Sebastian . . .' In her summery lavender and white dress, Kate was still glowing. The recent fine weather had given her a tan and brought out her freckles. For an hour or two, meeting new people, swept up in Margot's hospitality, she had been taken right out of herself. 'Lucy is loving it . . .'

'I'd no idea where either of you were. You could at least have left a note . . .'

But we didn't know that you were coming, did we? Kate screamed at him inwardly, her anger meeting what she sensed was his; the warmth she had felt on seeing him dissipating. He jerked back towards the light and she saw his face clearly for the first time. He was haggard. She turned to Sebastian.

'We don't want to keep you from the party . . . you must go back to it . . . thank you so much, Sebastian. You and Margot must come and see us soon. For a meal. We'll be in touch . . .'

After more thanks and a wave – from Kate alone – she and Robin went into the house. Kate followed the trail of light into the sitting-room. There were newspapers scattered around Robin's usual chair, an empty glass on the table beside it. He picked this up and made for the drinks tray.

'We didn't know that you were coming,' Kate said, sitting in the chair opposite. 'We wondered . . . but you didn't let us know. Lucy had no idea either.'

The light behind her head was off; she was sitting in half darkness. Robin, splashing whisky, did not reply. He came and sat heavily. He looked dreadful. Kate saw that – and ached somewhere. All the years in the City since he was a young man had left their mark. The struggle with Condicote which had ended in success. Now the huge push towards a new technological concept of the Stock Exchange – millions and millions of the enlarged American firm's money riding on it. So much of this, despite his aggression and his will to win, went against the grain; the long days spent on and off the phone, in and out of meetings or watching a computer screen; belying his true nature which craved the outdoors and physical activity.

Then – Guy.

Kate understood all this, but she was powerless to bridge the gulf that had opened between them; and neither, in certain ways – her own hurt, her stubbornness which was also her strength – did she want to.

'It looks as though the house has been sold,' he said, holding his glass, not looking at her directly. 'A young American couple. I've accepted the offer.' He mentioned the price. 'It's as good as I'll get. And I've found another flat – the right price, very central, immediately available. I put the particulars over there . . .' He waved towards her desk where a pile of bills and personal letters still lay – unopened. 'I've already made a bid.'

Kate inclined her head.

'I see . . .'

'The house will have to be cleared, belongings labelled, given away, brought here . . . all that. You're prepared to do it?'

'Of course.' She thought again how terrible he looked. 'It is, after all, my home,' she said with dignity.

'Yes – well.' He smiled without kindness. 'One forgets these things . . .'

Kate leant forward – aghast.

'Whatever do you mean, Robin?'

'Forget it.' He drank – and set the glass down on the table. 'We can go into all this when I get back. Kate . . .' He hesitated. 'Look, I don't know how to . . . I don't want . . .'

'What don't you know . . .?'

'Oh nothing . . .' He sounded inexpressibly weary. 'I just want to tell you that I'm off to Turkey – probably for a month. It's the last chance I'll get for God knows how long. There's a boat,' he said vaguely, rubbing his eyes. 'Rupert and Jill, some others . . . we'll sail down the coast, in and out of ports. It'll be pretty rough living. Frankly, it sounds like a bit of heaven to me just at the moment.'

'When – when will you be going?'

262

So it was to be Turkey this time. She, without question, excluded. And – 'some others'? She had too little strength, and too much pride, to ask.

'Next weekend with luck. I'll phone before I leave. The office can get in touch with me. Anything you need, my secretary . . . In a couple of weeks you'll have Lucy down here for the summer. She's leaving school early, no point in her staying on after exams – nobody seems to mind. You'll be all right – won't you?' He stared.

'I suppose so.'

'And you've got your new friends – the Sinclairs.' The very sight of her with that actor son Sebastian, helping her out of the car, holding her arm, had sickened him. For two pins he would have attacked the fellow, set on him, torn him limb from limb, never mind he had no right nor reason. None what-soever.

'Yes . . .'

'Laura can come down. Your parents will be back . . .'

Her hands and wrists, narrower than ever these days, lay in her lap.

'I said "yes" Robin . . .'

He drummed his fingers on the arm of the chair.

'I'm going up.' He stood and drained the glass. 'There's some gear I'll want – jeans and sweaters.' Kate did not move. He looked at her – and quickly away. He was in torment.

Kate – dimly – perceived this. Unaware of the depth and complexity of his feelings she said quietly, 'All Guy's books and toys from here went this week. Mrs Bundy and I packed them up. Pa made enquiries – and they've gone to the chil-dren's ward in the hospital. That's good, isn't it?'

He could not answer. He blundered out of the room and up the stairs. Kate heard him moving about in their room above. Soon, she sighed, turned out most of the lights – and went up after him.

Lying sleepless, her hands behind her head, Kate heard foot-steps on the gravel, Lucy calling out to someone, a male voice answering . . . Not Sebastian's, she was sure of that. Perhaps it was his friend who played the guitar. Lucy had spent some time talking to him earlier in the evening . . . The front door shut, fairly quietly, and Lucy clomped upstairs and into her room. Kate heard her turn on the shower in her bathroom.

'Lucy's in,' Robin muttered into a pillow.

Kate had thought he was asleep.

'I know. I heard her too.'

Some time later, 'Go to sleep Kate . . .' He threw off the blanket – restless. Instinctively, she turned to him; the sound and feel of him beside her was overwhelmingly familiar. All of a sudden, she wanted him urgently – touched him in the way she always did. She slid beneath him, her arms across his shoulders.

He groaned out loud. 'I can't,' he choked into her neck. 'Kate – I can't . . .'

She slept on and off, after all, waking fully only when it was getting light. She knew she wouldn't sleep again, so there was nothing for it but to get up and go down to the kitchen. She made herself some tea, and still in her dressing-gown, stepped out into the dewy garden. The birds called noisily. Walking softly round the sleeping house, she came to the seat from which, between the trees, the river was visible. Now, it was hidden in a soft blue mist.

It was the mist that did it . . . Her heart hammering dangerously, Kate remembered a time in Paris, years ago, with Robin; when their future together stretched ahead – to this moment. She sat there with her eyes closed, hands clasped round the mug of hot tea. The day, little by little, strengthening around her.

What, exactly, did he want of her?

Dear Robin, I am sorry that on account of me our son died . . .

Was that it?

Or, *Dear Robin, I am sorry that after our son died I was no longer, at least for a while, able to go on living in the same house from which Tony Martin carried him to the hospital, even though it meant our being separated during the weeks . . .*

Which? Or was it a bit of both – plus something, or someone, else?

She was crying now, excruciatingly, the tears pouring down her cheeks, splashing onto her dressing-gown; rocking gently back and forth.

264

Dear Robin . . .
Where, oh where, was love?

Robin did as he said and phoned before he left – several times.
He wanted, he said repeatedly, to be sure that she and Lucy
had everything they needed. Lucy would be coming down for
the summer the following week; they could deal with packing
up the London house when he got back. A neatly typed
itinerary of places where he could be reached arrived in the
post. Kate barely glanced at it and dropped it on her desk with
the rest of her untouched correspondence.

'Have a wonderful time,' she said gaily, the night before he
was to fly to Istanbul. Although it was after eight, he was still
in the office, clearing his desk. 'Don't worry about Lucy and
me. We're all right. As a matter of fact, we're going to be
working. Both of us . . .'

'Working? Where?'

'For Margot Sinclair,' she said calmly. 'She's consolidating
and expanding her knitwear business in the old barn she
bought on the north road out of Laverton. It's going to be her
headquarters and showroom all in one. She wants to open it
as soon as possible. Lucy and I have offered to help out . . .
Lucy is rather looking forward to it.'

'I see.'

'Sebastian is down at Thrush Cottage for the summer,
before he goes to Hollywood to do a film, and he's a handy
decorator . . .'

A few moments silence . . .

'Kate? Kate, listen, I want to talk to you . . .'

Was this the moment he had tried – and failed – to summon
last weekend?

'Yes?'

She was upstairs in their bedroom, standing by her dressing table, her head only inches away from a small framed
etching of Paris. There was a golden evening light and she
looked out of the open window, down past the lawn and
the shadowed flowers to the orchard where the long grasses
had been cut and left to dry. Briefly, she imagined Robin in
the dusty London office with the traffic rumbling past.

265

Worlds apart now. She entirely missed the desperation in his voice.

'Kate? Are you there?'

'Yes, of course . . . And I've got the itinerary. I told you. Have a lovely time . . . sailing, exploring, walking, roughing it, all that sun . . .' She laughed recklessly. Not caring, as she thought, any more. Let him go as he'd always wanted to; let him do anything he damn well pleased. 'Everything you like best, Robin. That you always have.' She felt as free as one of the birds she could see wheeling against the pale sky. 'Send us a postcard – if you're ever near civilisation.'

'My secretary will have all the ports of call,' he said soberly, the vital moment lost between them. 'I can always be reached.'

'Goodbye, Robin, goodbye . . .'

Later that week, Kate drove over to Yarnston for an appointment with the headmaster. He was cordial and sympathetic. He knew about Guy's death, murmured appropriately, cleared his throat – and agreed that the change of scene from a London day school for her final year would undoubtedly be good for Lucy. He was also delighted to welcome a pupil of her academic record. Cambridge, he thought . . . Hadn't her father been there? He was sure she had every chance of getting in, providing she applied herself and kept her standards up. He had no doubt that she would easily adjust to Yarnston. She seemed a very confident young woman indeed.

He then arranged for Kate to be shown round the school by one of the senior pupils. Admiring the fine old house and the grounds in which a theatre and a new art department had just been built, Kate was both impressed and reassured. All the opportunities would be there; it was up to Lucy to make the most of them. She told Lucy this when she next saw her, adding, 'I can see we won't have to bother about a uniform of any kind. They all seemed to be wearing any old thing, the boys *and* the girls . . .'

'Oh Mother, you're so old-fashioned. What on earth did you expect?' September and Yarnston were light years from her mind.

For Lucy, who had developed something of a crush on

266

Margot Sinclair, was now passionately involved in every aspect of her latest project. Watching this, Kate could only feel relief. She didn't seem to have any plans for the long summer weeks – and this gave her an opportunity to occupy her time and use her wits. And as Margot soon shrewdly realised, there wasn't much Lucy couldn't do efficiently once she set her mind to it. Within days, she had her helping with the mail-order catalogue, checking the garments as they came in, choosing sketches and making lists of invitations.

On her own initiative, Lucy sent the newly printed brochures off to all the magazines with appropriate letters, each one different, all composed by Lucy – and written in her stylised script. As a result, one of the simpler sweaters was taken up as a special knitting offer for the Christmas number which was then being planned. Encouraged by this success, Lucy took over the entire opening programme, leaving Margot free to rush up to London and 'do the rounds', as she put it, with a few of her outstanding samples.

So Sebastian was left in charge of putting the barn to rights, which he did – superbly. This was his period of 'resting' before he began the heavy workload ahead. Most days, he called for Kate and took her with him. And she watched, delighted, as the large vaulted building, stripped of partitions and sham interior balconies, was returned to starkness and simplicity, and the walls whitewashed and lighting installed unobtrusively behind the dark beams.

The knitwear was to be displayed on tables and wooden coatracks placed in groupings round the room. A treasure of a carpenter, found by Margot, was building simple wooden slatted shelves to hold the rest of the merchandise. At one end, Margot had a large semi-screened office to deal with the orders and the business. And it was here that she or Lucy, or both of them, worked away for hours, in apparent chaos, with much noisy camaraderie – each knowing precisely what they were about.

The month was warm and dry and cloudy. Kate received a long and gushing letter from Felicity Holford – every other word underlined – saying that they were having the most marvellous time in Italy, Pa was enormously better, and they

267

had decided to stay on for another month. Relieved, Kate stuffed the letter into her pocket; she would show it to Lucy later. And Kate, too, was caught up in the excitement of bringing Margot's business into its new Laverton phase. She helped with folding the garments as they came in and chatting to the outworkers who brought them, making tea and typing letters. Margot and Lucy seemed to be perpetually in a whirl – on and off the phone, elated one moment, cast down the next, meeting any problem head-on. They both had creative minds; both came to decisions quickly. Margot told Kate one day that she really didn't know what on earth she would have done without Lucy at this crucial stage. And she was insisting on paying her a modest wage.

Through it all, Kate was intensely aware of Sebastian, calmly directing the workmen, helping to paint the walls and doing odd bits of carpentry and electrics himself. Jeans splattered with paint, his T-shirt soaked with dust and sweat, he hummed away as he worked. Kate noticed this; he was naturally musical, it seemed. And he never fussed; he got along marvellously with the small band of regular workmen, joshing them about this and that, appearing with cans of beer from time to time. Often, he would catch her eye or whisper something – and they would go off to the pub for a bread and cheese lunch, leaving the others behind. And they would chat about progress that had, or had not, been made that morning, and laugh affectionately at Margot's sometimes eccentric ideas. Or Sebastian would talk about a particular part or a stage personality. But only if Kate insisted could he be drawn to talk about his career; he seemed to be happy having this interval at Laverton, away from it all.

As Lucy was so often poring over something with Margot at the end of the day, it was Sebastian who usually brought Kate home – staying to have a drink outside, knowing now where the ice bucket was kept and the corkscrew and the wine Kate liked.

'It's fun, getting it all together,' said Kate – who had thought she would never have fun again. 'Margot's enthusiasm is catching – she's taken Lucy right out of herself. Which is wonderful . . .'

268

They were on the terrace, watching a streaky pink sunset, waiting for Lucy and Margot to appear as that evening they were all having a cold supper at Knyght's Wood.

'That's Lucy . . . And what about Kate?' Sebastian turned to her. He looked young and relaxed and healthy. Long legs stretched casually, arms hooked over the back of the chair. After all the work on a muggy day, the first drink had gone down well. He felt it – pleasantly; and so did Kate. They were sitting very close. Kate saw that Sebastian had a smudge of white paint down one side of his face. This moved her strangely.

'Sebastian – look . . . you've painted your face today by mistake, not the wall . . .' She laughed and reached out, her fingers feathering down his cheek . . . he caught her hand and held it.

'And what about Kate then?' he repeated. The voice made her tremble; it could always do that. But it was his gentleness which made her heart turn over. She said softly, 'In limbo . . . and I'm liking it . . .' Then, 'I had a card from Robin this morning, from somewhere along the coast of Turkey . . .'

'That's what I meant.' His eyes did not leave her face. 'Oh Kate . . .' He leant across to kiss her. She gasped. And it was only her quick awareness of the time and place which stopped her from kneeling beside his chair, slipping her arms round his neck – and kissing him passionately in return. Which was what, at that moment, she wanted most in life.

While they were having supper in the kitchen, pleasantly tired, all of them still in their oldest clothes, the phone rang. Lucy answered. It was Laura. She came back to the table a few minutes later to announce that she and Nico were coming down on Sunday. Kate saw that she was wearing an old shirt of Robin's . . . she looked grubby – but good humoured.

'You must meet her, Margot, she might have some good ideas . . .'

'Quite right, Lucy. I will . . . Oh do give us some more wine, Sebastian . . .'

'We'll all have lunch here,' Kate said quickly. Under the table, Sebastian's hand felt for hers. 'And then you can show Laura round the barn . . .'

Chapter 25

Nobody bothered much about lunch on Sunday after all. Laura and Nico arrived while Kate was still in church. Lucy marched them straight over to Thrush Cottage – and they all went off to inspect the barn. Sebastian was waiting when Kate came out of church. Lost in her own thoughts, not expecting him to be there, she gave a start of surprise when she saw him.

'Sebastian,' she called, hurrying over to him. 'What on earth are you doing here?' The sight of him cheered her. Although informally dressed, his usual working togs had been replaced by slacks and an open-necked shirt. The fresh air and intermittent sun had given him a good colour, despite his fair skin. He must have washed his hair that morning, Kate thought, because it was still plastered to his head; for once, not falling over his forehead.

'The others, including Laura and Nico, have all gone to the workplace – so I came to fetch you. You've not been deserted.' He smiled engagingly. 'Shall we go and join them?'

'Well – yes . . .'

When they arrived at the barn, they found everyone shouting at cross purposes, their voices reverberating around the high structure. Nico had brought wine down for Kate – and this had already been opened and was being drunk out of tea cups. He had taken to the idea of the ancient barn being transformed into a modern showroom and speciality shop with his usual flamboyance . . . He was now perched atop a ladder, waving his arms, hair sticking out at right angles – urging Margot to get huge batik tapestries to decorate the stark walls.

Laura, used to his lunatic rantings, was telling Margot, equally loudly, to take absolutely no notice – except he did often have rather good ideas – when Kate and Sebastian walked in.

'Hi Katie . . .' Laura pecked her cheek. 'We got here earlier than we thought. We're very impressed with all this industry – and the barn. Isn't it fabulous?' And to Sebastian, 'Hello again . . .' They shook hands. 'This is a tremendous combined effort, what fun . . . you must meet Nico once I can get him down off that damned ladder – and make him shut up for a moment . . . he gets these rushes of blood to the head. As Kate knows.'

Late in the afternoon they all ended up at Knyght's Wood – eating slices of cold ham which Kate had intended for lunch and drinking tea. Margot and Laura had hit it off instantly, as Kate had envisioned. They had arranged, with Lucy, to meet soon for the day in London. Laura thought she could well add one or two of the more sophisticated items to her stock – and see how they went.

In the end, it was agreed that Tuesday would be the day. Sebastian could drive them to the station and meet them back later. There was plenty for the decorators to be getting on with at the barn.

'Lucy is having a great time, I can see that,' Laura told Kate just before they left. 'She's really involved in the whole thing . . .'

'Yes – yes, it's been a godsend, Margot and her business,' Kate agreed quietly. 'You've no idea how I was dreading the summer . . .'

'I do know, Katie. And it's turning out better than you could have hoped. For both of you.' Laura looked at her carefully. 'Have you heard from Robin by the way?'

'I've had two cards.' The second had arrived the day before. 'It's very remote, wherever he's been. He must be loving it. This kind of travel is what he always dreamed of. Remember?'

'Yes – well . . . he was badly in need of this kind of change,' Laura said reasonably. 'He's been overdoing everything for months. This tremendous pressure towards the October deadline for the Stock Exchange . . .' She felt it wiser not to mention

271

Guy that day. Whatever else, Kate's life, and Lucy's, did seem to be moving on from that tragedy. And as Kate didn't respond, she pressed, 'Robin did need to get away – from everything – don't you think Katie?'

Speaking very slowly – looking instinctively over to where Sebastian was standing by the car talking to Nico, Kate said, 'I don't know what to think about Robin – any more . . . Should I?'

After watching Kate and Sebastian all day – any excuse was enough for him to get close to her, and she had seen Kate's limpid smiles in return – it was Laura's opinion that she and Robin needed their heads knocking together. But she said cheerfully, 'That's entirely up to you, Katie. Isn't it?'

And she wished, as she told Nico later in the car, that she felt as confident about that as she sounded.

Lucy left early on Tuesday, looking well groomed and attractive in a black cotton suit – her huge tapestry bag, which she lugged everywhere, packed with brochures, price lists and colour samples. She was taking her first job experience very seriously indeed. Still in bed, half asleep, Kate heard the Sinclairs' car picking her up at the bottom of the drive and sputtering off towards the station. The day yawned ahead . . . As the sounds of the car faded, Kate could feel the sickening drag of depression – kept more-or-less at bay these past few weeks – rumble back. She pulled herself out of bed . . .

She spent the morning in the garden; the post, which included a card from Robin and some bills, stuffed into her pocket. The weather was partly overcast and humid. It was her faithful old part-time gardener's day to mow the grass, so Kate chatted to him, without much conviction, about various beds and what needed doing later in the year. All her gardening passion was gone, she realized sadly as she wandered round – languidly admiring this and that, deadheading a few roses. Even the raspberries, which she had looked forward to year after year, failed to pierce her massive indifference. Another casualty – memory stabbing; the future that had been lost with such brutal suddenness . . .

Behind her, the old man, his back bent and puffing hard,

272

shuffled up and down the velvety lawn, imprinting wide, smooth paths. He was slowing down all the time now. Kate could see this. Even the simplest tasks were taking him twice as long. She and her father both doubted whether he would be able to do the work much longer.

'Just get the grass finished – and go off home,' Kate called out to him, shading her eyes against the glare. The sun was slanting through high thundery clouds. 'I'll see to the beds. And Lucy can help with the watering . . .' She had had to do that this year. It was too much for Kate now – and she accepted it.

'Wha's that, then?'

The mower stopped. The old man cupped his hand to his hear. He's deaf as a post these days, Kate thought impatiently. And I don't have much tolerance left. She yelled, 'Just finish off the grass . . . that's enough for today.'

He nodded and touched his cap and started up the mower.

We're all going to pieces round here in one way or another, Kate thought despairingly . . .

Around midday, Sebastian came springing jauntily up the drive. Kate was sitting on the lawn, her hands clasped round her knees – staring sightlessly and not thinking about much either.

'Kate . . .' He was in front of her – very spruce, arms akimbo. Looking interesting and stylish; the way an up-and-coming young actor, already spoken of as one of the best of his generation, should. He bent and touched her shoulder. 'Hey there . . .'

Kate raised her head. For once, that mellifluous voice affected her not at all. Her head had begun to throb – and she felt achingly tired.

'Hi Sebastian . . .' She smiled wanly. 'No work today? I thought . . .'

He collapsed beside her – all his movements were fluid and elegant – his shoulder touching hers.

'There was a cock-up,' he told her cheerfully. 'Wrong timber delivered, the usual thing . . . so I told the fellows to leave it until tomorrow. As a matter of fact, I thought that while the

273

others are having a ball in town, we'd have one of our own.'
He leant, deliberately, hard against her. 'I came to take you
out to lunch. Somewhere nice if there is anywhere – otherwise,
a good pub . . .'

'Sebastian, I . . .'

'What's wrong, Kate?'

She wanted to tell him: everything, absolutely everything in
my whole life – with the possible exception of Lucy and my
parents . . . My darling Guy, Robin off somewhere. The pain in
her hip which never quite went any more. And Guy. And
Guy . . . This was the truth of the black dog of despair which
had haunted her since she wakened.

But she didn't say this. Instead, she shook her head.

'I don't know. Everything. Nothing.' She pushed back her
hair. She looked strained and weary. There were dark circles
under her eyes.

'Have you heard from – Robin?'

She nodded, feeling the bulging pocket in her cotton skirt. It
was his third card. 'He'll be back soon. Any day . . .'

'Good God, I should think so . . . he's left you for long
enough,' Sebastian burst out. 'Four weeks is it? Five . . .?'

He and his mother had touched on this subject more than
once. 'You mustn't judge, Sebastian,' Margot had told him
quite severely. 'You show your youth that way, your inexperi-
ence . . .'

'Something like that.' Kate agreed. 'Only *he* would say that I
had left him. For longer.' Still gazing into space . . .

Sebastian made no comment; he pulled angrily at some
grasses which had pushed between the stone steps – and
threw them violently aside. It was the first sign of anger Kate
had seen in him.

'Is that what's making you so sad – his card?' He sounded
truculent.

'Perhaps . . .'

He sighed. 'And you've been so much better, Kate. You've
come to life again. Margot thinks so too. And Lucy. You've
been – wonderful . . .' Sebastian sounded gentle and concerned
again.

Kate smiled slightly at this. 'Another time, Sebastian. We'll celebrate – something or other. All right? I'm sorry I'm in this black mood . . .' Realising as she said it that it was Sebastian and Margot who had done so much to fill the unfillable gap; who had made her feel, despite herself, that there was something ahead after all. Revived by their vitality, their gaiety, their warmth. They were alike in this. She could never express what their friendship had meant to her at that terrible time.

'Of course. I understand, Kate.'

When she got up, brushing grass off her skirt, he followed, walking into the house behind her. Was there anything she wanted? he asked. What about some food . . . And she looked as though she needed a good rest. She shouldn't worry about Lucy. Margot was phoning later to say what train they were catching – and he would meet them.

'Thank you, Sebastian, so much. And I'm fine – really.' They stood facing each other, yards apart, in the dim, quiet hall. Shadows fell across Kate's pale face and her yellow cotton blouse. All the windows were wide open and the scent of newly mown grass wafted through.

'I heard from California this morning,' Sebastian said softly. He had his back to the light so Kate couldn't see the intensity of his expression. 'They want me there by the tenth of September. We start shooting at the end of the month.'

'Oh Sebastian – that's marvellous.' She tried to sound it.

'I would have thought so too – once . . .'

'What do you mean?' She blinked.

'I mean – before Kate . . .'

She must have made a gesture, put out her arm towards him, done something. Because otherwise, it would not have happened. He was too sensitive, too controlled. But as it was, they came passionately together – hands, lips, tongues everywhere, his body pressed against hers; the things he whispered against her hair, her cheek, her neck. His urgency . . . She wanted this loving moment never to end; to blot out the past and take away the future. To be drunk on Sebastian. *That* was what she wanted . . .

But it was she – not he – who pulled back.

'You must go, Sebastian, you must . . .' She pushed him away, panicked, her hands against her flaming cheeks. 'Don't

275

you see – you must . . .' She was beseeching him – against everything she felt, that he knew she felt – to leave her.

He grasped her hands. They were breathing very fast. Eyes locked; only inches apart.

'Must I, Kate? Must I?'

They both knew one thing: if he stayed now, both of their lives would be changed beyond recall.

'Yes . . .' Kate tore her hands from his – and moved clumsily through the hall and up the stairs, pulling herself on the bannisters, not looking back, feeling her way blindly to her room.

Sebastian watched until a door banged shut somewhere above him.

Flung on her bed, fists clenched, eyes tight shut, Kate heard him walk away from the house.

When Kate came downstairs, much later, she was fully composed. She had slept on and off the whole afternoon – and she had done some hard thinking. She had also come to a number of important decisions. Perhaps for this reason, she felt clear-headed and controlled.

In the kitchen she poured herself a glass of wine and found some dry biscuits in the cupboard. She took these and went to her desk in the living-room. Although it wasn't five yet, the day had turned cloudy and the light was going. There must be thunder about . . . She turned on a lamp. Sipping the wine, she started to go through the heap of unopened mail – and as she separated it into piles, she came across the particulars of the London flat which Robin had said he liked. She perused it . . . A converted early Victorian house overlooking a square garden . . . a maisonette . . . large first-floor drawing-room, two bedrooms . . . recently redecorated . . .

On an impulse – and following closely on a couple of major decisions she had just taken – she took it and went to the phone, dialling the estate agent's number, making a note of the name written across the top.

'Mr Simon please,' she said when she got through. She looked at her watch; it was a little before 5.30.

'Just a minute, I think he may have gone for the day . . .'

A pause . . . he hadn't.

'Hello? Jay Simon here . . . Can I help you?'

'Yes, I think perhaps you can,' Kate said clearly. 'I'm phoning about a flat my husband saw last month . . .' She gave him her name and the details of the property. 'I was wondering if it's still available? If so, I'd like to make an appointment to come and see it. As soon as possible really . . .' Silence at the other end. 'Hello? Mr Simon – are you there?'

'Well – er – actually, Mrs Faraday . . .'

'Is it or isn't it – still available? That's all I want to know . . .' Looking at the roses through the window, Kate thought: I must water them poor things, can't wait for Lucy, heaven knows when she'll be back . . .

'As a matter of fact . . .' Then, unctuously professional, 'It's not currently available. It has in fact been sold . . .'

'Oh dear . . .' Still half concentrating on the roses – they hadn't had any rain to speak of all month.

'To your husband, Mrs Faraday. I'm sorry if . . .'

Kate dragged her eyes from the garden.

'My husband. I see.' The room tilted this way and that. 'I know he liked it, thought it suitable, was considering . . .'

'Oh indeed, he was very keen . . .' Relieved and confident now. 'He moved extremely quickly. In fact, contracts were exchanged before he left the country. We expect to close sometime this week.'

'I see. Thank you so much. Well – goodbye.'

Kate replaced the receiver, poured herself more wine and returned to her desk. She paid ten bills and wrote several notes, all answering sympathy letters for Guy – received months ago now. She wrote fluently and with ease. Saying all the right things; giving nothing away; sipping her wine. The roses, she had decided, would have to wait until tomorrow.

When the phone rang about eight, Kate doubted it was Lucy. They had all been invited to dinner with Nico, in one of the fashionable London restaurants that he adored. And she wouldn't want to miss that. So it was probably Robin.

It was.

'Kate? Kate? Are you all right?'

'Perfectly, thank you.'

'And Lucy?'

'Oh yes. She's fine too. She's in London for the day – but she'll be back later. Did you have a wonderful time?'

'Yes. Yes, it was very good. Just got in this minute. Kate . . .'

'I'm so glad . . . Turkey, wasn't it?' Careful, she told herself, careful. 'We got your cards. Thank you so much. Er – nice people?' she asked innocently.

'Kate – I've got to see you. As soon as possible.'

'That does sound suitable.' She suppressed a hiccup.

'Can you meet me in London for lunch tomorrow?'

This seemed inexpressibly funny to Kate . . . Why did everyone – suddenly, desperately – require to take her out to lunch? First Sebastian and now . . . She sniffed and wiped a tear of helpless laughter from her eye.

'Kate? Is that all right?'

'Oh yes – that's all right . . .'

She felt gloriously light-headed, and after only two glasses of wine. Or was it three? On an empty stomach, of course . . .

'I'll book at . . .' He mentioned a quiet, old-fashioned fish restaurant that she happened to know he had always considered deadly boring – where her father had taken her and Laura since they were children. 'Let's say 12.30 . . .'

The laughter was catching hold. She had an insane urge to say: Robin my love, do excuse my asking – but have you been buying any flats lately? I was just wondering . . .

'Kate? I'll see you then . . .'

'Yes . . .'

And as soon as she replaced the receiver, the laughter burst out – pealing and pealing, her eyes watering, red in the face. Soon after, she picked at some supper standing up in the kitchen, left a note for Lucy and went up to bed.

That night, she had her dream again. It had haunted her, on and off, for weeks. But this time it was different. In this dream, she ran and ran, her arms outstretched to this now familiar young man ahead of her, touching his arm, longing – so badly needing – to give him whatever it was that she was carrying. And this time – the first – she grabbed him . . .

278

He stopped and turned slowly, slowly . . . Kate gasping with
fear . . .

But it was not Guy, as she had always hoped and feared.
It was Robin, when he was young.

Chapter 26

Kate arrived at the restaurant about a quarter of an hour early. A doddery waiter showed her to a dark, panelled corner of the bar – where she politely declined to order a drink. 'I'll wait for my husband, thank you,' she said, looking round. She hadn't been there for years. The whole place had a fusty, bygone air about it. But it was decently quiet – and almost empty.

Separated from London by six secluded months of mourning, Kate had prepared carefully for today's expedition – looking up trains which she once knew by heart, arriving at the station, parking, much too soon. And she had dressed accordingly, with forethought, in a cream linen suit – unworn since the previous summer – and a navy silk shirt. Once in London, the noise and the crush had stunned her; she had stood outside the station, breathing unaccustomed fumes – confused, dithering about buses, looking at her watch, while the traffic blared and crowds jostled. She felt like an invalid, only partly recovered from some terrible disease. In the end she took a taxi – which was why she was early, even though she had asked to be dropped several streets away.

Robin arrived at 12.30 on the dot. Kate saw him for a moment or two before he spotted her, sitting in solitary state in the gloomy wood-and-leather corner.

'Kate . . .'

Tears started in – and left – her eyes.

He came purposefully towards her. She scarcely moved. He looked at least ten years younger; deeply tanned; his hair, nicely grey at the sides, was immaculately trimmed and parted – he could well have come straight from his barber. He never turned up from the wilds of Turkey looking like that . . .

'You look well,' Kate said pleasantly, sitting still as a statue as he kissed her on each cheek and slid into the opposite chair; signalling at once for the decrepit waiter.

'You too . . .' He smiled, not quite meeting her eyes. 'What will you drink?'

'Oh,' she said, 'I don't care – anything . . .'

He looked straight at her then – eyes very blue and lined at the corners. A clean thrust to his jaw. She caught his expression – mouth set firm, very business-like; hard.

That was when she knew that he was going to leave her.

'In that case . . .' He turned to the waiter who was shifting and peering beside them. 'A glass of white wine – dry, very cold . . . and a gin and tonic. Plenty of ice . . . Oh – and we'd like the menus now . . .'

No long, leisurely lunch this; that was plain from the outset.

They ordered when the drinks were brought – and sat like distant acquaintances talking stiltedly of this and that: Lucy, his father's illness, Laura and Nico, the marvellous time her parents seemed to be having in Italy. They still hadn't returned. The weeks sailing off the coast of Turkey, or wherever it was he had been, were not mentioned.

Knyght's Wood was fine, Kate said, and the roses were lovely even though there hadn't been any rain.

Robin stood rather too quickly when they were told that their table was ready, touching her elbow as they walked into the dining-room. One or two other couples were already lunching, everyone – even the waiters – talking in hushed tones. It was that kind of establishment.

Once they were seated, 'Kate – there's a lot I want to . . .' He looked at her gravely. Everything about him was so heartbreakingly familiar to her; if only they could put the clock back, erase whatever it was that had happened between them . . . Her courage began to falter. She interrupted, playing for time, talking – wildly – about Lucy. 'I hope she really does like Yarnston, she's not used to being cooped up and she's coming in at an awkward stage . . .'

'I'm sure she'll be all right,' Robin said impatiently, picking up a carafe of wine. 'It's what she's been wanting for a long time, the change will do her good. She's a bright girl and very

281

strong, is Lucy. And she'll be able to go to Knyght's Wood at weekends . . .'

'Laura thought it was a bit strange, Yarnston. But I was very impressed when I went there. I liked the headmaster. Oh – I *do* hope Lucy will be happy there . . .'

From the side, a waiter was approaching with a tray loaded with silver tureens. Robin looked at his watch. He's hating this, Kate thought – good.

This calmed her. 'Off the bone, please,' she told the waiter. That would slow things up a bit too. Anyway, she preferred it.

'All right, and for me,' Robin agreed reluctantly. They had ordered, as so often in the past, similar meals.

During the fuss of being served – spooning vegetables, de-boning, lids clanking – Kate drank the wine and recovered her nerve. And when they were finally left in peace, she looked down at her plate with genuine pleasure. The grilled fish was perfectly browned and oozed butter; crisp mange-touts; she had refused potatoes. A small dish of lemon halves, each covered in gauze. She picked one up, pricked it with her fork, and squeezed.

'Oh Robin,' she said, quite as though she was starting a perfectly normal conversation, 'I didn't know that you had bought the flat, the one you said you were considering . . . before you went abroad . . .'

A short pause. Kate thought he squared his shoulders.

'I'm extremely sorry about that, Kate. I never intended it. I'm sorry.' For the first time that day, he was talking in a way she recognised. 'You must believe that.'

'Never intended what, Robin?'

'That you should find out like that. About the flat. Through Simon.'

'Oh . . .' The fish was delicious. She drank some more wine. He must have been in touch with the estate agent that morning. He didn't seem to be eating and he looked wretched. Good, again.

'I wanted to tell you – everything – before I went away. I couldn't bring myself to. That's the fact of it.'

'Oh,' Kate said again. 'I see . . .' She went on eating. The restaurant was filling up; ancient waiters who had been there for years weaving between the tables. Kate dimly remembered that the last time they came here Robin had complained to the manager as they left that their waiter was drunk.

'I bought it because I'm going to live there. With someone who – who I have become very attached to. I have no doubt at all you will have gathered this. I get possession this week – so it will be soon.' His voice was so low and hoarse that she had to strain to hear. 'It kills me to do this to you, Kate . . .'

Did it? Well – he looked agonised enough. Another plus . . .

'I see . . .'

She had known, of course she had – deep down – for a long time now. She wasn't going to be able to finish the fish after all. Pity. But the wine was going down well. She couldn't think of anything whatsoever to say.

'I thought . . . Oh God, Kate, I thought I could have an affair – like other men – underhand, lies, business trips . . . But I couldn't do it when it came to the point. Not to you, not to me . . .'

Not to her?

A bit of anger suddenly on Kate's part. Delayed reaction perhaps. He was looking desperate now, the years piled back on.

Oh excellent . . .

'No . . . no I couldn't . . .'

Kate fiddled with the silverware.

'Who is she?'

'No one you know. I met her – through the office.' The office . . . Something stirred at the back of Kate's mind. Rupert talking after dinner; a drawl in the background during a telephone conversation. Something Laura said, warning . . . Inspiration flashed . . .

'That American,' she said loud and triumphant. 'Over from New York for a year, that one . . .' Kate was crowing at her cleverness.

'Quiet, Kate . . .' glancing round surreptitiously. 'There's no need to shout . . .' He spoke through gritted teeth although no one in the room was taking the slightest notice. You could probably die here and they'd walk round you, Kate thought. Robin had chosen the venue well. This was death of a sort.

'Well – is it?' she asked boldly.

'Yes.'

He sighed heavily. Kate, with the wisdom of intimacy, suspected it was going worse than he had imagined. This pleased her. Didn't it? Oh Robin . . . and he was wearing a plain pale blue shirt, the kind she always liked him best in . . .

Tears started – and stopped – again.

'Lucy must be told,' she said icily.

'Of course. And your parents . . . Laura . . . My father's too ill . . . I'd be grateful if we could keep it at that for the moment . . .' He was looking as tired as before he went away. 'Can we do that, Kate?'

Anger taking hold again, she demanded, 'What do you think I'm going to do? Put an ad in the papers? Scream from the housetops? Call in the lawyers?'

He didn't answer.

'I've got a life going too you know . . . *As* a matter of fact . . .' She was angry all right. She was furious. Trembling with rage and her hands shaking. 'What am I supposed to do? Sit in the country doing nothing while you carry on in a flat in London with this – woman . . . as though nothing had happened?'

'Please, Kate.' He closed his eyes briefly. He looked dreadful, drained beneath the tan. 'Not a scene. We've been through too much. Both of us . . .'

'*Don't you dare bring Guy into this sordid mess you've made . . .*'

'*And don't you speak to me like that. Ever. Do you hear me?*' His fist banging onto the table; his anger matching hers now. 'You left me first, remember. Don't you ever forget that . . . and you've got your own life now. You said so yourself. Knyght's Wood – it's yours. Anything else that's reasonable. It's what you always wanted, isn't it? Your precious garden . . . new friends . . . the actor – Sebastian Sinclair . . .'

He was looking at her with such yearning hunger – and such dislike – that she was shocked. She felt sick and her mouth went dry. The elderly waiters dodged about, taking plates, whisking imaginary crumbs.

'Coffee?' Robin asked distractedly, breathing hard. 'Something else?' He glared at a waiter – who still hovered.

'I'm leaving now,' Kate said faintly. 'Don't come after me . . .'

'You can't . . . I can't let you . . .' She was thinner, more fragile, than he'd ever seen her. Her skin was like paper – finely lined around her eyes and taut across her cheekbones. Her face was the colour of her suit.

The room turned round Kate's head. She prayed she wouldn't pass out.

'Yes . . . now . . .'

She picked up her bag and he half rose as she left the table.

When Kate got back to Knyght's Wood late that afternoon, she found a sheaf of two dozen superb cream roses, loosely wrapped in cellophane and stuck in a bucket of water, by the back door. The card read simply, 'Sebastian'. The bucket, presumably, belonged to Margot. Kate immediately undid them, cut the stems and arranged them in a large green vase, one of her favourites – given to her, she remembered wryly, by Doris Faraday. She carried them through into the sitting-room – and placed them on a low table next to an armchair. Robin's chair, as it happened.

She then telephoned Laura who was at her flat. Her shop was closed for the whole of the month of August on the grounds that 'my sort of people simply aren't around in London then'. Kate told her briefly that she had lunched with Robin that day, he had bought a flat – and was about to move in there with someone else. An American woman to whom he was now deeply devoted. That was all she knew about the situation – or wanted to. So they were, she supposed, separated . . . although Robin seemed to want to keep quiet about it for the present . . . just the family etc etc . . . and yes, it had been awful, although she had sensed it was coming – belatedly. She left out the short sharp shock administered, unwittingly, by the estate agent. 'I think it was worse for him than me today,' she added, sounding pleased – and feeling it.

'Oh God Kate . . . no . . . I can't stand it. Look, I'm coming down . . . immediately. I'm not doing anything in particular and you're not to be there alone. I can tell you about Nico and me if you don't want to discuss – the other . . .' Tense with

285

suppressed indignation; desperately protective as she always had been. Although she didn't sound as surprised as she might have. Kate supposed that she was the last to know, which was the usual thing. If only she could be left alone . . .

'Laura, don't bother . . . please . . . I'm all right, I've got Lucy . . .'

'I'll throw some things in a bag and stay the night. That's that. I'll just tell Nico – and I'll be in the car . . .'

'Well – all right,' Kate agreed reluctantly. She had had quite enough emotional confrontation for one day; the mere thought of Laura arriving in full dramatic flood exhausted her. She could have done with a quiet evening thinking about nothing in particular and perhaps speaking to Sebastian, just to thank him . . .

But Laura, the extrovert, would never understand that.

And what, if anything, had Laura known about Robin's life? Quite a bit, Kate suspected. That stung. And she didn't feel strong enough for any further revelations, not then; she simply did not want to know.

'I'll expect you when I see you then . . .' The creamy roses, plunged deep in water, were already picking up.

Bombing down from London – she had consistently driven at 80 mph along the motorway – Laura found Kate changed into jeans and calmly watering the rosebushes with the garden hose.

'Katie . . .' Laura slammed the car door and came racing over to her. 'Are you all right?' – looking very smart in white trousers and a black top; and for some reason, despite the hour, enormous dark glasses.

What on earth did she expect?

'Yes – of course I am . . . watch out, you're standing on the hose – and your lovely trousers will get soaked . . .' Laura hopped onto the path. 'That's better . . .' Kate adjusted the nozzle and went on watering. 'You were quick . . .'

'I flew. I hated to think of you being here by yourself . . .'

Kate smiled gratefully over her shoulder.

'Bless you for that. But I'm not too bad, truly, not yet at least . . .' This was true. There had been the odd painful twinge, but the anger had gone. The nub of the situation, and all its implications for the future, hadn't yet begun to penetrate. Coming down in the train, she had even regretted the delicious grilled sole she hadn't finished. She turned off the water and began to wind up the hose. 'Let's go in and have a drink – and there's plenty of cold meat and salad in the kitchen . . .'

Laura looked disconcerted. Kate thought she must have expected tears and hysteria; but she was beyond all that these days – wasn't she? Laura, of all people, should have known.

'Well,' she said, looking at Kate oddly, 'as long as you feel like that . . .'

'Look, Laura' – Kate faced her, pushing back her hair which needed cutting again. 'No more drama today. That's what I mean. We'll get to a few things by and by. God only knows what I really feel, *I* certainly don't. So tell me something cheerful, what you and Nico have planned for instance . . .'

'I will do that. As requested. We've even got a wedding date . . . and a drink would be divine. Where's Luce?' she asked, curling up on the sofa.

'She phoned about an hour ago. She's gone out with some people she knows locally. She'll be back later.'

'To be told nothing – about Robin?'

A tremor passed through Kate's body.

'Not yet.'

'You and Robin will have to work that out together.' Laura looked stern.

'Yes.'

'Heavenly roses, Kate. I can smell them from here . . .'

'Yes – aren't they? Absolutely ravishing . . .' She hurried on, 'I saw Lucy very briefly this morning and she told me she had a marvellous time in London yesterday. It was terribly kind of Nico to take her out, with Margot . . .'

'We had *such* fun . . .' Lucy always did with Laura. 'And I gave Margot lots of introductions . . . she's got the most marvellous ideas, and a tremendous personality . . . As long as she can keep her workers up to scratch, she should do well. I'm going to take a few of her things in the shop . . . and it's a wonderful experience for Lucy . . .'

'She's loving it.'

287

'Margot is very fond of you, too, Katie. She adores you. And she suspects Sebastian has fallen in love with you,' Laura teased, watching her closely.

'Don't be mad,' Kate said sharply.

'She does . . . and she thinks it shows very good taste on his part . . .'

'Ridiculous.' Kate felt herself colour. 'Now tell me properly about you and Nico . . .'

At last – 'at long, long last', as Laura put it – they were getting married. The divorce and the settlement were all tied up – and Arabella was perfectly friendly. She was cocooned in the country house with the children coming and going, which was what she had always wanted. Nico swore that the last time he saw her she offered to make the wedding cake.

Even Kate, that night, smiled at this. 'She always was eccentric, Laura. Don't you remember? Burying all that food, the flowery child's name . . .'

They were planning on the last Saturday before Christmas. Registry Office, family only, and a lunch after. The four eldest of Nico's children were coming – and, of course, Lucy. Ma and Pa. A dozen close friends including one or two from the gallery. And that was it.

'I'll have to tell Mother and Pa when they get back,' Kate said quietly, going hot and cold. 'About Robin.' She stared at Laura.

'I'll come with you,' Laura said, 'When you do.'

'I wish you would . . .'

Then they returned to discussion of the wedding. No fuss – that would be absurd, Laura said, under the circumstances. They were in the process of selling both their flats and finding somewhere bigger. Probably a house which would be useful for showing pictures to prospective buyers. She looked so contented, sitting in the lamplight, beside the open window, enjoying her drink. Kate felt a spasm of envy. All the years when she had been the settled one, the one with the husband, the home, the children; Laura up and down emotionally, mooning about during holidays when Nico was with Arabella and the children . . .

Kate could feel her confidence – her self – draining away . . .

The agony of Guy's death; now Robin . . .
This couldn't be happening, it couldn't . . .

'And the best part is Nico's wedding present . . .' Laura threw back her head and laughed. 'You'll never guess what that is . . .'

'What?' Kate asked dutifully.

Robin, Oh Robin, what am I going to do . . .?

'He's selling that damned plane of his. He's promised before – but this time it's definite. It's been nothing but trouble – I never trusted it. One more trip to Italy next month – and then it's being sold.'

'I know you hated him flying,' Kate said vaguely. 'You always went on about it . . .'

'He takes too many risks. He swears he doesn't but he does. He's so impatient.' She laughed again – indulgently. 'We've been lent a house in the Bahamas for a honeymoon . . . St Lucia . . . So we'll be going straight there after the wedding until the middle of January.'

And Lucy. Telling Lucy . . . how could they? Her world destroyed – again . . .

In terror, fighting down panic, she jumped up. 'What about getting something to eat? Put your things in the spare bedroom, Mrs Bundy keeps the bed made there . . . Lucy won't be in for ages, she said . . .'

It was when they were sitting in the kitchen drinking coffee that Kate asked the inevitable question.

'How much did you know – about Robin?' She looked down at the table.

'I suspected something a few months ago when I was at the house so much. He was never around when I phoned, or when I was there. Always vague excuses . . . something twigged after a bit . . .'

'I know, I know,' Kate said wearily. 'And I was down here . . .'

'Well – you were. I was never happy about that, Katie. And he was dreadfully depressed – and vulnerable. After Guy . . .'

'But not me, of course,' Kate said sarcastically, looking up. 'Not me?'

289

Sebastian had left those lovely roses, today of all days . . . he must have thought there was something to forgive . . . as if there was . . .

'*Of course* – you. But not together. You weren't with each other, physically, when you should have been. That's my point,' Laura said gently.

Moths flew about the light and the clock on the dresser ticked loudly.

Kate said, 'You've seen her, haven't you?'

'Yes . . .'

Only the shape and colour of their eyes marked them out as sisters now; no one would believe they were twins. Laura's stylishness and soft, bouncy curls bore little resemblance to Kate's waif-like appearance. Her wispy hair was flecked with grey and her collarbone protruded at the neck of her shirt.

'Well?'

'Once, briefly. They came into a restaurant just as we were leaving . . .' A knife turned somewhere in Kate. 'Robin didn't see us. She's spectacular all right – blonde, mid to late thirties, about ten feet tall . . .'

'*Laura* . . .'

'Well – the Amazon type. Nico thought so too . . . Oh Katie-Kate . . .' Laura replaced her coffee cup. 'He always spoilt you, treated you like a doll. I hated that. But I could *kill* him . . .' She almost spat the words. '*I could kill him with my bare hands* . . .'

'I'm going to bed,' Kate said unsteadily.

Kate thought, lying awake, much later: Laura hasn't called me Katie-Kate for years, not since Lucy was a baby. She always believed it was Nico who had put an end to the affectionate, babyish nickname. Tonight, it made their shared childhoods come rushing back – and with it, a certain comfort. She turned on her side. It had started to rain at last. She could hear the drops pattering against the windows. She was dreadfully tired. The wind was stirring gently among the trees in the Knyght's Wood above. Tomorrow, she would write a short thank-you note to Sebastian . . . And she would sleep after all.

Chapter 27

To her surprise, Kate found that life went on much as usual. She tried not to think about Robin and this unknown woman who was now sharing his life – and for much of the time, she succeeded. Even the memory of Guy was becoming faintly veiled; as though the mind and body did have some natural, merciful, defences after all. It astonished her to realise that it was only last winter that her life had been so different. Sometimes she thought she was living through an unending dream. Or had those bright successful years, when everything went their way so effortlessly, been the mirage after all?

Mrs Bundy did her twice-weekly stint in the house. In the village, dutiful questions were asked and answered about Robin; nothing given away. Everyone knew the top people in the City were working harder than ever these days. Lucy was almost continuously absorbed with Margot; the opening was only two weeks away now. Sebastian had disappeared to London for a week, closeted with his agent, Margot said, and giving interviews to the press. 'He'll be back at the weekend and stay on ... Kate, love, could you help sort out this consignment that's just arrived, do you think?' Which Kate immediately did – surprised, and slightly disturbed, at how much she missed Sebastian's enigmatic presence.

A letter arrived from Robin. He had moved into the flat – and gave his address and telephone number; he had arranged to have everything from the house, which had been sold, put into storage – it seemed simplest for the time being. And he suggested that she and Lucy meet him at a West End hotel one day the following week for an early drink. This way, they could tell Lucy together about the separation. He felt this was right and he was sure she would agree.

Kate stared at the word 'separation' for some moments before ringing Robin at his office. She got through immediately. As far as she was concerned, his arrangements over the house were perfectly satisfactory, she told him coldly. And then made a date for the three of them to meet. Yarnston started the week after next. Surely they would have to do some shopping and need to be in London. And whatever excuses Lucy might make about her job, Kate would insist that this date was kept.

When she told her that night, Lucy, opening the refrigerator door, said, 'I suppose he's going to be living in London from now on. That's it, is it – what I've got to be told?'

She slammed the door shut. Kate winced.

'Yes – we wanted to tell you together. Although frankly, Lucy, your father is the only one who has anything to tell.'

'Silly fool,' Lucy said, spearing a piece of ham. She glared at her mother. That goes for *both* of you, her look implied.

'Don't you need to get some clothes for Yarnston?' Kate asked, ignoring this. 'It's less than two weeks now . . .'

'I've got plenty of skirts and things. Nobody pays any attention to clothes there. You saw that.' Kate had indeed. 'After we've seen Dad, I'll stay up and spend the night with Lucinda.'

Sebastian came back from his few days in London and threw himself into the final preparations for the opening. All the invitations had been sent and the response had been better than Margot could have reasonably hoped. Kate waited until she and Sebastian were having a drink alone together at Knyght's Wood before she mentioned the roses, although she had written immediately. The gesture, and particularly the timing – which he could not possibly have divined – touched Kate. It was so like Sebastian – gentle and romantic and giving. Since he returned from London, they had met daily but there were always other people around.

'There was no need . . .' she told him, colouring slightly. 'But they were lovely and it was a charming thought . . . Look –

I've kept them going . . .' They were still in the huge green vase beside Robin's chair. 'You can't imagine how they pleased me, waiting for me when I got back from dusty old London . . .'

And from so much else, Kate thought ironically. The end of a part of my life, you could say. But she told him nothing of this – then.

'Have you forgiven me?' Sebastian asked.

'There's nothing to forgive.' She met his ardent look.

He lifted her hand and kissed it. 'Loving friends still?'

'Loving friends – Oh yes, Sebastian . . .'

'That's particularly cheering . . .' His voice dropping. 'Because I don't have to be in LA until October now. That was one of the things I was discussing in London last week. The filming has been put back because of the director's commitments. Personally, I'm delighted. It gives me more than a month here to persuade you . . .' He leant towards her – as high-spirited and charming as his mother. His hair carrotty in the evening sun.

Feelings that Kate had thought dead inside her responded to him. She laughed. She felt young and strong, able to face anything – even the ordeal with Lucy and Robin tomorrow.

'Persuade me what?'

'Why – to love me of course.'

Kate, Robin and Lucy all arrived separately, within minutes of each other, at the excessively grand West End hotel that Robin had suggested. It was almost six, still early for the theatre and cocktail crowd, so they had the cavernous and elegant room practically to themselves. In one corner, a trio was playing – very soft, very discreet – pre-war show tunes.

Robin arrived, chauffeur-driven, straight from his office.

Kate came by taxi after spending more than an hour on a bench in Hyde Park – thinking disjointedly about this and that.

Lucy came from the noisy discotheque beat of a series of hot and crowded Oxford Street shops.

Kate arrived first.

'So nice to see you again, Madam,' the flunkey said,

293

infuriatingly. She smiled dutifully and looked round for Robin – without a quiver. He came in with Lucy whom he had met at the entrance. He looked much better – composed, assured, still very tanned. A man getting on for fifty; in the prime of life. Handsome – radiating competence. Anyone looking at him would know that he was successful at whatever he did; it was written all over him.

'Kate . . .' He barely touched her cheek, sitting between her and Lucy. 'What about a drink everyone?'

He ordered a double scotch for himself, a glass of wine for Kate. Lucy said she would have a vodka and tonic. Robin looked at her hard.

'A *what*, Lucy?'

'Vodka ton – not too much ice,' Lucy repeated casually. The waiter scribbled, inclined his head and left. Lucy hiked her ancient tapestry bag onto the remaining chair, crossed her legs and fiddled with the strap of her sandal. She looked, Kate saw, her worst. Her natural good looks – her height, her marvellous figure – almost disguised by the drab black skirt and loose khaki-coloured top. Her make-up was white, like a mask. She was hardly recognisable as the vivacious girl who had been acting as Margot's right hand for weeks.

Settled with drinks, Robin turned to Lucy. 'Look, Lucy, we've got you here to tell you something that I hope isn't going to upset you too terribly . . .'

'Oh?' said Lucy, looking down into her glass.

'Yes. It's this. I'm going to be living in London now – all the time. Your mother and I have discussed it all. And we wanted to tell you together. That's right, isn't it?' He looked at Kate who smiled faintly and said only, 'Yes.' She had decided, sitting on her park bench, that she would say as little as possible. This was Robin's decision, his mess. Let him deal with it.

'We're not looking too far ahead, but it is a separation. It's been a terrible year for us all. I'm sorry to land you with this extra sorrow, Lucy . . .'

'With what?' Lucy asked, looking at her father with raised eyebrows.

'Well – sadness, then – difficulty,' Robin looked annoyed.

294

'But it is what I have chosen for the moment. Your mother already knows this.' He avoided Kate's glance.

'That's OK' said Lucy quite cheerfully. 'I'll be away at school anyhow. Then university, if I get in somewhere decent, then working . . .'

'What do you mean, if you get in somewhere decent?' Robin demanded. This wasn't going quite the way he had intended. He looked across at Kate – who said nothing but picked up her glass. 'Of course you will. You're going to Yarnston to work,' he told her sharply. 'It's got an excellent reputation – and the fees are exorbitant enough.'

'Spare the lecture,' Lucy said, looking bored. 'I know the form . . .'

'I'm glad to hear that . . .' Robin sounded exasperated. 'You've been nagging about going there for years.'

'Anyhow,' Lucy asked, dismissing Yarnston. 'Where *are* you living – now that the house has been sold?'

Kate hadn't even told her that much. That was Robin's business, she had decided. The Amazonian American too . . . And if he was happy with her, the woman with the initials for a name, said by Laura to be six feet tall, it wasn't showing just then.

When he told her, Lucy said, 'That's not far from here is it? I don't have to be up at Lucinda's until later. So I'll come with you and have a look. OK?' Kate thought she detected a whiff of interest on Lucy's part and Robin looked uneasy.

'Well – all right. I'm not exactly settled,' he said stiffly. 'But if you want to . . .'

'Sure. I'd like to . . . Mother's going straight back to the country. Sebastian's taking you out somewhere for dinner, isn't he?'

He was. Kate smiled brilliantly at her trying daughter. 'That's right – I'd like to catch the 6.45 if I can . . .' She could feel Robin glowering at her. 'So why don't you two go off together – and I'll get myself to the station?'

After some minutes of indecision on the pavement outside the hotel, it was decided that the driver should take Kate straight to the station – and Lucy and Robin would walk to his new flat.

'Many thanks,' Kate said as the driver held the door. 'Now I'll certainly get the train . . .' Robin stood about looking furious.

Dinner with Sebastian; how good that she had made a point of mentioning this, very casually, to Lucy. She had managed the meeting excellently, saying so little. Her confidence soared. Lucy had made it perfectly clear the night before that she had no intention of being much affected. And perhaps she wasn't. Kate had long suspected her of being as hard as nails – and perhaps she had been right.

She sat comfortably behind as the driver got in. Robin, scowling, told him which station. He's furious, Kate decided, with great pleasure. He's genuinely furious . . . Dinner with Sebastian; good for Lucy. And what, she thought, in the swell of her triumphant anger, did he expect?

She smiled sweetly at them both as the car moved off. Lucy waved casually and Robin nodded curtly.

Goodbye, old life, goodbye . . .

'We should have plenty of time as long as the traffic's not too bad . . .' She leant towards the driver. 'Waterloo thank you, that's right.'

Robin's flat was on the second and third floors of an early Victorian house, overlooking one of the prettiest Squares in central London. The drawing-room, with bow windows and ornamental balconies, was large and beautiful.

Walking in, Lucy thought – and said, 'What horrible furniture . . .'

The stark, ultra-modern matching white sofas and chairs clashed glaringly, so it seemed to Lucy, with the traditional proportions and mouldings of the room. Ditto the chrome and glass tables. She had learnt a lot about looking at things from Margot that summer. And Mother, to give her her due, wouldn't be seen dead with this stuff. There were piles of American newspapers and magazines – the *Wall Street Journal*, *Businessweek*, *Time*, *Harper's Bazaar*, *Vogue* etc, some curiously elongated lamps – and not much else.

'Don't be rude, Lucy.' Robin told her crossly. 'We – er – I have scarcely moved in. I'm still living out of crates and suitcases.' A row of large cardboard boxes were stacked against one wall.

The telephone, also shiny white, rang. Robin answered.

'One moment,' he said, covering the mouthpiece with his hand. And to Lucy. 'It's business, from New York – and this may take some time . . .' He pulled a pad towards him. 'Make yourself at home. All right?'

'Sure.' Lucy nodded. 'I'll have a mosey round . . .'

Robin looked at her warily, but had no choice other than to continue with the call.

Lucy sloped off up the poky interior staircase. The master bedroom was above the drawing-room; a second bedroom, very small, looked out over a mews. This was empty except for piles of Louis Vuitton luggage in a staggering plethora of shapes and sizes. Lucy made for the large bedroom. This had a kingsize bed, minus headboard, and a large television on a stand; nothing whatsoever to sit on. Built-in cupboards lined one wall from floor to ceiling. Mousey grey fitted carpet and heavily draped curtains in faded rose were obvious leftovers from the previous owner.

The bathroom next door was big and old-fashioned. Not bad, a bit tatty, thought Lucy. Nice soap and big, fluffy towels; twin towelling robes – 'How sweet,' said Lucy out loud, pulling a sarcastic face. They must look daft, padding around the place in those things. There were several kinds of expensive bath oil and pots and pots of Estée Lauder cosmetics in neat rows. Washing her hands, Lucy caught sight of a bottle of Georgio scent in its bright yellow box. She had heard good things of this; Lucinda, reliable in these matters, had told her it was The Best. And it was wildly expensive. Lucy investigated, sniffed, tightly replaced the top and slipped it into her bag. On the landing again, she listened. Dad was still droning on down there to New York; it must be costing a fortune . . .

Back in the main bedroom, she opened the vast cupboard. It was entirely filled with jackets, skirts, trousers and shirts, all in shades of beige or black or white, all carefully hung in sections on appropriate hangers. Some two dozen pairs of plain pumps, all quite low-heeled, stood neatly below. Lucy scrutinised the clothes labels which were mostly designer and

297

mostly Italian. They were all on the large side. She pulled out a black silk shirt with lace inserts. Valentino, said the label. Lucy held it against herself and stared into the floor-length mirror. It was very sexy, very adult, she decided. She rolled it carelessly and slung it in the tapestry bag, along with the Giorgio scent. She had by now compiled quite a satisfactory mental picture of her father's mistress – which was why she had asked to come to the flat in the first place. She guessed . . .

A tall American female, probably blonde, on the large side, who wore Italian clothes, Lauder make-up and Giorgio scent. She probably had some crashingly good job too – hence the stack of American publications downstairs other than *Vogue*. And although she was clearly well put together – Lucy couldn't fault her personal possessions – she had zilch taste in home furnishings. The mystery was: how come she had fetched up with Dad? A divorcée grabbing what she could get on the rebound? Falling for the Brit accent? Or perhaps she was quite young and had a father fixation. Lucinda was always going on about that.

Further brief investigation of their bedroom revealed her father's suits stuffed into some three feet of cupboard space. From this, Lucy concluded that the lady, whoever she was, had a healthy sense of her own importance.

Tiptoeing out onto the creaking landing, there was silence. The call to New York must be over.

'Hey, Dad,' Lucy shouted down. 'Is it all right if I watch "Cousins" for a bit? It's my favourite soap – I'm lunatic about it . . . I'll push off to Lucinda's in about half an hour.'

'What? What's that, Lucy?' Listening harder, she decided that her father was on the phone again . . . speaking more quietly this time. To *her*, probably . . . 'The television? Of course you can . . .'

Lucy turned on the correct channel and sat cross-legged on the floor, twiddling her hair. She wondered when a meeting with this dame her father was obviously living with would be 'programmed'. Frankly, she could wait . . . She concentrated on the show for a few minutes – but found it unusually boring. On the whole, reverting to her family, she thought her mother seemed to be having the better deal . . . down in the country with Sebastian. Even at middle-of-nowhere Knyght's Wood, spelt with a 'y'. How corny could you get? Anyhow, thank God for the lovely Sinclairs.

About the time Lucy was arriving at Lucinda's, Kate had just finished changing into a pink silk dress. The sky was darkening; the nights were already drawing in. Sitting at her dressing-table, having put on a good deal more than her usual make-up, she heard through the open window, 'Kate . . . Kate . . .' – quite low, totally clear.

She looked down onto the terrace below. The roses which climbed up that side of the house reached almost to the window-sill. Sebastian stood, head thrown back, looking up.

'I saw your light on up there. I'm a bit early, but there's the most marvellous sunset. Come on down and look or you'll miss it . . .'

'One minute . . .'

Kate went back and brushed her hair into a smooth cap. She never thought she could feel happy or excited like this again. She picked up her bag and shawl, switched off the light, and floated down the stairs, through the hall and out into the scented evening air – and Sebastian's arms.

299

Chapter 28

After their meeting with Lucy, Kate heard nothing at all from Robin; and neither did she make any effort to contact him. Most days she woke up much too early, her heart pounding with anxiety – and a sense of dread. She lay in the quiet bedroom, in the bed that now seemed much too big, gradually steeling herself into facing the day ahead . . .

Margot's opening at the barn was a smash hit. Everyone agreed on that. The revamped Margot Sinclair Knitwear designs took off with a bang. Laura, as she had promised, had pulled all the publicity strings she could and the day-long party was featured in one of the weekend supplements of a large circulation paper.

'And now that's over, we can all enjoy ourselves,' Sebastian said, looking at Kate. 'Do what we want without Margot ordering us about every minute of the day.'

'You'll be in Beverly Hills in a few weeks, forgetting all about us,' Kate challenged. 'All that sun and luxury and beautiful girls and casual chic on Rodeo Drive . . .'

He caught her arm in mock anger. 'What are the odds? How much do you bet me?'

They laughed – as they did a lot those pleasant, sunny weeks. The trees were beginning to turn. There were chrysanthemums and the first frost and lingering roses. They were often together – helping Margot with the paperwork, making expeditions to nearby parts of the countryside they both wanted to see. Once, Sebastian took her to the theatre in London to watch actor friends of his. After the show, they went backstage and had a late supper with the cast, driving down to Laverton in Margot's dodgy car in the early hours.

They were both skirting – just – the sexual friction between them. Kate bruised and wary; Sebastian, subtle, waiting . . .

Lucy had gone gloomily off to Yarnston at the beginning of September. She was going to miss the freedom and the excitement of the summer; they were all sure of that. The night before she went, she negotiated a generous allowance from Robin on the phone. Half listening while this was going on, Kate reflected that Lucy was canny as far as money was concerned, like Laura. And she knew for a fact that every penny she had earned that summer had gone straight into her savings account.

She came home for the day every Sunday but she was moody and uncommunicative. Ultra-protective, Kate watched and worried. Lucy didn't seem to feel the teaching was up to the standard of her old London day school; and she was silent on her fellow students. She never asked to bring anyone home with her, although not many of them could have lived so near. When she was at Knyght's Wood she disappeared after lunch with the local friends she had taken up with during the summer. Dean, who worked at the hardware store, was her great buddy now – a silent, hulking youth who had just bought his first secondhand car. She spoke at length to Lucinda on the phone. She was going to London to see her during the half-term break, she told Kate. She would see Dad then and stay at the flat perhaps.

'I don't see why you shouldn't,' said Kate – who did. She didn't believe Lucy had any inkling of the unknown American who was now sharing her father's life.

'I'll think about it,' Lucy said cautiously.

Laura and Nico took to spending quite a lot of time down at Knyght's Wood that autumn. The art world hadn't geared up for the winter sales yet, Nico told Kate. He had an important visit with a collector in Milan in November. The gallery was ticking over nicely for the present; his eldest son was working there and he was a competent lad. He and Laura had both sold their flats and were negotiating for a house in Kensington. Kate also suspected that neither he nor Laura liked her being alone too much now that Lucy was away . . . Without Robin . . . Without Guy . . .

301

And to her surprise, Kate found herself liking Nico more and more. He really was the most extraordinary man, as she said to Laura frequently. He turned out to be good at such unexpected things – making tomato chutney, recognizing birds, and doing tapestry. He made Kate a superb needlepoint cushion in blues and terracottas, perfect colours for the sitting-room.

Kate and Laura went over to their parents together, a couple of days after they had returned from their extended stay in Italy. It was a visit Kate had dreaded. The Holfords looked rejuvenated and wonderfully fit and it broke Kate's heart to give them yet more bad news.

But once she had blurted out the bare facts of her separation from Robin her father simply said, 'Poor darling, poor Robin too . . . hold on, both of you, don't do anything precipitate . . .' And then, eyes narrowing, slipping on his professional mask, 'We'll have to go and see what's-his-name in Harley Street again. About the hip, Kate. That's right, isn't it?' It was – and Kate nodded. He had always gauged her physical state precisely. She would have told him soon in any case. 'I'll make an appointment. It will probably take a few weeks, he's a busy man . . . I'll get on to his consulting rooms first thing tomorrow morning.'

Felicity Holford took the news of the separation with sad serenity.

When Kate and Laura got back to Knyght's Wood that day, they found that Nico had turned all Kate's frozen raspberries into jam; the pots stood in neat rows on the kitchen table. Laura and Kate both laughed and laughed – and felt obscurely better. And that night, they insisted on taking Kate back to London with them. They wanted her to see the house they were buying and a night away would do her good.

Kate got back to Knyght's Wood late the next day, having spent the morning and most of the afternoon with Laura and her architect and decorator at the new house. There were no half measures for Laura when it came to doing over a home – a new kitchen was planned; there were two bathrooms to be completely done over; a conservatory to be added. Worn out by Laura's energy and the thought of all that work, Kate was glad to get back to the peace of the country. In the kitchen, drinking coffee, she caught up with the morning papers. Amused – and excited – she spotted a long interview with Sebastian. She found herself staring at a casual and smiling photograph of him taken at Thrush Cottage. He answered questions about his part in the new picture – a young Englishman in India at the time of Independence, the end of the Raj era. His co-star was an extraordinarily beautiful French actress . . . he had high hopes for the film, great respect for the director . . . And yes, it was the most marvellous opportunity, he would love working in the States and in India particularly . . . They would be filming there early in the new year . . . He was off to Hollywood late in October.

It struck Kate forcibly that she would miss his friendship – and, yes, his physical presence – more than it was comfortable to admit. He was a marvellous companion and there was no point in pretending otherwise. She drank her coffee and turned the page . . .

The phone rang in the darkened hall.

Leaving the cosy kitchen, Kate went to answer it. There was a lot of crackling and buzzing. It sounded long distance . . . Then, 'Kate – is that you?'

A pause . . .

'Sebastian? Sebastian?' Where on earth was he?

'Kate? God, this is a terrible line . . .' His voice fading . . .

'Sebastian – where *are* you?' Kate was shouting now.

'That's better . . . Kate – I'm at the airport . . . Heathrow . . . I've been trying to get you all day.'

'I was in London with Laura and Nico.'

'Kate – I'm off to LA . . . I was desperate not being able to get hold of you . . .' He sounded frantic. '*Desperate* . . .'

'Already? But I thought . . .'

Kate's spirits dropped; the house, in darkness, creaked around her.

'There's been a sudden change of plan. My agent got hold of me this morning . . . I've had to fly out straight away . . . they need me there at once . . .'

'Oh Sebastian, I'll miss you . . .'

'That's what I wanted you to say – me too. Terribly. You must come out and see me . . . Do you promise? Oh Kate . . .'

He meant it. This too-sudden parting was more of a wrench than either of them had anticipated. Kate could detect his seriousness. 'I might . . .'

'Darling Kate . . . you promise? The moment I'm settled . . .'

'Oh yes . . . Sebastian . . . take care, good luck . . . I'll miss you . . .'

'Kate . . . I . . .'

The line went dead.

Chapter 29

Robin told Lucy, when she rang him from school, that the caretaker in the basement would let her into the flat. It was half-term soon; she would be spending a couple of nights with Lucinda. But she would like to see him first. It had been weeks, Lucy said, absolutely weeks since she had.

'That's wonderful,' Robin agreed, sounding genuinely pleased. The caretaker had the key – and he would tell him to expect her, late that Friday afternoon. If she came around, say, 5.00 p.m. he would try to be back by six. He had been working ridiculous hours, they all had in the City with the Big Bang deadline . . . he was dying to see her and hear all about Yarnston. They'd go out and have a good dinner; she ought to look in the paper and see if there was a film they might both enjoy . . . and he'd drop her at Lucinda's after. He had missed her terribly, he said. Lucy thought he sounded as though he really had. God, the mess adults made of their lives these days with their so-called post-sixties freedom of choice . . .

The flat was much the same as it had been when Lucy was there the first time in the late summer. The furniture looked just as incongruous. There were now a few chrome-framed, splashy modern prints on the walls; even higher piles of all the latest American magazines. The *Herald Tribune* and the *Wall Street Journal* lay unopened on the coffee table. There was no plant or flower – or ornament of any kind – in sight.

Lucy had more than an hour to kill before her father was likely to turn up. Bored by trawling the shops, which was all her room-mates at Yarnston seemed to care or talk about, Lucy had arrived early. Once the caretaker had left, she mooched about looking at magazines and examining the messages left on the notepad by the phone. There was only one that was slightly interesting: 'Late meeting – have fun with Lucy – love, love . . .' It was signed with unidentifiable initials. Big, round, bold, feminine handwriting. She might as well, she thought, have another look in the cupboards up-stairs . . . The persona of her father's live-in girlfriend did intrigue her – particularly as she had not been officially told of her existence.

It was while Lucy was perusing the clothes cupboard with one eye on a ridiculous television panel game, that she heard the front door of the flat open. She deftly shut the cupboard – and left the television on. The panellists were gushing and giggling inanely.

'Hi Dad . . . that you?' She called down the stairs.

Silence. A door decisively shut.

Lucy started down the creaky staircase which curved into the cramped hall. Up in the bedroom, the forced laughter still cackled . . .

A woman in her late thirties leant with her back against the door. She was exceptionally tall with a proportionately large frame. Her sleek, streaky blonde bob curved just beneath her chin. She was wearing a khaki-coloured suit, cream silk shirt and heavy gold jewellery. She had her hands on her hips, head on one side, legs crossed at the ankles. By any standards, her appearance was stunning. Perfectly poised, she watched Lucy quizzically, half smiling.

'Hello,' said Lucy nonchalantly. She had been half expecting such a visitation. 'I'm Lucy . . .' She slouched down the remaining stairs. 'Faraday,' she added unnecessarily. 'You must be my father's friend . . .' She walked into the drawing-room, flung herself down on one of the blindingly white sofas – and stared.

'Hi there Lucy . . .' Whoever it was pushed herself effortlessly away from the door. Her voice was soft, decidedly Southern – and pleasing; she sounded on the verge of laughter. Her wide red mouth curved into a grin which also wrinkled her short, straight nose. After a brief hesitation she said, 'I'm BJ – BJ Carson – it's so nice to meet you, Lucy . . . at last . . .'

Lucy smiled back. She blinked rapidly several times. Immediately, and against all her expectations, she liked her.

'Hi . . . same here . . .'

BJ, arms folded, sat on the arm of the sofa opposite Lucy, tossed back her head and started to laugh. This was deep and throaty and humorous, matching the seductive drawl.

Lucy went on staring. She was a knock-out all right – and Lucy hadn't been quite prepared for *that* . . .

So that was what the initials were; Americans went in for these shorthand names she had been told.

'You're a lot taller than I thought . . .' Lucy told her calmly – BJ was six foot two in her stockinged feet – 'but I got everything else right. Almost.' She sounded pleased.

'Meaning?' – that amused, questioning look again.

Lucy took a deep breath. 'American. Blonde. Tallish . . . Good clothes . . .' She glanced round at the chrome and glass whiteness of the large Victorian drawing-room. 'And very, well, modern taste in furniture,' she finished politely.

BJ gave another peal of easy laughter – which made Lucy feel like laughing too. 'Well, Lucy Faraday . . . I have to tell you that of the two of us, *you* were the one who got it right . . .'

'More-or-less,' said Lucy modestly. She was wondering how on earth BJ managed to achieve such silky smooth skin with just the hint of a tan – which showed off her manicured hands and collection of rings to perfection. Lucinda swore that lashings of baby oil did the trick . . . 'Why? Didn't you – about me?'

BJ shook her head. 'I certainly didn't. Such self-possession for one thing . . .' Lucy smiled blandly. 'Because you are nothing, absolutely nothing, like I had imagined. You don't, for instance, look one little bit like your Daddy.'

'I'm not like my *father*, no,' Lucy said sharply, giving her a sudden black look. She had no time for middle-aged women – and BJ was certainly that – calling fathers 'Daddy'. She stretched out her long legs in skin tight, tapered jeans. 'I'm not at all . . .'

'But as a personality perhaps?' BJ pressed. 'You seem to be a young lady with a lot of confidence . . .'

'We're quite different,' Lucy said decisively. She'd never thought herself in the least like dear old Dad . . . although he had been very jolly, she recalled regretfully, when she was

307

younger; before he got so stuck into the American company; his own chauffeur; self-important, snapping about the place as though he was God. 'I'm not like my mother either for that matter . . .'

'No?' BJ raised well arched eyebrows. Lucy noted her excellent, slightly muscular legs in the black-toed beige pumps. She was probably tremendously sporty – tennis, riding, that sort of thing. Well, that should suit Dad all right. He was always banging on about fresh air and exercise. Poor old Mother-dear. No competition there. 'But Lucy . . . you must *look* like her at least . . . if you aren't like your Daddy – I mean your father . . .'

'I suppose so – I mean, I suppose I am. Like my mother. To look at . . .' The conversation was getting boring. Yawn, yawn.

'Is she dark?' BJ, leaning forward now, sounded obsessively interested. 'She's very slim, isn't she?'

'*Slim?* She's practically anorexic . . .' If she wasn't like her father, she certainly wasn't, for God's sake, like Mother either – mooning at Knyght's Wood. No Sebastian now to take her about a bit and cheer her up. Still, one had to make allowances for the limp and the arm and whatever the hell else it was that made her what was once described as 'delicate' . . . And Guy, always Guy . . . 'Actually, I'm like my aunt, Laura, my mother's twin sister.' She fluffed her hair with her finger tips. 'She's great . . . What are you doing in England?' she asked curiously. 'Other than living with Dad, that is . . .'

BJ flashed a gorgeous smile. She had magnificent teeth – even and dazzlingly white. 'I'm working for a living, Lucy . . .' Bracelets jangled at her wrist. 'And enjoying myself at the same time . . . London's wonderful . . . I'm just crazy about the life here . . .'

Lucy considered . . .

'Are you in advertising?' she asked.

'No ma'am . . . I'm with your father's firm – on the American side . . . but they brought me over for a year so I could learn what was going on here. And I sure am doing that . . .'

'Oh I *see* . . .' said Lucy, who suddenly did. Glamorous female executive sent over from the New York office; making a pass at one of the bosses who – and this was probably whispered – had recently lost his small son, pathetic wife pushed off to bury herself in the country – which he'd never much liked. That sort of thing. Enter BJ, wildly attractive, stylish, plus – and this was what Lucy thought she really liked about her – a marvellous sense of fun ...

End, or beginning, of story.

Lucy sighed.

'I *see*,' she repeated.

'I don't know quite what ...' BJ looked a trifle disconcerted. 'But anyhow, I've been lucky and I seem to be making my way in the financial world these days ...' Lucy could believe that; everything about BJ bespoke glossy success. 'I'm good with figures – always have been, since I was a little kid ...' Can't imagine *that*, thought Lucy. Nothing little about this one ... 'I graduated from Duke University and I got through law school in two years – but I set my sights pretty high ... I believe that's what your father hopes you'll do, Lucy ...'

'Does he really?'

'He sure does. He thinks a lot of your ability and your drive ... Anyhow, it was after the Harvard Business School – I decided the Law really wasn't for me – that I joined Morton, Paine, Pearson, Black ...'

'Which gobbled up Condicote – the company my father started with some Cambridge mates.'

'That's right ... And we met here in London ...' She paused. 'By any chance, do you know anything at all about this, Lucy?'

Lucy shook her head.

'I guessed not.' BJ sighed. 'They don't get to talk much about anything emotional, do they – Englishmen?'

'No,' said Lucy. 'They don't much. That's the way they are.'

'So tell me, Lucy Faraday ... how *do* you communicate with them?' She bent forward, smiling, hair swinging onto her face. 'I'd really appreciate the answer to that one ...'

'Oh you don't much,' said Lucy – deadpan. 'You either accept this – or ...' – and here she looked straight at BJ – 'you leave ...'

BJ swung herself off the arm of the sofa and stood in the centre of the room. Lucy saw she wasn't smiling any more.

309

'Oh well,' she said quietly, 'I guess no one gets everything they want out of life . . . do they?'

Lucy's mouth dropped open. They don't, she thought? BJ, it seemed to her, was doing pretty well in that direction – great looks, terrific job. Dad at her beck and call. A wonderful flat, even if she did have it weirdly decorated.

'But – but don't you . . . have everything important that *you* want?'

BJ looked her right in the eyes. Her expression was serious, almost wistful. 'Not exactly, Lucy,' she said softly, 'Not exactly . . .' She turned abruptly. 'Now listen . . .' – light and brisk again – 'I came to pick up my briefcase and notes for a meeting. And I don't believe your Daddy – er, father – would be terribly pleased for us to be talking away like this – do you?'

'I don't see why not.'

'Well – you just take my word for it . . .' She walked across the room, scrutinised by Lucy, and bent to pick up a slim briefcase which was propped against the side of a chair. 'So I'll be on my way . . . but before I go, Lucy honey, two things . . .'

'Yes?'

The room was quiet. There wasn't much traffic outside.

'You just enjoy the Giorgio – but I'd appreciate the Valentino shirt. Returned . . .' She slung the briefcase under her arm. 'OK Lucy?'

Beneath the lazy drawl, the ice stung. Lucy thought: she must be a tiger in a boardroom with a posse of men – those looks, that elegance, that height. That toughness underneath – *wow*. Lucy admired assurance. No wonder she had taken to BJ instantly.

'OK,' Lucy agreed, not batting an eyelid. 'Actually, the blouse didn't fit – it was miles too big,' she grinned innocently. 'I lent it to Lucinda, a friend. I'll ask her for it back . . .' Some chance, thought Lucy. Lucinda wasn't exactly famous for her generosity. 'I'll ask her to have it cleaned and send it here.'

BJ headed for the door. A neat Chanel bag – like Laura's, thought Lucy – dangled from her shoulder.

'Great, Lucy. You do that. I'm glad we understand each other. So long for now.' She had picked up some keys and opened the door. 'Now you have a good time with your father this evening, you hear. He's been really looking forward to having you to himself.'

'Oh I will. Nice to have met you, BJ,' Lucy called. 'And remember what I said about Englishmen. I don't think communication is really their thing . . .'

BJ gave her a broad, conspiratorial wink – and swept out.

Robin arrived soon after BJ left – and hugged Lucy warmly.

'Lucy – you haven't grown again. Or have you?' He held her away from him, smiling. He looked full of vigour. Handsome, well set up – as though he had thrown off all his desperate preoccupation.

'Hope not . . .' Lucy extricated herself. She found she was very pleased to see him too. And he looked much less tetchy and awkward than at that grim meeting with Mother at Claridges. 'I wouldn't want to be as tall as BJ – although I suppose,' she added thoughtfully, 'it has its advantages – unusual height – in a woman . . .' She took the evening paper which Robin was carrying and immediately turned to the entertainment pages. 'BJ proves that point all right.'

After a few moments Robin said quietly, 'I knew she was coming here on her way to that meeting. She told me. She's absolutely straight is BJ. She's a very special person to me and I'd wanted to introduce you two myself. I promise.'

Lucy looked up at him. He was standing rigid; looking tense again. Oh God, Lucy sighed, shuffling through the movie ads, these adults . . . here we go again . . .

'I believe you, Dad. Not that it mattered in the slightest. Naturally I didn't think you were living in this pad entirely on your own. I'm not that daft. Anyhow, she forgot her briefcase – I think that was what she said – and dropped by to get it. I came a bit early – so we had a chat . . .'

'Lucy darling, she's been wanting to meet you for ages. I was waiting for what I thought was the right time to get you two together. I didn't intend you to meet her like that. I'm sorry it happened this way.'

'That's OK Dad.' She looked up and saw him watching her. Like Mother – like everyone else, really, for months, since Guy died – he seemed to expect her to react in some hysterical

311

manner which they considered suitable. 'I liked her – really.' Lucy smiled briefly and blandly. 'She's a stunner. Have you seen *A Cat Called Lulu?* Everyone says it's a hoot. And it's playing at the Coronet, round the corner . . .'

Over dinner, Lucy told her father, reluctantly, something about Yarnston. The kids were terribly cliquey, she said, sounding depressed. There were some she got on with – but not many. It mattered very much who your father was – and he'd better be rich. And seriously rich too – houses scattered about, use of a private plane . . . That, really, was the bottom line. And if he had some whizz-kid connection with a recognizable High Street chain-store, or if he was about to take over an American business and was seen being interviewed on a weekend T V programme – so much the better. The Yarnston son or daughter was perceived as a princeling, head of clique etc etc.

'I was afraid of that,' Robin told her.

'And it's so silly,' Lucy said, cleaning her plate and already eyeing the sweets trolley. 'Because at my London school so many girls had fathers – and mothers – who were terribly well known. Politicians, journalists, ambassadors . . . and nobody bothered about them much. It was just accepted. At Yarnston, what ones parents do – or rather what they have – is the number one topic of conversation. And the boy/girl thing is a bore. One girl has already been expelled for being pregnant . . .'

'Oh, Christ . . . What about the teaching, Lucy?'

'Patchy. Some excellent, some unbelievably bad. I'm miles ahead in maths . . . and I'm having to work out the Latin and Greek more-or-less on my own. In fact, they're talking about getting someone local in to teach it. Only three of us do the subjects – and the other two, although they're bright, simply haven't had good grounding. Which I have.'

Robin frowned. All his worst fears were confirmed, but it wasn't long, only another year and a half. Lucy would have to stick it out. He changed the subject.

Later, while they were having coffee, he asked, 'Is your mother all right?'

'So-so . . .'

312

'What do you mean?' Robin asked brusquely. 'She loves being at Knyght's Wood, she always has . . .'

'Maybe . . . Sebastian Sinclair has gone off to California. Did you know?'

'No – no I didn't. When was that?'

'A couple of weeks ago. He's making a movie out there. I think Mother gets a bit lonely – I mean, I'm hardly there and Margot is heavily involved in the business now . . . and she's completely cut herself off from everything in London. Gran and Grandpa come over sometimes . . . but they're very perky again, always out and about. Being away in Italy all summer seemed to give them a new lease on life.'

'I see . . .' He started drumming his fingers on the table. 'Well, have you made up your mind about that film?' He looked at his watch. 'We'll have to get a move on if we don't want to miss the beginning . . .'

After the film, which relaxed them and made them both laugh inordinately, they walked back to the Square to pick up Robin's car which was parked outside the flat. Robin made no move to ask her in although Lucy could see lights on in the drawing-room. He would drive her up to Lucinda's. She was not, he insisted, going to take the underground as she had suggested; because she was missing her old London haunts, even the grotty old subway, more than she cared to admit now that she was stuck down in the country all the time.

'Can I ask you about BJ?' Lucy asked as the car shot up towards north London.

'Ask away . . .' Robin, negotiating a difficult corner, smiled at her sideways.

'Well – is she married for instance?'

'She was, briefly. She's divorced.'

'Children?'

'No, no she hasn't.

As a matter of fact, I think she would like to have a child. Very much.' He spoke slowly and deliberately.

After a silence, during which she thought hard, Lucy said, 'She's very bright, isn't she?'

'Very. She's got the most tremendous IQ – or so I'm told.

Something quite extraordinary. And she's ambitious. She's got a first-rate brain – and great grasp. And presence. Well – you saw that. She could end up as president of the entire company . . . I'm not at all sure she won't. This was one of the reasons she's been sent over here . . . To learn the London market – and the European for the future . . .'

'I see.' Lucy was hunched in the seat. 'Superwoman herself.'

'Lucy . . . don't say that . . .' Robin put his hand on her arm. 'She's very human, you know . . . just as vulnerable as the rest of us, despite the way she looks.'

'I bet,' Lucy said sourly.

Robin laughed. 'Did she tell you about her racehorses?'

Racehorses . . .

'No.'

'She's mad on horses – on any sport really, she's a very adventurous lady – and she's bought into a syndicate. They've got five horses, and in the last month, every one has come in last or not finished the course. We went down to Ascot to watch one of them last weekend . . .'

Lucy didn't answer. Here was Dad, all go, squiring BJ to the races; Mother, pottering about Knyght's Wood, swooning over Sebastian. She must have been wrong about the two of them all along. Tonight, how they ever got together in the first place baffled her.

As for BJ . . . *Vulnerable*, he thinks she's *vulnerable* . . . I bet she eats these high-powered men – men like Dad – on toast for breakfast . . . That was brilliant the way she pulled her up over the scent, which she disliked, and the tarty shirt, now Lucinda's. Lucy approved of tough talking. And she had the feeling that she and B J could have had a good laugh together, given the right circumstances.

Just before they got to Lucinda's house Lucy said, 'If one got a good degree from Oxford or Cambridge, and a bit of commercial experience, would it be hard to get into the Harvard B. School, do you think? I mean – if you're woman?'

Chapter 30

The airline ticket lay on the kitchen table. It was nine o'clock on a stormy morning in late November. Outside, the trees heaved and keeled, throwing off the last shrivelled leaves. Rain battered the windows and black clouds scudded.

And there, pristine, slipped out of its air-mail envelope, lay a passport to sun and brightness. And fun. And Sebastian . . .

He had done exactly as he promised. He telephoned at least twice a week and wrote often: long letters when he had the time, or whimsical notes with funny clippings. As soon as he was settled – they had agreed this during that heart-stopping phone call from the airport, both shocked by the sudden loss of each other – she would come out for a visit. There was no reason not to. The warmth would do her good; she would manage the journey. And they would be together, as they had learnt to be, all summer.

So here it was . . .

Through his agent, he had rented a house in Bel Air, high in the hills, overlooking the ocean. It was a rambling bungalow with masses of rooms, vivid flowering shrubbery all round and a swimming-pool. He wasn't working every day, so they could do some gentle sightseeing. It was one of the most beautiful places on God's earth, she should forget all she had heard about the glitz. Whatever scenery you chose, it was there for the taking. Marvellous food and delicious Californian wines. Air like nectar away from the city. Blue skies; sunlight; brilliant sunsets. And he missed her. He missed her dreadfully . . .

'Oh Kate, Oh Kate, my love . . .' – that liquid voice, still potent across a continent and an ocean. 'I want to make you laugh again. I always have . . .'

Hence – it was he who insisted – the first-class return ticket, London–Los Angeles; arrived at Knyght's Wood, by express mail, that morning.

Margot, who was now getting down to the gritty daily round of making the business work – and slaving at it fourteen hours or more a day – was emphatic. 'Go, Kate. Go on – for once in your life break out and do what *you* want to do . . . You know Sebastian adores you. He did from the minute he saw you – and you were a poor sad little lamb then . . . accept it, for now, for what it is . . . don't think about tomorrow. My darling, when life offers you something lovely – and this is – take it, for God's sake, *take* . . .'

It was lonely at Knyght's Wood these days; and Kate had never felt lonely there before. Even the garden, which had always been Kate's solace, was drear with approaching winter. And the house, which she had loved for years, cared for and enhanced, was hardly used. She moved from kitchen to bedroom to a chair in the sitting-room in the evenings. Apart from Lucy's short Sunday visits, it seemed to Kate as though the place was slowly dying round her.

All the tragedy of Guy which she had somehow managed to keep at bay during the busy summer came hauntingly back. She now had hours of blackness and despair. Mrs Bundy had started to worry again. Kate had gone back to wearing the same sweater and skirt day after day after day. Mr Faraday had not been seen in the village for months now; nothing much had been said openly, of course, Kate Faraday was too popular for that. But the people who knew her best felt that all was not well between them.

And Robin? In her worst times, tears streaming in the terrible dark hours when she couldn't sleep and her whole life seemed to have collapsed, she shouted out for him. Often frightened; always angry. And in the morning, after she had wept herself into an exhausted sleep at last, she would find herself curled into a ball – on his side of the bed. She didn't dream any more either; or not that she remembered. Even that loved and hated fantasy sequence of Robin and Guy, melted into one, walking on ahead – unreachable, for all her burning determination – had left her.

Fighting desperation she thought: so it was to be California. And she was lucky to have the chance. She would go for two weeks early in December and be back in time for Laura and Nico's wedding and Lucy's school holidays. Back too for the unimaginable Christmas, without Robin, that must somehow be faced . . .

California, here I come . . . Tonight, she would speak to Sebastian . . .

She was meeting her father for lunch in London tomorrow. After, he was coming with her to see the specialist about her hip. That, too, would have to be faced. So also would the old gardener who had told her that he wouldn't be able to carry on in the spring; she had half expected that for months. And she knew he was irreplaceable . . .

She got up and looked out at the depressing wet, grey morning. Perhaps after two weeks in sunny California, with Sebastian, all these agonies, which seemed insurmountable now, would be more manageable.

She snatched up the ticket; she wanted to tell Laura.

'Katie, it's a madhouse here . . .' Laura was in a whirl, trying to get the builders out of the house in time, working with decorators, getting clothes together for the wedding and the month in the Bahamas after. She sounded deliriously happy. Nico had gone off on his important visit to the collector in Milan. She had spoken to him last night. He had unearthed a secret, very special collection . . . he knew just how he was going to market the pictures. . . He sounded excited; more than that – elated. This was the last trip in the dreadful plane that had caused so much trouble. They had left it at an airport near Milan last summer for maintenance and repairs and it was fixed at last, he said. They had the mechanic on board as well as a second pilot; the British buyer was satisfied. They were flying it back to London. And that was that with Nico and private planes – or so she hoped.

Kate could hardly get a word in edgeways – and when she did, there was a silence, followed by a shriek . . .

'Katie, that's absolutely marvellous . . . California – you'll adore it. When? As long as you'll be back for the wedding . . . Oh fine . . . that's the best news from you I've heard for ages . . . you'll be a different you . . . Now don't you dare even think of copping out of it . . . God Bless Sebastian . . .'

And let Robin, running round town with that brilliant blonde American – looking for all the world like the cat that had swallowed the canary – put that in his pipe and smoke it. Worms could turn . . . even, it seemed, Katie Faraday . . . Hmm, just what the doctor ordered, Laura fancied . . . In more ways than one possibly.

'I couldn't be happier about it, Katie, enjoy every second . . . and with divine Sebastian Sinclair . . . lucky old you . . . and get yourself some pretty clothes, and for God's sake get your hair cut properly. Lucy's nail-scissors really won't do,' she added severely.

'No, Laura,' Kate said meekly.

Kate told her father when they were having lunch in London two days later. He, too, was approving.

'A change . . . Do you good, my darling. He must be a nice chap, Sebastian, or you and Lucy wouldn't like him as you do. Warmth and swimming won't hurt either.' He shot her a canny look. 'And Robin? What does he say?'

Kate shrugged. 'He doesn't know a thing about it,' she said coolly. 'I mean – why should he?'

'Quite.'

The conversation turned to other subjects. It amazed Kate to see how her parents had recovered their equilibrium after Guy's death. During the early part of the summer she had doubted this was ever possible. But her father was continuing with his committees, his charity work, and his passionate interest in art. He never missed a good exhibition. There was something he had his eye on that was coming up for auction next week, he told her. And Felicity Holford was at that moment lunching with her editor, reworking the book which she had abandoned in despair during the spring.

Kate thought she knew what it was that had got them through the crisis of their only grandson's death. They were not unscathed; they had both endured long stretches of depression. They had both aged physically. But what had pulled them through was: love. Of each other.

318

'Yes,' she said brightly. 'More coffee please. The appointment is at 2.30 isn't it? We've got plenty of time . . .'

The doctor, whom Kate had seen before, was straightforward and firm. He did not tell either Kate or her father anything they didn't already know. The right hip, that she had been favouring most of her life, was arthritically affected. He wanted X-rays; it was a question of timing. He would operate, of course, but he couldn't predict when. Frankly, he'd prefer to wait as long as possible because of her relative youth. He gave her a prescription for the pain – and arranged to get a set of X-rays after Christmas. They would make the decision sometime after that.

They came out of the consulting rooms and stood on the pavement in weak sunlight.

'Well,' John Holford said, taking Kate's arm. 'That's that. It was more-or-less a formality, Kate darling, but we're putting the operation in motion. It's inevitable. You know that.'

'Yes, of course. I do know.'

'He won't want to do it until he must . . . And he's a top man.'

'It's bearable for the moment,' Kate said quickly. 'Bad sometimes – but it is bearable . . .'

'I know it is. And so did he. But it won't be.'

'No . . .' She gave her father a kiss on the cheek. Not even this cloud hanging over her was going to spoil a bright spot of happiness. She said gaily, 'But I'm off to California first. Don't forget to tell Mother. And I'm not going to think about anything unpleasant, including the wretched hip, until I come back rejuvenated – with the most marvellous tan . . .' She then hopped into a taxi and told the driver to take her straight to the station. She had taken Laura's advice and had her hair washed and trimmed that morning; it was amazing how that alone had raised her spirits. Even the doctor's gloomy prognosis hadn't cast her down. She had already made a list of clothes to be looked out and essentials to be bought: sunglasses, sandals, new make-up . . .

Her mind ablaze with California and sunshine and Sebastian, she flew through the station – with just enough time to

319

snatch an evening paper before she pulled herself onto the train with only minutes to spare. And they had already swayed and jerked out of central London, shot past rows of grimy terraced houses to a greener suburban landscape before Kate casually picked up the paper.

She glanced at the headlines – down the page – and then she saw it. A stop-press item squashed into the bottom right-hand corner . . .

WELL-KNOWN WEST END GALLERY OWNER IN CRASH OF PRIVATE PLANE

Mr Nicolas Kirilov . . . flying from Milan to London early this morning . . . plane crashed into a mountainside near Milan in dense fog . . . pilot and another man, in addition to Mr Kirilov, believed to be on board . . . it is not known whether there are any survivors . . . The Kirilov Gallery was founded in the early 1920s by Mr Kirilov's grandfather . . . Mr Kirilov recently obtained an uncontested divorce from his wife, Lady Arabella Kirilov, daughter of the Earl of Elvin . . . there are seven children of the marriage . . .

The rest of the short journey was a horrified blur to Kate. She sat rigid, staring, too shocked to panic, thinking: Laura, Laura, Laura, over and over again . . . She had taken the car from the station car park and driven to Knyght's Wood, just as she would have done on any other day. She remembered nothing of all this.

The first moment of reality came when she saw Lucy's note on the kitchen table, scrawled on a notepad she kept by the phone. It read:

Mother – don't know if you've heard but Nico's plane crashed early this morning. Somewhere near Milan. It was on the one o'clock news. Someone has been rescued, badly hurt, but they didn't say if it was Nico. Very confused. Laura must have left. I couldn't get hold of her. And I'm going too. I must be with her. Whatever happens. I've got plenty of

320

money and I've collected my passport. Dean is driving me to Heathrow. I'll phone as soon as I've got any news. Please don't worry. I'll be OK ... Laura's the one to think about. Love, Lucy.

P.S. Could you or Dad tell Yarnston? They won't start to flip for a few hours yet. Thanks.

'I must speak to Mr Faraday. At once. It's urgent. This is his wife ...'

'I'm sorry Mrs Faraday, but Mr Faraday took the afternoon off. He's gone to the airport. He wasn't sure whether or not he'd be coming back to the office – but it's 5.30 now. So I would imagine he would go straight home.'

This must be a new secretary; Kate didn't recognise the voice. She swallowed. Oh Robin – where *are* you ...? It must be someone very important for Robin to have bothered to meet off a plane these days.

The prim voice went on, 'I could leave a message for the morning. Or' – sounding reluctant – 'I suppose I could give you his home number if you wish ...'

'That won't be necessary,' Kate said coldly. And rang off.

She flung off her coat and her bag and started pacing. What on earth should she do? Her parents were in London for the evening. Would they see, or hear, the news? Would Robin? Surely ... And where – a sharp pang – was Lucy?

And why – Oh why – were her nearest and dearest, both of them, at the airport, for God's sake ...?

An hour or so later – it seemed a lifetime to Kate – the phone rang. It was Robin. He had heard the reports, he'd been out of the office most of the day, and as soon as he got in he'd been phoning everyone he could think of in Milan. He'd managed to get some information. Nico had been pulled clear. The two others as well. He was alive. Badly injured but alive. He was in the hospital and Laura had arrived. That was all he knew.

'Thank God ...' Kate could feel her knees buckling and tears of relief beginning. 'Oh thank God ... and Robin, Lucy – she heard it on the news and she ran away from Yarnston and she's gone out to be with Laura ...'

321

'She's *what?*'

Tears pouring down her face now. 'You heard . . . I was in London and I got back and found her note . . . she's probably flying over now. She'll get in touch as soon as she knows anything, she said. She said not to worry about her . . .'

'Not to *worry?* And what about the school may I ask?'

'She asked us to phone. Will you, Robin, please? Explain that she hasn't been happy there and she felt that she had to be with her aunt. With Laura. When this happened. Say whatever you like. Will you, Robin? Will you?'

'Of course. I'll have to . . . My God, they must have missed her by now . . .'

'I expect she left a note . . . in any case, you'll have to speak to them. You will – won't you?'

'Christ, what a mess . . .'

'But I – I love her for this,' Kate sobbed. 'It's so like Lucy. It's gutsy and brave and decisive . . .' She could hardly speak.

'I think you've got very strange ideas of bringing up children, I must say,' Robin sounded exasperated. Kate also sensed that he was distraught. His mind, somehow, wasn't on all this.

'I'll let you know if I hear anything from Lucy . . .' Kate brushed her wet face with her hand. 'And you'll phone the school, won't you? Tell them – Oh tell them anything . . .'

Events started happening in a strange sequence. Lucy rang, very late. She had found Laura in the hospital, don't ask how she got there, and they were sitting about waiting. Nico was badly burned and had spinal injuries. The pilot and the mechanic weren't too bad. Nico was critical. That much they had made out. No one spoke much English except for one doctor – and Laura had made herself felt. If he made it through the night, he had a good chance. He might be paralysed. She had spoken to Arabella – 'so I saved Laura that. She was very good, very calm, and is organising a service of prayer tomorrow so the children, the younger ones, will have something to do. She sounded nice.'

'What about Laura?'

'Well – we're just clinging together and hoping for the best.

322

It seems to have been engine failure – that bloody plane. Laura always hated it. Although the flying conditions were risky apparently. It's going to be a long night.'

'I'm so glad you're there, Lucy, so glad . . .'

'Me too . . . despite the ghastly circumstances. It's a nightmare all right.'

'Dad is phoning Yarnston. He got on to the hospital, by the way. Someone he knows in Milan . . .'

'Oh good. Bugger Yarnston. I'll ring in the morning . . .'

Kate, composed at last, contacted her parents when they arrived back from London. They had already heard the news and their thoughts were only for Nico's survival and Laura's pain. Neither showed much surprise when Kate told them that Lucy had run away from school – and was in Milan with Laura. Perhaps, after facing Guy's death together and coming through, only the basics of life were important to them now. Or perhaps it was simply growing old. In any case Felicity Holford merely said, 'We must hope for the best, Kate darling . . . Laura is with him – and he's alive. Now do go to bed and get some rest . . .' And her father added, 'Icarus . . . I warned him – Nico – years ago . . . But it sounds as though he's going to make it, thank God.'

After hours of indecision, Kate phoned Sebastian and told him the news. He was terribly shocked – but at the same time, he hoped it wouldn't alter their plans. Kate said she didn't see why it should, as long as Nico started to recover . . . She would let him know what happened in the next couple of days; she thanked him and yes, it all sounded heavenly and she was tremendously excited; she had never done anything like this in her life before . . .

'And about time you did,' said Sebastian.

But in some indefinable way, Kate's enthusiasm for the trip was already beginning to ebb . . .

Laura phoned in the morning. She sounded strained and exhausted. Nico survived the night and was out of immediate danger. It was too early to say whether or not he would

323

be paralysed. The doctors seemed excellent, very concerned. There was no question of her moving him for the present.

'And Lucy,' she said, 'wonderful, difficult, law-unto-herself Lucy' had literally saved her life – mentally – and quite possibly Nico's as well. She really didn't think that without Lucy's grit she would have had the strength to pull Nico through those difficult hours when he could so easily have let go. And didn't.

There was nothing more Lucy could do there and it wasn't good for her to hang about. She was putting her on the late afternoon flight to London – arriving about 6.00 p.m. – and she wanted Kate to meet her. Robin too. 'She's been through a lot, Katie, and it hasn't been pretty. And the school business has got to be sorted out. So you'll be there, both of you. She needs you *both* – desperately. You promise?'

Kate did.

PART 5

Concord

Chapter 31

They arrived at the airport, separately, much too early. Kate
had come by train and bus; Robin had driven himself straight
from the office. They met at the arrivals barrier. Kate's face was
white – accentuated by the cherry red scarf which she had tied
over her warm grey wool coat. Robin instinctively put his hand
beneath her elbow and steered her towards a seating area.

'There's plenty of time.' He glanced at his watch. 'I checked
on the board and the plane's on time.'

Kate nodded. After hanging around for an hour by herself,
she already knew that.

'No more news of Nico?' Robin asked. 'Look – here are two
seats . . . let's grab them . . .'

They did.

'I've heard nothing since this morning. Lucy might know
something more . . .'

Kate glanced at Robin. He appeared distracted and ill at
ease; fidgeting, continuously glancing round. Every inch the
City businessman in his dark suit; that good head of straight
hair. Kate's arm ached painfully . . . He was carrying an
evening paper – which he opened and skimmed.

'There's nothing in this about the crash. I thought they
might have followed it up . . .'

Kate wondered bleakly what – if anything – he had told the
dazzling BJ person about this bizarre and tragic turn of events;
how he had explained this early evening meeting of the plane
from Milan. Perhaps they had plans for this evening which
had to be cancelled. Perhaps this personal intrusion from
Robin's former life had caused – what? Hard words? Sulking?
A flaming row?

Was this why Robin seemed so agitated? She had sensed this even when speaking to him last night, too; as though something troubled him that was deeper than the crisis of Nico's accident and Lucy's absconding from Yarnston . . .

She turned away, gazing sightless at the milling airport crowds. I know nothing about his life now, she thought helplessly, nothing at all . . .

She had insisted that he meet Lucy with her tonight. Laura was right about that and Kate had been prepared to exert herself if Robin had shown the slightest reluctance. But to her surprise he had simply said, quite gently, 'It would be helpful if you could get out to the airport yourself – I've got a meeting, but I'll leave early. Then I can take you and Lucy down to Knyght's Wood . . . it shouldn't be more than an hour's drive at that time of day . . .'

He then told her that the headmaster at Yarnston had been relieved to know that Lucy was safe – she had apparently left a note making up a story of some kind – but they were beginning to worry all the same. He didn't, Robin said, sound particularly interested in the situation otherwise – which surprised him. Kate hardly cared.

The minutes wore awkwardly on until Robin, who had been strolling restlessly about, came back and told her that the plane had landed; she couldn't have any luggage to speak of so perhaps they should go and wait at the barrier.

Kate got up stiffly. Again, Robin took her arm as they pushed through the scurrying crowds. Now that Lucy was to appear so shortly, Kate's nervousness grew. Emotion was never far from the surface these days. She must have been shaking slightly because Robin's grip on her arm tightened.

She dared not – could not – look at him . . .

They stood at the barrier, not moving, not talking – waiting for their only child to appear among the straggle of dishevelled passengers, weighed down with handbags and duty-free carriers, calling, waving, looking about anxiously. Robin continued to hold firmly onto her elbow.

They were looking straight ahead, standing just as they had at Guy's funeral; Kate was even wearing the same coat as she had that pitiless winter's day. They were intimates – they had been for years. They were also total strangers. Only Robin's touch at Kate's sagging elbow united them.

That – and Lucy.

And there she was – black leather jacket flapping; long, skinny legs in thick black tights; hair frizzing around her pale face. There were dark smudges under her eyes. She looked very young and very forlorn. The inevitable tattered hold-all was hoisted onto one shoulder.

She saw Kate – only Kate – and her face crumpled and she started to run and came flying into her arms ... And there they were, mother and daughter, clinging as though nothing could ever drag them apart, both talking and sobbing at the same time, both faces streaking ...

The single spot of colour was Kate's red scarf which was now somehow wound round Lucy's neck too.

They were crying together in this public place for many things: for the hardness there had been between them, on and off, through the years; for the missed opportunities of childhood; for the love they had always felt towards one another – but been unable to express. There was joy in Kate's tears too – for this overgrown child who had miraculously been restored to her. And Kate knew instinctively that mixed up with everything else, Lucy was also crying for Guy. Sitting with Laura, watching Nico through the still hours poised between life and death, had started to release her inner anguish.

Robin stood by them, his expression inscrutable. The emotional scene was nothing particularly unusual in a crowded international airport. A few people glanced at Kate and Lucy sympathetically – and went on their way.

After a few minutes, Robin touched Kate's shoulder. 'I'm going to get the car – go over to the entrance and wait and I'll pick you up there. Can you do that?'

Lucy's head was buried on Kate's shoulder, still sobbing. Kate, more or less in control now, looked up at Robin over Lucy's head and nodded.

Lucy, who seemed to have reverted to babyhood, insisted that Kate sat in the back of the car with her. She clung to her all the way down to Laverton, bursts of unrestrained crying

329

punctuated by hard information. They learnt that Nico was stable, and that although Laura had been prepared for the worst, the doctors did not now think that he would be paralysed. They weren't certain of this yet; his back had been severely crushed – and it would take some time to be sure. But there were hopeful signs. Laura knew of a marvellous rehabilitation centre near London and if necessary, when he was well enough, she would arrange for him to be moved there.

Then, after another bout of weeping: the pilot and the mechanic were also recovering – badly shaken but not in danger. Nico had been by far the most seriously injured. It was astounding, even the nurses said, that any of them had got out from the crash alive. More weeping, then: Laura always hated Nico flying because she said he took risks. It had been implied that flying a small plane in those foggy conditions round Milan was unwise – although they had obtained all the necessary flight permissions. Nico, Laura thought, had been wildly excited by the secret collection he had just seen – and frantic to get home – to her . . .

Another long and painful fit of crying while Kate rocked and soothed and murmured and pushed back the straggly dark hair. Then – Yarnston . . . She hated it, she would never go back. She would have left at Christmas, so this just made it a bit sooner. She was sorry – very, very sorry – to have caused all this trouble and expense over it. She had wanted to do well there; they must know that. But there it was. The teaching was awful – and the values 'stank'.

Kate, both arms still clutching Lucy, spoke up clearly for the first time.

'That's that then. If you feel like that about it, Lucy, you shouldn't go back. You mustn't.' Laura's instincts, not hers, had been correct after all.

Robin, looking grim, met Kate's eyes in the driving mirror. She looked defiantly back. Groping in her handbag, she had found some tissues and was attempting to mop Lucy's livid face. But she was beyond it now. Sobs were punctuated with hiccups. They had just reached Laverton when she said, incoherent with tiredness and grief, the words wrenched out of her, 'I miss him, Mum, so terribly . . . Guy . . .'

330

Between them, they got Lucy out of the car and into the house. Kate and Lucy went straight upstairs, arms round each other, to Lucy's room. Kate turned down her bed and ran her bath and helped her to undress. She would come up and see her in a little while in case she wanted something to eat or a hot drink.

'What you really need, Lucy darling, is a good night's sleep . . .' They would talk again in the morning and perhaps try to get through to Laura. Also, perhaps she could contact Arabella and the children.

Lucy nodded and headed for the bathroom.

'Have a lovely hot bath, Lucy, I'll be up soon,' Kate told her. Then, standing by the door she said quietly, 'I admire you so much for doing what you did, Lucy. Laura needed you – and you were there. Well done you . . .'

Kate was aware of Robin's presence in the house while she was upstairs with Lucy. All the time she had been listening, surreptitiously, for the car – which she hadn't heard. When she came down, she wondered uneasily what his reaction to all this was going to be. Lucy wasn't going back to Yarnston – that was final. She had made a mistake, they all had, out of the best motives and at an excruciatingly difficult time. There was no reason for her to go on being as unhappy as she clearly had been. But she couldn't face another showdown tonight.

He was in the sitting-room, standing with his back to the door, looking down and reading something he was holding. He had switched on all the lights, but the room looked cheerless. Kate realised that for the first time, there wasn't a plant or a flower anywhere. These past few weeks, she had given up on the house. She said wearily, 'I think she's all right, Lucy. She's having a bath which should make her feel better and then I'll go up and see if there's anything she wants . . .' Robin still had his back to her. Kate felt suddenly overwhelmed by it all – Lucy, Laura, Nico. Lucy's passionate outburst of grief, however therapeutic, had been terribly draining . . .

She pulled herself together. 'Is there anything you want? Coffee or something?' Presumably he was about to take off for London again; it would be a relief, the way she was feeling, to have Lucy and the house to herself. She had been faintly surprised to find him still there, with all the lights blazing.

He wheeled round and faced her. She had never seen him look like that. His chin thrust out, his eyes narrowed with anger. His hands were shaking visibly with whatever it was he was holding. He said – his voice like a whiplash, 'And *what* is this?'

'What is what, Robin?'

She sank into the little Victorian nursing chair that they had bought in a country market soon after they were married. Her hip was acting up, throwing hot sparks up and down her side. Was it too late to phone her parents and tell them Lucy was safely home? She thought perhaps a cup of tea . . .

'This . . .'

He thrust an envelope at her – and she saw it was her air ticket to Los Angeles. She leant across to take it – when he whisked it away from her.

Instantly furious, Kate said, 'Give me that. It's mine, I tell you, mine. How dare you, Robin . . . Where did you find it anyhow?'

'On the kitchen table as a matter of fact . . .' He probably had; she lived in the kitchen these days. 'And what exactly does it mean?' – his tone rising dangerously.

Spots danced before her eyes. 'It means what it says,' Kate yelled back. 'That I'm going to California for two weeks at the beginning of December. As you see, it's all arranged. Providing Nico's accident doesn't prevent it. I have some right to a life of my own too, you know, while you're wining and dining around London with your glamorous American mistress . . .'

Kate glared at him. She forgot all about being tired. Rage had given her a high colour. Her precise new haircut showed off the fine high cheek bones and her dark almond eyes flashed.

Without a word, Robin handed her the envelope – and slumped in the chair opposite. 'Why,' he asked quietly, 'are you going?' He held a hand across his eyes.

'I am going,' she told him, heated with her new found mettle, 'to stay with Sebastian Sinclair . . . and I cannot see, as a matter of fact, that it is any of your business.' She stood up,

332

pushing herself out of the low chair with her good arm. 'I did ask you before – would you like a coffee?'

'No. Thank you. Kate, sit down. Please.' This was his normal voice.

She sat. 'Well?'

He had loosened his tie. She thought without so much as a tremor: he's still a handsome man. He looks – so competent; but then, he always did.

She waited for what seemed like some time.

'I have a lot I want to say to you,' he said at last. 'But if you are seriously involved with Sinclair . . .'

Still she waited, not moving a muscle. He had flung himself back in his chair. He was looking at her differently now – achingly, she could see it in his eyes. And like the old Robin. With love.

'He is, and always will be, my friend,' she said quietly.

'Friend – only?'

'My friend – I've told you . . .'

He leant forward. 'Kate . . .' His fingers were clasped tight at the knuckles. She had never seen his expression so set. He was desperate to say whatever it was he wanted to – desperate. 'BJ – she's gone. Back to the States. She'd had enough – we both had. And in any case her time here was up . . .' The words blurted out. 'It could never have worked for either of us. I must have been mad.'

Kate stared – wary, saying nothing. She wasn't even sure she was hearing properly.

'It is completely over. I wanted you to know that. I had hoped – that if I was truly honest – about everything – it could make a difference. Between us.'

'Gone?' Kate said stupidly, as though she couldn't understand what he had just said. 'When did she go? Where to?'

'Yesterday. I saw her off at the airport for New York. It was an amicable parting. There were no hard feelings. She's a remarkable woman, I shall always think that.'

The airport . . . that was where he was when she tried to get him – seeing BJ off. It struck Kate that they had all been extraordinarily involved with airports, one way or another, these last few days.

'Oh – I see . . .'

'I had hoped you might. Apart from Nico's crash, I have thought of little else except you and me for weeks now. It started – with BJ . . .' He took a deep breath. 'It started, in a casual way, some time ago . . .' His whole being was focused on her. There were deep lines across his forehead that she hadn't noticed before. Kate looked away.

'When?'

'Before Guy died. We skied together all that winter. I wanted to break it off – it meant nothing much. I told her. I hated doing it to you, Kate. I hated it.' He was vehement. 'After that dinner party in Bryanston Square when we drove down here and it was my idea. I wanted to make a clean break of it then – I was going to tell her . . .'

This, Kate thought unsteadily, is getting painful. And really I've had enough . . .

Then she remembered. His lovemaking that night had been shocking. It was because of her. He was involved with her. Then.

She had stifled her misgivings. She had not probed – missed the now obvious warning lights. Trusting; happy; naïve. Absorbed in her own lovely life. No questions asked.

'I see,' Kate said in a hard voice, looking clear across the room. 'Do go on . . .'

'If I do – say everything – however dreadful it seems . . . If it's truthful – is there hope for us then? Is there, Kate?'

'I don't know.' She rounded on him, anger erupting again. 'You blamed me – for Guy.'

He dropped his head in his hands. He didn't say anything for a long time. When he looked up, his eyes were wet.

'Never. Never in any important sense. I said – thought – things that were unthinkable and unsayable. They can never be totally retracted. I know that. The truth is – I couldn't accept Guy's death. And you were the nearest . . . I didn't have – don't have – whatever it is you do. Steel. Inner strength. However one describes it.'

Silence . . .

'All the same,' Kate said at last, very slowly. 'All the same, it might have made a difference, those couple of hours, if I had

334

taken him straight from school . . .' He lunged at her – out of his chair, on his knees beside her. His arms around her waist. 'We'll never know, there's no way we could. But it might have been a mistake . . .'

His shoulders were moving, his head bowed. Kate thought he was probably crying. *She* was long past tears over Guy.

'And then you left, wouldn't come to London, cut yourself off from everyone and everything – from me – down here . . .' His face was still buried; she could hardly hear.

'Yes.' She accepted this.

'I was too weak for that . . . to be left alone when I needed your presence, your strength, your loving . . .' His face was pressed against her side. 'I resented it terribly, Kate . . . I thought you didn't care . . .'

'I can't blame you for that, Robin.' It wasn't easy to say – but she couldn't.

'BJ was around . . . at the office, meetings, dinner – I'm nearly fifty, Kate. And I'm as vain as the next man – probably more so. I was physically dazzled . . .'

Kate winced. 'Please, Robin, I don't want to . . .'

'But you must,' he said fiercely. 'Don't you see . . .' Raising his head. 'If there's ever to be trust again between us . . .' His head dropped. 'Of course I was – flattered and gratified. And there's worse . . .'

'What?' Kate asked faintly.

'She wanted a child – my child. Desperately. This was, she said, the most important thing in her life.'

I might be sick, Kate thought. I might . . . She closed her eyes. That Amazon, Laura had described her. If there was such a thing as ultimate cruelty, then this, she supposed, was it.

'Why are you telling me this?' she asked coldly.

'Because I love you. Because I never stopped loving you. Not for an instant. BJ knew this. She was right.'

Kate was starting to shiver. She must put a stop to all this – really it was past bearing . . .

'Can you forgive disloyalty, temporary madness? Can you, Kate?' He was as urgent as she had ever heard him. Some hard core eased in Kate; she could feel it going.

335

'I was stubborn . . .' – very low, as though she was talking to herself. 'I put my own feelings above yours – and Lucy's . . . I did do that . . .'

Lights started flickering before her eyes. She didn't think she was going to be able to stand much more of this . . .

'Can you, Kate, forgive?'

Above them, at that moment, something stirred – some grinding noise. Startled, they both looked up. It began with a thump and a wail, grew louder, settled into a steady beat. Da-dum, da-dum, da-dum . . . Lucy's heavy rock . . .

Robin sat back on his heels. He was grinning – in the midst of all this. His eyes crinkling at the corners the way they always did. The unbearable tension was diffused and a semblance of normality restored – by Lucy's awful music.

'The young have the most amazing recuperative powers, don't they? I'm going to get us both a drink. Don't move – not an inch . . .'

'Robin – I couldn't . . .'

'You could – you will . . .'

He handed her a glass. The beat was loud and steady now, the whole house reverberating . . .

The brandy burnt and warmed after all. Within seconds – she hadn't eaten for hours and hours – she felt as though she had some blood in her veins again.

Robin pulled over a stool and sat beside her. He warmed his glass between his hands and tossed the brandy off in gulps. Lucy was really letting it rip upstairs now . . . That was a good, cheerful sign, so she must be feeling better after the trauma of the last two days. She would go up and see her in a minute.

Kate sipped her brandy; it was going straight – and quite pleasantly – to her head.

Robin said, his voice intimate against the rocking beat above, 'I'm asking you, again, to forgive my vanity. That was what it was – that was *all* it was. Can you, Kate? Can you?'

'I – don't – know.'

She didn't know anything much any more. Sebastian . . . She peered round for the air-mail envelope . . .

'Won't you try to, Kate? Won't you? There's so much riding on this – our lives – Lucy's . . .'

336

His face was very close; he was utterly sincere, she knew that. Eyes boring into hers; that determined mouth and chin.

She said again out of nowhere, surprising herself, 'I *was* stubborn . . . it gave me strength – but it's a weakness too. I made mistakes,' she said vaguely. She had forgotten for the moment what they were.

The brandy . . . she drained her glass . . .

Did they matter so much – her mistakes, his mistakes, BJ, Sebastian, pride, hurt?

Did they?

Guy was dead. They must make their peace, live with memories – such vivid and lovely memories – and move on in their lives. His toys and games, his bear, were all in the children's ward now . . . She hadn't expected to cry again for Guy. And yet she was – tears running helplessly down her cheeks . . .

She was getting muddled. Thinking – lulled by the artificial warmth? – that nothing mattered at all in the end except for Robin's face and eyes, Lucy's loud presence upstairs. And Laura and Nico's present trouble.

Her hip was giving her hell now; nothing helped that. She moved – and grimaced. Robin saw. He said steadily, 'I think you can forgive, Kate. I think we will go on – together.'

He touched her wet cheek gently with his fingers. And when he put out both his hands to hers, she took them.

They were sitting like that, hands held loosely, not talking, when Lucy padded down the stairs, across the hall and into the kitchen.

Idiots, she thought amiably. Complete idiots, the pair of them. All the same – if she was honest – in her opinion, it had been a close run thing their getting together again. Poor adorable Sebastian languishing in sunny California . . . Ah well, there'd be no shortage of takers there . . . She also thought she might – possibly – have played a part in seeing BJ off the scene – which was presumably what had happened. Or was about to . . .

She opened the refrigerator. Neither she nor Laura had had a thing except a couple of stale Italian rolls with a bit of salami stuck inside which she had dashed out and bought very late last night. They weren't hungry, in any case. And today, the food on the plane had been revolting. As per usual.

She rummaged about. Some cheese that had seen better days, a wedge of pâté, fruit . . . loading a plate, she shut the door with care – and crept off upstairs again. On her way, she looked into the sitting-room. They were talking now, quietly and seriously. She could have listened, of course – they were dead to the world – but frankly, she'd rather not hear . . .

Back in her room, she turned down the deafening volume slightly and prepared to start on the food.

Pity about BJ in a way. She'd found her wildly intriguing. Amazing, really. She had no intention of losing touch alto-gether . . . one never knew . . . she was a good contact all right, and she had a brilliant sense of humour . . .

Which made her think: heaven only knew what she had been doing with dear old Dad in the first place. It must have been the Brit accent and the City gent look. A child too, possibly. She must be pushing forty – and Dad had hinted at something of the sort. She would have to consult Lucinda. In any event, she was afraid she would have to whistle for the Valentino shirt or buy herself a new one.

When Kate eventually made her way up to see her, the plate was clean, the music turned off – and she was tucked in bed with the covers pulled up to her ears, almost asleep. Kate dropped a kiss on the dark mop of hair, took away the plate and put out the light.

Just as she was shutting the door, a sleepy voice came from the bed, 'Good to be home, Mum 'Night . . .'

After Kate had reported to Robin that Lucy was in bed, almost asleep, they went into the kitchen – both like sleepwalkers now, both white and emotionally drained. Lucy's foray had depleted Kate's meagre supplies. Alone for so much of the time, she hadn't bothered about food. They found some fruit and cheese and biscuits – neither of them was hungry – and while they picked at it, they talked soberly.

Both had come, separately, to major decisions. At the end of the summer, Kate had decided that Knyght's Wood must be

338

sold. It was one of the problems she had confronted lying on her bed, distraught, on a dull and sultry afternoon. The house and the garden were too big for her now, she told Robin. Peters was leaving, they would never replace him – and it was only a matter of time before she would need surgery on her hip.

'I suspected that,' Robin said, reaching out for her hand. 'But Kate – Knyght's Wood . . . you've always loved it so, put so such of yourself into it . . .'

'I have . . .' Kate shook her head. 'But not any more. It's a part of my life that's over and finished with.' She thought briefly and piercingly of the small grave in the churchyard nearby, where the cherry trees blossomed early in the spring. She must leave that too. Everything that she had loved in Guy was in her, a part of her, now. 'It's a sort of letting go, Robin . . .'

'I believe I can understand that . . . Then it will have to be London – somewhere new – a fresh start for us all . . .'

'Yes . . . and that's better for Lucy too. We'll have to find her the best tutorial place we can.'

Robin pushed aside his plate which he had scarcely touched.

'And I'm leaving the firm,' he said abruptly. 'I meant to tell you before. I'm already negotiating the terms, and they should be generous.'

'You never enjoyed it,' Kate said slowly. 'Not since the Condicote days . . . did you?'

'No – and it seems terrible to spend one's life feeling that . . . all that money grubbing . . .'

Light years ago, in another life, he had hinted as much to her – that he was sick and tired of it all despite his success.

'What will you do?'

'Something else . . . perhaps quite different this time.' They had been through much the same conversation years before. In Paris. She had supported him then – and she would, Robin knew, do so again. They smiled at each other wanly, deflated by the evening's wringing emotions – Lucy's and their own. And the question mark of Nico's full recovery hanging over them all . . . 'To tell you the truth, I haven't been able to keep

339

my mind on anything recently – except us . . .' This time, it was Kate who put out her hand. 'And I've been wondering,' he said seriously, 'about Laura. Don't you think your father should fly out at some stage? He has excellent judgement and his medical background . . . Is he up to it?'

'Oh yes – he's in great form now. Mother too. The summer in Italy, together, did them so much good. I think we should definitely suggest that he goes . . .'

Although it was getting late, Robin insisted on lighting a fire in the sitting-room while Kate checked on Lucy. She was dead to the world and hadn't moved since she left her before. So they brought their coffee and came and sat close to the fire. It was almost winter again and the old house had always been chill in the evenings.

They talked, like the old friends they had always been, of this and that . . . Kate said that despite the plane crash, Laura would cope, however serious Nico's injuries were. He was her life's blood. As long as he was alive – and they were together – she would survive. Robin agreed. They touched on selling Knyght's Wood – and this gave Kate a pang – which must be, and he made this clear, her decision alone.

'I mean it, Robin. I've been thinking it through for months now. And once the decision's made, the sooner the better . . . and we can start looking for a house in London. As long,' she said wistfully, 'as long as it has a garden of sorts, however small . . .'

Robin sprang up and began pacing the room, hands clasped behind his back, as he had done so often when pondering some problem or other. It was very quiet in that familiar setting with the darkened garden and the tranquil countryside around them. Only the fire crackled. All of a sudden Robin stopped. He turned . . .

'Kate,' he said. 'I've had an idea. I know exactly what we're going to do . . .'

His shoulders were back – he had thrown off the years – he sounded young and buoyant and exhilarated.

'What's that?' looking up, surprised.

Two strides and he was beside her chair, half kneeling.

Kate's features were softened in the glow of the lamp behind; her skin was luminous. There was beauty – and character – in her face. Robin drew his hand gently down her left arm and rested it on hers, in her lap.

'What, Robin?'

'I'm going to take you to Paris. Everything else in our life can wait for a bit – to hell with the office. Tomorrow if we can. Or the day after. Your parents will keep an eye on young Lucy for a day or so.'

'Well, yes . . . I suppose so . . . but what are we going to Paris for, Robin?' She had always found his ebullience hard to resist. She did then. She was unutterably tired – although it didn't seem to matter. 'What for?' she repeated.

'Because I'm going to propose to you – again. On the quay near one of those bridges on the Left Bank. Very, very romantic. Notre Dame, the boats on the river. Perhaps a stray artist or a fisherman or two. The works. I wanted to the first time, years ago. Did you know?'

'I *hoped* . . .'

By then, she had caught his vigour and the glint in his eye. She couldn't help herself smiling back. They had always had the knack of having fun together. Kate had the curious sensation of all the strands of her life coming together again. Lucy fast asleep upstairs . . .

'The shadow of your smile . . .' he hummed softly.

'Oh Robin . . . dear Ina . . . and remember Manou?'

But he didn't hear, he hadn't taken his eyes off her.

'And when I propose, this second time – it's going to be in one of those marvellous velvety blue twilights you loved . . .'

He looked exactly like Guy – his eyes, the way his hair grew. That wicked smile. Kate's heart flipped – and righted itself.

'But that was in the spring . . .' She was tremulous. 'It's late November now . . . you won't find any hours of blue along the Seine these days . . .'

'*Of course* we will.' A world of confidence in his voice. 'When it comes to blue Parisian twilights November – late November – is the choicest time of all . . .'

And as it happened, so it was.